The Flower Garden

A Tale of the Home Front

Jane Cox

Published by

MELROSE
BOOKS

An Imprint of Melrose Press Limited
St Thomas Place, Ely
Cambridgeshire
CB7 4GG, UK
www.melrosebooks.co.uk

FIRST EDITION

Copyright © Jane Cox 2018

The Author asserts her moral right to
be identified as the author of this work

Cover designed by Melrose Books

ISBN   978-1-912333-33-2 Paperback
       978-1-912333-34-9 epub
       978-1-912333-35-6 mobi

Printed and bound in Great Britain by:
TJ International Ltd, Padstow, Cornwall

MIX
Paper from
responsible sources
FSC   FSC® C013056
www.fsc.org

This book is based on the reminiscences of my mother and her two sisters and my grandmother's letters; some considerable flights of fancy are thrown in.

For my cousins Rick and Kate.

Main characters

Smart family:
Lil (Mum)
Sid (Dad), oil shop man
Lily (Ooly)
Pansy (Pan)
Rose (Mog)
Dot (Aunty) Sid's sister
Ed (Edward Victor Davids) Lil's brother
Billy (Sid's brother)
Flo' (Billy's wife)
Elizabeth (Todge)

In Bow:
Miss Ruth Bagwell (Baggy), mistress at Skoriers.
Fanny Bastaple, her husband, Harry, a blackshirt.
Edward (Teddy B) and Mrs Billington-Smythe, vicar and wife.
Johnny Bowyer, Ooly's husband.
Derek Bowyer, Johnny's brother.
Nell Bowyer/Waters, Johnny's mum.
Veronica Brackenthorpe, a socialite.
Doomandgloom Davies, undertaker.
Edie, Mossy, Mossy Jnr. and Aaron Goldberg, next door neighbours.
Bert Gum (ARP warden), Mrs Gum (flower shop next to Emporium),
    and Timmy Boy Gum.
Rabbi Hotzner, customer in shop.

Ethel Jiggins, from Old Ford, Wesleyan.
Vi Kerridge, husband Will, a docker, and communist.
Dai Lewis, dairyman.
Douglas Mitchell, Ooly's paramour.
Lady Mitchell, mother of the above.
Sir Henry Mitchell.
Old Morgan, non-conformist minister.
Archie Mosley, a cousin of Douglas Mitchell.
Norah, Derek's girl friend.
O'Brien family, next door neighbours: Paddy & Kathleen, daughter
    Maureen, Ooly's best friend, Denny, Pan's friend.
Sarah Posnanski, old customer.
Sam from the chippie.
Tom Tittler, (Poor Old Tom) teacher, admirer of Mog.
Albie Walters, Johnny's step father.

In Suffolk:
Dom Sci., colleague at school.
Aelgifu Drayman, friend of Pan.
Father Jessop and curate.
Jenny Kilminster, pupil of Pan's, her parents and brother.
Jocasta Meredith, headmistress.
Elsa Rush, friend of Pan.

In Woodford:
Mrs Plunket, neighbour.
Mr and Mrs Spoon, neighbours.

In Somerset:
Pete O'Malley, evacuee.
Sir Horace Tillingham bart.
Edmund Tillingham, his son.

Isabella Duboulay Tillingham, his daughter.
Bob, the gardener.
Mrs P, the housekeeper.
The stable boy.
Jake Campbell, Canadian air force.
Pooty (Percy Poultney) of the War Office, friend of Dougie and Edmund.

Contents

Chapter 1:
Christmas Eve in Old Ford 1938

'Come on Missus, treat yerself to a nice pair of drawers for Christmas!'

'Bootiful little canary bananas – only a tanner for seven.'

As the rose of a snowy dusk was deepening into purple, Lil Smart was crossly pushing her way through the crowds "up Roman". The flaring naphtha lamps blew in the wind, filling the market with a golden light which played on the stacked arrangements of glossy fruit, the piles of sticky toffee, pink coconut ice, tubs of jellied eels, racks of cheap fur coats, piles of sheets and pillowcases, china, kettles, buckets, toys and trinkets, fat turkeys with coloured rosettes hanging in rows on wide steel bands, strings of sausages, all set about with bunches of mistletoe and holly. The hot chestnuts smelt good and the baked potatoes steamed invitingly.

Roman Road market, known to all and sundry as "the Roman", bustled and shouted its way right through the heart of Old Ford, it was its life force.

Once, long ago, Old Ford was a hamlet of the ancient baking town of Stratford Bow, a cluster of cottages around the banks of the lazy River Lea, forded here even before the Romans came, quite a beauty spot, where the apprentices of Olde London went to bathe. It lay just north of Bow, and the great Colchester – now the Mile End – Road. By the 1930s Old Ford had become part of the London Borough of Poplar and was scarred by factories, workshops and railways, its meadows covered with monotonous rows of tiny houses, wedged in between two branches of the LNER, its being sucked into the grey, amorphous mass of the East End.

For some of its older inhabitants, whose parents could remember the days before the Jews came, it still has a village feel about it. Not so long ago you could go blackberrying along the lanes that are now care worn, sooty streets, or idle among the irises in a rowing boat on the river. For Sid and Lil Smart (born some thirty years before the Great War) it had a separate identity from its neighbours; they were very conscious of being Old Ford residents, while for their daughters, their home was just "Bow".

'Plaice, cod, haddick – luverly, luverly fish, fresh as a daisy.'

She stopped at Solly Isaac's fish stall, which boasted haddock two foot long:

''Erd one of yours is gettin' 'itched, Mrs S. Would that be the pretty one or the funny one?'

As a matter of fact, Lil had three daughters, all born in the spring, Lily, Pansy and Rose. Sid had chosen their names – he was a soppy old devil – dreamed of raising three beautiful blooms in his backyard at 29 Selman Street, a turning just off the market. The other kids in the street used to call them the "Flower Garden".

Lily (they called her Ooly) was the eldest. Mad about music, Sid was, and Ooly was put to the piano when she was just a tot. She took to it like a duck to water and, by the time she was eight, she was giving concerts. Her teacher had a maid and big house in Tredegar Square. Lil had never met him, of course, Sid dealt with all that sort of thing. Later on came the singing. When Miss Harrison from school sent a note home about her "astonishing voice", and said she had been chosen to sing on her own in front of the Duchess of York, up at the People's Palace, Sid was beside himself with delight. Lil made her a special frock for the occasion from a nice bit of gold velvet and some cream lace from a stall up Roman. She didn't go to the concert herself, didn't think it was her place. Sid went with Old Dot, his sister, both done up

2

to the nines. They told her all about it when they got back.

Lil never said anything much to Ooly about her triumph, but managed to mention it, quite cleverly she thought, to Elsie Fairbrother at the Post Office, 'Oh yes, that was the Tuesday after my Lily sang to the Duchess at the People's Palace', to Mrs Gum at the flower shop, 'That chrysanthemum is just the colour my Lily wore when she sang to the Duchess', to her snooty sister-in-law, Flo', 'Sorry I haven't been over since Easter, I was 'ard at it makin' a dress for Ooly to wear for the Duchess', etc.

But Ooly got fed up with music; Lil thought perhaps Sid had pushed her too hard. At all events, she took to larking about – it might have been something to do with her nose. She had been such a pretty little girl, tinkling and trilling away but as she got older a large, hooked hooter (like her dad's) appeared. It was quite soon after she started at Skoriers and the girls there called her Caligula, some Roman geezer whose bust stood in the school hall. Skoriers was a posh school – nothing but the best for Sid's daughters. Never mind about the nose (she did), she had yet another gift, she could make people laugh. Ooly became the funny one.

Rose (called Mog), Lil's youngest was a blue eyed stunner. Up Roman they said she looked like Greta Garbo and everywhere she went, even Up West, people gawped. She was, of course, the pretty one, also blessed with a fine singing voice (soprano), a sweet nature and a lot of pluck; she was only redeemed in Ooly's eyes, by her fat legs, large bottom and short, stubby fingers – Ooly's elegant hands were her pride and joy. At Skoriers, never as popular as her eldest sister, Mog worked hard and got a place at a college, where she was known as "the Great Belle of Bow". She taught seven-year-olds at a school in Wapping.

In the middle, there was Pansy, named after the buttonhole that Sid gave Lil the first time they walked out. It wouldn't have been so bad if she had been called something else. In fact, no one called her Pansy; she was Pan, at home, at school, at church and up Roman. Pan was tall,

3

strong and handsome; her eyes were green, she sang contralto, wore suits, had an Eton crop and smoked small cigars. She had a bad back, bad temper, boils, and taught biology at Harpisfield Grange in Suffolk. No chance of a wedding here.

Lil snapped at the fishmonger: 'It's my eldest who's gettin' wed.' She hurried on – it was "no ruddy business" of street traders to call her daughters names.

She, Mrs Smart, was married to a proper retailer, with a shop in Roman Road – the girls called it Dad's Emporium. Out the back he kept his job-lots of damaged kettles and saucepans which he soldered into good use for the very poor. He was purveyor of his own patent bug blinder, to purge the hovels of his neighbours and sold paraffin in tiny ha'penny bottles to those who couldn't afford a pint or a gallon. Sid Smart was oil and colour man extraordinaire, Lord of Roman Road market, interior design consultant to the poverty stricken East Enders, recommending, inevitably, a "nice light stone" paint for the wash houses of Old Ford (he had an on-going job lot). He sold pickles and jam, tea and soap, nails and wire netting, string and carpet beaters, tacks for catapults, brushes and buttons, glue, fly papers, gas mantles, buckets and practically everything else, he gave the children lumps of toffee, and dispensed wisdom and comfort to his customers.

'My Jack's gorn orf again, Sid, I'm at my wits' end – 'ow am I supposed to feed the kiddies? They're bawlin' the place down they're so 'ungry.'

'Just take yourself over to Old Sylvia's place (Pankhurst) – they'll sort you out, mate, and there's a soup kitchen up near the Troxy, open early in the morning.

'I've come out in that rash again, Sid, can't stop scratchin''

'Just a mite of Jeyes will do the trick, brother. I think I've got a tin left out the back.'

The Emporium was a news exchange :

'What abaat that Simpson woman? – bleedin' well comin' over 'ere

4

with her Yanky swank and nickin' our King!'

'Good luck to 'im, that's what I say. Why shouldn't 'e 'ave the totty he wants withaat them snotty-nosed buggers pokin' their noses in?'

'Bit unfair on that poor little Dook of York, 'avin' to take over and 'im not able to string two words together.'

Goings-on in Europe were much discussed; terrible stories came from the Jewish customers. 'Oh, Mr Smart, Mr Smart,' wailed Sarah Posnanski, long in the tooth with tragedy in her eyes, 'I have seen it over there, it is coming here, vot vill become of us?'

'Nothing like what's going on over there will ever happen here, rest assured, mate,' said Sid, sagely.

'What abaat that Jew boy found tied up to a wooden cross over near the gas works? Poor mite – some say 'e was only a little kid yer know.'

'That's them Blackshirts at it again. They're nestin' all round near Stepney church. No Jew dare go near Duckett Street, I've 'eard. Lot of out of work lads, struttin' abaat in their uniforms, throwin' their weight abaat, beatin' up anyone that takes their fancy … Jews, Reds, even innocent kiddies. No better than thugs – they say that most of the Shoreditch gang are ex-cons.'

To be honest, Sid wasn't sure about Jews; his brother Billy, the bombastic butcher and poulterer of Bethnal Green, said you could never trust them. Pushy and nicking the trade – they were all for money, he said. It was true that the new Sunday trading laws had given them the edge and the cut price shops they were opening – selling all manner of stuff – that was a worry. Billy said that Mosley's outfit had some good ideas for associations of shopkeepers being set up to stop chain stores and cut price trading.

Another brother, Tom, had tried his luck with a shop in Grove Road, selling socks and stockings, but the only time he got any trade was at Passover and such like, when the Jewish stalls up Roman were not out. Stories flew around about Jewish landlords evicting poor devils who got behind with their rent. Harry Bastaple, one of his regulars,

5

was always full of these tales. But the Goldbergs next door were good people – although Lil didn't agree. Edie Goldberg was a fine figure of a woman with flaming red hair and flashing black eyes. Sometimes she would take a hot dinner over to the shop for "dear Sidney", and her husband, Mossy, had given him a hand on more than one occasion, even offered to help out in the shop, but Sid didn't think that was quite right. Old Beattie Cohen made clothes for the girls – she was a good sort. Rabbi Hotzner would always stop for a chat; he was a wise, educated old man – did quite as much in the way of good works as any of the local parsons. And now this latest – poor little kiddie strung up. Sid hated bullying.

Lately it was all talk of war, as the monster bogey man of Europe starts his relentless march towards Bow, and the prime minister flying off to Germany every five minutes to try and "appease" him.

'Old Chamberlain's off again. Reckon it'll do any good, Sid, lettin' that blighter get away wiv murder like he's doin' ?'

'Anything's better than war, brother.'

Lil was lucky in Sid, although she would never tell him so; he was a good provider, never touched a drop – well – one glass of sherry at Christmas: 'Just a drain, mate.' He was handsome, with aristocratic aquiline features, was gentle, undemanding in certain quarters and fond of doing a comic turn or two. Being a Methodist, he addressed all men as "brother"; he loved Shakespeare, Wordsworth and, above all things, the books of Charles Dickens. He had a good tenor voice, played the fiddle and had aspirations for his daughters which he had not been able to fulfil himself: 'You are leaving when you should be just starting,' remarked his school master at Roman Road School when he left, at twelve.

Sidney Smart was a "new man", before such commodities were generally available. He loved children and firmly believed, and was often quoting "But trailing clouds of glory do we come From God who is our home." He played games with his girls and made them laugh,

6

took them to the doctors, when they needed to go. If any approaches were to be made on behalf of the Smart girls to the gently reared mistresses of Skoriers (founded in 1702, where dinner was "lunch" and break "recess"), it was Sid who did it.

Like all the Smart brothers (apart from Billy) though, he was a shocking worrier – when Ooly started to toddle he wrapped all the sharp corners in the houses up in felt so she wouldn't hurt herself. Going to catch a train with Sid was an ordeal. When they went down to Margate for their annual week's holiday, he had them at the station a good two hours early "just in case". He collected pieces of string, kept his cash in a safe in the kitchen, having no truck with banks and, when the TB season approached, washed the whole house down with Lisol. Sometimes the worrying got so bad that he got stuck in his chair, couldn't swallow, couldn't leave the house without checking at least three times that the guard was up around the fire.

Lil thought it was probably the worrying which had kept Sid out of them ruddy awful trenches. Her nephew, Albert, the son she never had, went off to France with the Poplar and Stepney Rifles; she remembered seeing him off – looking so smart and proud in his uniform – just a kid he was. She fainted right away when the bad news came. Some papers had come for Sid; he hadn't said anything to her, but was stuck in his chair for a couple of days, and then there was coming and going, involving his brothers and Old Murphy (the doctor) and he never went away. Reserved occupations kept some blokes at home, but they were usually policemen or firemen or something like that and she didn't believe that making bug blinder was something of "national importance".

Lil was glad to have Sid safe at home, but couldn't help thinking that if she'd been a bloke she would have been out there with her tommy gun, shooting at those blighters. This worrying was a mystery to her; she had always just got on with things and kept her pecker up and, for the most part, enjoyed herself. She couldn't make it out – Sid's life had always been quite comfortable, as far as she could see, and it certainly

7

was now. They had proper furniture (not just orange boxes), vases to put flowers in (her mum had used old tins), a whole house, with a tiny back garden, with enough soil to grow marigolds and pansies and even a few vegetables. It wasn't like when she was a kid, hungry most of the time, going out on the streets to sell fire wood to make what she could, moonlighting from a shabby room in one street to a worse one in another. Her dad had died young and the only time they had any cash was when her lovely elder sister, Esther, smart as paint and pretty as a picture, had taken herself off to the match factory and brought home a good wage. They had oranges then and sometimes even a nice piece of scrag end. But Esther had got that horrible disease that the match girls got and died, when Lil was still a little girl.

Her mates were more than surprised when Lil landed a Smart brother. 'Come on up Bow Baths wiv' me,' she had said to her friend, Ethel, 'there's this swanky bloke who's singin.' Lil was not much of a looker, she was very short, with small, beady black eyes and a square jaw. But her eyes twinkled, her dark brown hair was glossy with red lights, her tongue sharp as a razor and her determination as strong as any you might encounter east of Aldgate Pump.

She bought her fish, three huge pieces of plump cod, just right for Christmas Eve supper for the seven of them, some fags for Ed – she always forgot to get her brother's present – and two dozen oranges. You could only get the tiny, thin skinned yellow ones at that time of year; they were so sour that the only way you could eat them was by sucking the juice through a sugar lump. All the family loved oranges, but not Lil. They reminded her of that time when she was little and was sent by her mum to get what she could from the Sunday School of the East London Tabernacle in Burdett Road, whether it be holy stuff or learning or hand-outs. She was proud, even in those days, and when the lady in charge of the Sunday School tried to give her an orange, she turned tail and fled, running all the way home.

With her purchases tucked into her shopping bag, along with a

8

copy of *Peg's Paper*, she left the market and hurried through the slush. Christmas was fun and she felt quite excited, but rather tired. Sid did all the tree and decorating stuff, and he wrapped up the presents – she always thought all that wrapping in silly paper a bit of a waste of time, fiddly ribbons and labels that got lost.

As she turned into Selman Street she spotted the vicar ("Teddy B" they called him) and the tribe from St Alphege all gathered around outside the Duke of Cumberland("sparkling ales and genuine porter"), belting out 'Good King Wenceslas'. The girls were there, of course – they spent too much time at that blinkin' church, Lil reckoned, especially Pan.

Teddy B (Rev. Edward Billington-Smythe) was a looker, a serious looker, but a bit girly, Lil always thought, with his whiney parsonical voice and mincing ways. No doubt he was brave and good – he had been a pilot in the war and worked very hard with his struggling parishioners, but he was not Lil's cup of tea. Mrs B was there too, a large floury faced woman, her cloche hat snuggled down into a fluffy fur collar, a monumental bosom heaving up and down to the strains of the carol. She was so big and her voice was so small, a thin, reedy warbly thing, winding its way out of her pursed lips in a manner suited to one who could trace descent from some nobs somewhere in the country. It was hardly any competition for the thunderous blasts with which Pan and her sisters rent the snowy air.

Lil was looking forward to getting home, to putting her legs up over the fire and reading *Pegs Paper* with Old Dot, her sister-in-law. Old Dot, also known as "Aunty" was, of course, not really old. The epithet "old" was used liberally by the Smart family and their like, a slightly patronising term of endearment, applied, only to those who were to be slightly pitied or possibly mocked. Usually it was reserved for those who had the misfortune not to belong to the Family, but were, nevertheless, worthy of some sort of regard. Hence Old Morgan, the congregational minister who was hopelessly in love with Mog, Old

Murphy, the family doctor, Old DB (never known by her full name) who fawned over Pan, Old Mrs Gum, who kept the flower shop next to the Emporium, Old Sylvia (Pankhurst), who had such funny notions but worked hard for the women and children of the East End and, of course, Old Chamberlain, the Prime Minister. Pan acquired the epithet after she left home.

Old Dot was of a different category. She was, of course, a Smart, Sid's sister, said to have been nearly as beautiful as Mog at one time, but there was not much sign of it now – her black hair had gone grey early and was thinning and tied back in a knot.

She was the youngest and only daughter of the family, much prized and closely guarded by her doting and over anxious father, Tom Smart, manager of Smithson's Oil and Colour (the only man in Cardigan Road with a live-in servant or, indeed, a servant at all). She often recalled one Christmas – she was ten – her brothers, Tom, Billy, Jack and Sid, were taken off to the pantomime at Drury Lane, and she was left behind. An outing to the theatre was considered most unsuitable for a nicely bred young girl. The boys came back with tales of fantastic transformation scenes, of shimmering fairies (real ones) dancing in the air, of fountains playing on stage, wonderful costumes and music to make you tap and twirl. Sid sang some of the songs to her and described the Enchanted Crystal Garden and the Fairy Parliament. She begged and begged to be allowed to go next year, but it was not permitted, next year or any other. Suitors were, of course, discouraged. The story was that a brave fellow had come courting once and her father received the visitor, sitting with his feet in a tub of water, wearing a paper bag on his head and gibbering in a convincing manner.

Dot's teacher had suggested that teacher training would be possible for this bright and capable girl, but dad would not hear of that so she stayed at home, keeping house for him after mum died. When Smithson's got rid of him and money was tight, they shared a house (number 29 Selman Street) with Sid and Lil. Dorothy Smart remained single, became Old Dot; she shared Lil's fireside, her home, her kitchen, her children and *Peg's Paper*. Perhaps it was really the other way round.

Dad, in retirement, proved a problem for the two women. It was whispered that old Tom Smart had a drink problem in his youth, but his wife, Dot and Sid's adored mum, a docker's daughter of strong Baptist principles and a firm hand, had him take the pledge. All was well, even when Fanny Smart departed this life (reciting all the verses of "Peace perfect peace" on her death bed) he remained firm in his resolve. Then came the Smithson's Christmas party and Tom succumbed to a glass of port wine and that was that.

Dot and Lil found whisky bottles under his bed and did their best to conceal his staggering and slurring from the neighbours. He was never a pub man so it was possible to keep his secret, or so they thought.

'Yer grandad's on the sauce, yer know, drunk,' said Maureen O'Brien from next door to Ooly. The O'Briens couldn't afford to drink, except on Paddy's Day, of course.

'He's not so. He's just a poor sick old man.'

And, so it turned out he was. When the cancer took him, Lil pressed Dot and Sid to take in her youngest brother, Ed, who, though a grown man, was not able to look after himself. Lil's tough and rough old mum, had died round about the same time as Grandad Smart, leaving Edward Victor Davids, (21 years old, a wood chopper, lame and a bit silly) to the mercies of the workhouse. Dot was appalled at the thought of this dim and dirty creature occupying her father's room, but Sid caved in and Ed was installed.

The shop was really Old Dot's, a lease having been purchased with a small legacy left by her father. She worked there with Sid, and Ed (not that he was much use) and kept an eye on both men. Underneath her sweetness, and willingness, just a hint of bitterness might occasionally be detected in a steely glance – rarely a sharp word, mind. After all, she had it better than most, much better. Surrounded by a loving family,

11

children supplied without that business that Lil had to put up with, there was enough money to keep up the Smart standards. No queuing up at the fish and chip shop for them, no recourse to "uncle" (pawnbroker) on Monday mornings, and most certainly no hopping. In late August, Bow was quite deserted when the exodus to the Kentish Hop Fields took the mums and kids, (dads at weekends) off to the only holiday they ever had. Some holiday! ''Oppin' is 'ell Miss Smart,' said Vi Kerridge, the docker's wife, when she came into the shop to buy a billy can and spirit stove for the expedition. They camped out in nasty little huts and worked hard at picking from dawn to dusk, but the money was welcome. Dot had heard of some rather scandalous goings-on down in Kent, but she shut her ears to that sort of thing.

Lil put the fish and the oranges in the pantry, and tucked the fags away in the dresser drawer. Old Dot put the kettle on and stoked up the fire, 'Come on Lil, let's have a bit of a sit before the 'erbs[1] descend, you look all in.' They could have some peace with Pan out of the way at the carol singing and Sid and Ed wouldn't be back from the shop until late.

The goose (courtesy of Billy the Bombast) was stuffed, the pudding on the boil in the copper and the mince pies baked. Sid liked to leave the tree to the last minute, as he had done when the girls were small, so that when they came down on Christmas morning it would be standing there, a shimmering surprise, with all the candles lit. Sid's gentle but obstinate insistence on sticking to his custom, had caused trouble. There was often trouble between Sid and Pan. She had brought home some very special tree decorations that she and her chum, Gif (short for Aelgifu), had got in Austria on holiday, and she wanted to get the tree dressed and then shown off as soon as she arrived home from Suffolk:

'For God's sake, Dad, we aren't kids anymore.'

'Don't use language like that, mate.'

---

1 *Pot herbs, contracted to 'erbs' was a term for family members.*

'Can't you at least try and address me properly. You talk like a street trader.'

'Here we go again,' said Ooly to Mog.

Doors slammed, the sound of sobbing came from upstairs.

Quietly and firmly Old Dot started unpacking the precious glittering glass balls from their tissue paper. Pan always got her way.

Chapter 2:

Pan

She had always been such a trial. Too clever by half, strong as a horse, should have been a chap, Lil thought. She and Sid would have liked a son, to help in the shop and take the business over when the time came, but Pan turned up instead: 'Good heavens, Mrs Smart,' commented Old Murphy, 'the baby is bigger than you!'

Pan burst upon Bow at a time when Sid was often getting stuck in his chair and the amusing, kindly chap was replaced by a shadowy, withdrawn character, whose raw nerves were lacerated by the incessant screaming of the new arrival. Pan's cot was moved into Old Dot's room; little Lily (four) stayed in her parents' room. When Pan was two and tantrumming in earnest, the pretty one was born. The new baby was gurgling and delightful; her cot stayed in the room with Lil, Sid and Ooly. Old Dot and Pan fought it out along the passage.

'Can't you do something with that blitherin' kid – she screams day and night and my Mossy needs his sleep,' shouted Edie Goldberg to Lil over the garden wall. Mossy had a fruit and veg. stall in the market. 'There's sommat 'up with 'er. It's not natral for a kid to be carryin' on like that.'

Relations between the two women had been less than cordial, since Lil had let Aaron Goldberg (14) climb over the yard wall and get into the house, and raid the pantry, while they were off at the synagogue for Yom Kippur. 'Poor lad was starving. I don't 'old with that fasting business.'

'Their ways aren't our ways, duck,' Sid had said, always the peace maker.

Lil drew herself up:

'If your Mossy 'ad a proper job 'e wouldn't 'ave to get out of bed in the middle of the night. And I'll 'ave you know there's nothin' up with my daughter.'

Kathleen O'Brien, at number 27, blessed with four children and one on the way, was not much more sympathetic:

'Jeezus, Missus, yer cheilde is screamin' like a banshee, 'tis an ungodly sound for such a little babe. Be sure she's cheilde a' God?'

'I'll 'ave you know, all my kiddies 'ave bin christened proper at St Alphege.'

'Well 'tis no church of St Peter; the divil's got a grip on her cradle, for sure.'

In the early days it was rare for Old Dot to have more than a few hours' sleep and the little house was shaken by the tumult. Lil would sometimes shove a gin-soaked rag into the baby's mouth, when her husband and sister-in-law weren't around. No jigging or cuddling, no rocking or cajoling seemed to pacify the child, only in one way would she oblige. She ate. She ate and ate and grew and grew. By the time the Pretty One was born Pan was as the size of a five year, though only two. The wider family called her the Monster of Selman Street.

Ooly was the main target of her rages and clumps of her elder sister's brown, silky be-ribboned hair were to be found in Pan's angry little fists. Uncle Billy and Aunt Flo' (childless) had bought Ooly a doll from Hamleys, up west; it was, the last German doll sold there before the Great War broke out. As soon as Pan was old enough to see it for the treasure it was, she started screaming for it and when she could talk a bit, 'Want dat!' was her unending cry.

'Ooly, do let her have it for few minutes. You're getting a bit old for dolls now, anyway,' Old Dot advised, worn out with her charge's demands. Pan smiled smugly and cradled the creature in her arms, briefly, then, quick as a flash, it was on the fire, its Teutonic curls going up in smoke and the kitchen filled with acrid fumes. Princess Ooly, swept out of the room and went off to play the piano, as she did in times of distress.

From an early age it was clear to Pan that it was the piano (to which Sid had devoted several seasons of the income from his bug blinder) that made Ooly special. One morning, Lil was heaving heavy, steaming sheets out of the copper and chatting to Ooly. Mog, who had survived several Pan attacks in the early weeks of her life, was smiling away in her high chair and banging her spoon in a friendly fashion. Pan was, as usual, whining and pulling at her mother's skirts. 'For Gawd's sake leave me be, will you!'

Pan flew into the parlour and kicked as hard as she could at the offending instrument, until there was a good big hole in it. Raging around to see how else she could make her mark, she noticed a tin of paint ('nice light stone') sitting there. She kicked and kicked, her green eyes bulging, her jaw set firm, until the lid came off. The contents ran all over the floral patterned carpet, making a lovely squidgy lake. She stomped around in it for a bit and then ran around like mad, all over the house, so everywhere you went there were little cream boot prints.

That was when Lil shut her in the cupboard under the stairs. The shrieks could be heard as far away as Bow Road, or so it was said. Sid and Old Dot, called by some busy bodies, rushed home from the shop and what a to-do there was.

After that was the incident with the carving knife, which was followed by the business of the matches and the kitchen curtains, and a new batch of night terrors. Sid eventually took Pan to see Old Murphy.

The doctor rubbed his chin, 'I don't know what to advise, Mr Smart. The child is really quite disturbed. Have you considered an institution? She is clearly causing some upset in the family.'

Pan was squirming around in Sid's arms, shouting for her aunt and digging her nails into her father's neck.

16

'Oh no, we couldn't put her away, Brother, she needs her family's love. She's a bright kiddie, brighter than most. Isn't there any medicine which we could give her, just to keep her steady?'

'Well, Mr Smart, I don't usually prescribe that sort of thing for a child of such tender years. She would probably profit from some firm discipline (fat chance of that, he mused). I wonder, is there some member of the family, a grandmother or aunt, who might take her on, get her away and give you all some peace?'

'Lil and Dot wouldn't hear of such a thing,' said Sid (meaning he wouldn't), 'and, in any case, I doubt if anyone would take her.'

Dr Murphy scribbled out a prescription. 'Look, give her just a tiny drop of this when you need to, and we'll see how we go. But be sparing and try and keep her occupied as much as you can. You may find that she improves when she gets to school.' A good belting was probably in order, he thought, but knew full well that was never going to be part of any Sidney Smart regime.

Old Dot sniffed warily at the contents of the small bottle which Sid brought home. 'I don't like this, Sid, drugging a little mite.' Lil took the bottle and put it in the cupboard. When she was out Dot got the bottle out and poured the contents down the sink, meanwhile Sid bought a rocking horse and went off to see the headmistress at Malmesbury Road, to see if they could take Pan early. 'Pleeeese can I go to school with Ooly – pleeese, I want to go *now*.'

She would be five in March. On a chill January day, clutching Old Dot's hand as tight as she could, and stuffed into brand new gaiters and boots, she started off with a light heart on her first walk to school. Ooly, who had been ink monitor at Malmesbury Road for some time now, and was in the "big girls", went ahead, swinging her school bag. Pan had a little bag too, made of American cloth. In it was a slice of cold buttered toast to eat at break time, a slate rag and a penny for the starving Europeans. Whoever they were.

School turned out to be a hard, sharp, cold place, loud and clattery, and you had to sit still and not fidget. If you dared to talk you had to stand on the desk with your hands on your head. She shared a double desk, and spit for the slate rag, with Mossy junior from next door. A good job his mum didn't know about the spit. Miss wore a long black skirt and a striped blouse with a little frill at the neck and there were some funny little half glasses on the end of her cross nose. 'Pansy Smart, if you do not stop crying you will be whipped!'

When Old Dot collected her she shot like a bullet into her arms, her face swollen, her eyes red. After that, mornings at Selman Street started with a violent tummy ache, refusal to get dressed and toast and marmalade thrown across the kitchen. Old Dot could only get Pan out of the house after she had mum, dad, Ed, Mog and Omo the cat all had lined up and crossed their hearts, and sworn scouts' honour 'surficial' (it's official) that they would all be still there when she came back. It made Lil mad, but Sid said if it was the only way to get her to school, they'd best do it.

Although Pan quickly finished all the tasks set by Miss Frilly Collar, she was never able to please her and was frequently reminded that her elder sister never answered back – such a pretty, quiet, well-behaved, child, couldn't Pansy follow her example? When she shot her hand up to answer a question, she was never chosen, and her clumsy attempts to "dance like a snowflake" were scorned. The sobbing went on, day in, day out. Things were no better in the playground. Because she was so tall everyone thought she was much older than she was and the big boys teased her and called a dunce. 'Leave my little sister alone, she's only five and she cries a lot.' Ooly, as ink monitor, commanded some respect. Pan might drive her to distraction, but family was family and bullying was bullying.

That afternoon, when Lil went out to whiten the door step, she was astonished to find her two elder daughters sitting together companionably, deeply engrossed. Ooly was taking a snapdragon apart and showing Pan the different bits, petals, sepals, stamens – they had been taught about it at school that day. She liked nature study. The little one was still, quiet and absorbed in her first botany lesson. 'Ooly, can we learn 'bout the flowers again?'

Sid was summoned to the head mistress – she was a formidable woman – children had to salute her if they met her in the playground. 'I am not sure, Mr Smart, that we can continue in our attempts to educate your daughter. Have you thought about a special school?'

He hadn't and he didn't. The head reluctantly agreed to give it another try. Sid bought Pan a metal hoop with a stick, for which she had been crying for weeks – Lil had said it was a boy's toy and was quite cross.

A miracle happened in Pan's second year at school. Mrs Hughes was now her teacher, a young war widow, with ginger curls and freckles, and snub nose. She sat with her feet up on the desk and sang Welsh folk songs to the children, she read them stories from books with lovely pictures, *The Making of the first Opal* was Pan's favourite. Best of all, she took to Pan and praised her efforts. From now on Mrs Hughes and school became her life; the sobbing stopped and the morning inspection was no longer called for.

Selman Street breathed a sigh of relief. These were the good days. The Flower Garden rode Dobbin the rocking horse; he was nearly life size and painted dapple grey. Ooly was the west wind, tossing her long, silky hair; Mog, the little, soft south wind shook out her fluffy fair curls; Pan, the east wind pulled out the brown strands from behind her ears, making the most of what she'd got. Pan didn't much like being the east wind; she preferred it when her sisters were two princesses and she, Pan, was the prince, whipping her steed with the poker.

What summers these were. In the long afternoons Pan and Mossy Jnr., with Denny O'Brien in tow, raked the streets, hopping up and down on Pan's pogo stick, batting their iron hoops under Tom Thumb's Arch, shooting potato pellets at passing carts. When their mums could be persuaded to part with sixpence for a "bowl of mixed", off they ran up Roman to find Angelo the Italiano with his little cart of delights. Denny never got a sixpence – his mum said that was enough to feed the whole family for two days. Angelo's cart had two sunken tubs with handled lids, and when they were lifted, there, glowing in the sunshine was the most golden ice cream in one, and in the other the glistening white lemon-ice. Never would they taste such ice cream again, never was there such a summertime treat.

On Saturdays Pan would sometimes be allowed to help in the shop; she loved that, standing on a wooden box so she could see over the cluttered counter (with Dot keeping a wary eye) spooning out measures of pickle or jam into customers' cups, tucking tacks and nails into screws of paper with her tough little fingers.

'Go and find a tube of box maker's glue for Mr Atkins, would you mate? You should find a couple under the watering cans.'

She buzzed about, glad to be busy and, it has to be said, delighted to be getting one over on Ooly, who would certainly never dirty her elegant hands with such menial work. Ructions with dad were few and far between:

'Pleeeese, Dad, pleeese teach me how to solder.'

'Much too dangerous, mate, perhaps when you're older.'

Stomp and slam.

'Can't I pour out the paraffin?'

'Best left to Uncle Ed – that's his job.'

'Why is it his job. I could do it faster than him. I would be really careful. Pleeeese, Dad.'

'No, mate, if any paraffin is spilt we might all go up in flames.'

'But he has a fag hanging out of his mouth all the time. That's much more dangerous than me pouring it out *really* carefully.'

'Pan, leave it, leave it.'

She contemplated setting fire to the shop for a minute or two, but changed her mind when Mrs Jiggins came in and needed serving with some whitening. The big chalk blocks were kept at the back under the counter, and you had to burrow through all sorts of stuff to get at them – that was fun.

Sundays they might pile up on dad's push bike, with a little home made trailer, a large wicker basket on wheels, Ooly sat on the seat with Mog on her lap and Pan crouched at her feet and ride off to Wanstead Flats, Hackney Marshes or Temple Mills. Expeditions to Epping Forest were the best, with a picnic of blackcurrant jam sandwiches and ginger beer. Pan loved the woods, the tiny, fragile wild flowers, the bracken, the beech trees. Best of all she loved clambering up into the branches, a pirate on the rigging, calling triumphantly from the crow's nest, "Ship ahoy".

'Be careful, mate. Pan get down from there – you'll fall. Don't get yourself dirty –mum will be livid.'

Ooly, meanwhile, sat demurely on a tree stump in a pretty dress and pristine white socks, reading her book, and Mog made chains of buttercups and daisies.

On winter days, when the freezing market traders wore woolly mittens with their fingers poking out, and slabs of snow weighed down the canopies over the stalls, the girls rushed home from school to a warm kitchen smelling of cinnamon on baking days, to *Tiger Tim* and the *Children's Newspaper*, to mum and hot buttered toast. In the pre-Christmas days, so excited were they that they couldn't even say the word –'Chimma! Chimma!' they whispered to each other, as mum and Dot smuggled the tantalising parcels upstairs and into the wardrobe.

Uncle George always came on Christmas Eve, an annual visit. He was dad's uncle really, Grandad's brother, a great lumbering man with mutton chop whiskers and a beard, a person of importance and fat cigars. Settling in the best chair, he would take a glass of port and regale the company with tales of his triumphs and those of his sons and daughters. He would then push his fat fingers into his waistcoat pocket and pull out three gold sovereigns, one for each of the girls.

'Why is Uncle George so rich, Dad?' asked Pan one time, after he'd gone. 'And why did Genie and Sophie and the others go to such posh schools? And why does he live in Ilford, in such a great big house and keep showing off about it? And why does Aunty Eugenie never come out and keep sniffing all the time?'

Just once the Flower Garden had been taken to visit the plush and chenille-draped, dark house in Goodmayes, all enclosed with laurel bushes. Aunty Eugenie sat in a great stiff, stuffed chair, with her handkerchief always at the ready.

'Uncle George was the lucky one, mate. He was taken up by his aunt Eliza, my grandad's sister. She had a refreshment house in the Bethnal Green Road, inherited from her mum, my great-gran. Made a lot of money and she handed it over to George to run about ten years before you were born.'

'Can we go there?'

'No you cannot. Terrible ruddy place,' said Lil. 'Refreshment house my bum! A stinkin' coffee shop, full of drunks, stuffin' their faces with sandwiches and pickled onions, swilling beer and throwin' skittles at each other in the basement. I've 'eard that Old George gets a bit tight 'imself and throws eggs at the customers – 'es still good with 'is fists – 'as to be in a joint like that!'

'Is that how you get rich, then?'

'Some people do, mate,' said dad. 'But it's not a very good thing to do.'

'Is that why Aunty Eugenie sniffs a lot?'

'No, mate. She's very sad because her youngest boy, Albert, was killed in the war. He was only a lad – ran off and volunteered, joined the Gordon Highlanders.'

'So Uncle George isn't really the lucky one, is he Dad? Why did you say he was? Mum's nephew Albert was killed in the War, too. Did everyone called Albert get killed?'

22

Pan excelled at school and came top in the exams which earned her a place at Skoriers (where fees were paid for Ooly) and Lil cooked her favourite supper of baked potatoes, sausages and onions to celebrate. A new world opened up. Genteel ways were dispensed at the old established institution, there were visits to art galleries and the theatre, field trips, a choir, an orchestra.

It was Miss Bagwell the art mistress, who she talked about most. Baggy this and Baggy that – 'Baggy says I'm really good at drawing. Baggy chose me to be silk worm monitor. Baggy took me up into the tower to watch the sunset over St Paul's. Baggy wears the most beautiful floaty dresses, all different blues and greens, and earrings which dangle and sparkle. Do you know what she said today? – "Pansy dear, I'm having a little tea party for some of my best gels at my house in Woodford, and you are invited."' Sid was delighted. Lil was dubious.

Lil wasn't quite sure what university was and how it was different from school. When Pan got a place to do something called "botany and zoology" at King's College (London) there was a terrific song and dance. As well there might be. Sid and Old Dot were overcome with pride, though Sid was concerned that it might "overtax her strength". Years of hopping up and down on a pogo stick had wrecked her back and there were still "incidents". The three girls had gone off on holiday to the Lakes, on their own, and had to come home early because the landlady of the B&B couldn't stand Pan's screaming at night times. At least she would be living at home and they could keep an eye. Ooly had hoped she might make it to Oxford or Cambridge or somewhere even farther away.

Chapter 3:
Back to Christmas 1938

As Lil settled down comfortably in front of the blazing fire, to have her bit of a sit and relish the hush, she was content. A good fish supper lay ahead – there might be a tussle over Midnight Mass, though.

Mog pleaded: 'Mum, you must come – it's such a lovely service.'

Pan thundered: 'Dad, for goodness sake, it's Christmas – we should all be together, especially this year, our last as a *proper* family, as Ooly has decided to desert and Hitler is on the rampage. God knows where we'll all be next year, and what will Vicar think if half the family is missing. You're ready enough to go off to that wretched chapel at all hours of the day.'

Lil didn't have much truck with church, gloomy old places where you went for buryings with snooty busybodies telling you what to do. As far as she was concerned, Sunday was a day for everyone to put their feet up and get round the table for a hot dinner. She usually got a nice piece of sirloin up Roman, put it in an enamel dish with a little drop of water and, with the lid tightly fixed, she'd pop it in the oven and let it simmer away all morning. Billy the Bombast told her it was the ruination of good beef, but she took no notice – it was what her mum had done, on the very rare Sundays when they had a joint. For special occasions, Billy might come up with a plump fowl (a real treat) and she made onion puddings, delicious little suety balls, sizzled in fat, her mum's recipe. They all had a drop of pale ale, apart from Sid, and if Pan wasn't playing up, or wasn't there, Sunday dinner was a jolly occasion, all together, safe in the Selman Street fortress – Sid called it a "nest of doves" – silly old bugger.

He went off to Old Ford Wesleyan on Sundays, all done up; sometimes he went twice. The girls went to afternoon Sunday School at St Alphege, where there was a better class of person – Lil wanted the best for her kids. Now and again, at Christmas, Easter and Harvest Festival she and Old Dot would put on their hats and go to a service, but she didn't know when to stand up, sit down, or kneel and as reading was never her strong point, she just opened and shut her mouth silently in the hymns.

Lil wasn't quite sure when Pan got religion. She remembered her rushing into the house one time and screaming that God was writing in the sky. 'Mum, Mum come and look – the world must be coming to end!'

'Don't be so bloomin' daft,' she said, and got on with flouring her pastry board.

'Mum, come and see, we're all going to die – I know we are.'

She wiped her hands on her apron and went out into the yard. Sure enough, there was writing in the sky, "Players Please" it said.

When they were too old for Sunday School the girls were sent off to church, showing little enthusiasm until Ooly found it a good market place for courting, Mog, somewhere to show off her looks, and Pan got into Teddy B.

She was about seventeen when the new vicar turned up, young, Oxford educated and a glamorous war hero, standing up there in his starched white surplice, with his coal black hair and pretty face, talking gently of love – who, with racing hormones and academic aspirations, would not be entranced? From then on you couldn't keep Pan away from St Alphege.

Teddy B was delighted to have the Flower Garden on board; they were an ornament to his congregation, rather a different type of girl to

25

the rest of them, better dressed, much better spoken, better educated – quite cultured for the East End. They brought his choir to life and were always ready to give a recital or sing solos for weddings, funerals and festival services. Lily and Rose were exceptionally good looking girls and Pan – she was something different. So vibrant, so forceful and handsome and strong enough to do, single handed, all the necessary heaving around of tables and chairs and the collection of jumble, ready to clamber up and hang bunting, and to run the tombola. When Pan read the lesson, which she often did, her mellifluous tones filled the whole church, stirred the souls of his congregation and disturbed the vicar in a way he did not care to admit.

Mrs B, too, was quite taken with this strange, clever, boyish girl, though the family were certainly not her sort – but then who of their parishioners were? The father was, regrettably, a nonconformist, and the mother was – well – she was rather a rough diamond. The eldest daughter was undoubtedly talented, but rather shallow, she thought, and always surrounded by a cluster of males. Rose, the young one was very pretty, if bulbous, quiet and accommodating – but then there was the dreadful halfwit uncle, and the grave old maid who seemed to be in charge. And that horrible little house – cramped and rackety, smelling of Lisol, littered with half mended saucepans!

Her vicarage was a gracious rambling place, with good old family furniture and a garden large enough for parish fetes. Wrapped in trees and high box hedges, which did their best to keep out the East End, it was an oasis of gentility, sitting uneasily among the mean, squalid houses, appalling public houses and noisy workshops which were its neighbours. Not exactly what Mrs B had in mind when she became Teddy's lawful wedded wife – she was horrified when he took this humble slum cure – but she did her best. At least they had a maid – Pater's generosity allowed them to live decently – and she had put a stop to Teddy's inclination to offer shelter to the hoi polloi. It was, she believed, no part of their duty to encourage dependence on church bounty – they were there to bring light and enlightenment to the poor, not to look after their daily needs.

Seduced by intellectual talk and Mrs B's chintz and lamplight, not to mention the glitter in Teddy B's eyes as he handed her a bone china tea cup or touched her hand as he showed her some old leather bound volume, Pan was often at the vicarage. One summer evening she was there for supper and the three of them sat chatting into the twilight. Mrs B fell asleep in her chair. Pan and Teddy, engrossed in each other, talked deep into the night, until Mrs B woke with a start, hastily rose and broke up the party.

It was not until the small hours that Pan got home.

'Late night, mate,' said dad anxiously.

'Vicar and I have been discussing plans for Harvest' she snapped.

Sid had thought that going to Suffolk would at least keep her away from Teddy B, but as soon as she was home, off she went to church or vicarage. This evening she was, of course, singing carols with Teddy B around the snowy streets of Bow.

Lil had nodded off and Dot was engrossed in her book when the 'erbs descended, their cheeks frozen and flushed, their coats, hats and scarves sprinkled with snow, all excitement and noisy squabbling

'You really mucked up the descant to 'Hark the Herald' – Vicar was furious.' said Pan to Ooly.

'Your soppy vicar wouldn't know a descant from a donkey and I doubt if he's ever been furious in his life, he hasn't got it in him,' said Ooly. 'Pansy, my dear,' she went on in a high-pitched voice, 'could I prevail upon you to join me for a few moments in the church, I am anxious to have your opinion on the new bit of ecclesiastical tat which I have procured to gladden the hearts of my starving parishioners.' She minced about, adjusting an invisible surplice.

'How dare you speak about Vicar like that! How dare you! Just because you've got that teeny weeny diamond on your finger you think you're God Almighty. Well I can tell you, Teddy B knows more about life and suffering than any of this self-regarding household. Unlike *some*, he fought in the War – fought gloriously and …'

'It was all lovely,' Mog interrupted. 'Nobody noticed anything wrong with the singing and we got loads of cash for the children's home.'

'Hark the herald angels sing, Mrs Simpson's pinched our King,' cackled Ed, who had just come in from the shop.

'"Hark the herald angels bicker, Pansy Smart's keen on the vicar," more like it,' said Ooly, under her breath.

In came Sid: 'A merry Christmas, one and all. Who's for a tale of Dingley Dell?'

'Oh, Dad, not Pickwick now, we're starving and we must eat before we go off to the Midnight. You can read it to us tomorrow.' said Mog.

'Yes,' said Pan threateningly, her eyes bulging. 'We are *all* going to the Midnight.'

Here we go, thought Lil.

Christmas Eve supper was rowdy. In the scullery Dot had a quiet word with her sister-in-law and it was decided that for the sake of peace and quiet they'd better go to church. Sid was agreeable, and at eleven fifteen off they set, all of them, apart, of course from Ed.

Along Selman Street there was a tree in almost every window, even some of the Jewish ones, with candles still flickering – Bow went to bed late on this most magical of nights. More snow was falling, transforming the grim little houses into fairytale cottages and the Duke of Cumberland, even at chucking-out time, into a glittering castle. Sid was galloping along, pretending to be the stage coach which took the Pickwickians to Dingley Dell, hallooing seasonal greetings to his neighbours, Jew and Gentile alike: 'A Merry Christmas to you, brother.' Lil was tired and achy and trudged along grumpily, while Dot trod warily on the slippery pavement. Pan marched in the van, high with religious fervour and triumph. Mog was glowing and dreaming, wearing a fur hat which set off her film star looks. Ooly was subdued.

Mog and Ooly linked arms, 'You excited about the wedding, Ool?'

'I suppose it will be like being in a play. Hope dad doesn't decide to do a funny turn, though that might be better than his pious mode. I suppose he *has* to make a speech – just imagine it: "It has been my privilege today, brothers and sisters, to stand before you in the sight of the Lord and give away my daughter, Lily, who has, since early childhood been accomplished at the piano, and has sung before the highest in the land. As she embarks upon the blessed state of matrimony we must all hope that she never abandons the gifts she has been given and that she holds fast to the Good Book. I give you the words of Tiny Tim 'God bless us, Every One'."'

'Ooly, you are wicked. Have you decided on your dress? I suppose Old Beatie will make it?'

Beatie Cohen made their special occasion clothes, while Old Dot and Lil ran up the everyday stuff.

'I'm not sure yet.' She was, however, quite sure that Old Beatie would not have anything to do with this particular garment.

'What will it be like? When I marry, it will be May and I shall wear a gown of gossamer with real flowers in my hair – forget-me-nots to match my eyes – and a necklace like droplets of dew and silver satin slippers. The wedding will be in a tiny medieval country church, probably in Sussex, folded in green hills, and decorated with frothy cow parsley gathered from the lanes.'

'You'll look a right daisy,' said her sister. 'And cow parsley doesn't last two minutes once its cut – and it stinks. What about the groom?'

'Mm, Clark Gable-ish – his mother will have a Georgian silver teapot and his father a pedigree that goes back to the Conquest. Mum will wear lavender lace.'

'She won't like that,' Ooly laughed.

'Anyway – it's your "do" that we should be thinking about. I am

29

going to be a bridesmaid, aren't I? I shall wear palest turquoise and a circlet of lily of the valley. And what about Pan?'

'Blimey – can you see Pan with flowers in her hair? Have I got to be followed up the aisle by that sniffy bugger in a tweed suit? Can't she be an usher or something?'

'Ooly, don't be daft. Pan will *have* to be a bridesmaid. I'm sure we can find something that she's prepared to wear.'

'Well, only if you promise to keep her under control.'

If anybody could, Mog could. For reasons which were hard to fathom, Pan loved her little sister as much as she resented Ooly. After the initial attempts to smother her baby sister with a cushion and a clever plot to roll her up in a rug and put her out with the rubbish, Pan had become her staunch defender. It probably started when two year old Mog became very ill with appendicitis and the poor scrap was stuck in the "London" for weeks, with no visitors allowed. Mum, dad and Aunty went along every day and were allowed to view her at a distance through a glass panel. Pan was sure she would die and when she came tumbling home with her golden curls rubbed off at the back from crying and tossing on the hospital pillow, there was nothing but cherishing and tender watchfulness from her turbulent sister. She even gave her the special purple sweet that she had been given at Sunday School – well she nearly did, carrying it home carefully wrapped up in her handkerchief, but when she and Ooly got as far Tom Thumb's Arch she succumbed and popped it into her own mouth.

Mog was, of course, no rival in the performing stakes, being two years younger, and her voice, when it developed and joined the family choir, though high and silvery, was no match for Pan's or, indeed, Ooly's. Her exquisite face posed no problems for Pan, who saw, and treated her, as a rather simple angel.

Further discussion of the wedding plans were curtailed by their arrival at church.

A shaft of light splayed out from the west door onto the snow and

Teddy B stood there, beaming, wrapped in a thick wool cloak with a frosting of snow on his glossy black hair:

'Mr Smart, Mrs Smart, Miss Smart, girls – welcome, welcome, one and all.'

'Vicar looks like he's something out of The Bride of Frankenstein,' whispered Ooly to Mog.

'Shut up, she'll hear you'.

When Christmas Day dawned the snow was deep and 29 Selman Street yawned into festive mood.

The major spat came early. Sid lit the candles on the tree so that it would be ready for the girls when they came down to breakfast. It was, as usual, a tall spruce with gangling arms, which took up a good deal of the parlour. Lil, bustling by with an armful of parcels, brushed against it and over it went, flames shooting up, making a good Christmas crackle. Quick as a flash, and proud of himself, Ed stomped all over the flaming tree with his heavy boots. Down rushed the girls to see what the commotion was all about, and beheld Pan's treasured glass baubles smashed to bits.

'You stupid, stupid old fool – look what you've done.'

'I've put the fire out,' he stammered.

Pan lunged at him, picking up the poker as she did so, and took a swipe at his head. It was a narrow miss and Lil managed to seize the implement out of her hand.

'Get out of 'ere you ruddy maniac – get out of this house and if you show yourself 'ere agin' you will find yourself in the nick. Out – out!' She opened the front door and pushed the hysterical Pan, still in her pyjamas, out into the snow.

'Mum, I didn't mean it – I didn't mean it.'

The door was slammed.

'Before any of you whey-faced wimps say anything, I've had enough. She is off 'er blitherin' 'ead, always 'as been. Let 'er go and

31

smash 'er posh friends up with a poker or those toffee nosed items up at the vicarage.'

No one said anything.

The sound of wailing and screaming brought Mossy junior out from next door: 'In trouble, Pan? We 'eard your mum shoutin' about the poker. Wanna come in to ours?'

No reply. Pan lay in the snow battering the door with her fists.

Sid crept out the back way and over the wall and took her some clothes, a warm coat, a scarf and some gum boots: 'You'd best get yourself off to the vicarage – mum's really riled.'

She did, and number 29 got on with Christmas, Ooly's last Christmas as a Smart – thank the Lord.

By Boxing Day morning history had been re-written. Lil had calmed down and Dot went off to the vicarage to bring the miscreant home. Not that she was, any more, accounted a miscreant, least of all by herself.

'Poor Pansy, fancy that terrible man smashing everything up!' said Mrs B.

' I spent hours choosing those baubles. Ones like that are only made in one Austrian village – they were like spun gold with beautiful tracery. I so wanted you to see them.'

The word "poker" was not mentioned either in the vicarage or at home and everything at Selman Street went on much as usual, with the ham, beef and Sid's home made mustard pickle laid out ready for the party: Uncle Billy, Aunty Flo' and Old Morgan were invited, as they always were on Boxing Day. Pan was back on form, shouting orders about the table settings and Ed cowered in the corner while Sid disposed of the offending tree and got his fiddle out ready for the musical entertainment which would follow the meal.

'I suppose that silly old Billy will make us say grace,' said Lil, who only put up with her brother-in-law for the sake of the poultry and the lavish presents he had always given to the girls for birthdays.

In they came, Billy resplendent in his gold fob watch and chain strung across his fat chest – the butchering business was doing well. Flo' wore purple with a long string of pearls dangling down over her pendulous bosom, her hoity-toity double chin wobbling with Christmas cheer.

Old Morgan was fun – he had curly red hair and a smiley, wide face. 'Happy Christmas, folks. Here's a bottle or two to see us on our way. Where's Mog?'

Mog emerged from the kitchen and allowed herself to be hugged. She liked Old Morgan, but that was all.

'I gather congratulations are in order, Ooly – where's the lucky man?'

'He's spending his last family Christmas with some relatives in the country somewhere,' said Ooly vaguely.

'Have you fixed a date?'

'Not yet.'

'St Alphege, of course?'

'Oh, yes,' She allowed herself a glance at Pan. 'The Reverend Teddy B will officiate in all his glory, I have no doubt.'

Pan glowered menacingly and Dot hastily took round tiny glasses of sherry with plum cordial for Billy and Flo'.

Billy took the best chair: 'I could probably get Cutter and Butter to do the wedding breakfast; they don't normally do anything in the East End, but for my niece I'm sure something can be arranged. Splendid outfit; they cater for our company dinners. (Billy had recently become Freeman of a City livery company, the Honourable Society of Wax Chandlers.) Harry Cutter has graced our abode many a time, hasn't he Flo'?'

'Oh yes, Billy.'

'We want something better than bridge rolls and dad's home made ginger beer,' (hearty laugh) 'don't we Ooly?'

'Oh yes, Uncle Billy.'

'We dined at Hall only last week – Lord Brackenthorpe was guest speaker, wonderful chap – marvellous speech. Makes you think about what Hitler is really up to. He's certainly got Germany on its feet. Flo' wore silver lamé, didn't you Flo'?

'Oh yes, Billy.'

Ooly winced.

'It'll have to be tail coats, of course – can't have a Smart wedding with anything less. A business contact of mine has a hire place in the City – rather pricey, but top notch. I'll introduce you, Sid, but you'll have to mind your manners, these people are used to dealing with the quality.'

'Doing a good trade in black shirts, no doubt' whispered Ooly to Mog, who saw her mother bridling and quickly introduced a new topic.

'Tell us about your new house, Uncle Billy.'

Billy had come up in the world; he now had several shops and had decided that it accorded with his new status to evacuate the flat over the Bethnal Green butchery and make for the sunnier climes of Forest Gate, where they had bought (not rented) a palace (neat little semi) with self-closing doors (whatever they were) and all manner of modern conveniences. Flo' had a vacuum cleaner and rose beds.

'You ought to try and get away from this dump, Sid. Nothing like the fresh air of Forest Gate, is there Flo'?

'There certainly isn't, Billy.'

'Handy for the park, the cemetery, good clean shops. Plenty of room for an air raid shelter if the worst comes to the worst. You should think about it, Sid,'

'We're more than content here, mate,' said Sid.

Lil was thinking about rose beds.

After the meal came the music: Ooly at the piano, Sid with his fiddle and everyone singing except the outliers, Lil and Ed. Lil was proud of her performing family, but she didn't really care much for music herself and thought classical stuff sounded like ants running up and down the window. When the girls and Sid got together round the piano, which they often did, the noise was deafening and made her head ache. Ed usually sat in the kitchen and did the pools (much to Sid's disgust).

Dot was no musician but she listened dutifully and every Christmas, after a good deal of practice, she played 'London's Burning' on the piano with bells on her wrists, for a joke. But this parlour concert was no joke – it was serious business. At no time was the competition in the Flower Garden so keen, with Mog trilling her soprano, proud of the high notes she could reach, higher than anyone else, Ooly engulfing the room with her magnificent mezzo, Pan oozing out the liquid gold of her deep alto, pulling such extraordinary faces, as if she was in an agony of labour for each note:

'Come unto me all ye that labour ...'

They sang carols and other things, solos, part songs and choruses. On and on it went. Billy had no voice but he joined in with a gruff and hearty, if toneless, noise and Old Morgan added a jolly baritone-ish sort of sound.

'Come on, Flo, give us 'Now sleeps the crimson petal'.'

'Must I, Billy?' she simpered.

'Everyone must do their party piece at Christmas.'

Off she warbled:

'Now folds the lily all her sweetness up,
And slips into the bosom of the lake:
So fold thyself, my dearest, thou, and slip
Into my booo-sooom and be lost in me.'

'At least it ain't encased in silver lamé tonight,' whispered Lil to Mog.

Ooly sang the Kerry Dance:

'Oh for one of those hours of gladness
Gone, alas, like our youth too soon.'

Sid gave a good rendering of 'I hear you calling me':

'I hear you calling me

35

Though years have stretched their weary length between
And on your grave the mossy grass is green
I stand, do you behold me listening here
Hearing your voice through all the years between
I hear you ca-alling me!'

Followed by 'Thora':
'I loved you in life too little
I love you in death too well.'

'Blinkin' miserable all these old songs,' said Lil, to no one in particular.

There was a thunderous rendering of the Hallelujah Chorus which made number 29 shake and Edie and Mossy Goldberg, next door, put their fingers in their ears.

'Let's do "The Gypsy's Warning", cried Mog – 'It's such fun.'

They usually finished off with 'The Gipsy's Warning'.

They had been at it for several hours now and Lil was praying that this was the signal for celery and paste sandwiches, followed by departure and bed.

Mog (the gypsy):

'Do not trust him, gentle lady, though his voice be low and sweet
Heed not him who kneels before you, gently pleading at thy feet
Now thy life is in its morning; cloud not this thy happy lot ...'

All:

'Listen to the gypsy's warning, gentle lady, heed him not
Listen to the gypsy's warning, gentle lady, head him not.'

Pan (the dastardly suitor):

'Lady, heed thee not her warning, lay thy soft white hand in mine
For I seek no fairer laurel than the constant love of thine.

When the silver moonlight brightens, thou shalt slumber on my breast

Tender words thy soul shall lighten, lull thy spirit into rest.'

All:
'Listen to the gypsy's warning, gentle lady, heed him not
Listen to the gypsy's warning, gentle lady, head him not.'

Roars of laughter from all – except Ooly.

Chapter 4:

November 1936 to August 1937, Ooly

The first flush of the Lily might have faded, but Ooly was, nevertheless, undoubted Queen of Old Ford, with her singing and her prowess at the piano; now she took to the stage as well.

When she was fourteen dad had taken her up west to the Regent's Theatre see *Romeo and Juliet*. They had all been to the pantomime, of course, but it had been nothing like this wonderful tragic tale of love. She was overcome by the magic world – the fairytale building with its fantastic turrets, the boxes with their gilt chairs, the plaster cupids and glittering chandeliers, but, most of all by Gwen Ffrangcon-Davies, sweeping in with her high-crowned tiara, all in palest green chiffon over a corn yellow satin under dress.

After that she got it into her head that she would become an actress. Sid wouldn't hear of that: 'You stick with your music, mate. The stage is no place for a respectable young woman.'

But, reluctant to get down to the learning part which might make her into a concert pianist, or an opera singer, she ended up being a typist, somewhere in the City. Lil thought it was a good job, but Ooly hated every minute and went in for amateur theatricals in a big way. The Alphege Players were all she talked about now – she was Cinderella in the Christmas pantomime; nearly all the starring roles came her way. Audiences were from as far afield as Ilford. In spite of her nose, which wasn't nearly as bad as she thought, she got a flock of admirers and always seemed to have at least two in tow.

All three of the girls had their dad's wonderful, large eyes, only Ooly's were dark, almost black, and her skin pale and translucent and her hair deep brown. She had the very best clothes in Bow. Lil saw to that. One time the vicar's wife found a pair of fine lavender kid gloves left behind in church; she knew they had to be Lily Smart's.

There was a very grand concert at the People's Palace, with Sir Malcolm Sargent ("Flash Harry") conducting, bringing culture to the masses. Ooly was singing with the sopranos and had a little bit of a solo part. She wore a clingy deep-crimson frock of chiffon velvet and looped her glossy chestnut hair into a loose bun, instead of its daytime rolls. 'Blimey, Ool, you don't look too bad,' was Lil's comment, when she came down the stairs. It was the nearest mum had ever got to a compliment.

'You look quite beautiful,' said Dot, 'no one will notice your nose.' Her skin was creamy, her dark brown eyes soulful, and her figure such as might make Mog weep – but she was away at college, eating buns to cure her homesickness.

Dad wished Ooly the very best of luck – he couldn't attend the concert as he was performing himself at Old Ford Wesleyan. 'Mind how you go mate, there's pea-souper out there tonight, take this with you, just in case.' He thrust a police whistle into her hand. Since the terrible tumult of the Battle of Cable Street only a few weeks back, he had been even more anxious than usual.

'Dad, for goodness sake, don't fuss.'

When the concert was over and the sopranos were twittering with excitement, and comparing notes about which of them had been singled out for a kiss (blown of course) by the great conductor, a tall, dark young man with a fine Roman nose and an expensive tweed overcoat came over to the group.

'Excuse me,' he doffed his homburg, 'It's Miss Smart, isn't it? May I say what a jolly good performance you gave. Absolutely splendid. I w-w-wonder if I might accompany you home?'

39

Ooly was used to this sort of thing, but not used to this sort of person and thought that Selman Street was probably not his kind of terrain.

'Thanks, but my dad's taking me home.'

'Oh-er-righto. Good evening then, and many congratulations, again.' He wandered off, looking, she hoped, rather disconsolate.

'Cripes, Ooly,' said Maureen, from next door. 'He's some toff! And did you see the width of his Oxford bags! Your dad's not taking you home — why didn't you go with him?'

'What, and let him see our house, and dad calling him "brother" and treating him to a rendering of "I've got the Oopazootic", Old Dot putting on her lady muck act, mum nudging and winking and sticking on aitches where there shouldn't be any, Ed sounding off about how Ramsay MacDonald betrayed the workers? Not likely.'

She and Maureen fumbled their way home along the Mile End Road, through the dense fog, with only the occasional faint glow of moving lights, the smell from the fish and chip shop, and the drunks pouring out of the Bancroft Arms, to guide the way. Some shadowy figures were gliding about like ghosts; Ooly thought she saw him again, getting into a cab, and was very grateful for the fog which prevented him from observing that her dad was not, in fact, seeing her home.

Sid was waiting up: 'How did it go mate?'

'It was OK, pretty good, I think.'

A few weeks later he of the Roman nose turned up again, came round to the stage door at the parish hall, when she had been starring in *The Passing of the third Floor back*. This time he asked if he m-m-might take her to the flics, if she wasn't too busy, any day to suit – there was a Ginger Rogers and Fred Astaire film playing at the Majestic. That was safe, she thought. Dougie was his name.

She didn't mention him at home, or even to Maureen, but sitting over her hated typewriter she whiled the days away, dreaming of the way his black hair flopped over his brow and his elegant hands entwined with her elegant hands, as they walked around Vicky Park, soft little kisses,

40

laughing as their big noses collided.

Sometimes, after work, she met him under the clock at Charing Cross and they did a show, but were always impatient for it to finish so they could just be together, walking along the Embankment, having a pot of tea at Lyons Corner House, going home, tucked up on top of the number eight.

He told her he was a doctor at the "London", and shared a house with his cousin, also a doctor, in Tredegar Square. She told him about her dad, not all, about mum and Pan and the others, a tidied up version, of course, but never took him home. He never mentioned his immediate family, which got her wondering if they were mad or dead or just too beastly for words.

As the days lengthened and Selman Street daffs were making quite a show, Ooly was at home even less than usual and, when she was, she mooned around the place like a sick cow, Lil thought. In lilac time Dougie took her down to Kew on the train; they carved their initials on a tree and had tea at the Maids of Honour. Afterwards they lay on the grass and the kissing got strong and insistent. Lil knew there was something seriously up when Ooly turned down two really quite plum parts for Alphege Players.

One afternoon in early summer they went boating on the Serpentine; he had rowed when he was up at Oxford, he said. As he seized her round her tiny (18 inch) waist and swung her out of the craft there was a loud hallooing from across the flower beds;

'Dougie! Dougie Mitchell – well I'm damned – fancy seeing you here! And who might this delightful creature be?'

Introductions were made: 'This is my old pal, Dickie.' Ooly was struck completely dumb.

'Still at the doctoring, are you?'

'Look, why don't you and the little lady join us later at Claridges? I'm picking up Vron Brackenthorpe – remember her? She's gone shopping somewhere. Pooty and Snooty are going to come. It'll be good to have a chinwag about Oxford and everything.'

Dougie hesitated: 'Well – I d-d …'

'Come on, old fruit, it'll be just like old times and Pooty's footing the bill, his old man has just popped his clogs.'

Ooly froze. She knew of Claridges, of course, and was only wearing a plain cotton dress, a bit muddy from the boat, and a cardigan.

'Dougie, mum's expecting me home,' she whispered.

'Well you go home now, darling, and I sp-sp-spose we might meet up later, if you like. If you'd rather not …'

'No, I'd love to come.'

'Okey doke,' said Dickie cheerily, 'it's cocktails at eight o'clock then.'

Dougie and Ooly parted company at Bow Road Station, Selman Street being a no-go area, and she flew home.

Pan was there, in a rage, home for the weekend.

'Where the devil have you been? I told you Vicar's coming over for some music this evening – we ought to practice something suitable. Something from the *Messiah* or *Elijah?*'

'I'm busy tonight,' said Ooly.

'What d'you mean busy? If it's just that amateur play-acting you can just put it off. We need you to play the piano. For God's sake have you no consideration for anybody?'

'Ooly, duck, surely you can spare us just one evening,' wheedled Old Dot.

Sid came in, rubbing his hands.

'All ready for a spot of musical entertainment, everyone?'

'Dad, I have to go out.'

Pan flung a plate across the room. Ed ducked.

'Now, now, girls, lets calm down.' said Sid 'Perhaps we can manage unaccompanied – there's my fiddle.'

'You're damned fiddle's no good. Ooly's just determined to ruin my weekend. I'm never coming home again.'

She fled upstairs, and met Lil, coming down to see what this particular scene was all about.

'Any more lip like that, my girl, and you go back to Suffolk and ruddy well stay there.'

Ooly dared not go into the bedroom, so she sent Old Dot up instead.

'Aunty, I need my new apricot silk and the coat that goes with it, and the long cream gloves – they're in the second drawer – and those amber earrings – they're in the box on top.' Oh – and the gold medal I won at the Bromley Music Festival – it's on a chain in the same box.'

She got dressed in the kitchen.

'Where are you off to, all dolled up?' asked Lil.

'As a matter of fact, I'm going to Claridges.'

'They'll be shut, you dope.'

'Not Gamages, Mum, Claridges. It's this very posh place up west. Maureen's rich cousin is taking us there.'

'I didn't know Maureen had a rich cousin – thought all micks were as poor as church mice – livin' like pigs. You make sure you keep your hand on your 'a'penny.'

As Ooly left, Teddy B arrived, and Pan was all charm and smarm, pulling faces at Ooly behind his back.

'Good evening, Vicar, so sorry Lily has to go out. She's got a hengagement at Selfridges,' said Lil, importantly, ushering him into the parlour.

Dougie met Ooly outside the Pavilion Theatre and they took a cab.

He cuddled her and told her she was an absolute stunner. 'Vron can be problematical but you'll love Pooty and Snooty, they're bags of fun.'

Bags of fun was not how Ooly would have described the evening. It started off with yellow coloured cocktails – and Vron. Vron wore a cloche hat covered in sequins and a tight emerald green dress which showed off her fashionably flat chest. Her face was large, too large for the hat, and flabby; her mouth was bright scarlet.

'So, Lily, you play the piano and sing, do you? And what, pray, does your Pa do, dance?'

Befuddled by the unaccustomed drink, Ooly looked hopelessly at Dougie.

'L-l-lily's father's in r-r-retail.'

Out came a shagreen cigarette case, and black Russian cigarettes were offered around.

'I don't smoke, thanks,' said Ooly. She did, but didn't like the look of the black things, and thought perhaps she was supposed to have a holder, like Vron's.

'And, you live in the East End, like darling Dougie. How quaint. My Ma went down there once to do some good works, but it was so frightful she never went back. Do you do good works?'

'Oh yes – all the time.' Ooly managed, thinking of the church jumble sale – they were now on their third yellow drink.

'Have you known Dougie long? I expect his Ma and Pa find you quite adorable – I've known him simply yonks. Lady M is one of my Ma's oldest chums, in fact.'

Lady M – *Lady* M – Ooly felt dizzy and tried to articulate something sensible, horribly aware of her cockney vowels. They were OK when she was singing – Old Matthews who trained her voice saw to that, but, unlike Pan and Mog who had learned well how to speak "proper", Ooly had never bothered much. Any polishing up of her speech that was achieved had been ruined when she joined a girls' club at church where mockery of her posh voice sent her scrambling back into her native modified cockney, where she stayed.

'Dougie and I met at a concert last November,' she said carefully, avoiding any mention of Ma and Pa of whom, of course, she knew nothing whatsoever.

44

Pooty came to her rescue at this point:

'Come on kiddiwinks – time for nosh.'

Through the marble halls they went, past the most extravagant fantasy of delphiniums and peonies Ooly had ever seen, and across a deep pile carpet to a round table, sparkling with silver and glass, with waiters hovering around.

The menus, huge and formidable were distributed.

'Lily and I like to st-st start with asparagus, followed by sole meunière and then perhaps some fillet of beef – if that's OK with you, darling – we'll have our usual, shall we?'

Vron snorted and Ooly gave a dignified nod. She was unfamiliar with asparagus, however, and when it came was most surprised to see her fellow diners pick it up in their fingers. She followed suit and dropped a blob of melted butter onto her apricot silk.

'Oops,' said Vron, 'that's your best party frock in the wars!'

Ooly was feeling more in command of the situation since the champagne had arrived; Pooty had started to question her about the gold medal she wore around her neck, Snooty asked her if she might like to accompany him to the Wigmore Hall, if Dougie didn't mind, and Dickie had rubbed his leg up against hers.

'Oh goodness – don't worry about this old thing. Lady M is taking me to be fitted for a new wardrobe at her cootoorier's – she wants to treat me to some really splendid gowns for my next tour – I'm off on the Queen Mary next month. I've got masses of frocks, of course, my Ma sees to that – but its so kind of Lady M, I can hardly not accept her offer.'

Who said that? Must have been Ooly Smart of Selman Street, Bow. After all, she was an actress.

The sole and the beef went down nicely, as did the Corton-Charlemagne, the La Tâche, and the Château d'Yquem. Vron kept ominously quiet and everyone else had a hoot of a time, dancing and smooching to smoky, soft romantic music under the crystal chandeliers in the great ball room.

They rolled out into cabs, variously.

'Dougie – is your mum really a Lady?'

'Mm. Shush – I must kiss you all the way home. He did for a while and she had to let the driver go to Selman Street, but by that time they were both asleep.

'Here we are, ladies and gents, next stop Tredegar Square.' Dougie was spark out.

Dad was waiting up. 'Good night?'

'I think so.'

'Cocoa?'

'No thanks, Dad, I'll just go up.' She found the stairs.

Dougie was going to see her the following Monday – dad liked them all at home on Sundays. She waited outside Bow Road station for an hour. She thought of walking round to Tredegar Square – she was pretty sure she knew which house it was – but decided against it. He had probably got held up at the hospital, anyway.

Not wanting to go home, she wandered about, returning to the station every now and again. It was a hot evening, there as a smell of tar and the kids were playing hopscotch and marbles in the streets. She met some of the crowd from the Alphege Players. 'Where have you been, Lily?' asked Johnny Bowyer, hesitantly, 'we haven't seen hide or hair of you since "Passing". We're auditioning for *Berkeley Square* soon, why don't you come along?'

She said she'd think about it and went back to the "nest of doves".

No word came from Dougie. As the days passed her stomach knotted up more and more and she started a stye. Mum thought she looked a bit peaky, but that she was best left be.

On Friday of the second week an envelope addressed to Miss Smart plopped on to the mat. It had been re-addressed, having gone first to number 39. With trembling hands she tore it open. It came from somewhere called Barrington Gardens and, oh joy, oh joy! it was from

Lady Mitchell. They were having a little do – would she like to come? – perhaps she would play the piano – just some background jazz and songs from the shows would do nicely.

Dear, dear Dougie. He had been keeping this as a surprise. She was being invited to meet his family.

'Good news, Ooly?' Dad was putting on his hat ready to leave for work.

'Oh it's just someone wanting me to play at a party up west.'

On the appointed day she set off, wearing beige slipper satin. A uniformed person opened the door and she gave her name.

'Oh yes. Her Ladyship asked me to show you the piano.'

It was a concert grand, white, with a bowl of lilies on it. Especially for her, no doubt.

'Her Ladyship says you might like to practice.'

There was no sign of any guests, but after an hour or so Lady M swept in, tall and dark, in brown and gold lace, all affability. Ooly thought she looked rather like a hawk.

'Miss Smart! How kind of you! And how delightful you look! Someone will bring you a glass of champagne – but perhaps you don't drink when you're playing.' And off she wheeled.

The guests started to arrive – Ooly tinkling away – no sign of Dougie yet. Perhaps he might turn up with a diamond ring in a little velvet box.

She tinkled on – some jazzy stuff at first to jolly them along and as they settled in to chat and clink and the air was a haze of blue smoke, she turned to something gentler, popping in dad's favourite, 'Silent Worship' ('though I could never woo her, I love her till I die') and some Ivor Novello tunes.

Still no Dougie. Should she ask?

Dickie was there. He came and leered over the piano. 'Well, well – if it isn't the little lady from the boating lake! Thought you'd be on the Queen Mary by now,' he chortled.

'Where's Dougie?'

He laughed. 'Dispatched.'

'What do you mean?'

'Dispatched. A foreign trip or something, with his Pa. They didn't seem to like the way the wind was blowing.'

'The way the wind was blowing?' she repeated, her stomach twisting and her stye burning.

'W-why am I here?'

'It was Vron's idea – thought it was a good way of letting you down lightly, I suppose. She and her Ma are very pally with the family. And curiosity – the Hawk wanted to give you the once over, and a pay off.'

Lady M came up and put a bunch of crisp bank notes on to the piano. 'Thank you Miss Smart, and goodbye. I trust our paths will not cross again.'

The maid showed Ooly to the door. The party was over.

Ooly never cried, even as a child – well only once, for some white court shoes she saw in a shop in Margate. She did now – great racking sobs – all the way from Mayfair to Bow. Never much of a one for walking, but tonight it was the only way to make the pain bearable. As she trudged along Oxford Street it came on to rain and her beige satin dragged through the puddles. When she got to Charing Cross Station she simply had to sit down. As she sat with her head in her hands a tramp came up and settled down on the next-door bench, all wrapped up in newspaper. She took the soggy bank notes out of her coat pocket and thrust them into his grubby paw and went on her way.

'Hey – missus – bloody … blinkin' 'eck – there's a hundred smackers 'ere.'

It was the early hours by the time she got to Selman Street. Dad was waiting up.

'Had a good night, mate? You look like a drowned rat.'

'Oh Dad, it was awful.' She flung herself down on the settee and out it came, all of it – well, most of it.

'Never you mind. Just drink this hot cocoa – Aunty and I will sort it all out.'

She was too exhausted to protest.

The very next day Sid closed the shop early and they set off for Barrington Gardens, Old Dot in her best hat and Sid in his Sunday suit. They took umbrellas, as rain threatened, and several buses.

The footman said that Her Ladyship was busy, but they might wait, and they were ushered into a book lined room which Sid took to be the library.

'Just look at those leather bindings – wonderful craftsmanship. They must do a deal of reading here. I'd like old Pan to see this.'

Lady M kept them waiting a long time and finally came in.

'I imagine this is what you have come for?' – she sat down at writing desk (finely inlaid), took out a mother-of-pearl fountain pen and wrote a very large cheque, with a flourish.

Sid calmly removed it from her outstretched claw and tore it up.

'I have heard something of the way you and yours have treated my girl, Lady Mitchell, and my sister and I are here, not for your lucre, but for an apology and an explanation. What about this young man of yours – what's he been up to I'd like to know? Dorothy and I would like a word or two with him, if it's convenient to your Ladyship, of course.'

'Convenient! Convenient! It is most certainly not. His father has taken him away. If you choose to spurn my generosity there is no more to be said.' and she rang the bell.

'Pardon me, your Ladyship, but in our opinion there is a good deal more to be said.'

'I suppose you are trying to tell me the wretched girl has got herself into trouble.'

'I'll say she has (Sid hadn't quite understood) – getting herself mixed up with a cad like your blessed son, who drops her just like that, and then you make a fool of her like you did.'

'Come, come now, Mr Smart, you can't possibly imagine that an East End oil and colourman's daughter – that's what you are I gather? – has any place here.'

'It's a good honest trade – and we are straight folk with plain, honest values. My Lily has sung before the Duchess of York, she's no ordinary girl – she was giving piano recitals when most kiddies are still …'

'Look, Mr Smart, if your daughter is pregnant …'

'What?' gasped Sid, 'Haven't you done enough to my girl without insulting her? Come on Dot, I'm listening to no more of this. May God forgive you, Lady Mitchell – if you want to learn to mend your ways, I can recommend the first seven chapters of Jane Eyre. And I would be obliged if you would give my compliments to your husband and ask him to call at 363, Roman Road at his earliest convenience.'

They left.

'How did it go, Dad?'

'Oh, pretty well, I think. You won't be troubled with that crew any more.'

Ooly's heart sank.

'I 'ope you gave them what – for,' said Lil, suspecting that this was unlikely.

'But, what about Dougie? What did she say about Dougie?'

'Aunty and I think it's for the best if you forget about that young gent,' said Sid, gravely.

She didn't. She couldn't. Every morning she rushed down to catch the postman. After a few weeks she even swallowed her pride and went up to the hospital. No, Dr Mitchell had left, rather suddenly.

Dougie would never have just gone – after all the things he had said. All she could think about was the way his eyes tipped down at the corners, the blue-grey tweed of his over coat, that bit of a stutter when he was nervous, the smile when he met her, that glorious, happy smile. Over and over again she went through it all, sitting on the bus, walking

50

along Bow Road, at her typewriter, during Teddy B's sermons. Her anguish was played out on the upright in the parlour, hour upon hour.

'Wish she'd knock off that bleedin' jo for a bit – it's drivin' me mad.'

Lil had never been one for romantic love. Just find a suitable bloke and make the best of it was her creed.

Sid knew about heart break, Ooly had always thought: 'Have you not seen my lady go down the garden singing … though I could never woo her, I love her till I die.' On the other hand, as she knew full well, he didn't want his girls taken from him, especially not by another man; nobody would ever to fly the "nest of doves" if he had his way.

Ed said it was only to be expected if you tangled with toffs, and Old Dot, kind as ever, was all sympathy and re-assurance, with much talk of pebbles on the beach and fish in the sea. Very secretly, she wondered if perhaps the Queen of Bow had got her come-uppance.

No word came. Sir Henry Mitchell never turned up at the shop for Sid to administer the dressing-down he had in mind and the days dragged on through hot and sticky summer evenings, endless in their despair.

All the family knew about Ooly's trouble now. Sid wrote to Pan about it in his twice-weekly missives and Dot and Mog chewed it over. Lil kept mum. Everyone agreed that Ooly needed taking out of herself and Mog took her off to see a Fred Astaire film, but when he sang 'Suddenly I saw you there, and through foggy London town the sun was shining everywhere', it was too much for Ooly and they had to come out.

When Pan came home in the summer holidays they talked of little else but the Barrington Gardens Humiliation. Pan railed against men in general, while Mog, who nurtured a particular aversion to society women who had their pictures in magazines, reckoned it was all the fault of that Veronica Brackenthorpe. She brought home a copy of the *Tatler* and they all had a good look at her photograph and pronounced her hideous.

'Leave it be, mates,' said Sid (often). 'Ooly's well out of it.'

'Leave it be! Leave it be!' roared Pan. 'She's only been made a public fool of and us with her.'

'Poor old Ooly,' said Mog. 'I think she really was in love with him.'

'Love and stuff,' said Lil. 'All I know is I'd like to wring their ruddy necks, all of them.'

'Up the workers!' cackled Ed.

Ooly auditioned for the autumn production of *Berkeley Square* and got the female lead. (autumn 1937). Wearing a flattering white wig and swathed in a gorgeous eighteenth century gown, she started to heal, and a hard crust began to form over the wound, pierced only now and again by the sight of a grey-blue tweed coat, the scent of lilac or the words of the "Gipsy's Warning".

Chapter 5:
October to November 1938

Pan kept up with some of her old teachers from Skorriers, Baggy in particular, who was now headmistress. When she was home from Ipswich she occasionally went off to the pretty regency house on Woodford Green, for an afternoon of culture and gossip.

'Now, my dear, tell me about the family. I suppose Rose is as beautiful as ever, and Lily – does she still play?'

'Not as much – she's too busy with her acting and her men.' And she outlined the story of last year's Humiliation.

'My dear, how positively frightful for your poor sister. I have some slight acquaintance with the Brackenthorpes – the father's a fascist – has spent some time in Germany – great admirer of the regime. The Mitchells, I regret to say, are remote relations of mine, very remote. Hawky Mitchell is my mother's third cousin – awful woman, has her family completely under the thumb – or claw. They're all part of the Cliveden Set – you know the crew who congregate at the Astor's place and are all for cosying up to Hitler. What dreadful, dreadful goings-on one hears of these days. Dear Austria – you've visited haven't you? –heavenly Vienna – Mozart, Beethoven Strauss – taken over by that brute. Where will it all end?'

Pan didn't know much about politics, but she had heard of the Cliveden Set and, of course, Lady Astor, first woman MP, who had come to present the prizes at Skoriers one year. She hated the Germans with a passion, however, having been born into the world of the trenches, was terrified by the sinister goings-on in Europe and ranted a good deal about the feebleness of the British government. Pan was never one for appeasement.

'What about the son, Douglas?'

'Suffers with nerves, I think, and who can wonder, with a mother like that. More tea?'

'Thank you, Miss Bagwell.'

'My dear girl, not Miss Bagwell, please, we are no longer mistress and pupil. Do call me Ruth. Now, you must stay to supper, we have so much to talk about.'

After several glasses of elderflower wine there was more discussion of the Barrington Gardens Humiliation.

After Pan had left, Baggy put her mind to business.

Prize Day was a great occasion at Skoriers, held, unusually, in November, on the anniversary of the founder's death, which meant that girls who had left at the end of the previous year came back to receive their prizes, dressed in their very best finery. Some celebrated and influential lady was usually invited to give the prizes away. Baggy had something up her sleeve, which she decided to keep to herself.

'Who? Who might Veronica Brackenthorpe be?' asked the deputy head.

'Well, she's nobody, really, but she happens to be a viscount's daughter and I have some relatives who know her quite well, so we could easily get her,' replied Baggy.

'Is there any connection with the school?'

'Well – I'm sure we could dredge something up. I think her mother did a very brief stint of "East Ending".

It was agreed and a letter was sent to Brackenthorpe Towers.

'Oh Ma, how terrifically silly – some East End school wants me to present their prizes! I've had a letter from that eccentric woman, Ruth Bagwell.'

'Darling, that's splendid. Time you did your bit. I'm sure your father would approve.'

'But, what can I say? I shall have to make some sort of speech.'

'I'm sure Dougie will help – he knows all about the dreadful place – especially since he had that liaison with that Semitic looking girl who played the piano.'

'You know perfectly well, Ma, that Dougie is totally incommunicado.'

'Well – it doesn't really matter what you say – they're only guttersnipes. Just tell them how fortunate they are to be getting an education at all.'

Vron agreed, and turned up on the appointed day wrapped in silver fox, having practiced some words of pleasant condescension. Baggy met her: 'My dear Veronica, how delightful! How *very* kind of you to join us – you got my letters of course? Come along and meet my colleagues.'

Dignitaries and staff gathered on the platform and the girls twittered in excited anticipation. Miss Bagwell, large in aquamarine chiffon, rose to speak.

'We are delighted to welcome back our old girls who have come for their prizes and I would like a special accolade for Lily Smart, one of our most distinguished older old girls, who has graciously offered to play for us today.'

Roars of approval and applause. Ooly took her place at the piano, unaware of Veronica's presence. Miss Brackenthorpe looked on with horror.

Mog, who had come to turn over the pages for Ooly, said, quite loudly 'My God, isn't that the Brackenthorpe woman sitting next to the mayor!'

'And now for our treat ...' went on Baggy. 'We are *immensely* honoured to welcome our celebrated guest. She has *most* generously taken time out of her busy schedule to grace us here today and present our prizes.'

Veronica preened a little. At which point the school captain appeared at the back of the hall and conducted an elegant figure up to the front.

'Cripes, she's only got Lady Diana Cooper – how on earth did she manage that?' whispered Ooly to Mog.

'She's meant to be the most beautiful woman in the country,' said Mog. 'I don't think she's all that ravishing.'

Veronica flushed bright scarlet with outrage and the hall burst into a paroxysm of delight as the girls recognised the woman who was probably the biggest celebrity around, socialite, film star and acclaimed, except by Mog, as the most beautiful woman in the country.

Lady Diana did her stuff while Veronica stewed, firmly wedged between the mayor and the deputy head, she was unable to bolt.

The prizes were handed out to the lucky girls, while Ooly tinkled away. Baggy concluded proceedings:

'Before we go our separate ways, our new old girls off to take their places in the world, I would like a round of applause for Veronica Brackenthorpe, who so generously stood down in favour of Lady Diana. In view of events in Europe and the very public and unfortunate pro-German stance taken by Lord Brackenthorpe in recent months, we agreed it would be most unsuitable for his daughter to speak to us today. With immense courage, she has, in spite of this agreed to join us for our celebrations.' She waved a chiffony arm in Veronica's direction. 'Thank you indeed, Miss Brackenthorpe.'

There was a deathly silence in the body of the hall, broken only by the splat of a rotten egg flung expertly at the silver fox fur by an unseen hand.

Lady Diana, who had agreed to the engagement months ago, looked puzzled.

Veronica fled.

Baggy explained to the governors, who were less than pleased with the debacle: 'With so many Jewish girls in the school, even some refugees – little Anna Hollaender arrived from Vienna only last week – we couldn't possibly have that woman speaking. Everyone knows about Lord Brackenthorpe's anti-Semitic tirades.'

'Surely it was rather ill-considered – making a public pronouncement as you did?' said the chairman of the governors sternly. 'You were not appointed to play politics, Miss Bagwell. And who exactly threw the offending missile, we would like to know?'

'I really have no idea.' (She had.)

'Well, gels,' said Baggy, disengaging herself from the chairman of the governors, and going over to the piano. 'I think that dealt quite nicely with the initiator of the Barrington Gardens Humiliation, Lily.'

'What!' said Ooly, 'How did you know, Miss Bagwell and how did you get Lady Diana Cooper?'

Baggy winked and floated off.

Johnny Bowyer, Johnny-Come-Lately, as he was speedily christened by Pan and Mog, didn't have eyes that tipped down at the corners, they were very pale and bulged ever so slightly. He had a medium sized straight nose, set in a rather long narrow face, and his hair, blond, not black, didn't flop about, but was sleeked down with Brylcreem.

Johnny had been pursuing Ooly with shy determination, ever since his mum had seen her singing 'I know that my Redeemer Liveth' at some church do, and fancying she would make a suitable daughter-in-law, started dropping hints. There was competition among the Alphege Players, and at church; Ernie Atkins, who worked at Charringtons, was mad about Ooly, and so was Owen Lewis from the dairy. Then there was Harold Lemay, of Huguenot descent, or so he said; he taught Sunday School and played the organ at church. Rumours had spread about the toff she'd got mixed up with – but nobody knew any details.

One Sunday morning, a few months after the Humiliation, Ooly was at church for the harvest festival service. It was a glorious autumn day and the sun was streaming through the stained glass windows onto the rows of shiny apples and banks of bitter smelling gold and red chrysanthemums. Johnny went up to read the lesson. He had a fine non-Bow voice, having learned to speak "like a rich man", (as Mog used to say) when, after his father's death, he was sent away to the Masonic School. His green and brown tweeds (not blue-grey) were well cut and his Oxford bags were said to be the widest in the East End.

The sunlight glinted on his sleek golden head and the rich, stern words of the old prophet rang out; 'He'll do,' thought Ooly. Undoubtedly he was the best looking of the bunch and, even though his mum had taken in washing when she was widowed, and then married a docker, Johnny was certainly a cut above the rest; on his father's side he had two uncles who were school masters and a cousin who was a vet. The Masons' schooling, moreover, had done a good job, fitting him for a professional life. Yes – he would do.

After a fairly brief courtship, the flics, some outings up west and to Hampstead Heath on the train, she took him to number 29.

'Dad, Mum, Aunty – this is Johnny Bowyer.' Ed was kept in the kitchen.

'Pleased to meet you, brother. Lily tells us you work in a bank. Good solid job.' Sid was wary. 'Your step-father is on the docks ?'

'Yes, the gov'nor is a foreman in the West India Docks.'

'Ah, a foreman, yes,' said Sid. 'Church goers are you?'

'Oh yes, we all go to St. Alphege. Mother does a turn at the tea urn and the gov'nor carries the cross – on special occasions.'

Johnny's voice got lower and gruffer as it did when he was nervous and he blew his nose, several times. He suffered from catarrh.

'Would you care to take some port wine ?' asked Dot.

'Perhaps you'd rather have a nice cuppa?' said Lil.

'I'm really a beer man – but tea would be fine.'

Johnny perched awkwardly on a squashy armchair and declined a biscuit. His nerves also went to his stomach.

Sid went on. 'What is your instrument – or do you sing?'

'I'm afraid I'm rather non-musical – rugby is more in my line. I play for the bank – was captain at school. Jolly good fun.'

58

'I take it, as an educated man, you are familiar with the works of Charles Dickens ?'

'Oh yes' said Johnny, not realising that this was *the* leading question. 'But I never got on with the books – rather dense and turgid for my taste. My English master went in for the picaresque and he was quite keen on Milton.'

Ooly winced and thanked the Lord Pan was not around.

The formal introduction of Ooly to Johnny's mum, Nell, was more of a success, as well it might be, Nell being the prime mover in the whole business. She thought she would keep her new husband, Albie Waters, the docker, in reserve for a future visit.

'Mother, this is Lily. Everyone calls her Ooly.'

'I'm so pleased to meet you Miss Smart ... er ... O-ooly.'

Ooly flashed her most brilliant smile, for which she was celebrated in the town of Bow, and risked a peck on the cheek.

Nell was rather taken aback.

'I've heard your lovely singing, of course.'

'Come on,' said Johnny, 'Let's get inside the house.'

The table was laid with homemade scones, arranged on a doily, the best china (three Worcester cups and saucers, all that was left of a service given to Nell when she married Johnny's father) and three neatly folded linen napkins.

It was a chilly, quiet, dark house, smelling of damp and faintly of lavender water. Unlike the other Bow houses, which were mainly all-of-a-piece, built about fifty years ago, it was one third of an older, rather bigger house, erected in the more spacious days. Nell maintained that it had once belonged to a bishop.

There was a garden at the front, quite long by Bow standards, with a straggly, sooty hedge fronting the road, a sumac tree and a rusty wrought iron gate which bespoke former glory. At the back the garden had been obliterated, built on by workshops which came right up to the house, blotting out the light. Just inside the front door was a glass-fronted cupboard, full of trinkets, a little green china boot with violets in it, a coronation mug, the wooden butter pats that Nell had brought from her country home, and a cracked plate embossed with a picture of her village church. Once the cupboard had been a window which looked out over the fields, but it had been bricked up long ago.

It felt sad to Ooly – not the sort of place where you could imagine children having grown up. No rocking horses or picture books like they'd had at home, just a pile of yellowing boys' comics, neatly stacked up on an unused kitchen range polished up and used as a sideboard, in a room which had once been the kitchen, but now served as a sort of dining room. Cooking was done on a gas stove tucked into a narrow passage, along which ran a wooden working surface with open shelves above and below. At the end of the passage was the scullery, with an ancient cracked sink (no hot water, except by boiling kettles) and a tin bath hanging on the wall. In the parlour was a door that had been nailed up which led to the middle part of the old house (now next door).

Like her house, Nell was used to fields and trees. Unlike the Smarts, who had been town folk for ever and a day, she was a country girl, whose childhood memories were of skating on the village pond, of larking in the woods with her brothers, helping with the harvest. After a short spell in service with a comfortably-off aunt in Stourport, she took up with Johnny's father, son of the village school master. They married and he brought her to Bow, where he worked, gave her two sons and died, leaving her poverty stricken and stranded. After a ten year struggle, only made feasible by the boys being sent off to the Masonic School, where everything was paid for, she had, much to the horror of her in-laws, married the "boy next door". Albie Waters was considerably younger than Nell, a large, awkward lump of a man, low on book learning and from a family which went hopping. Still, he was kind, pious, earned a good wage, and, best of all, revered and cosseted the long neglected Nell, protecting her from the harshness of the East

60

End and keeping the bailiffs at bay.

Johnny's glamorous young woman, with her scarlet nails, fashionable clothes and effervescent charisma warmed the shabby, still house into life. Ooly was an enthusiastic listener and adept at putting sympathetic gasps of horror or approval in the right places, very polished at the art of making anyone feel in total receipt of her undivided attention. For Nell it was love at first meeting; she was soon at ease and chattering on about the happy days when she had milked her aunt's cows and run about in the corn fields in a floppy sun hat.

As for Ooly, if this was to be her new family, she would make the best of it. There was absolutely no competition here. Johnny's younger brother, Derek, was keeping rather reluctant company with a kindly girl from East Ham who typed. Norah was one of those individuals who dealt with the terrors that crowded into her world by moaning about incidentals, more or less incessantly. Her gripe of the moment was continual mention of an almost invisible rash on her arm, which really meant: 'My dad is a drunken bully; my mum never stands up for me; I'm not very pretty, we live in a hovel; Derek doesn't really love me and his mum treats me like dirt.'

Over the ensuing weeks Ooly brought all the force of Smart charm to bear on the Bowyer/Waters clan. This might be a passionless match, on her side at least, but it would provide a good audience and she would be queen. She brought some Jeyes ointment from the Emporium for Nora's rash, and listened soothingly and reassuringly to her complaints about the catch on her powder compact, the cheekiness of the butcher (aren't all butchers given to sexy badinage?), and the torture of waiting twelve minutes for a tram. Nora was soon captivated. Then there was Old Albie. Ooly admired his new Sunday suit, enquired about the West India Docks and said that if Teddy B had any sense (which she doubted) he would have Albie as church warden. With Derek she flirted and he adored her at once, as most young men did.

At number 29 battle lines were drawn. Pan was home for the weekend.

'Johnny, these are my sisters, Pansy (we call her Pan) and Rose (we call her Mog).'

'Delighted to meet the rest of the Flower Garden.' He kissed Mog in a brotherly fashion and decided to shake hands with Pan. 'Lily has told me so much about you. You are both teachers, I gather?'

Mog giggled and showed her best profile coquettishly: 'I struggle with the brats of Wapping, but Pan is much more important – she's a scientist – went to University!'

Advantage Smart.

'Most impressive,' said Johnny. 'I was offered a place to read chemistry at Oxford, but decided it was time I pulled my weight at home – so got a boring old job in the bank. What's your line, Pan?'

Advantage Bowyer.

'Botany and zoo' snapped Pan. 'I had thought of going into medicine, but I've always felt passionate about the education of girls.'

Fifteen all.

'Sport is my real forte –rugby mainly. D'you play anything?'

'I used to row for King's.'

'My cousin rows for the Royal Vet College – he's a vet you know.'

Slight advantage Bowyer.

'And you both sing, like Lily?' He took a new tack.

'We're all in a concert at church on Saturday night,' said Mog, arching her perfect brows. 'Perhaps you'd like to come along?'

'Sorry – we've got a match – and then we make a night of it in the pub.'

'It's just as well we know what your priorities are,' muttered Pan.

Chapter 6:
Pan and the Drayman visit,
November 1938

Pan took against Johnny in a big way. Ooly might have been her bug bear – but she was her sister, a part of home – not to be removed by any man, let alone such a surly bit of bully beef. She was scared of her safe home nest being broken up. Truth to tell she was scared most of the time.

Her childhood night-time fears had been legion; she remembered listening to the rhythmic drumming of her heart beat and knowing that goblins were marching under the bed, waking in the pitch dark and screaming that she had gone blind, rushing hell for leather out of the lav before the water flushed and brought the hissing snakes up with it.

Things calmed down a bit when school became her passion, especially when Baggy and Skoriers took over her life.

She suffered, gloriously, from pashes, the first object of her fantasies being a stately sixth-former called Delia. Pan grew into her skin, became known for her melodious, deep singing voice, her academic excellence and flower paintings. Her strong, long limbs, flashing green eyes and masterful way with a hockey stick, made girls and staff alike go weak at the knees. When she played Mr Darcy in a production of *Pride and Prejudice* the whole school went "horn mad" and girls in blazers and boaters were to be found hanging around 29 Selman Street at all hours of the day and night. Two years running she was school captain – elected by the girls.

In her late teenage years the mirror cracked from side to side. It was soon after she had taken her matric, she came home from Skoriers and went out into the yard and sat on the wall by the marigolds in the sun. Always she would remember those marigolds, holding up their cocky, vicious orange heads beneath the low, crumbling brick wall. Framed for ever, an anatomy of madness, hanging in her relentless, cruel hall of memory. There was a fizzing, a fuzzing a sudden thumping of her heart and, from nowhere, came the fear to end all fears – the fear of fear itself. The backyard swayed and rocked. Dad's shed brought its face hard up against her. She opened her mouth, but nothing seemed to come out, but she could hear screams. Shadowy figures appeared with wondering, sad, bewildered eyes.

Waiting for the bus in the Strand, walking along Bow Road, sitting at the kitchen table – always they were there. Her head was full of death. Sitting on the beach at Margate she would see the sea rise into a towering wall of water roaring towards the Smart picnic and deck chairs. For months on end she was unable to swallow anything for fear of choking. Any pimple or bump was cancer; if she had a cough it was TB. Her biological training made matters worse and a good deal of time was spent diagnosing fatal ailments not just in herself, but the rest of the family.

She absolutely refused to see a doctor; Dot and Lil came up with various nerve tonics and everyone battened down the hatches and somehow weathered it through her explosions of rage and violence. The outbursts seemed to alleviate her agony, as did the arrival of Teddy B.

King's had not been such a good time for Pan. The work was hard – Skoriers was all very well for making ladies out of slum girls, but academics? – not really. "Blue stockings" were still something of a rarity and almost unknown in Bow, except among visiting do-gooders. Most of her fellow university students and all tutors and profs were men and no one at all was from the East End. Not that she admitted that she was, she let it be thought that she came from Purley. The prospect of the annual ball was excruciating but attendance was *de rigeur*. She borrowed a frock, which made her feel like a scarecrow, and one of Ooly's hangers-on for the evening. Awkwardly she tottered around the dance floor in unaccustomed court shoes, holding the hanger-on at arm's length. At least rowing and the choir made life bearable.

A degree was awarded, not a good one, and it was with relief that she went off to teacher training, at which she excelled, and "back to school". Teaching practice was at a convent in Hampstead. At first she was wary; mum had always told her to run fast past the convent near home in case the nuns got her. She remembered her tales of going with her brothers and putting soot in the holy water so when the "old mickeys" crossed themselves they would have a black mark on their foreheads. As a matter of fact, her Hampstead days turned out to be the greatest of fun; she soon had the nuns swooning.

Leaving home for her first job, in Suffolk, was a terrifying wrench, not least for Sid. Lil and Dot packed her up with home-made cakes and warm underwear, Ed gave her some "fag money" and Sid came up with warnings and saucepans, expertly soldered.

'These may come in handy, they've got a lot of use in them.'

'How on earth do you think I'm going to manage that lot on the train?'

At Liverpool Street there were nearly tears. As the monstrous puffing giant pulled out, taking Pan out into the great unknown, Sid was running along side. 'Remember, mate, "Those friends though hast, and their adoption tried, grapple them to thy soul with hoops of steel".' Polonius's words were lost in the blasts of steam, but this was one piece of advice Pan did not need.

School provided a safe enclosed harem, a good audience, a fawning coterie of colleagues and adolescent girls, deprived of male company.

When she came home for a visit, a not infrequent occurrence, she often had two women in tow, colleagues from school. Pan was now sure enough of herself to reveal her East End origins. What a scrubbing and polishing, fumigating and fuss went on in preparation for these occasions. Ed was often packed off to relatives – they didn't want him coughing up lace curtains, making daft comments or getting into one of his "up the workers" monologues. Ooly took herself off to Maureen's and Old Dot gave up her double bed and slept downstairs. If Mog was there she slept with Lil, and Sid took the narrow bed in the box room vacated by Ed.

Lil didn't know what to make of the visitors; Sid was impressed by his daughter's clever, classy chums, and relieved that there was no man on the scene likely to steal Pan away, seeing nothing untoward in the surreptitious handholding and whispering which went on.

Gif (Aelgifu) Drayman was the main contender, an enormous woman with a motor, no less, a gleaming dark red Vauxhall, which she named "Amun" (the sun god). She taught history. Her voice was deep and hearty, with a firm hand shake to match, 'Delighted to meet you, Mr S, Mrs S, Aunty – if I may be sold bold – Piggo has told me so much about you.' For reasons which were never revealed, Pan and Gif called one another "Piggo" or "Pig" for short. There were no men in Gif's life, except her dad (Pa), who was an archdeacon in Devon, and her grandfather who had been a brigadier general.

Number two was Elsa Rush, thin, sharp and handsome, immaculately dressed and coiffured. Like Gif, she had a motor, just a tiny one – it never ventured far – just taking trips to school, church and local shops. She called Pan "My little love" and Mog "darling", screeching with delight when she met or re-met any member of the Smart family, was presented with a plate of sausage and mash, or shown the marigolds in the backyard. Elsa's father, who had bolted, was a rear admiral, she was High Church and had been jilted by a dashing Pole (male).

Gif and Elsa were at polite daggers drawn, and addressed one another as "Drayman" and "Rush". Pan shouted at Gif a good deal and

66

Gif shouted back. Elsa was more circumspect and chose to give in to Pan's demands. When it got too much, she would announce that she was off to spend time with her friend in Chelsea, but she wrote letters every day, sometimes twice a day. Gif just hung around, eating butter brazils, which she kept with her pig-skin gloves and her camera in the glove compartment of her Vauxhall, and hoped for the best.

Mercifully, the invasions were usually of short duration; as they sped off in Gif's shiny motor – a very rare sight in these parts, the net curtains of Selman Street would be all of a twitch and Lil would breathe a sigh of relief. She and Dot warmed to Elsa, although rather dumbfounded by the delighted screeching at first, they grew to quite like it, and she sometimes put on a frilly pinny and helped with the washing-up.

Gif was something quite beyond their ken. Half the time they didn't know what she and Pan were talking about. "B squared" meant brassiere, they detected "yellow tigers" in the lav, and talked a great deal about "the curse". ('The curse is come upon me,' cried the Lady of Shalott.) "My sainted aunt" was Gif's chosen expletive, the plum stone rhyme was "army, navy, medicine, church" instead of "tinker, tailor, soldier, sailor". When she was around the whole family were expected to join in parlour games, charades was the favourite, and the customs followed by the Drayman family were adopted – like crowning whoever was the "birthday girl" with a circlet of flowers. One time she sent them a book called *The Well of Loneliness*. Dot was glued to it and Lil had a go, even though she wasn't much of a reader. Sid proclaimed it a, 'very well written tale, good piece of literature.'

One Thursday, early closing, dad, Dot and Ed were home early and the family had settled down for the evening. Ooly was out, as usual, Mog away at college. Lil was knitting, Old Dot and Sid were making out price tags for the shop, beautifully inscribed in their impressive copper-plate hand, Ed was engrossed in the *Daily Worker,* occasionally spitting and muttering to himself about "bloody Baldwin". Ed was the only member of the household who took any real interest in politics. A knock came on the door.

'Mr Smart?'

'Yes, brother, what can I do for you?'

A portly gent, with spectacles, a booming voice and a dog collar stood before him.

'Fitzwilliam Drayman. May I come in? I think you have met my daughter.'

Lil and Dot, hearing the boom, hustled Ed out of the room, pinned up stray bits of hair and plumped up the cushions.

'Pleased to make your acquaintance, brother.' May I introduce my sister, my wife?'

'Good evening, ladies.' Dot resisted a temptation to curtsy.

'Cuppa' tea, sir?' offered Lil.

'Oh, no thank you, Miss Smart, I am here to have a conversation with your brother. I think perhaps we should withdraw ...' He looked around for somewhere to withdraw.

'Oh that's all right, sir,' said Lil, thinking of the tripe boiling in the kitchen. '*Miss* Smart and me will make ourselves scarce so you can 'ave a quiet chat with my '*usband.*'

Off they scuttled, shooing Ed upstairs.

'Well, Reverend' said Sid, 'It is certainly a pleasure to receive you in our humble abode. Aelgifu has been a visitor here on a number of occasions, of course. She and my daughter Pansy are such good chums.'

'Quite so, quite so,' replied the cleric, 'I am concerned, I may say deeply concerned, about their er- er-friendship.'

'I can put your mind at rest on that score, brother,' said Sid, starting to bridle. 'Pansy is a well-educated girl, with a fine singing voice and quite accustomed to mixing with quality. Our parson and his wife entertain her to tea, and even to supper, regularly, and Miss Bagwell of Woodford, the archdeacon's sister, you know, has been a great influence in her life.'

'I am not concerned with your daughter's social pretensions,' replied the other. 'It is her – how can I put this – her demeanour.'

'Pansy's a very well mannered girl, in company.'

'No, no, Mr Smart,' said the parson, getting irritated. 'I am referring to your daughter's dress, her …'

'I can assure you, brother, Pansy has the best tweed for her suits.'

'No, no Mr Smart. Are you familiar with the term "invert"?'

'I have heard the word, naturally, it means turn upside down, as far as I know.'

'It has another meaning. It may be used to refer to what might be described as a moral issue.'

Sid was perplexed and getting hot under the collar:

'I can tell you, Reverend, this household is as God fearing a one as you could wish to meet. All my girls have been brought up in the sight of the Lord; since childhood they have attended St Alphege. Pansy taught Sunday school, sang in the choir and has always walked in the paths of righteousness I have no idea what you are suggesting, but whatever it is, there is no truth in it.'

'Look, Mr Smart, there are some women who, shall we say, turn to their own gender. I have been concerned about Aelgifu ever since she went to university and acquired some very dangerous notions about earning her own living and setting up her own establishment without benefit of matrimony. My wife and I are worried about the hold your daughter seems to have over her – to be more blunt than I had wished to be, we are of the opinion that their friendship is of a sexual nature. I shall say no more.'

He rose to leave.

'I would advise you that I intend to withdraw Aelgifu's allowance if she and your daughter continue to consort. I have heard there are members of the medical profession who can deal with this sort of thing.'

'Look here, brother, you may be a man of the cloth, but I have never heard such baloney. If you wish to take steps to break up our daughters' innocent friendship, you are, of course, at liberty to do so. My compliments to Mrs Drayman.'

The ruffled clergyman took a hasty leave.

'What was that all about, Sid?'

'The Reverend thinks Pan isn't good enough for his daughter. Better keep mum about this – we don't want Pan going off on one of her tirades.'

And so they did.

Chapter 7:
2–3 September 1939, Ooly's wedding

It was hot on Ooly's wedding day, perfect, with a light breeze. Lil, up early, getting the house organised before the commotion started, opened the shutters and let in the hazy, smoky Bow sunshine. The windows had been polished within an inch of their life and the whole place was neat as a new pin and stinking of bleach. That was something that would set Pan off, she thought.

Pan came down stairs, red eyed from lack of sleep.

'For God's sake, Mum, we shouldn't be going ahead with this show. Doing ourselves up like characters in a pantomime, eating and drinking ourselves stupid while children are being shipped off to the country with gas masks and the big boys in the playground are rolling up their sleeves for the fight to end all fights.'

'Shut up. It's Ooly's day. Let's just make the best of it and face what we 'ave to face when we 'ave to, if we 'ave to. Take this tea up to the bride and keep your ruddy gob buttoned and don't go upsetting dad.'

'What's the point of it – what's the point of anything. We'll all be dead by their first anniversary. You know they have stacks of coffins, thousands of them, piled up ready. London will be bombed out of existence. And why are you letting her marry that surly, beer swilling rugger player, anyway?'

Lil opened the kitchen door and sniffed the unpleasant sickly, sweet aroma that always wafted their way from Charrington's Brewery in Whitechapel, when the wind was in the west. She couldn't do anything about that, at least the wind wasn't coming from the east, bringing the smell from the gas works, from the soap factory and the glue from the Yardley box factory in Stratford. The southeast wind was the worst – that blew across Barking Creek bringing the stench of sewage outfall.

Out at the front the brewer's dray was delivering at the Duke. Two great horses were feeding, tossing their nosebags to get the last mouthfuls and pigeons were pecking around at the scattered grain and chaff. What with the clanking of harness chains, the crooning of the birds against the backdrop of trees around St Alphege, it felt almost like the country. Lil had only been to the proper countryside a couple of times – to visit some remote relatives of Sid's in Great Hormead. It was lovely there. She sometimes dreamt of a cottage in good clean air, and a nice plot of garden where she could grow roses and runner beans.

This wedding was going to be some do. Sid (and Billy) had made sure of that and Ooly wouldn't have settled for anything less. Sid was going to be done up in coat tails with a topper and a camellia in his button hole – Ooly said that carnations were common. Old Dot's hat was a fancy confection from Wickhams in Mile End. Lil had seen one that she thought would do on a hat stall up Roman, but Mog dragged her off to Wickhams and made her get some great, piled-up shiny thing which, she thought, made her look like a ruddy grenadier guard.

Cutter and Butter were doing the spread at the parish hall, arranged by Billy – there was going to be all sorts, Lil wasn't quite sure what. When Sid suggested that his homemade pickled onions might be a good accompaniment for the cold salmon, Pan told him that he was ridiculous. Mog said it was a lovely idea, but better to save them for the evening get-together at home. Ooly looked pained and Lil decided to keep out of it. The selection of hymns caused the most trouble, second only to the choice of flowers, not to mention the champagne furore, the guest list and the bridesmaid business.

Mog would look lovely in a brown paper bag, of course. Pan was resistant to the whole idea of dressing up: 'If you think I'm going to get myself up in some frilly nonsense and make a complete fool of myself …' But, remembering the snapdragons on the doorstep, long ago, she finally acquiesced, and Mog said she would wear anything that could be found to suit Pan.

After many trips to the shops up west and more arguments round the kitchen table than you can imagine, they settled on duck egg blue crepe which clung and draped and fell elegantly around any shape. They would wear enormous plain cart wheel hats of the same hue. Mog was all for tiny Victorian posies of miniature roses and pansies, for obvious reasons.

'Mum, Mum – she's done a bunk! She's not in bed! Ooly's gone!' Pan shrieked down the stairs.

The rest of the household tumbled into life.

'Now, keep calm, everyone, I'm sure there's some perfectly good explanation.' said Sid. 'She may have gone for a walk to calm her nerves.'

'Ooly, walk! Don't be so stupid, Dad.'

After a good hour's panic and a thorough search of the streets Mog thought they'd better go round to Johnny's house.

Pan was all for warning Teddy B.

'No, leave it mates,' said Sid. 'We don't want to get them in a state yet. There's five hours till the wedding.'

The hours ticked by. Ed set off grimly, armed with an old pistol (not loaded) which he kept under his bed in anticipation of the Revolution to come. Dot went round to the church and Sid to the parish hall to see if Ooly was doing a last minute check. They decided it was best not to mention the loss of the bride to anyone they met – rumours spread like wildfire around the streets of Bow.

Mog went round to Maureen's.

'She seemed rather pre-occupied last night – but you would be?'

With two hours to go to the wedding, the bride, looking strangely calm, if rather dishevelled, walked into the kitchen.

Lil was livid: 'Where the bloody 'ell 'ave you bin? Your dad and I 'ave bin worried witless.'

Pan flew at her sister: 'For Christ's sake, do you never think of anyone but yourself? Aunty has been beside herself. Isn't it enough that I have to get myself all dolled up in ridiculous garb, that dad is laying out goodness knows how many years of bug blinder profits on your big performance, that we're all preparing to dance to your tune while the civilized world is teetering on the brink of total disaster – you just take yourself off and ...'

'Leave her be, leave her be, mates, she's all nerves.' said her father, 'Let's just all go and get ourselves into our finery. No harm done.'

Without a word Ooly went upstairs and slid quietly into her ivory velvet wedding dress, with its long rows of tiny pearl buttons from cuff to elbow and from neck to hem down the back.

Mog went up to fix the orange blossom and arrange the veil.

'Are you OK?'

'Oh yes,' said Ooly. 'The show must go on.'

The organ creaked into life with the Clarke's trumpet voluntary – "Here comes the bride", had, of course, been dismissed out of hand as common. Ooly had favoured the soulful tones of Tallis's "If ye love me", but you needed a choir for that and, as the main protagonists were going to be otherwise engaged, it was not really an option. Pan wanted Handel's firework music, but, for once was over-ruled.

Down the aisle, on the arm of Sidney Smart, oil and colourman extraordinaire, the "only gent in Bow", came the leading lady, trailing a fabulous lace train (the longest anyone had ever seen) and bearing a sheath of arum lilies (the largest anyone had ever seen). Mog looked like a film star and, to everyone's surprise, mainly her own, so did Pan. Teddy B, standing up in the chancel, specially starched for the occasion, was knocked for six when he saw her, although he thought he probably preferred her in her tweeds.

The leading man stood splendid in his tails, handsome in his high white collar and grey silk tie. Derek, his best man, grinned cheerfully – round faced and jolly with rosy cheeks. It struck Ooly that they looked a bit like a lemon and an orange.

Teddy B did his stuff; vows were taken and St Alphege smiled with pride. Out they all poured into the golden afternoon, watched by a straggle of well-wishers – most of them.

'Good old Sid – what a luverly show.'

'Good old Sid, my arse; 'es makin' a fine packet, floggin' them rubbishy "expertly soldered" pots and pans to poor old ducks as don't know any better. And what abaat them tiny little bottles of paraffin – what sort of a mark up is 'e makin' on them, I'd like to know?'

Mossy Jnr. from next door (now Goldberg and Co. 323, Mile End Road, Society Photographer of Paris, New York and London) was hopping around and crouching down to get the best shots: 'All the family together now, ladies and gents.' Somehow Nell got missed out – when the photographs were developed, there was Dot, sitting in pride of place where the mother of the groom should have been. The Bowyers never forgave the Smarts; even in the 1970s it was still spoken of with venom.

'Where's old Ed?' went up the cry, but no one bothered to find out – he was still prowling along the canal bank with his pistol.

A limousine, courtesy of one of Billy's wholesale clients, swept the stars around the corner to the parish hall, while the rest of the cast babbled and bobbed their way through the grimy streets: Pan clutching her cartwheel and grinding her teeth; Mog sashaying elegantly, for all the world as if she was thus attired everyday of the week. Lil in a nice navy two-piece, topped with the swirly satin thing from Wickhams, went arm in arm with Dot, in lavender. Sid and Billy, the smartest the Smart brothers had ever been, strode along with Flo', who was very fine in crushed strawberry, which enhanced her florid complexion. Then came Nell in brown shantung, with a modestly brimmed straw from the Roman, Albie, trussed up uncomfortably in suit and tie, Norah in powder blue, topped with a tiny feathery pill box, hanging for grim death on to Derek's arm, complaining about the heat and hoping to catch the bouquet.

There were country cousins – a few who risked the journey – and East End aunts and uncles. Uncle Will was not there, of course – he was in the workhouse, not cousin Sam – he was in the territorials and had been called back to his barracks – church and chapel, choristers and costers. Past the hoardings outside the paper shop, "Germans invade and bomb Poland; Britain mobilises", past the sweet shop where the girls had bought gob stoppers and liquorice pipes on the way home from school, the chip shop (forbidden), Lewis's dairy, the Duke, they went, like gaudy butterflies against the grey back-drop of Bow, weeping for her children. Bereft mothers in overalls, their children taken off in trains to God knows where, stood in at their doorways, gawping at the parade, their menfolk scanning the newspapers to see what terrors the morrow might bring.

But for the wedding party there were matters of more direct concern. The parish hall, scene of so many of Ooly's theatrical triumphs, was finely dressed for this, her finale, hung with garlands of pale roses, the long trestle tables unrecognisable from their jumble sale selves, clad in heavy white linen. All among the Cuttery and Buttery, the sparkling glass and gleaming silver, the towering fairytale cake, fanned napkins and bowls of lilies, pansies and moss roses (expensively procured from Moyses Stevens up west, to Mrs Gum's disgust) stood, here and there, a bold kilner jar of pickled onions, each with a browning label: 'S Smart, October 1937'.

'Good Lord alive,' shrieked Pan, 'Look what he's done!'

'Never mind, duck,' said Dot, 'No one will notice.'

'Not notice! Vicar and Mrs B will be appalled – after all the trouble

Mog and I have been to with the flower arrangements – all the cash paid out to the caterers – all the fuss about getting the menu just so – and dad puts his spoke in and ruins everything!'

She made a grab for the nearest jar, but was neatly fielded by her mother:

'Just leave things alone, will you. Today of all days just try and keep the peace and keep your blitherin' trap shut.'

Everyone did notice, of course; the country cousins opined that it might be an old East End custom. Nell, having been in service, knew exactly how things *should* be done, as did the more elevated branches of the Bowyer clan and, of course, Uncle Billy, who had learned his lessons well at Wax Chandlers' Hall.

Cocktails were dispensed and sherry for those who feared the coloured concoctions, with cordial for the stricter members of Old Ford Wesleyan and Billy's Baptist cronies. Performers and audience settled down together for the next act, those who were unfamiliar with such proceedings, anxiously wondering which knife, fork or spoon to use. It was a banquet indeed – *nonpareil* in the annals of St Alphege parish hall, which was more accustomed to sausage rolls, cheese straws and scones than salmon in aspic, chicken galantine and charlotte russe, happier with fizzing tea urns than with silver champagne buckets.

And what of the leading lady? Her ivory velvet was a dream, the long tight sleeves and embroidered cuffs showed her elegant hands off to perfection, the pearl droplets, a present from mum, complemented her skin and her stye had held off. Dispensing sweet condescension to all, before taking the throne, she floated around among her public, treating even the most lowly to a glorious bridal smile, a soft and grateful word of thanks, a joke or two. Mog might be the beauty of the family, but no one could out-do Ooly in the charm stakes.

She surveyed the scene. Pan, cartwheel removed and eyes flashing, was firmly wedged between Teddy B and Mrs B – that should keep her in check. Mum was next to them, sitting tight underneath her glossy hat and remarking in her very best "Lady Bow" voice, 'Hoffly shockin' this news from the continong, isent isn't it, Vicar?' Dad was regaling Nell with the tragic tale of Miss Havisham, while Dot tried to find something to say to Albie, and Mog flirted with Derek. Johnny-Come-Lately was nervous and kept blowing his nose.

All was clatter and buzz as the company ate and drank with relish, all apart from those who still had to perform.

Ting, ting went the spoon on the glass and Sid rose to speak.

'Brothers and sisters, may I bid you all welcome to the nuptials of my daughter, Lily. There is no better way to start than with some words written of such events by that great chronicler, Charles Dickens,: "Mixed up with the pleasure and joy of the occasion, are the many regrets at quitting home, the tears of parting between parent and child, the consciousness of leaving the dearest and kindest friends of the happiest portion of human life, to encounter its cares and troubles with others *still untried* and *little known*".'

'Dad, no!' (Ooly, under her breath.)

'Oh dear,' muttered Mog to Derek, 'I'm afraid he's in solemn mode. A good rendering of "I've got the Oopazootic" would have been preferable.'

'As you all know, Lily has a rare talent; she has performed before the highest in the land.'

Ooly winked at Mog.

'She has won gold medals. She has.' There followed a catalogue of her triumphs.

'Now she has chosen to fly our "nest of doves", we must pray that she holds fast to her music and to the gifts which the good Lord has bestowed upon her.'

'Can't someone shut him up? He'll be singing "At Trinity Church I met my Doom" next.' (Pan.)

Sid continued: 'In the words of Samuel Pickwick's toast at the wedding of his dear friend, Tupman, I ask you to raise your glasses to that "very amiable and lovely girl", (Pan gave forth her famous snort.) "well qualified to transfer to another sphere of action the happiness which for twenty years (actually nearer 30) she has diffused around her, in her father's house." And may the good Lord guard and keep us all in the days to come.'

A heckler/country cousin: 'What about Johnny?'

Clap, clap, clap – murmur, murmur, murmur.

Johnny's prepared speech of thanks to parents et al. with a few rugger jokes seemed rather out of place now that Ooly had been presented as a musical offering on the shrine of matrimony. 'What can I say – except I promise to keep her at it – ' (roars from the audience.)

Derek's parting shot, he was a quick witted lad in the old days (before North Africa took away his humour and shredded his nerves): 'So here's to the bridesmaids and a toast to the founder of the feast and his extra special pickled onions.'

'Good gracious me,' commented Mrs B to her husband, 'who would have thought the Smarts would put on a show like this. One might, apart from the onions, even take it for a society wedding.'

The Sunday after the wedding was another glorious sunny day. Following the rigours of the pageant and the feast, number 29 dissolved into post celebratory chaos. Every cranny of the house was crammed with bedding and relatives. Lil and Dot bustled about with tea, toast and marmalade and Sid organised the breakfast welcome. Ed, who was in everyone's bad books for missing the wedding, was crouched over the crackling wireless set, fag in mouth.

'They're sayin' we've got to "standby for an announcement of national importance," he ventured to his sister.' They keep on sayin' that old Chamberlain is goin' to speak at quarter past eleven.'

'Oh my Gawd – this is it.'

As the wedding guests and residents crowded into the parlour there was music from the wireless and a talk on, "how to make the most of tinned foods. More music followed. No one spoke. The clock on the mantelpiece ticked ominously. As the long hand touched the twelve the Prime Minister addressed the company at number 29:

"I am speaking to you from the Cabinet Room at 10 Downing Street. This morning the British Ambassador in Berlin handed the German Government a final note stating that, unless we heard from them by eleven o'clock that they were prepared at once to withdraw their troops from Poland, a state of war would exist between us. I have to tell you now that no such undertaking has been received and that consequently this country is at war with Germany. Now may God bless you all. May He defend the right. It is the evil things that we shall be fighting against, brute force, bad faith, injustice, oppression and persecution and against them I am certain that the right will prevail."

Pan screamed. 'I told you, I told you we shouldn't have had that stupid affair yesterday,' – as if Ooly's remaining single might somehow have halted the march of the jack boot.

Then came the wail of the air raid siren.

Chapter 8:
September 1939 to September 1940

There would be no more weddings like Ooly's in Bow for a long time to come. Not that there was any lack of marriages, here or anywhere else – quite the reverse. The outbreak of war brought many a couple scuttling to hastily tie the knot before the groom was sent off to fight. Norah even got Derek to St Mary Mag. of East Ham through the piles of sandbags. It was a sad affair – a rainy day, a skimpily cut beige costume for the bride, with a corsage of pink "cars" and "gip", cups of tea, some slices of Battenberg cake and just one bottle of Cornish mead that someone had once brought back from a holiday. Her dad stayed in the pub; her mum kept sniffing into a hanky, and Nell did nothing to hide her disapproval. Johnny, now in the RAF and busy with barrage balloons in Barking, got an eight hour pass and Ooly, feeling rather queasy, did her best to jolly things along. For Ooly, you see, as for Bow, as for the country at large, these were those long months of waiting.

This was the time of terrified anticipation, known then as the 'Bore War' and to posterity as the "Phoney War' with no observable military action, just a confetti war of propaganda leaflets dropped on Germany.

'If we only gave that swine 'itler a good bashing instead of dropping all that rubbish.' said Lil. 'There's no reasoning with them blighters!'

In the shop Sid did a good trade in blackout stuff and sticky tape to keep the households of Bow safe from poisonous gas.

'I never thought we'd live to see another war. The only thing that's the same is Jerry – the same old dirty dog with his mines and submarines.'

''Ow long is this goin' on? I want my kiddies back.'

Bow was shorn of its children – mums hung around, not knowing what to do, just waiting for a letter which might tell them where their children had been sent. Derek, was called up and joined the army; the sky was full of Johnny's great silver blimps frolicking in the air – blown by the wind – there to ward off the bombardment to come. The streets were crowded with men in tin hats, lorry loads of soldiers rumbled ceaselessly along Bow Road. The People's Palace, scene of Ooly's early triumphs, and now a college, was taken over by the military and also served as a temporary town hall. Giant anti-aircraft guns moved into Vicky Park and the flower beds were dug up for allotments, while trench shelters were dug in the garden of Tredegar Square. They wouldn't let you in the Majestic without a gas mask.

Sid plastered up the cracks in the walls and blocked off the fireplaces to make number 29's ground floor safe from gas. His blackout was the most secure in all the East End, and he pinned to the back door a list of items to be taken into the air raid shelter when the time came: I D cards, gas masks, ration books, wallet, candles in flower pots, *Great Expectations,* Bible, hymn book, blankets, bread and jam, thermos flask, valor stove. While Albie made an expert job of building the Anderson shelter in Nell's front garden and covering it with a nice rockery, Ed was put to digging the hole in the backyard at number 29, with help from Mossy.

'Me garden, me marigolds – all that work gone to waste,' Lil loved her little patch.

'We'll never get Pan into that tiny tin box – she'll have hysterics and shriek that she's going to be buried alive,' said Ooly, 'Thank the Lord she's gone back to Suffolk.'

Ooly had decided to stay with the family until Johnny came back. The brand new Come-Lately semi in Buckhurst Hill, with its long garden, back and front, was rented out, and the ebonised Chappell baby grand (mum and dad's wedding present), the silvery brocade three piece suit (from Pan and Mog), the monk's bench, the Tudor style dining table and side board, along with the canteen of cutlery (silver plate), the cut-glass, the vacuum cleaner and the toaster were packed up and put into store. Escape and stylish modern living were put on hold.

Dot said it was not right to bring a child into the world at such a time and wondered how the Queen of Bow would cope with the wrecking of her figure, all the demands and mucky toil. Pan reckoned it was an act of gross irresponsibility; Lil started knitting and Sid dreamed of the next musical prodigy which the Smarts might offer the world. Mog was thrilled to bits and Ooly just plain scared. No one asked Ed his opinion, needless to say, but he cut down on his fags and started putting a little bit by for the baby. When the proud Johnny told his mum, he was disappointed by her grave looks; Nell supposed it wasn't going to be much of her business.

'Aren't you excited about the baby, Ool?' asked Mog. 'It'll be wonderful to have a little one around to take our minds off everything. If it's a girl I shall make her a white silk dress with red French knots and she shall have a matinee jacket of the finest wool, like lacy cobwebs. I shall sing to her: "The little white horse came scampering scampering." – I will jiggle her up and down on my knee, "This is the way the ladies ride, trit, trot, trit trot, trit trot." – and read to her from *My Days with the Fairies*, the one with the Edmund Dulac illustrations. When she's old enough I shall take her into Epping Forest and teach her about wild flowers and buy her a box of beautiful Lakeland coloured pencils.'

'Hold your scampering horses. It might be a boy.'

'Well – the "Galloping Major" will still be on. I suppose it'll be all rugger and tin soldiers.'

Ooly was thinking of baby gas masks.

It was May when the new Smart *recte* Come-Lately first saw the light of day. Churchill (Old Winnie) had taken over the war, which had now become a present terror. Just as the customers in the Emporium were beginning to say that the gassing and the bombing might never come to pass, and many children were brought home from their country exile, Hitler's tanks started rolling across Belgium, across Luxembourg, the Netherlands, and France towards Bow.

A name debate raged when the baby arrived – a girl. Sid was all for an addition to the flower garden: Iris, Violet and Primrose were tendered. Mog had been canvassing for Catherine (as in Earnshaw) for months, in the event of it being a girl, and Pan wrote demanding that her niece should have a name that could be easily abbreviated – Henrietta or Frederica perhaps. Ooly stood firm and, mindful that the nose might be inherited, opted for a plain name that wouldn't embarrass her daughter. When Johnny arrived to inspect the bundle she was introduced as Elizabeth. He was permitted to add a film star to the equation and when Ooly registered her it was as Elizabeth Marlene. From day one they called her Todge. Johnny's name for her was Mini Lizzie.

Mog missed the arrival of Todge and her displacement as the darling of the household, which was, perhaps, just as well. She had been dispatched to Somerset, to Tillingham Newall, where the ancient family of Tillingham had offered to provide accommodation for a modest number of East End children with their teachers in their nearly stately home, New Hall.

She had always been a good girl, Sunday's child, everyone's favourite at home, the baby of a family which adored children, the beauty of a family which had an exceptionally high regard for looks. But, it has to be said, she had neither Ooly's glamour and talent, nor Pan's brains, and had always felt rather over shadowed in Bow, and she was a bit shy. At Skoriers there was no competing with Pan's success and Ooly's popularity, but she did win the most coveted prize of all, awarded to the girl whose price was "above rubies" – her sisters never had. She excelled at elocution and three years in a row she won the poetry reading competition and played Titania in the school's production of *A Midsummer Night's Dream*. Poetry became an abiding passion and, under Baggy's tuition, she learned to do passable flower paintings.

Hard work and determination paid off and she got to college to train to be a teacher. She missed mum and dad a great deal, too much to enjoy herself, and comfort ate herself into the Great Belle of Bow. As soon as may be, she came home, lost weight and took a post in a school down by the docks where she soon had even the most recalcitrant Wapping youngsters eating out of her hand. Like dad she had a gift with children. There were puppet shows, sing-songs, games and stories, patience, kindness and a very firm hand. Behind her pretty, gentle facade, she was, as much loved children tend to be, as tough as old boots. Cross Ooly and she would clam up and capitulate after a bit, cross Pan and she would fight, rage and sob, cross Mog, and God help you.

A colleague at school, one Tom Tittler (Poor Old Tom), took over from Old Morgan as Mog Worshipper Number One. Tall, dark and handsome he may have been, with a Clark Gable-ish moustache, but he wore thick specs, collected stamps, played the piano (not in Ooly's league), and went to church a good deal. Poor Old Tom, he tried his best. Mum thought he was a "good old stick", dad was tentative, but not hostile and even Pan found him tolerable. But Mog's dreams were fuelled by the flics and her head still full of Bagginess – of Pre-Raphaelite fantasies, of the Brontes and Elizabeth Barrett Browning. ("How do I love thee? Let me count the ways. I love thee to the depth and breadth and height …") Poor Old Tom was up against Heathcliff, Rupert Brooke and Errol Flynn. What chance did he have with this ravishing girl who dreamt of an all consuming passion, probably with a bounder, and was becoming well aware of the power of her wide blue eyes?

She was glad to be doing her bit, but it was awful, leaving her little mum, standing there on the doorstep in her flowery overall. There were no tears – it was not their way. 'Keep your pecker up, mate, your tail too – when you come home my marrow will be sitting down to dinner.' Off she went, loaded up with blackcurrant jam and cake, a tin or two of Jeyes ointment and a copy of *David Copperfield*. Poor Old Tom, now in the army and stationed somewhere in Kent, had sent her a beautifully bound copy of W H Hudson's *Far Away and Long Ago*. She told Ooly: 'I had to read it about three times at college. Still – it's a lovely volume with wood engravings.' It was left behind.

The noisy hubbub, sobbing and confusion at Paddington gave way to the rhythmic song of the Great Western, as the train sped them away from the fearful city: 'When will we be there? When will we be there? Can we go 'ome? Can we go 'ome? Will there be chips? Will there be chips? Will there be jam? Will there be jam? Must we pick 'ops? Must we pick 'ops? And the long shriek of the whistle: 'I want my Mummeeeee.'

London petered out and the May sunshine, no longer filtered through a haze of smoke, lit up green meadows brush stroked with buttercup gold.

'Look at them cows, Miss, there's 'undreds of em.' Cows at home were few and kept in the backyard of the dairy.

They alighted at a tiny station called a "Halt", just a platform overgrown with clumps of ladies' mantle.

'This ain't a proper station, is it Miss? Not like wot we 'ave at 'ome. There ain't no cuppa tea place, and no lavs.'

Along the lane stood a row of carts, hay waggons, dog carts, ramshackle things with moth eaten looking ponies looking bored and resentful. The Tillinghams could no longer afford the Rolls, let alone a chauffeur, and petrol was hard to come by.

'Blimey, Miss, ain't they got no buses 'ere? 'Ave we got to get into one of them fings?'

Off went the waggon train, swaying and creaking, the children holding tight to their precious bundles from home; Mog and her colleague, Freda Lovell (a fierce and fiery red head from Ilford), holding tight to the children. St Mary the Virgin of Tillingham Magna, who remembered the Wars of the Roses, gave them a disdainful glance from her tall, lacy, rose coloured tower, as well she might – Pete O'Malley and his mate, Ernie Slack, who had been holding on for ages, had, in desperation hopped off the cart and wee'd up against her venerable walls.

'Keep those vermin off,' roared Miss Scott-Dickens, out in her front garden, pruning her Montana.

'Oh my God,' moaned Freda, 'This is going to be hell.'

On they went, observed by crowds of bluebells, with yellow cowslips and celandine peeping out, past stone cottages with tiny, watchful, windows, framed by fragrant lilac.

'Gawd luv us! That 'aas ain't got no roof – it's got a straw hat on!'

'That's thatch, stupid,' said Pete, who had been hopping and knew about the country.

Some old boys sunning themselves over their scrumpy outside the Tillingham Arms gave them a cheerful wave.

'That'll be they little vackies from Lunnun goin' up the 'all. Looks like they've got that Greta Garbo with 'em!'

'That other one's no picture, mind.'

Mog's first sight of New Hall was something of a disappointment. The ponies had taken them through an imposing gateway with enormous twin stone posts 'like ruddy Nelson's Column', topped with Tillingham lions, much fiercer than Landseer's bronze ones in Trafalgar Square. The carts turned into a wide gravel drive, flanked by banks of rhododendrons and two shimmering lakes, dotted with swans idling around among the sedge and water irises. There, beyond a crumbling ornamental bridge, the Tillingham mansion rose before them. Pete, hanging onto Mog's hand, whispered anxiously: 'Gawd, Miss, it looks like the blinkin' work 'aas.'

And so it did. New Hall had been built on the sight of some old medieval pile, by a be-ruffed Tillingham who had made a fortune bringing tobacco into Bristol from the New World. It had been added to by his son, the first baronet and by almost every baronet since. Thus a hotchpotch of a building, clothed in ugly Victorian pretentiousness, presented itself to the East Enders. There was a dull yellow-brick Edwardian wing and the windows were of all shapes and sizes. All that was left of the Jacobean structure was a magnificent dark, panelled hall, tucked inside, and some decorations over the main entrance depicting clay pipes.

Miss Tillingham – that is to say Isabella Gertrude Louisa Henrietta Duboulay Tillingham – met the invaders. Ever since the tobacco magnate had named one of his fine galleons Isabella, after his daughter, the eldest Tillingham girl had been given that name. She was a pale, rangy creature, about Ooly's age, who had given up on marriage when she was given a medical warning not to reproduce and, aware that she could give no one an heir, let alone a spare, devoted herself to New Hall. Her father was past it, her much older half-brother had been killed at the Somme and her slightly older brother, Edmund, the heir, had a wonky leg and nerves.

It was a shabby place of threadbare carpets and curtains which would not dare to be cleaned for fear of disintegration:

'Not very posh is it, Miss – my mum wouldn't be seen dead with curtains like that in our Peabody,' said Pete.

'Shush. Shush.'

Generations of lords more interested in their regiments than their family estates had brought the Tillinghams low; Lloyd George's taxes and unprofitable marriages had brought them even lower. So poor were they that the incumbent Isabella rolled her own cigs, keeping the tobacco in a silver box given to some earlier Isabella by Charles II. So poor were they that rents had to be put up in the cottages on the estate and some of the tenants, regrettably, thrown out. So poor were they that the paltry sum of money offered by the government for the accommodation of a bunch of cockneys was welcome.

Miss Tillingham seemed friendly enough:

'We thought the "pink" drawing room would do for lessons – used to be pink in the good old days – now rather browny, I'm afraid. What d'you think? Had to pawn the Bechstein grand, ha! ha! ha! – but there's an upright in there.'

They were shown their bedrooms – huge and gloomy – and a bathroom the size of a ballroom with a vast iron bath.

'No hot water, I regret to say. Boiler's had it.'

'Kiddies welcome to roam about – garden, stables, ponies – that sort of thing. They can eat in the buttery – Mrs P will lend a hand. We've only got her and the gardener left, oh and the stable boy – can't get staff. Can't afford 'em, anyway. Perhaps you would like to join us for supper? Nothing grand, these days. We eat at seven – Pa has to get his fodder in early.'

'Do you think we're expected to dress for dinner?' Freda looked aghast at Mog.

They decided that as it had been called supper this was not a requirement and, in any case, neither had brought anything remotely resembling a dinner gown.

The meal was served in the old panelled hall. Ranks of dead Tillinghams, in heavy gilt frames, looked down with disapproval at the sausages, glittering greasily between the massive silver candelabrae, on a table so long that Mog could hardly see the person at the far end. It was Sir Horace, frail and decrepit, attired in military garb with a row of medals. He, too, was friendly, very friendly indeed, and proclaimed himself glad to have some youngsters around: 'Where's the boy? Stuck in his damned books in the library, I'll be bound. Still – each to his own I suppose.' Sir Horace, formerly known as "The Horror" had softened up a lot since his blustering days. In fact, the villagers reckoned he'd gone soft in the head.

They had nearly finished the sausages – washed down with some very prized claret which Sir Horace had been keeping for a special occasion – when "the Boy" put in an appearance. Rupert Brook, for it was surely he – burnished gold-red hair, a silk cravat, slid into a late seventeenth century high-back walnut chair next to Mog, murmuring apologies.

He turned to hang his silver topped stick on the back of the chair and gazed, amazed, into her blue eyes.

'I am delighted to meet you, Miss er ... Welcome to our crumbling old edifice – I do hope you and your charges can put up with us for a while.'

'I think the boot may be on the other foot, Mr Tillingham. Some of them are rather rough round the edges. They're good kids, all of them really, but not used to minding their p's and q's, if you see what I mean?'

'Of course – of course, and it must be terrifying for them – being dragged from their mother's arms and stuck in a great barn of a place like this. By the way, do call me Edmund. You are ...?'

Mog, well aware that the gentry went in for silly nick names, thought it appropriate to own up.

'My name is Rose, but my family call me Mog.'

'May I? Mog? I do apologise for the lack of mod cons, and the Pater – he's just a bit bonkers. The uniform often comes out, usually on Thursdays – he's frightened that Bella is going to put his medals up for auction! He spends most of his time snooping around, counting the Gainsboroughs – she did get rid of one of them. Still we've got most of the library left – you must let me show you round, and your colleague, of course.'

Intermittent Labradors, as old as Methuselah, snored on the just-recognisably Persian carpets and the dying rays of the British Empire filtered through the armorial stained glass – Mog and Edmund were caught up in a loop of light.

She was Queen of the May, Titania and Merle Oberon. As the heavenly days unfurled, they would walk through the woods, not too far because of his leg. He would read her poetry, sitting on a bank among the wild thyme, oxlips and violets. When she sang in St Mary the Virgin on Sundays, he was entranced. It was the talk of the village. 'Reckon that Greta Garbo's got young Mr Edmund all of a dither.'

Now, you may wonder what the scion of the venerable house of Tillingham was doing consorting with the likes of an East End oil and colour man's daughter. Unlike Dougie's family, whose status was acquired only relatively recently, founded on Victorian industrial enterprise, the Tillinghams had been lords of all they surveyed when Mitchells were still making nails in a Black Country shed. Their superiority thus assured they had no need for snobbery and had felt able, generation after generation, to indulge their weakness for a pretty face, showing a dangerous lack of concern for consolidating their empire by suitable alliances. It was rumoured that Sir Horace's first lady had been a tweeny and his own mamma, the delicious Henriette Duboulay, had, according to gossip in the village, danced at the Moulin Rouge. Over the mother of Edmund and Isabella a veil was drawn.

As for the "littl'uns from Lunun", there were no chips, but there were delicious buttery pastries and even fresh eggs – they went and found them for themselves among the straw. There were ponies to ride and farm kittens to cuddle. The East Enders romped in the fields of Olde England, clambered up her hay stacks, climbed her oak trees and made dams in her streams, mostly missing their mums just at bed time, when the sun sank down over the lakes. Only were they reminded that this was no summer holiday when planes whirled and snarled overhead or when they encountered the old boys of the the Tillingham Parva cricket club, armed with shot guns and pitch forks marching along, ready to defend the Mendips against all comers.

Mog came upon Sir Horace and Pete chatting in what remained of the conservatory, with its cracked panes and straggly palms. Pete was very hot these days. It had been a chilly day for May when mum had waved him off at the station and she had told him to make sure he kept his coat on. He never took it off.

'Damn fine shooting parties we used to have here – no chaps around now and we couldn't afford it anyway. Cash very short.'

''aas worth a few bob, init, Sir?'

'No property market thanks to this damned business with the Hun.'

'Never mind, Sir, when it's all over, you can sell up and buy a nice little Tooder semi and live like a lord again – have some tinned salmon for tea – that sort of stuff. My mum's sent me a bit of chocolate – want some?

'Jolly decent of you, eald cheappe, but it upsets me guts these days.'

While across the Channel the real army, fought the battle for France and the brave little British pleasure craft chugged out in the face of enemy fire to rescue the soldiers from Dunkirk, the New Hall vackies chanted with the country children: 'Oak Apple Day, Oak Apple Day, give us a holiday or we'll all run away!'

What fun – what glorious patriotic fun it all was, rather like being at the flics, thought Mog, in that enchanted country paradise, cheering on their heroes at the coal face far away. They sat in the faded splendour of the blue drawing room and listened to Churchill's words to the Commons, read by the newsreader:

"…We shall defend our island, whatever the cost may be. We shall fight on the beaches, we shall fight on the landing grounds, we shall fight in the fields and in the streets, we shall fight in the hills; we shall never surrender."

'Good old Winnie – that's the stuff,' roared Sir Horace, announcing to the assembled company that the original Isabella had sailed with the Armada.

France fell. Britannia braced herself for the onslaught to come: 'If the British Empire and its Commonwealth last for a thousand years, men will still say, "This was their finest hour".'

Mum wrote: OK

Well we are doing grate –1 shilling 8 pennyworth of meat today – we had to put our glasses on – that is the first this week. he told aunty to go on Friday to get the rest of our rachon - 3 shillings and thruppence. i laugh when I saw it – he can't get any more. Still – Old Billy got me a lovely fowl it was grand. I cooked it on sataday. me and Aunty had it for lunch, dad had it hot when he came home 5.30 on sataday – clearks hours!

I wonder how you get on for meat – im sending some some sprats to help you on the road & I thought you would like a few biscuits – they are nice ones.

You would love our little Todge. Ool is managing alright – she broke her teeth and woldnt come out of the bedroom – said she looked like mr punch and put her head round the door, shouting 'that's the way to do it' – she was a larf – just like she used to before you know what – made me think of your puppets.

Keep yourself and them kiddies safe and don't go worryin about us old crocks. i wish you was at home tho – i miss you with all this terrible trouble about that swine (Hitler) seem to have all the gains – he seemes so powerfull doesn't he? and that daft, fat little Eytie Musso struttin' abaat in 'is silly uniform – weeve seen it on the newsreels. i just looked up at your photo grinning at me so i have got to be satisfied with that ...

Poor Old Tom turned up again – he had 24 hours and brought us a pot of creem on Thursday; we had it for tea with strawberrys. Old Albie Waters was on one of them boats that went to Dunkirk. Ooly says he was in a parlous state when he came home.

Well i cant wright much. burn this don't let it lay about because of the rotten spelling & writing. dad is going to finish a goodnight.
Dad wrote:

Just penning a few words adding a little to the Big Woman's epistle. This week with us as been about as usual – lot to be thankful for. Johnny had a pass and came to have a look at out little Todge. He amuses us with the tales of their sing-songs. They take things very much as they come.

I am attending the rehearsals for that choir where we sang at Easter. We are doing Elijah. I wonder how you're doing for victuals.

Ooly has broken her teeth.

God Bless and keep you safe.

Dot wrote:.

Johnny has had a day here. Ooly was in a bate – she's broken her false teeth and didn't want him to see her with her chin touching her nose. It was stupid business having all her teeth out for her 21st, if you ask me, and cost a fortune.

I wonder what you are doing this evening. Dad is trying to repair a revolving rolling pin for somebody – he has just finished making a music cabinet out of an orange box, mum is knitting, Ed is sitting as usual & I have been doing bills & labels for the shop.

Mog wrote home:

Mid week epistle – have got some more Swiss postcards but though I'd treat you to a letter this week. See how I'm economising with paper. You'll probably all have squints before you finish this.

Was pleased to get your letters & the goodies. Glad you're all soldiering on. Fancy poor old Ooly breaking her teeth.

You should see me these days – quite the Lady of the Manor – I even have a four poster bed. Not that it's all lah di dah – you would have roared at our Oak Apple Day do – me and Freda and the old village dames of about 665, all got up in enormous white rubbers, dancing 'Gathering Peascods' and such like.

Now about holidays, my old cockies. I am going to be able to get home DV for a bit in August, isn't it good!!! For the last two weeks Freda is going home & I shall be left here – if any of you intend coming down to see me that would be a lovely time & I should love it. But if you feel you can't afford it or you would like to have a really good rest or you've other plans, I don't want you to think that I would be a bit hurt or lonely if you don't come because I am extremely happy here with this family. They're not a bit snooty and have made us all very welcome.

The fare is 28s 7d return – praps that's a bit expensive isn't it – I could help you a little bit with the money – But if you think it would be nicer to have a whoopee time when I get home don't think I'll mind a bit. I should be everso glad to have one, two – or three of you at the same time, but will not be disappointed if you feel you can't manage it ...

I wonder what Baggy thinks about Italy joining in with Hitler!

As the roses in the arbour began to fade the incessant sound was of Sandy Macpherson's organ and public service broadcasts from the wireless, not to mention the menacing tones of Lord Haw Haw "Germany calling. Germany calling".

On 10 July, 400 German aircraft attacked the coast; the Battle of Britain had commenced.

"Never in the field of human conflict," Winnie announced to the blue drawing room, "was so much owed by so many to so few."

Dad wrote:

It would be wonderful to see you, but you're best safe down there in the country –these are difficult times. You just stay put, mate, and make the best of it.

Mum wrote:

Well – looks as if we shant get a look at you after all, not till Christmas at any rate. i was all for putting on my hat and getting on the train down to your place but dad and Dot didn't think it was safe to be gallivantin' all over the shop with all this goin' on specilly with little Todge around.

What about those bliters getting a real bomping from our lads! i would like to be a young man – i could'nt sit & make buttons – i think i would be after them. I would like to sit old Hitler on the busser & blow it right up his decayed tooth.

Ooly wrote:

'You make the most of it down in your rural idyll with your glamorous fancy man. It's fairly hellish here, with 24 hour a day baby worship from the old guard – mum and Aunty keep creeping up and putting extra blankets on the cot and dad's in a continual watchful dither about my every move – poor old Ed isn't allowed within a mile of her, in case he drops some fag ash on her head or infects her with his lefty notions. The child isn't given a moment's peace – one or other of them is always picking her up. What a song and dance there was last week when I suggested leaving her with Johnny's mum for a few hours – you can't imagine how they went on!

Don't breathe a word about your buddy to the old 'uns, by the way. You know how attached mum is to Poor Old Tom, and dad is likely to blow a fuse if he thinks you're getting yourself into a dangerous liaison.'

Chapter 9:
September 1940

Ooly's first wedding anniversary fell on a Monday, it being leap year, and it was decided that there should be a modest celebration at number 29 the following Saturday – with some plump kippers, a cake might be managed, and just a drain of sherry. Johnny thought he might be able to get a few hours away from his balloons. Ooly said they ought to ask Nell and Albie and grass widow, Norah.

'Best just keep it in the family,' advised Sid.

'For goodness sake, Dad, they *are* family. Nell is actually Todge's grandmother, you know.'

'I s'pose she *did* come up wiv' that pot of beef drippin' for us last week – she'd got it from some folk of 'ers in the country,' offered Lil, reluctantly admitting that there were occasions, just now and again, when Todge had to be shared.

The day dawned fair with a faint autumnal mist blurring Bow's rough edges, giving way later to blistering sunshine, tipping with gold the mop-head chrysanthemums which stood in a blue glazed vase in the bay of Nell's parlour window. Dot left the Emporium early so as to be on hand to help get ready for the evening. The shop was Saturday-afternoon busy; Sid was wrapping up some bars of Sunlight soap for Mrs Gum, when the siren set up its wail, just before five.

''Ere goes that whinin' bleeder agin, I don't take much notice – well I didn't until them raids in Enfield and Croydon last week. But my Bert is very particular now e's a warden. With his tin 'at and uniform, there's no speakin' to 'im. Orderin' everyone abaat is certainly 'is cuppa tea.'

'He's doing a fine job. We must just pray that things don't get any worse and trust that Old Winnie and the RAF boys will keep us safe. Now we best take shelter – come on, mates – off with you all.'

'Mark my words,' proclaimed Doomandgloom Davies from the Undertakers. 'These little bomps bompsare just the start. The big smash is comin – we've bin warned. That man will raze London to the ground. My cousin Fred was over there fightin' in Spain in '37 when Jerry 'ad his practice run – he saw what 'appened in Guernica – mark my words it'll 'appen 'ere. He smelt the burnin' flesh of those poor bastards; he saw the flames miles 'igh in the sky, he heard the screamin ...'

'Steady on, brother. Nuisance raids is all we've had and, God willing, all we can expect.'

'I've 'eard that all food will be on the ration soon.' said Fanny Bastaple from Victoria Buildings, ''Ow are us lot s'posed to "Dig for Victory" when we ain't got no soil, I'd like to know. Got a bit of sugar for me?'

'Sorry. Not today, mate. If you bring in a cup I'll put you in a mite of condensed milk – that'll sweeten your tea. Now we'd best get ourselves to safety, just in case.'

He took out his cash box and started counting up the week's takings. Down again thanks to Cohen's Cut-Price Kitchen Ware down the other end of the market. Good job he had managed to get hold of that stock of sugar, and some butter sometimes came his way. Customers who could afford it paid good money for under the counter supplies.

'Got any of that 'orrible waxy stuff that we've got to use for cookin?' asked Old Gert, the navvy-fisted landlady of the Duke.

'Plenty of that.' –And he went off to rummage out the back where Ed was measuring out bottles of paraffin oil.

'Oh – and some of that White Cardinal polish for me blackout door step,' she called out.

Lil was in the garden taking in the washing from the line; it had been a boiling hot day and they were bone dry – no need for airing. She stroked her cotton sheets – lovely and smooth, all ready for a good night's kip. When she was a kid they had to make do with newspapers.

'Moanin' Minnie can wait,' she muttered to herself, as she folded the sheets, neatly laying them in the basket and sitting down on the low wall to sun herself.

'My Gawd, Dot, come out 'ere,' she called out to her sister-in-law, who was fussing about in the scullery, cutting fat off some kidneys to make a suet pudding.

'Just take a gander at this.' She pointed at the sky over towards the east. 'Looks like a load of midges swarmin – the bloody sky's full of them.'

'For heaven's sake, Lil, let's get that baby into the dug-out.'

Bert appeared rushing up and down the street blowing his whistle: 'Take cover. Take cover. Planes overhead.'

Ooly grabbed the baby from her pram, before anyone else could, as the menace from the heavens growled towards them: throb, throb, throb.

Ed shrieked as he tumbled through the gate: 'They're comin' for us. Jerry's comin' for us. Fousands of them – the bleedin' sky is fallin.'

''Ark at our good old guns in Vicky Park crackin' away at them. There's genna be some fireworks tonight,' said Lil, as she was reluctantly hustled down into the shelter. Lil and Dot, Ooly, and Ed crouched in the dark, damp little metal box as the world came down overhead – crumps, crashes, the whine and snarl of planes. Ooly hugged the screaming Todge tight to her, shaking and white.

''Ere's to you, Ooly,' said Lil, raising a thimble full of sherry. 'And 'ere's to our lads fightin' it out, shootin' down those Nasty buggers. 'Ere Ed, have a drop of this – it'll calm your nerves.'

She then put a drop of sherry on her finger and stuck it into the baby's mouth.'

'Mum, for goodness sake …'

Sid, the while, had taken cover under the kitchen table with his Bible. Claustrophobia was endemic in the Smart family.

A thunderous noise exploded in their ears and the ground shook.

'God help us, God help us, Lord graciously hear us,' prayed Dot, her hands clasped tightly together.

'That'll be a proper bomb – not one of those insanitaries. Direct hit in our street I wouldn't wonder,' said Lil. 'I'll just pop out and check on dad.'

'Mum, get back in here!' screeched Ooly, grabbing hold of her mother and losing hold of Todge. The baby was neatly fielded by the gibbering Ed, who was hopping from one foot to another in a sort of dance: 'It's all right. I've got 'er safe.'

Dot snapped out of her orisons: 'Give that child to me, you silly old fool. And for heaven's sake put that fag out.'

'Leave him alone. He was doing his best. It's mum's fault for being so stupid.' Ooly took the baby, at which point Lil made her escape. She rushed through the din, smoke and flying glass and into number 29.

There sat Sid, with his trilby on, under the table, clasping the Good Book and singing 'Abide with me' at the top of his voice.

'You all right, duck?'

At 6.10 the All Clear went.

'Come on,' said Lil, who had returned to the shelter. 'Let's be up and doin' and 'ave a butchers' – see what's bin 'appnin.'

'I'm not movin' aat of ere,' said Ed.

'Well – you can stay put if you like. Come on, Dot, Ooly, let's go and do a recce.'

The three women clambered out into the choking smoke of the rushing, crashing, whistle-blowing world, Lil at the helm.

'Oh my Gawd – the Dook's copped it. Is that poor old Gert?'

Stretcher bearers were coming out from the smoking wreck of the grand old public house. Lil rushed across the road to get a closer look.

'Keep back, missus. Keep back. There's more of that wall comin' dahn.' She was hustled out of the way.

'My bleedin' Gawd – it *is* 'er – that's 'er turban poking out. Ruddy Jerry bastards.'

Sid joined them. He stood quite still, deathly pale and drawn: 'Poor old devil. I was only serving her in the shop a few hours back. She always said she was as safe as houses down in her cellar.'

'Come away, Lil', said Dot. 'Come and get inside and let's get away from all this smoke – it's hurting the baby's eyes.'

They went into the house.

'It's not much better in here,' said Ooly. 'How on earth are we going to get rid of all this dust.'

Dot set to work grimly with a dustpan and brush, while Sid swept the floor.

'Let's get the kettle on and 'ave ourselves a nice cuppa,' said Lil ' – and we must get them kippers on the go. Guests will be 'ere soon.' Lil turned the gas tap on the stove and lit a match under the kettle.

'Mum, for crying out loud, they'll hardly be turning out in all this – they might not even be alive.' She wondered about Johnny.

'Hm. No gas comin' aat.'

'That'll be a gas main hit,' said Sid. 'We'd better get the valor going.' He tipped some paraffin into the stove and carefully turned up the wick, trying to keep his hand steady.

Lil applied a lighted match: 'There we go. We'll soon 'ave a good strong brew to cheer us up.'

'Mum, the tea caddy is full of dust – and so is the sugar bowl,' wailed Ooly.

'Well get some new packets out of the cupboard – Dot's got some put by,' said Lil as she washed the kippers under the tap.

Tea was made and distributed and in due course, the kippers. No body ate much …

101

'Shouldn't we go and see if Nell is OK?' asked Ooly.

'We'd best keep together and stay put,' said Sid. 'What about some music?'

'Oh, Dad, not *now*.'

'Well, I'm not just genna sit 'ere – I'm genna find out what's bin goin' on,' announced Lil. She blew the dust from her everyday felt, plonked it on her head and set off, with her husband in hot pursuit.

'Come back here, mate. We'll know soon enough. We should stick together. Don't you go putting yourself at risk. Come back – come back …'

But she had gone, bustling along, dodging between shards of broken glass and lumps of masonry, splashing hoses and flying cinders, finally disappearing in the pall of greasy, black smoke.

With the departure of the "onion in the stew", as they called the mum in the matriarchal society which predominated in these parts, the brave little company at number 29 fell into some disarray. Ooly shrieked at her father for not taking a firmer line; Dot blamed Ooly, who, being younger, should have been the one to go for news; Ed emerging from the shelter and finding his sister gone, screamed abuse in all directions. Sid froze in his chair and Todge bawled her head off.

Stumbling along, Lil encountered a knot of people gathered round the doors of St Alphege. At the heart of the huddle was Mrs Gum's youngest, Timmy Boy, sixteen and important in his tin hat, a Fire Brigade Messenger, sitting astride his yellow painted bike and proudly holding forth:

'The 'ole bleedin' docks is on fire, from the Royals (Victoria and Albert Docks) right up to St Cath's (St Catherine's Dock). Woolwich Arsenal copped it first and now the 'ole bleedin' East End is in flames – Whitechapel – everywhere – rivers of tar, ware'ouses crashin' into Old Farver Thames. You ought to see it like I 'ave. Rats the size of dogs swarmin' out. Ragin' fires at every turn. Even my tyres was burnin' as I come up from Wappin'. 'Ouses round Stepney Church – gorn, smashed. You've 'ad nuffin up 'ere – nuffin compared to what I've seen wiv my own eyes. *And* they say 'e ain't done wiv us yet.'

Not to be outdone, Doomandgloom, who had it from someone who had got off a bus at Bow Church, who had it from someone else, enlarged:

'Dogs (Isle of) is like a ruddy refugee camp. Families roamin' around, their 'ouses gone, no money, no food, no nuthin' – kiddies sobbing their 'earts out –mums not knowing where to turn.'

Lil thought she would go and check on the shop. On her way she met Teddy B hurrying from the public shelter where he had been offering what comfort he could.

'Luvaduck, Vicar, what a todoo! The Dook's 'ad it yer know. I'm just off on a tour of inspection. They say a 'aas 'as gorn in Glebe Terrace and one of the schools is all ablaze.'

'You get back to your family, Mrs Smart. This is no time to be out and about. Just thank the Good Lord that your loved ones are unharmed – I take it they are?

'They're all right. I left them with a good pot of tea. What abaat them poor perishers who've lost their 'omes? They say there's 'undreds of 'em daan Poplar way.'

'The authorities are doing what they can. We must just pray that the Lord will provide.'

And he strode off through the smoke to give the Lord what assistance he could.

The Emporium was still there, looking a bit shaken, with some glass blown out of the windows. Lil peeked inside and what did she see but Fanny Bastaple making off with a bag of sugar.

Lil scrambled through the broken glass and grabbed hold of her overall:

'Put that daan, you, wicked cow!'

'I'll pay for it, missus. Your Sid said he 'adn't got none!' She

103

struggled free and did a speedy bunk, not relinquishing her prize.

Lil thought she'd better get back home and get Sid to come and board up the shop's window.

It should have been dark by now but, as twilight turned into night the sky was lit with a fiery red glow.

Dot was tight lipped: 'Where the dickens have you been? Sid has been stuck to the chair and Ed has been dancing about like someone possessed.'

'That's as maybe. I just appen to 'ave caught someone who shall be nameless looting the shop! Nickin' sugar. And you'll never guess what – 'undreds of 'aases gorn in the Dogs, all Stepney and Poplar burnin' up, corpses lyin' around, 'eads sliced off by falling glass.'

'Mum, stop it – stop it – stop it.' Ooly put her fingers in her ears.

'That'll do, duck,' said Sid. 'Just take off your hat and we'll put the kettle on. When I've had a cuppa I'd best go and see what I can do to secure the shop.'

As Dot was rinsing the cups, it started again – the wail of the siren: 'I told you so. I told you so.' It was 8.30.

'Gawd all bleedin' mighty – not again,' Ed rushed for the shelter, Ooly brought up her kipper and Dot passed out.

'Sid, get out of that chair and get the smellin' salts. Ooly, keep your ruddy mind on the kiddie – get her bottle and some milk. Come on – everyone ready for the fray.'

'Dad, for pity's sake come into the shelter with us.'

'Leave 'im be, Ooly,' said her mother. 'It's a good strong table.'

For seven long, sickening hours it went on – crashing and thumping, the nee-naw of fire engines, the whine of planes, the crack of guns. In the early hours of Sunday the All Clear sounded just before five: 'Come out if you dare.' Bow lay bleeding and a great pall of smoke was coming up from along the river.

Again that night, Sunday night, came the birds of death. They would return to their prey night after night.

104

Early Monday morning Sid and Dot opened up. Ed was put to clearing up the dust and Sid did what he could to board up the smashed windows.

A trickle of customers came in, battered and care-worn, a few excited by the momentous events, most terrified out of their wits.

'Church bells 'ave bin ringin' all over. They're sayin' Jerry's landed down in Kent.'

'' Ope 'e blomin' well 'as – then praps we'll be left alone.'

'No chance, mate. Them bells 'ave made a mistake. That Man'll never get his bloody tanks rolling over good old Blighty. Old Winnie and our lads will see to that. D'you know 'ow many Jerry planes was shot daan last night? Fousands – blinkin' fousands.'

'Ford's copped it down Dagenham and the Beckton Gas Works was 'it. That was a sight.'

'They're sayin' nigh on 'undred died in the Peabody daan near the London Dock last night.'

'And what abaat the so-called safe shelter up Columbia Road Market. Forty killed.'

'Good Old Winnie was down in the docks dinner time Sunday. They say he blubbed at the sight of it all and when they called out "We can take it, Winnie. Give it 'em back!"'

'Good Old Winnie, my bum. It's 'im and his posh cronies we've got to blame for all this. If those nobs at the other end wanted war why the 'ell didn't they go and fight the same people in their set in Berlin.'

When Sid and Dot got home from the shop Lil announced:

'The Goldbergs have 'opp'd it.'

'What d'you mean?' asked Dot.

'Some of their lot – rich – turned up in a taxi and took them off. I think they've got some folk out Epping Forest way – Wanstead I think. They say them Jews can always find a few bob to help their own.'

'I wish Uncle Billy would send a taxi for us,' muttered Ooly.

105

'Anyway,' went on her mother, 'it won't do them no bleedin' good. Stick with them as you know nearby I say. 'Ome is 'ome. The Fairbrothers ave gone up west, yer know. Dunno whose genna run the post office.'

Sid came in with an envelope in his hand: 'Old Mossy seems to have left us a letter.'

'Well I'm blowed. He says some relative of his has got a nice house to rent, out Woodford way. He's asking if we are interested. What d'you think, Dot?'

'We would be well advised to take up the offer. Better class of place, clean air and safety for the kiddie and more respectable for Pan to bring her chums home.'

'For a good price no doubt,' said Lil.

'No, no, mate. He says it's quite reasonable. Bit more than our rent here, but the shop's not doing too badly.'

'What *about* the shop?'

'There's trains, buses. We could manage. We can't go on risking the kiddie's life like this. Mossy said we could move in immediately.'

He looked again at the letter and then hard at his wife: 'There's a long garden and it's quite near to Ooly's new house – where Todge will be living when the war's over …'

They set about packing up and arranged for a taxi to take them away the very next day. Furniture and the large household items would follow on later when it could be arranged and Johnny might have a few hours leave to lend a hand.

It was raining when the Smarts made their departure from Selman Street, leaving behind the friendly Old Ford summers, when all doors were open, so you could hear the bagel man shouting out his wares and the twangy melodies from the barrel organ grinding gaily along the dear old streets.

'Oh Blimey,' said Lil, pretending to wipe some soot out of her eye.

106

'Poor old 'ouse. See you agin sometime – I 'ope.'

'Pastures new, mate. Pastures new.' Sid adjusted his trilby and tied an expert knot in the good, firm string that he had used for the parcel of precious books, which he was not going to let out of his sight.'

'What about Pan's old school books?' Dot was concerned. 'She really prized them, you know.'

'They're all packed up in the wash house – they'll come with the stock of tinned stuff.'

Ooly came out of the house with Todge.

'Bit glammed up aren't you?' said her mother.

'We don't want our new neighbours thinking we're a bunch of gutter snipes.'

'Just a troop of sluts,' Dot grumbled to herself.

Ed staggered out carrying the wireless.

'Leave that for the van,' said Sid sharply. 'Just put it down and go and post these letters – Pan and Mog must know where we're going.'

'We need the wireless for the news, duck,' said Lil, ' and Dot can't be doin' without Old Sandy Macpherson bangin' away on that organ and keepin' 'er goin.'

'No bleedin' point in postin',' grumbled Ed, as he put the wireless into the taxi and went off to the post box on the corner. 'It's all up the spout.'

'Dad, for goodness sake, surely your violin can wait – or d'you want to fiddle while Rome burns?'

The taxi, piled up with Smarts and Smart paraphernalia, finally drew away. Number 29 watched sadly as her rowdy family were carried off, leaving her to face the nightly terrors alone. Dobbin watched from the parlour window and hoped they would come back for him.

'So, Sid Smart, you've left us to it 'ave you? remarked Mrs Gum tartly when she went into the shop a few days later to get some soda.

'Dot and I will be opening up same as ever we did. No change here.'

107

'Never thought you'd abandon ship. Blimey – even the King ain't run away. 'Es a good old bloke.'

'More than can be said for Fanlight Bloody Fanny,' added Vi Kerridge. 'Done up regardless in her feathers and furs, flapping her paw. She comes daan 'ere doin' 'er lady muck bit. One tiny bit of bomb on Buck 'Aas and she says she can "look the East End in the the face" – ha! She don't 'ave to go and sleep in some poxey church 'all – it's just off to some other bleedin' palace.'

'That's no way to speak of the queen, mate. She's doing her bit as best she can,' said Sid.

Chapter 10:
14 September 1940

'Piggo, it would be insane to drive to London. We're told not to drive anywhere unless it's absolutely vital. The police will stop us. In any case – I don't know if I can rustle up enough petrol. The little we've got we need to get to School. And what use would we be?'

'You're as hard as nails aren't you? Does it not occur to you, my dear good woman, that I *must* find out what's happening to my family. I've heard nothing since the night the docks went up – it's been a week! I've tried ringing the vicarage time and again – the lines must be down. If it was your stuck up tribe it would be a different matter, wouldn't it? You'd be out there in your shiny show-off motor hooting your way to Devon like Mr Toad – come what may. Typical – just typical – you fat, self-centred bitch. I'm going to Elsa's – she'll take me.'

Pan flung herself sobbing onto her bicycle and started peddling furiously.

Gif ran after her, puffing and heaving her great body along on its tiny feet, she managed to catch hold of the saddle bag.

'OK, Piggo, we'll give it a try. But I will not have you insulting my Ma and Pa. Apology *now* or no trip. And, don't imagine for one second that your precious Rush would risk her mimmsy self or her ridiculous "bath on wheels" for such an enterprise!'

Sid and Dot, and Lil had feared for the fragile Pan in these dark and threatening days. They need not have worried. Remarkably, the total collapse of normal life and the imminent threat of global annihilation perked her up no end. Her own private anxieties were taken over and abated by real tangible terrors and they were all in it together. No body would say, "Don't be so silly – there aren't really any planes flying overhead dropping bombs. It's all in your head." There were more urgent things to do than whisper about her "nerves" behind her back and tiptoe around her, acquiescing to her outrageous demands. What is more she had the adoring, sensible, clever Gif, to soothe her fears, keep her under control (perhaps) and coach her in the mores of the gentry.

Pan and Gif rented (unfurnished) a pink-wash cottage in Radswick which had once accommodated the local blacksmith. It had been slightly modernised and lay amid wide cornfields, a little way outside the village, where they could be private. A lean-to on the back of the house served as a store for tins and dry goods, cans of oil, tools and a collection of different sorts of string; Pan christened this "the shop".

Pan started work on the garden, manuring, fertilising and cursing the poor soil. It was also her job to put out the rubbish, change light bulbs and do painting and decorating and general repairs. Gif was in charge in the culinary department, managing the laundry and rations, giving orders to the char. They had a bedroom each. Pan's was the large one, facing south, with new plate glass windows overlooking the garden, bookshelves spilling over with papers, scientific journals and sheet music. If you looked inside the wardrobe you would find, pinned to the door, a whole host of photos: Teddy B in the vicarage garden, all the "old chinas" on a church outing, St Alphege *en fête*, mum, dad and Aunty off on an trip to the seaside, smiling in a charabanc, the hockey team at Skoriers, Baggy on prize day. Gif's room had tiny original windows and was rather dark and overborn by the few pieces of heavy Victorian furniture of Drayman provenance. A leather bound prayer book, a sewing basket, and two small faded silver framed photographs stood on the bedside table.

Each woman had a narrow single bed, neatly made each morning, corners tucked in, and covered with a patchwork quilt, exquisitely worked by Gif. Never the twain shall meet – unless there was a thunderstorm or a screaming nightmare which had to be soothed.

Pan did flower painting and prepared her lessons in a cosy beamed study. China cats, jugs of various shapes and glazes, bits and bobs of coloured glass, bowls of butter brazils and sugar almonds (before the war) ornamented the chintzy sitting room where Gif sat in a winged arm chair to do her marking and write plays for the girls to perform. Blacksmith's Cottage was full of re-assurances that all would be well, perhaps very well, if you behaved yourself: "Act so in the valley that you need not fear those who stand on the hill ..." warned a china plate hanging in the hall; "*Begin de dag met blijde lach*," encouraged a little blue and white Dutch dish on the mantelpiece. "Yea though I walk through the valley of the shadow of death, I will fear no ill", insisted a plaque, inappropriately decorated with pink hollyhocks and hanging in the lavatory, or "aunt" as Gif (and soon Pan) called it.

Silver cutlery (courtesy of some long dead Drayman) was kept carefully in a new mock Tudor dresser – they had saved up to treat themselves to just one piece of furniture – Mrs B would have considered it vulgar. It also housed Gif's greatest treasure, a set of Nymphenburg china cups and saucers.

The tiny kitchenette was Gif's domain; there she squeezed in and attempted the good plain meals that had been dished up by Ma's cook. Sometimes, she would branch out into a more venturesome dish; rationing tested her ingenuity and some of the results were less than successful. "Rubber in vinegar" was how Pan described her casserole of some small birds offered on the shrine of Pan worship by one of the "Others at School" whose father had an estate.

'You ungrateful creature.' sniffed Gif into her embroidered hanky, 'This was meant to be a special treat.'

'Treat! I'm thoroughly fed up being used for your ridiculous experiments. Can't we ever get some decent food like Aunty and mum serve up.' And she flung the offending dish across the dining room, striking the Nymphenburg with disastrous results.

The sobbing Gif boomed and blubbered: 'I've had enough of your tantrums. I've had enough. Get back to your deplorable East End hovel and leave me in peace.'

'How *dare* you ! No one speaks to me like that. No one. I'm going to Elsa's.'

As usual, Gif climbed down and there was a cuddly reconciliation; Pan permitted the opening of a bag of sweets and the early drawing of the sitting room curtains.

For the most part they kept themselves to themselves, apart from School Society. On Sundays they, naturally, attended church; for Pan the salt had lost its savour, however, and for both it was a less than uplifting experience. They would drive home through the lanes, batting, one to the other, noisy expostulations of disgust at some minor misdemeanour committed by the vicar, who was, of course, a man and not Teddy B.

They planned to set off for Bow very early on Sunday morning so as to make the most of the daylight and get back home again before the evening siren went off. Pan shouted at Gif if she drove fast, or, indeed at any normal speed, so the journey would take some time. As it usually did, bickering, fussing and the assembling of necessities delayed their departure. A country route was devised, avoiding, where possible, any main roads or built up areas, where they might be stopped, and they stocked Amun up with thermos, blankets and sandwiches, a can of petrol, a first aid box, a whistle and the pistol Pa had kept when they were in South Africa. Pigskin driving gloves and tin hat firmly in place, Gif finally pulled the starter and pressed down hard on the throttle; off to the front line – she was not a brigadier general's granddaughter for nothing.

Amun nosed cautiously through the autumn lanes of Suffolk and Essex, careful not to alarm or upset. Gif, as was her way, provided an historical running commentary, only interrupted, now and again, by the expostulation "My good man!" as another driver overtook, drove too fast or hogged the road.

'You see that church there – and the other on the opposite side of the road? They were built by two sisters – great rivals – St Margaret and St Catherine – during the Wars of the Roses. Margaret was …'

'For God's sake, Pig, do shut up. And stop munching those wretched sweets.'

'I'm only trying to educate you and keep your mind off things.'

After about an hour, the fuselage of a wrecked plane caught their eye, sticking out of a ditch, in a field not far from the road side, still smoking.

'My sainted aunt, there's a man in there!' Gif scrambled out of the car, her vast bosom heaving with anxiety.

'Come on, Piggo, give me a hand.'

'It might be a Jerry. Leave it – come on – we're never going to make it.' Pan sat tight.

Gif was gone, striding through the corn stubble.

A 'Come back you damned fool!' dwindled into a whimper: 'Don't leave me, Piggo, I'm frightened.'

Gif dragged the sticky body out of the still burning wreck and started pumping his chest and blowing into his mouth. As soon as there was some sign of life she took out the whistle and gave several blasts. A farm hand on a bike appeared in no time and was despatched to get help.

Huffing and puffing she got back into the car.

'Well – you were a lot of help.'

Silence from her companion, eyes flashing, fists clenched.

Now Gif put her foot down and they sped through Romford at an alarming pace.

'For God's sake, Pig, you'll kill us!'

'If you want to see your family you'd better put up with it.'

113

Through Stratford and over Bow Bridge, they went, through the grey, smoking desolation of the ninth day of the Blitz. Eerie and strangely majestic it was; they passed the unearthly shapes of blackened buildings – familiar yet unfamiliar – like a dear old face twisted up by a stroke.

'Struth – its the Great Fire all over again,' commented Gif.

Amun bowled along Bow Road – all forlorn it was, houses all tattered and torn, past rubble and piles of debris, past a sad cavalcade of the dispossessed making its weary way out of the East End: cars and milk carts, charabancs and taxis, coster's barrows and prams – loaded with mattresses, pots and pans, piles of clothes, cats in baskets, canaries in cages, babies in bundles.

Amun negotiated the turn into Selman Street.

'My God,' gasped Pan. 'The pub, the Duke of Cumberland – look – its just a pile of rubble.' They pulled up outside number 29.

Pan flew to the door and knocked. No response. She tried again. Nothing.

She fumbled frantically for her door key and opened up. Same old rosy wall paper, same old brown and green lino, same old hall stand. She cried out: 'Aunty, Mum, Dad, Ooly'. Silence. 'Mum – where are you? Answer me – for God's sake answer me.'

Meanwhile Gif had emerged from the car and gone round to see if the back door of the house was open. 'Piggo,' she said quietly. 'The back wall of the scullery – it isn't there.'

'Oh dear God – they're dead! My mum's dead! I told you we should have come before. I told you,' she screamed and thumped Gif's great chest with her fists.

'They might have taken off somewhere. Let's go and enquire next door.'

No response from the Goldbergs. No response from the O'Briens on the other side.

'Let's try the shop,' said Gif.

I'm going to the vicarage,' said Pan and she tore off.

'My dear girl,' said Mrs B. 'What on earth are you doing here?'

'It's mum and dad and Aunty – what's happened to them?'

'I'm afraid I have no news of your family. I believe your sister was at church the Sunday before last, or possibly it was the Sunday before – and, as you know, your aunt and parents only rarely grace us with their presence.'

'But you must have heard something – there's damage to our house in Selman Street and the public house is completely wrecked.'

'*That's* no bad thing,' said Mrs B, continuing to arrange some chrysanthemums in a vase by the fireplace.

'Mrs Billington-Smythe – please help me.'

'Pansy, dear, I can only repeat I have heard nothing. Teddy may know more, but I'm afraid he's over at the hall – it's now a ghastly rest centre for the homeless. May be your family are there? Are they homeless?'

Rage was boiling up into Pan's green eyes. Mrs B had never encountered this side of the Smart girl. It was rather alarming – and then the siren sounded.

'Come along, Pansy, we are using the basement as a shelter. You had better stay here.'

'What – and be buried alive. I'm going to find Vicar, he'll know what's happened to them – you hard-hearted bitch.'

'Pansy oh no! no!'

Gif, the while, having found the shop closed, had been doing a house-to-house and encountered Kathleen O'Brien and her three youngest, making for the shelter in Armagh Road.

'Excuse me, you're neighbours of the Smarts, aren't you? Could you tell me – do you happen to know where they are?'

'Aah, sorry – haven't seen one of 'um since the day of the docks, y'know – those dreadful flames? Black Saturday they're callin' it. Wouldn't have seen 'um anyway – yer know the rest centre ? The one at Corpus Christi? well I heard that they were givin' out soup and sandwiches to the needy – y'know – Christian charity like – so I taught to myself, with seven children I'm certainly in need. We packed a suitcase and was dere by tea time. Grand!

Look at me talkin' away at ya – better get aarselves down into the shelter before we all get blown to pieces.'

Down they went and with all the dramatic flare she could muster, Gif told the children stories, as much to keep her mind off Pan, as for their benefit. They were regaled with *The Elephant's Child*, *Sir Gawain and the Green Knight*, the story of the Tolpuddle Martyrs, Rapunzel, and the murder of the Princes in the Tower.

'That's grand ma'am. Those fellahs real?'

'Can we 'ave the one abaat the bloke who's head was sliced off and 'e put it back on?'

All the shelterers, grown ups and children alike, were enthralled.

When the All Clear sounded Gif set off for the vicarage. As she approached Church Road she was engulfed in smoke; giant flames were reaching up into the sky.

'Keep back! Keep back! Oh my Gawd – there's more coming down.'

All Old Ford shuddered a terrible shudder as the mighty St Alphege sank to his knees, taking his vicarage with him.

Gif pushed through the throng.

'Keep that woman back.'

Teddy B appeared – 'My wife's in the vicarage basement – for God's sake – we must get her out.' He forged through the melee of firemen, wardens and on-lookers and started scrabbling at the piles of smoking rubble with his bare hands.

Timmy Boy peddled like mad to round up a digging party, ringing his bell.

'Reverend's missus buried alive! 'E 'elps us. We must 'elp 'im. Come on – let's be seein' yer.'

From all quarters they came, with shovels, spades, trowels – anything they could lay their hands on. Gif got to work with Amun's jack.

After an hour's furious work, they got in by a side door which had burst open in the heat, crawled into the basement and pulled out an hysterical Annie (the maid) and her young man. No Mrs B and no Pan.

'I last saw the missus up in the parlour, Sir. She was talkin' to that Miss Smart, the odd one that looks like a fella.' They seem to be 'avin' a bit of a ding dong.'

A fireman called down from up aloft: 'We've got 'er. She's up 'ere.' The vicar's wife was found, unconscious, in what remained of the drawing room, her legs trapped under her grandmamma's burled walnut bookcase and her head smashed in. She died in the London a few hours later and had a Union Jack draped over her when they took her off to the cemetery.

Mercifully no one was in the church; it had no crypt which might have served as a shelter. Albie Walters risked his life and earned a hero's reputation by dashing through the inferno to rescue the cross from the altar. Every single piece of glass was splintered, except for one pane, that depicting the head of St Alphege himself – a miracle, surely – the old saint making his last stand.

Still there was no sign of Pan. Eventually Bert Gum found her gibbering under the kitchen table at number 29.

'Come on Miss Smart. Let's go and find yer dad – 'e's with yer auntie, they've bin in our 'ouse, but they're back in the shop now – doin' a bit of clearin' up. And your mate wiv the car – she's there too.'

'My mum – where's my mum?'

'All safe and sound – the 'ole lot of 'em moved out Epping Forest way a couple of days ago.'

Never had the little ramshackle, two storey shop, with its rickety stairs, heard such a commotion – even when the bombs fell – as when Pansy Smart's full fury was visited on her defenceless father:

'You stupid, thoughtless, idiot. Standing there in this filthy, disorganised apology for a shop – this hole in the wall – overflowing with insanitary rubbish, you disgusting, selfish, hypocritical old man, with your ridiculous Dickens worship, your empty cant …'

The brooms and brushes, carpet beaters and gas mantles which hung from the ceiling were all a-quiver.

'How dare you just take off and not tell anybody. How dare you put me through the hell I've been through. And where, may we know, are my books?'

Chapter 11:

End of September to December 1940

Mog *had* got the letter about the move and quickly replied in re-
assuring tones that it was for the best. Another letter came to New
Hall that day – it was for Pete O'Malley.

When Pete got the news it conveyed he set off to walk to London
by way of Tillingham Magna. There he planned to nick just a few dark
red velvety dahlias from Miss Scott – Dickens's garden – mum liked
them. He sat on a tussock by the war memorial and tied them up in a
little bunch with some string he had brought with him for the purpose.
St Mary the Virgin, who had been busting her guts, ringing out her
warning bells over the Mendips, wept for the little mite. The baronet
was taking a prized single malt or two with the rector and emerged to
find Pete sitting stifled in his coat.

'Hello eald cheappe. What's new?'

'Leave me be, you silly old blighter. Leave me be.'

'Come on now – what's up? That daughter of mine been bossing
you around has she?'

Silence.

'She's a bit above herself. Don't you take any notice of her. Come
on – let's go and see if we can find the badgers.'

'I don't care about no bloody badgers. And you said they don't come
out till dark. I 'ate this bloomin' bloody place. I 'ate you, I 'ate Miss.'

'Oh dear, surely the delectable Miss Smart hasn't upset you?'

'She said I shouldn't go – she said mum would 'ave wanted me to stay safe 'ere. What does she bloody know. I know you 'ave to put flowers when someone dies. I know that.'

Sir Horace put his head in his hands. 'My dear, dear boy. Of course you must go. Come back to the house with me and we'll find some petrol somehow and get the Morris on the go.'

And so they did, Sir Horace wrapped the flowers in some wet cotton wool and newspaper and they set off for Wapping, telling no one, as the sun was dipping down over the Mendips,

As soon as their absence was noticed Mog started frantically scouring the lanes on her bicycle. Bella set off on foot and alerted the village bobby and search parties were despatched. Edmund went into what remained of the chapel and had a word.

It was a dark, blackout dark, country-dark night and Sir Horace fumbled and squinted his way along the lanes.

'Can't see a damn thing. It's as black as your hat. Truth to tell – haven't been behind the wheel for donkeys.' Can't see too well at the best of times. But needs must. We shall make it!'

'I'll be your eyes, Sir. I'm good at seein' in the dark – mind out, mind out …'

Their mangled bodies were identified a few days later, crushed under a lorry, just a few miles from Wells.

Mog wrote home:

Poor little blighter. He was always so brave and cheerful. Why do innocent children have to suffer so? And it's my fault. If only I'd taken him instead of leaving him to the mercies of that old fool. Still – he was doing his best to help, I suppose – which is more than I did.

Dad wrote:

Don't you blame yourself, mate. Terrible things happen in war. They're saying there's more folk killed because of the blackout than by

bombs. *Man's inhumanity to man, that's what it is. It would have been folly to attempt a journey. Go and have a word with the parson down there – he'll put you straight.*

You ought to see the garden we've got here. It'll take some work, mind. There's a very fine monkey puzzle tree in the next door garden.

Ooly wrote:

At least the poor little kid won't have to face life without his beloved mum. It's all so cruel. I can't help thinking that it would have been better just to give in and let the Germans rule us. What difference would it have made? Better than all this suffering. I suppose your buddy is Lord of the Manor now."

Pan wrote;

Stupid old man, risking the child's life like that!

Mum wrote:

You stop frettin' – you'll make yerself queer. Yer kno how that pain in yer 'pendics comes when you get into a stew. i would get as much sleep in as possible and dont worry about things.

I am sending you a small parcel I sorry I could not make you a cake but I have made you a baked buddin – you can hot it up in the oven – put a basin over it – that is the best I can do this time.

Poor Old Tom was here – had a few days leave and cum to see our new place. He's a good old boy – reckoned it was like a palace. i suppose it is, and we only have the odd firework display – but i can't help missin Old Ford, whats left of the poor ruddy place. I have to keep remindin meself how lucky we are. if we adnt moved out when we did we would all ave coppd it. cant wait for you to see the garden ere – its like a bloomin park.

Dot offered her sympathy but could not conceal her excitement about their new home:

You should see the size of the parlour – I suppose we should call it a lounge here – and it's got lovely long windows opening out onto a terrace! There are four bedrooms, a bathroom, a separate dining room, at the front, and a good big kitchen, not like that piddling little kitchenette in Ooly's house. There's a sizeable scullery off it, too, and a good sized cupboard under the stairs for a shelter. And it's such a very nice area – not a public house in sight, no smoking factories, no market barrows, just beautiful, clean shops, only a step away, and even a few motors on the roads.

New number 29 (Chestnut Avenue), (Sid called it "the abode of love") was slightly senior to the Come-Lately house. It was set among interminable rows of like-minded properties and rather insolent young "Tudor" semis; there were even some superior detached residences. How smug they all looked, with their round rose beds, clipped hedges and neat lawns. Very pleased with themselves, they were – pleased that they had pert little pointy roof bits sticking out over their all-seeing bay windows, that the air around was fresh and clean and that chestnut trees spilled their autumn wares out onto their pavements. No rubble or smoke marred their serenity, no smashed windows, no loops of hanging brick, no charred beams, or mangled metal, no blackened, burnt-out eyeless terraces; the air raid shelters were quite hidden beneath tasteful rockeries shrouded by ornamental shrubs. All was quite in order in this pleasant land – or it was before the refugees arrived.

The Smarts were not alone. As the destruction of the East End proceeded, trickles of the homeless joined them in the leafy suburb, sometimes whole families crammed into just one room, tents were put up on the Green and washing lines strung across churchyards. Tut, tut.

Sid made himself known to the neighbours: young Mrs Plunket on one side and the elderly Spoons on the other (joined-up) side.

He thought an introductory offering of some of his bug blinder might be a good idea.

'Dad, for heaven's sake! They don't have bugs round here – it would be taken as a terrible insult.' Ooly sighed deeply.

'Perhaps I'll just offer to do some soldering if ever they need it.'

'It's them la-di-da buggers that should be welcoming us with something, in my 'umble opinion,' said Lil.

'Come on, now, duck, all men are brothers.'

'What, includin' them ruddy Jerries, I s'pose?'

Dot thought it was probably best if they kept themselves to themselves. Ooly kept on flashing her famous smile in the direction of Mrs Plunket and the Spoons, but, getting little response, left it at that. Ed was just glad he hadn't been left behind and Sid put on a brave face, hardly aware that he kept whistling to himself:

"Through pleasures and palaces though we may roam
Be it e-everso humble there's no-o place like home."

Lil scuttled past the neighbours, keeping her head down, for the most part. Fancy missing that crew of noisy, mucky micks, the O'Briens; fancy missing the Goldbergs! At least you could always feel you were a cut above them.

She found herself standing behind old Mrs Spoon in the queue at Bumfords the grocer one morning. There was no going "up Roman" here for a haggle and a chat; a polite trot to the Broadway for the rations was all that was on offer – you had to take your overall off and carry a decent basket. What a shop Bumfords was – more like a ruddy palace, with a long marble counter and fancy glittery lights hanging from the ceiling.

'Good morning, Madam,' she ventured. 'I ham yer next door – what a very fine monkey puzzle tree you 'ave aat yer back.'

'Oh, er – yes, I suppose it is,' replied Mrs Spoon, and found herself deeply absorbed in digging around in her bag for her ration book.

Harris Family Butchers was nothing like Billy's place – it was full of portly gents in straw hats and striped aprons and you had to pay at a separate counter from the one where you got your meat – such as it was. Here Dot encountered, face to face, Mrs Plunket with a little Plunket in a pushchair.

'What a lovely little kiddie. How old? I'm your new neighbour, by the way.'

'Yes, so you are. Will you be staying long? I expect you'll be anxious to get back to where you feel more comfortable.'

She swept her tiny piece of meat into a large wicker basket and made off.

There was no fish and chip shop, no pie and mash shop, no ice-cream barrows, just chintzy little Polly's Pantry, with warming pans and horse brasses, where customers wore their best hats to take a cup of tea and a poached egg. Lil and Dot never ventured in there. No sign of a pub, except the stately old fashioned inn overlooking the Green – not that anyone was looking, except Johnny when he came over on leave. Fancy missing the Dook!

The hardware shop was something to behold! Full of bright green lawn mowers, shiny folding step ladders, brand new sparkling pots and pans. Sid reckoned it was over-priced poor quality stock.

But heaven lay about the Smarts. At the front of the house was a patch of well mowed grass with bushes of lilac, syringa and forsythia. At the back was a terrace overlooking two long stretches of lawn divided by a rustic arch; there were wide flower beds on each side of the upper lawn and an almond tree outside the kitchen window; beyond the arch were apple, plum and pear saplings – they called it the orchard.

Lil wrote to Pan:

Soon I shall be pullin my own greens and pickin my own parclee – it'll be like on a farm – good int it?

124

Sid was dreaming of bright scarlet geraniums in tubs on the terrace, deep red carnations making a show under the almond tree and a glorious, full blossomed rose clambering over the arch. Ooly didn't garden, of course, neither did Dot, but Sid and Lil set to work with a will, with Ed put to digging a vegetable patch and moving lumps of stone around to make a rockery.

'For heaven's sake mind the kiddie. Ed, watch what you're doing.'

'Wish you all a good day!' called Sid as he left Chestnut Avenue for his daily journey to Old Ford, with Ed in tow. Dot had decided that she was needed at home and didn't relish the thought of a daily journey back into the abyss.

'Anyone we know copp'd it last night ?' Lil would ask when Sid came home, weary and battered. 'Come on, duck, tell us all abaat it!'

'Well Lewis's dairy is a gonna – a direct hit, they say little Minnie was cut to pieces – head sliced off – they hadn't got her out of her cot and down into the shelter in time. Ma Lewis has gone off her head apparently – they took her off to one of these mental clinics set up especially for the war.'

'Oh, Dad, please do shut up. Do we have to hear all these horrors?'

'We ought to know what's 'appenin' to all the old chinas, Ooly,' snapped her mother, 'Its no ruddy good putting our eads in the sand. Go on, duck – what else?'

Ooly flounced over to the other side of the kitchen, sweeping Todge from Lil's lap.

'Well,' went on Sid, 'young Doctor Murphy has moved away and the Kerridges have been bombed out – gone to live with her sister in Tredegar Road. Poor old Norah, you know Johnny's sister-in-law came into the shop with a black eye – I though her dad had been up to his tricks, but she had walked into a lamp post in the black out. A mite of Jeyes did the trick.'

'We must be grateful no one in *our* family has been hurt,' said Dot. 'I s'pose we'd hardly recognise Old Ford.'

'I can't 'elp missin' the old place,' said Lil. 'Stuck up lot raand 'ere won't give you the time of day. No chattin' when you go and get yer rations. It was so luverly and friendly up Roman.'

Ooly exploded: 'Friendly! Mum, come off it. Reds fighting Black Shirts, our lot at daggers-drawn with Jewish costers and shopkeepers, chapel against church, you and the uncles tearing round like hooligans, putting soot in the holy water.'

Sid shook his head sadly: 'All fighting for the same crust, mate,' said her father. 'That's what you get when kiddies are hungry and folk are desperate. But there was always some clinging together – old Ma O'Brien, even though she hadn't two brass farthings to rub together, always offered us a bit of a bread pudding when she made one.'

'Can't imagine that Mrs Spoon sharing 'er bread puddin',' said Lil.

'Can't imagine Mrs Spoon making bread pudding,' said Ooly.

The patriarch went on: 'There's certainly a good deal of camaraderie these days, but a deal of bitterness too. Doomandgloom says they're all up in arms in East Ham – he's got a brother with a fancy shop in the High Street – the shopkeepers there are locking up their basements to stop them being used as shelters. Everyone seems to think the tacky little public shelters aren't much cop – Bert Gum reckons its criminal that folk have been stopped using the Underground stations – says they're ideal – deep and strong. Anyway – some of them are taking matters into their own hands now.

Feeling against the Jews is running high with the East End getting all the stick, or most of it; Old Hotzner's sure the Jerry bombers are targeting us because of all the Jews – Mosley's lot are stirring it. Bert Gum says that Hitler made a big mistake doing some smashing up west; he reckons that if it had been *all* on our side there would have been real trouble.'

Ed, fists clenched, shaking with fury, chimed in: 'Yea – real trouble – Old Harry Pollit [*communist leader*] says there's a reckoning to come – not against the Jerry workers but against our own boss class who've

126

dumped us in it and keep tellin' us a pack of lies in their newspapers.

What abaat all them dooks tucked up snug in the Dorchester's basement – their families sent off to America to be safe – rentin' country cottages for as much as a worker earns in a year. And the bloody Savoy parasites – they got a bleedin' shock when that bunch of good old East End Commies marched in and said they were stayin' put.'

'Shut up, you stupid idiot,' said Dot.

But Ed was on a rare roll: 'Just read this …' He thrust the *Daily Worker* at his sister-in-law, pointing with his grubby forefinger at:

"The rulers who plunged the people into this war can neither stop the bombers nor protect the people from the bombs."

'That's quite enough of that,' said Sid firmly. 'If we don't stick together behind Winnie, it'll be the finish of us all. Pollit and the rest of the communists are putting the whole country at risk with their ranting.'

The leaves fell off the chestnut trees, and through the darkness of blackout winter, the nightly bombing went on and on.

'Shops are closing left, right and centre,' reported Sid. 'No stock being delivered, delays, customers gone. The only thing that's keeping the Gums going is selling wreathes and then it's only one for each coffin.'

Coventry was smashed to smithereens rivalling London in its suffering. Then came Liverpool, Southampton, Bristol, Birmingham.

In Chestnut Avenue Sid put the head back on Mrs Plunket's garden broom and it turned out that Mr Spoon's old dad had kept a pub in the Mile End Road and Mrs Spoon admitted to some remote relations in Bethnal Green. So that was all right. The neighbours also welcomed the odd pint of paraffin when things got tough and were quite won over by gifts of sunlight soap.

Sid wrote to Pan:

Have just been talking to Mr Spoon. He showed me a letter from his eldest son. It was a striking example of penmanship and a rare tribute to Mr and Mrs Spoon. Should like you to have seen it.

Lil wrote to Pan:

Now – about this Christmas business – you know as much as we all like you to come home – i dont think it is worth it. dad and i think the rest will do you good – you do to much chasing about. You should have some rest. you will be able to have a little party on your owne with Gif with all our thoughts ... when things quieten down a bit we can have a pice of cake & cup of tea together. that will be nice wont it?

Johnny went back to day – his two days went quick. their was know raid in London last night thank goodness – they have been through it – . Well I cant say any more about this rotten raids – we get fed up. you hear nothing else but war. Well don't forget I should not come if I were you.'

Pan spent her December evenings laboriously painting individual Christmas cards – this year's subject was a fox cub in the snow, decorated with holly and ivy. The one she sent home had a curt message:

Seasons Greetings – I trust you will enjoy yourselves "all together".'

Frantic preparations for school festivities took up most of the working day. Gif wrote and produced the sixth form nativity play and Elsa was wardrobe mistress. Pan taught the girls to project their voices and organised the music. The cast adored her; all the girls adored her, especially Jenny Kilminster, a sturdy farmer's daughter with long yellow plaits wound round her head, cast as Balthazar (frankincense). Although she only had one line, she found it necessary to do a great deal of practicing and was to be seen hanging around the biology lab. whenever she had a free period. At weekends Gif often spotted her flitting around the lanes in Radswick on her bicycle, hoping for a glimpse of Pan, or even an encounter.

'My sainted aunt, Piggo, can't you see that wretched girl off? We shall never be left in peace if you keep on encouraging her.'

'I do nothing of the sort. I am pleasantly friendly as I am with all the girls. Anyway you can talk.'

Gif had taken something of a shine to the Virgin Mary, a slim arrogant miss with a mass of glossy ebony hair, an evacuee. There was no reciprocity here, far from it.

'She keeps makin' me stay behind after rehearsals to practice me lines and make me talk proper. Can't keep her chubby 'ands orf of me. If my dad was 'ere ...'

The Kilminster farm came up with a fine duck for the Smart/Drayman festive table – Jenny brought it over to Blacksmith's Cottage on Christmas Eve, hoping against hope she would be allowed to share the fireside shrine just for a few minutes. Gif opened the door and she was firmly denied the privilege.

In Chestnut Avenue they prepared to celebrate Todge's first Christmas. Although she was not walking yet, Sid made her a dear little wooden wheelbarrow and a cart to pull.

'Isn't she a bit young for that, Dad?' said Ooly, irritated.

'She'll be up and about soon enough and I'm going to make her some bricks as well.'

'What's goin' on up Roman?' asked Lil, 'I s'pect its all fun and games.'

'Not like it used to be, mate. None of those lovely decorations, not a scrap of wrapping paper to be had – hardly any fruit or nuts. Trees on old Mossy's stall are all little tiny jobs – small enough for folks to take into the shelters. Not that anyone's going near the Jewish stalls, except their own kind. They're saying that the Jews are bagging all the best places in the public shelters and cornering the black market.'

They made a good fire in their posh lounge, lit the candles on a small tree ('Watch it, mate, be careful of the baby') and ate one of Mr Spoon's chickens in their posh dining room. Ooly tinkled away a bit, Sid got out his fiddle, but no one felt much like celebrating and they all sat round watching Todge play with the brown paper and string that had been so lovingly wrapped around her presents. Johnny had a day's leave on Boxing Day and Ooly and Todge went off to Nell's.

Lil (like Sid and Dot) was horrified: 'Surely you're not takin' the kiddie into that 'ell 'ole? For Gawd's sake make sure you're back before Moanin' Minnie starts up, if she does. Just because we've 'ad a couple of nights of peace it don't mean she's shut up shop.'

Nell had never been much of a one for Christmas – money had always been short and not to be wasted on frivolities, especially not now when Derek was away and in danger. The baby was much too small for presents, anyway; she got Ooly a pretty scarf up Roman, there were Players for Johnny, some bicycle clips for Albie (which he badly needed) and, for Norah, a comb in a pink plastic case. As usual she made her late Christmas Eve trip to Smithfield and managed to get a small turkey, for practically nothing. She and Albie would eat it hot, with enough left for the others to eat cold on Boxing Day. Her cousin on the farm had sent some mushrooms and a dozen fresh eggs which would make a fine soufflé to start. She had been saving coupons for weeks to make a special pudding.

Ooly tried not to compare the chilly house with its two lorn strings of paper chains with the cosy warmth and generosity at home. This was her family now and she must convince herself that it was just as good as the show-off Smarts. What with Pan going to university and Mog being Greta Garbo, she had long lost her position of pre-eminence in the family.

'Merry Christmas to you all,' said Albie, opening the door.

'What-ho, guvnor.' Johnny shook his step father's hand. 'I don't know about "merry", but at least those swine have knocked off the nightly battering over Christmas. You never know – perhaps it's going to let up now.'

Coats, hats, scarves and gloves were removed and stowed.

'But it's so co-old.' Norah shivered and sniffed into her hanky. 'Just look at my fingers – they've gone all purple. It's perishin' at ours – mum can't afford much coal – if only Derek hadn't taken himself off, leaving me to freeze …'

Nell bridled. 'My son is risking his life for us. No more of that talk, if you please.'

'You're in as much danger as Derek, I'd say, mother, more chance of you copping a packet here – I do wish you'd go down to the farm until things calm down a bit.'

'And leave Albie to fend for himself?'

'I'd cope, Nell – Johnny's right. I've tried to persuade 'er, but she's an obstinate old bird, aren't you, gel?'

Ooly thought it advisable to attempt a diversion and passed Todge to Nell.

She screamed and was hastily handed back.

'She's not too good with people she doesn't know very well,' offered Ooly.

Johnny was livid: 'For Christ's sake, she doesn't know her own grandmother ?'

Ooly shrugged her elegant shoulders and flashed a scarlet smile at Albie. 'Come on – let's open our parcels.'

And so they did, while sipping just enough sherry to allow a not uncongenial repast. At least Nell, having been trained up to it, was an excellent cook.

Mog wrote home:

Well, my old Maties, what a Christmas we had here – just like Dingley Dell. It wasn't nearly as good as being at home, of course – I missed you all terribly and the thought of midnight at poor old St Alphege with the candles flickering made me long to be back in Bow.

It all started here with the stable boy and some others dragging an enormous Yule log into the Hall – and we had the biggest, most roaring fire you ever saw. All the old wurzels came for a jolly on Christmas Eve in the Great Barn – we hung up Union Jack bunting and paper chains made by the children. Mrs P and I made a great bowl of hot cider with spices and we even put in a bottle of brandy still left in the cellar from ages ago. Some old boy brought his squeeze box and everybody danced – except Edmund, of course, because of his leg. Not so many young men, of course. I led carol singing round the tree – it was a giant, stretching right up to the rafters.

For Christmas dinner there was pheasant. It tastes a bit like chicken but has a stronger flavour. There was even a proper cake with dried fruit which one of the village women gave us – she had been keeping it for a christening. All our littlies ate with us in the Great Hall – we managed a small gift for each of them – just tiny things like gob stoppers and pea shooters, wrapped up in some old Christmassy paper Isabella found in a trunk in one of the attics. Some of their mums and dads had done them proud. Jessie Aubrey got a beautiful dolls' house which her dad had made himself – like the one dad made for us. Others weren't so lucky. One little chap opened his parcel excitedly to find a tin of sardines.'

Chapter 12:

Between Christmas and New Year 1940

On the fifth day of Christmas, a Sunday, on a bitterly cold, clear night, with a full faced bomber's moon lighting the way, the Luftwaffe struck hard at the City's Square Mile, the age old heart of London. Its fabled guardians, the giants Gog and Magog, were consumed by the raging firestorm, along with the medieval Great Hall at the Guildhall, eight Wren churches, and the headquarters of many a venerable livery company. This was accounted the worst night since the docks went up and was speedily christened "The Second Great Fire of London".

Tuesday was New Year's Eve; Billy and Flo' had decided to join Sid's family as they usually did. Sid and Billy shut up shop early.

'Not a bad place you've got here, Sid.' said Billy, making his first survey of Chestnut Avenue. 'Pity you have to rent, but better this than the smoking ruins of Old Ford. I'd do something about the scullery, if I were you; a good lick of paint and a new stove would be an improvement.'

'Come on,' said Lil, 'I'll put the kettle on. Settle yourselves down in the lounge and we'll 'ave a nice cuppa and a bit of cake – I've made it special'

'Mm. Good size room, but you need some draught excluder on those French windows.'

'We like a bit of breeze,' huffed Lil. 'Good for the kiddie's lungs, 'ave you seen our orchard? It's right down at the end of the garden, beyond the rose arch.'

133

'Oh, Lil,' said Flo', how naice.'

'Fruit trees need a deal of care,' advised Billy, taking the chair nearest the fire.

'Well, my Pan knows all about that sort of stuff.' Lil was beginning to boil.

'I think we should listen to Mr Morrison's broadcast,' interjected Dot hastily. 'He's going to say something important, the announcer says.'

At 6.15 they switched on and listened while the Home Secretary spoke of Sunday's raid.

"Thus is revealed the blackness of the heart, the beastliness of the spirit, of these contemptible foes, of all that is fine in human life. Such is the ugliness of Nazism."

''Asn't got Winnie's touch, 'as 'e?' said Lil, busying herself with the tea pot.

'Damn bad business Sunday night – our Hall went you know,' said the butcher.

''Have you seen this photo?' Sid proffered the *Daily Mail.* 'Old St Paul standing firm against a wall of flame. They're saying Winnie pulled out all the stops to keep him safe.'

'Dad, do shut up and listen – Morrison's been telling us we've *all* got to do fire watching.' snapped Ooly.

'Bloody conchie in the last war, 'es got a flamin' cheek.' Ed, (who usually kept mum when Billy was around) could not contain himself.

'Why are they suddenly telling us what really happened, I'd like to know? Monday's eight o'clock news just said that "some damage" had been caused in the south of England during the night. Why couldn't they tell us the truth?' said Ooly.

'Security, mate, security – can't be too careful,' said her father.

'So why are they telling us exactly what happened now?'

'I'm informed by those in the know,' said Billy wisely, 'that Winnie is all for publicity this time – there was no excuse for burning the City

134

– our Hall – not a military target in sight. You heard what Morrison just said.'

'Strikes me that killing 'undreds of poor perishers in the East End and makin' more of them 'omeless, is more worth shoutin' abaat than a few old churches and your blinkin' club 'ouse getting a bomp' Lil was really angry.

'Heritage, heritage – Lilian – our "club house" as you are pleased to call it has stood on that site for over 400 years. Jerry has ripped out the very heart and soul of England – of the Empire.'

Sid, although he had serious doubts about Wax Chandlers' Hall being the very heart of the Empire, took his brother's part: 'Billy's right, mate. This is a different sort of raid.'

'Raids is raids and bombs is bombs,' went on Lil. 'Just because 'e's gone for toff land this time, there's a song and dance in the papers – it's no different – what abaat all them poor buggers in the Peabody, what abaat old Gert from the Dook?'

'Up the workers!' chimed in Ed.

'Calm down, duck, calm down.' Sid addressed his wife. 'These are difficult days for everyone. Look the kiddie's started crying with all this shouting going on. Let's show Billy and Flo' the telephone.'

The shiny black instrument, prominently displayed on the hall table, was Sid's pride and joy.

'We've got them in the shops, of course,' said Billy, 'but Flo' wasn't keen on having our privacy invaded at home, were you Flo?'

'Oh, no, Billy.'

As they were settling down for a good meat supper, there was a knock on the door. Dot opened it and there stood Johnny.

'Managed to get away to see the New Year in! Thought Ooly and I would go up west.'

Ooly looked dubious.

'Up west! Is that wise, brother? You'd best stay here – you never

135

know what's going to happen and we thought we might have a bit of a sing song. Think of the kiddie – if anything happens to Ooly.' Sid had a low opinion of his son-in-law's protective instincts.

'Where *is* my little Mini Lizzie?'

'We've just put her down for the night, duck. Best leave her be.' said Dot.

'Oh, but … OK then. Come on Missus – jump to it – get your glad rags on!'

But Ooly had left the room and reappeared with Todge a few minutes later.

Lil and Dot exchanged glances.

'Say hello to Daddy Johnny,' said Dot. 'Come on, now, give him a smile. He didn't mean to disturb your beauty sleep.'

Todge's face screwed up and she let out a shriek.

'Come on Mini Lizzie,' coaxed Johnny, seizing the baby and tossing her up in the air.

'Oh, don't do that, brother,' warned Sid.' She's not used to rough play. Let her Nan take up to her cot.'

'I am quite capable of putting my own child to bed,' snapped Ooly, and did so, changing into her glad rags the while.

'Right, we're off now,' she announced as she re-entered the dining room. 'Come on Daddy Johnny, I'm sure our daughter will be well guarded in our absence.'

Sid saw them out: 'Now, make sure you wrap up warm and watch out for a warning.'

'Don't you worry, Mr S,' said his son-in-law wryly, 'If I can protect us all from bombs I think I can recognise an air raid siren.'

'Christ Almighty!' exploded Johnny as soon as they got outside.

They walked on in silence for some time.

'All right, Ooly? You seem a bit browned off.'

'I'm OK.'

'You don't seem very sure.' He squeezed her arm.

'Oh, you know … How are things in Barking?'

'Oh we're pretty chipper. Our boys are doing a great job – my cousin Jack flies a Spit. Sometimes wish I was up in a kite. He came down to visit last week – what tales he has to tell. Do you know …?'

'Oh, did he? Where are we going anyway?'

'Some of the chaps are going to some sort of a do at St Martin-in-the Fields.' Johnny was deflated.

'What – a service?'

'No – a party in the crypt.'

'OK.'

They made their way sullenly to Trafalgar Square.

It was dark, lit only by dimmed torches, and throbbing with the strains of dance music coming up from the Underground station and out from the crypt of the church. A vast concourse of humanity heaved and seethed, jitterbugged and puffed and stamped out fags, gripped by a sort of feverish excitement. Here at the nub of the Empire guarded by lions, they were dancing and jostling the bad old year out: soldiers, sailors, pilots and prostitutes, typists and WAAFs, nurses and firemen, butchers, bakers, armament makers and pedlars.

'Buy a bunch of white heather for luck for the lovely lady.'

'How much?' asked Johnny.

'Special heather – guard you against the bombs – only ten bob.'

'You must be joking. Come on, let's get out of this.' Johnny took Ooly's arm and wheeled her into the church and down into the crypt. The noise was thunderous – the beat insistent and inviting. Under festoons of fairy lights they jigged and swayed, drank and cuddled up.

'Hey, Bowboy,' called out a very posh foxtrotting voice. 'Come and meet my missus – and this is my chum, Mitch.'

Ooly has often imagined a moment like this – she, elegant on the arm of her tall, blond husband, chancing upon Dougie, would sweep by in glamorous disdain, perhaps flinging a fox fur over her shoulder.

Thank goodness she had done herself up …

It wasn't quite like that. Should have got some lucky heather to protect her against bombshells – the Gipsy's Warning.

Introductions were made. 'Dr Mitchell and I have met before,' Ooly smiled her most radiant of smiles – for which she was now famous in Woodford Broadway. 'He came to some of my concerts.'

Their eyes locked.

'Oh y-y-y-yes, I d-d-did.' He pushed his fingers through his floppy black hair. 'It is v-v-very good to see you again. You are a most f-f-f-fortunate man, Flying Officer.' His arm brushed against Ooly.

'Come on – it's the Lambeth Walk,' Johnny hustled Ooly off into the melee:

'Whose that gibbering idiot?'

'Oh, just one of my pre-war fans, Bowboy. I didn't know they called you that.'

Ooly felt she was walking on air, rather than in Lambeth.

Midnight approached and there was a hush as the parson led the whole gathering out on to the steps of his great church, facing the square. As the clock struck twelve they all knelt down, obediently, and sang 'Oh God our help in ages past'.

Johnny grasped Ooly's hand. She was scanning the crowd, singing fit to bust.

'Sufficient is thine arm alone
And our defence is sure.'

'A couple of WAAFs have invited us over to a chum's flat off Piccadilly – we might as well make a night of it.'

Ooly let herself be led away. As they passed by the place where Eros should have been, and wasn't, the strains of 'There'll always be an England' floated on the air, in brave desperation, coming up from the Underground.

'Must we go, Johnny? I'd really like to get back to Todge and dad will be worried.'

'Your bloody family!'

As the mighty wail of pleading had risen to the Almighty from the steps of St Martin-in-the Fields, the telephone rang out in the hall at Chestnut Avenue.

'Hello, Dad, its Pan. Just ringing to wish you Happy New Year.'

'Good to hear you, mate. We're all here – want a word with mum and Aunty? Ooly's gone up west with Johnny.'

'What! My sainted aunt, Dad, what on earth is that callous bastard thinking of?'

New Year was never much celebrated at New Hall – this year least of all. Isabella retreated to her room after supper to worry about bills; Sir Horace's estate was not yet settled. Edmund, who had been quiet and withdrawn since his father's demise, disappeared with a headache.

After the children had gone to bed Mog and Freda were at a loose end. Freda was restless: 'Come on Mog – let's go down to the Tillingham Arms – there might be something going on there. Isabella can keep an ear open for the children.'

'I've never been in a public house,' said Mog. 'My dad would go barmy if he thought I'd entered such profane portals.'

'A village inn is a very different kettle of fish from an East End boozer! Come on – it's New Year's Eve – we can't sit here and twiddle our thumbs all night. Perhaps Mrs P would join us.'

'Aah, no, Miss, we at the Hall aren't in the way of goin' down to that place.'

'Just this once Mrs P, can't do any harm. Do you good to have a knees up.'

But Mrs P was adamant.

'We can't really go in without a man.' said Mog.

'Let's get the stable boy to come with us. We could buy him a drink

139

– I suppose he's not really old enough, but I doubt if anybody will mind.'

The two girls went off to the stables to find their escort. There was no sign of him – in fact the stable door was locked, although there seemed to be a dim light inside.

'Oh well – what about old Bob?'

The gardener was only too pleased to accompany the ladies and they set off through the park, over the bridge, through the lion gates and along the pitch black lane into the village.

The Tillingham Arms loomed up out of the darkness; Mog shone her torch. It was a substantial, square property, built in the classical style in the days when Henriette Duboulay was a new bride at the Hall, covered in Virginia creeper which had even crept along the bar from which swung the sign board – sorely in need of restoration.

'Why is the sign not a coat of arms?' asked Mog. She had noticed before that it was the likeness of a woman.'

'Oh, that be old Lady T, the Horror's mother, a furrener, she were,' said Bob. 'Old Lord T were nuts about 'er and 'ad 'er face painted all over the place. Silly old bugger. She be Virgin Mary in the east window in the church an' all.'

'I think that's absolutely lovely,' said Mog. 'He must have loved her *so* much.' She thought about Edmund. He seemed so withdrawn these days.

In the entrance hall hung a gas mantle, shedding a hissing, yellow light on to a flagged floor, and walls dark with peeling brown anaglypta. Mog tentatively opened the door on the right, labelled "saloon bar" and peeked in. It was empty – a shabby, chintzy, parlour of a room, thick with dust.

'Not in there, my lovely,' called Bob. 'Kept for funerals and the like and strangers as don't know any better.'

He ushered his charges through the door opposite and there were a group of old wurzels crouched at cards over a smouldering fire and a few young lads wielding their cues at a bar billiards table. This was a workaday room, with a plain hatch serving as a bar, half tiled walls, wooden benches round a scrubbed table, a couple of rickety chairs and a beat-up ancient piano. The only decoration was a faded framed print of "Luther at the Diet of Worms" hanging next to the dart board. It sported a sprig of holly.

'What-ho, lads,' called out Bob. 'I've got the Lunnun ladies down from the Hall.'

There was shuffling and an embarrassed silence, nudging and giggling from the billiard table.

'What can I tempt you ladies to?'

'I'll have a small glass of beer, thank you,' said Freda, surreptitiously thrusting a note into Bert's hand.

'Miss Smart?'

'Oh er – I'm not sure. A sherry, perhaps?'

The Grumpy Face in shadows behind the hatch spoke: 'Only cider 'ere, missus.'

'Oh, I'll have some sweet cider, then.' said Freda.

'Only scrumpy 'ere, missus.'

'Oh, okey doke – scrumpy it is.'

'And you, Missus?'

'Oh dear. I really don't much care for cider …'

'Cider's good enough for us Tillingham folk,' growled the Face, 'We don't 'ave no fancy stuff 'ere, 'cept for funerals o' course. Might just 'ave some left from when we buried old mother Bratton in '38.'

The Face reappeared some fifteen minutes later and a tankard was duly filled with something out of a bottle.

Mog sipped tentatively: 'That's very nice, thank you.' She took a swig: 'Very nice.'

They sat down uneasily at the scrubbed table with their unaccustomed beverages to wait for the New Year. It would, they surmised, seem a long wait, but soon Mog, mightily emboldened by a second half pint of "fancy stuff" decided to tackle the locals.

'What game are you playing?' She asked.

'Read 'em and weep,' mumbled a wurzel.

'Goodness – whassat?'

'Came down off Mendip.' was the reply.

'Could we join in?'

The wurzels looked anxiously from one to the other.

'Oh, let's have a go. You can tell us what to do,' said Freda.

And so they did. And in no time there were gales of laughter and the merry snip snap of cards. It turned out to be rather a complicated game and the newcomers were not sure they really got the hang of it – especially Mog who was rather befuddled by now. But the ice was broken and everyone was enjoying themselves.

'Does anyone play the piano?' slurred Mog.

No response but a lot of guffaws.

'I can manage a bit of a chune – nothing like my sister – she's nearly a concert pianist – but I could bash out something, if you like.' Mog went over to the piano.

'Go on then, missus. Give us "Old MacDonald had a farm".'

'No – let's be 'avin one of Vera Lynn's.'

'What about "Roll out the barrel"?'

'I'm not s-s-sure I can manage any of those. I could sing them though.' And she started to sing, and went on singing, and even the billiard players joined in.

At 11.45 the Tillingham Parva Cricket Club turned up in force, all attired in their Home Guard uniforms, fresh from practicing rolling forward to avoid dizziness during combat, in the village hall. Out from behind the hatch, has if by magic, came whisky, gin and rum. One of the new arrivals could play the piano and the whole company fell to dancing, even the Face (who turned out to be female) emerged to take a twirl, while Luther looked on with stern disapproval.

At midnight they linked arms and sang 'Auld Lang Syne'. Mog

passed out.

They may have had their bomb stories in Lunnun, but the best tale told hereabouts, for many years to come, was the story of how that Greta Garbo got drunk on the fancy stuff and was taken up to the Hall in a wheelbarrow. That was some night.

Gif didn't want to go the party on New Year's Day. A rabbit stew with leeks and dumplings was slowly simmering on the stove; with any luck Pan would be happy to stay by the fireside. She loved a good blazing hearth.

'Come on, Piggo,' wheedled Pan. 'We've been stuck in this place for days and Elsa will be so disappointed if we don't put in an appearance. You can wear your new brooch.'

'It'll be a dreary affair, Rush's house is always stone cold and I want to get the French Revolution ready for the sixth form.'

'So, you don't like the brooch I got you. I spent days searching for that moonstone – you really are the most ungrateful and selfish of people. Do you *never* consider anyone else's feelings.'

They set off.

Elsa, who had been with friends for Christmas, had decided to host an early afternoon gathering on her return – just a select few were invited to partake of madeira (or elderberry cordial) served in tiny tea cups in silver holders which, long ago, Captain Rush had brought home from Turkey. As she laid out her mother's exquisitely worked lace doilies, she happily sang to herself the refrain from an old French folk song which she taught the girls:

> *'Il y a longtemps que je t'aime*
> *Jamais je ne t'oublierai.'*
> *(I have loved you long; I shall never forget you.)*

There were homemade meal biscuits sweetened with syrup, some cheese cut into miniscule pieces and put on cocktail sticks and a small "poor man's cake". It was a threadbare little house, convenient for school, genteelly furnished with old but not venerable pieces; after her glamorous sea-faring father had taken off there was much make do and mend. Being careful with what was available was nothing new for Elsa.

She dressed with even more care than usual, excited about the present she had bought for Pan. It was rather an extravagance, but it would be well worth it to see the delighted beam with which it would, undoubtedly, be greeted. Of course, she would much rather have had Pan to herself, but that was not on – there was the omnipresent Drayman, so she thought she might as well invite a few of the Others at School, and Father Jessop from St. Silas with his diminutive curate.

'Glad tidings, Rush,' boomed Gif offering her hand. 'Wretched year over, thank the Lord. Had a good break?'

'Excellent, thanks.' Elsa risked a lightening peck on her cheek and turned to Pan for a hug and whispered in her ear: 'You look gorgeous, darling, as ever. *Il y a longtemps …*'

The clergy were already ensconced in two stiff wing chairs, next to the madeira bottle.

Perhaps the gift should wait.

Introductions were made. The Others trickled in: Maths, Art, Eng. Dom Sci.

Maths, (a substantial figure with a shingle and just a hint of a moustache) had just returned from a daring visit to her family in London and was full of it.

'The mater's at her wits' end – absolutely no staff to be had. Pa's thinking of moving the family into the Savoy – if he can get in – full of foreign royals and such like.'

Art, who was perched prettily on the arm of Father Jessop's chair, wearing green shantung and long lapis lazuli earrings, addressed the company:

'Terrible, terrible the blaze in the City on Sunday. This must be the by far the worst raid yet – all those wonderful, wonderful Wren churches, the Great Hall of the Guildhall – the City's heritage wiped clean away.'

Gif, who did not care for Art, remarked to Father Jessop: 'As a matter of fact 20 churches were destroyed by the Victorians, under the Union of Benefices Act – half of them were Wren.'

The cleric added hastily: 'We must thank God, and Mr Churchill of course, that the extraordinary efforts to save St Paul's paid off.'

'Oh yes, wasn't that a mercy.' added the diminutive curate.

'The docks is one thing, but the heart of the city! Smart, your people are somewhere in East London, aren't they?' It was Eng.(Harriet Oxendale) who spoke, a tweedy woman from Norfolk, who had heard dark tales of the Smart origins.

Pan was uncertain as to whether or not to take arms against a sea of toffs and rage against their insensitivity. In the end she just said:

'Oh – they've moved out into the suburbs.'

Dom Sci., a plump red head, a regular and irritating donor of baked offerings at the shrine of the Great God Pan, bustled over to her side:

'Gosh, that's exciting, Pan dear – a new home!'

Pan snorted her famous snort, lit a Tom Thumb cigar and stalked over to the window.

Gif watched her warily and turned to Father Jessop with a show stopper:

'Well, Mr Jessop (Gif was Low Church) what is your opinion – are we going to be invaded?'

'Ah – the hosts of Midian – well I er ...'

They all went through the motions of deferring to the cleric's opinion although no body really did.

Maths interrupted: 'Pa says Hitler's more interested in the Ruskies.'

No one else offered anything and Gif now steered the company into their comfort zone: the trouble with refugee gels, the misdeeds of Geography, the shortcomings of Chemistry, and, of course their two favourite subjects – the appalling behaviour of the boys, masters and headmaster at the Boys' School, their twin and near neighbour, and the manifold offences committed by their own very new head, Meredith.

Father Jessop and his acolyte spoke softly to one another, the while.

'She's here. She's actually demeaned herself to come!' Pan called from the window.

Disengaging her slender legs from a glossy dark green Morris 8 was a tall, willowy woman, rather older than the Others, wrapped in palest lavender cashmere. She had vague, light grey eyes, and an undoubted air of superiority. This was Jocasta Meredith. There was talk of a fiancé who had died in the trenches.

'New Year Greetings everyone. What a delightful spread, Miss Rush. Look – I've brought some token gifts – just frivolities for you all.'

Elsa put on her best hostess smile. Gif groaned. Jocasta took centre stage.

She nibbled at a biscuit and sipped just a little madeira.

'I've heard Miss Smart has a magnificent voice. Perhaps she might treat us to something.'

'Oh – but I'm afraid I've no pianoforte.' said Elsa.

'I'm sure Miss Smart needs no accompaniment.'

Pan adjusted her tie and gave a perfect rendering of 'Blow the wind southerly'.

Rush and Dom Sci. drooled.

'That was quite delightful,' said Jocasta, 'Shall we have some more?'

The performance went on. Maths and Eng. made their excuses and eventually Gif decided it was time to call a halt.

As they were putting on their coats Jocasta drew Pan aside. She spoke quietly: 'I thought we might take a drive to the coast – next weekend, possibly? I want have a talk with you about the new curriculum.'

'Yes, of course.' Pan smiled her most charming of smiles.

Elsa overheard and quickly produced the present – a long, heavy item, wrapped in some very special pre-war Christmas paper. She thrust it at Pan:

'Something I spotted in an antique shop – I thought it might …'

'Come on Piggo,' shouted Gif from outside.

Amun growled and spluttered into life. His mistress roared:

'Fancy Hoity-Toity putting in an appearance. She's nothing – farming stock. Vulgar –complimenting Rush on those derisory titbits – and bringing everyone a Christmas present – not the thing at all. And turning up 50 minutes late to make an entrance. What were you whispering about, may we know?'

Pan was silent.

'What's that great parcel you've got?'

'Oh – it's just a present for from Rush. There's a bag of butter brazils for you

'Hrrmph.'

'But you like butter brazils …'

'And what have you got?'

Oh – I'll open it when we get in.'

They chugged along the frosty lanes, beneath a rosy sky and saw smoke curling up from the chimney at Blacksmith's cottage. As Gif turned her key in the lock she sniffed the savour of her stew.

'Looking forward to supper? I think I'll open a jar of plums for pudding.'

'I'm not hungry.' Tucking the parcel under her arm Pan made for the study.

'Perhaps you will be later. Let's see your present.'

'OK.'

Gif: 'Why – it's a companion set – quite a beauty – art deco.'

Pan: 'Get rid of it. Take it away.'

'But it's …'

'I said get rid of it-now!'

She tore up the stairs and slammed her bedroom door.

Gif ate her rabbit stew in miserable, uncomprehending solitude. By nine o'clock all the butter brazils were gone.

Chapter 13:
January to 13 April 1941

With menacing brow 1941 strode in. The nightly bombardment from the sky went on while the greatest army on earth gathered on land less than a hundred miles away. Press comment was gloomy:

"Had anyone a year ago ventured to predict that at the end of 1940 Hitler would be in possession of the Continental coast from the North Cape to the Pyrenees and hold Norway, Denmark, Holland, Belgium, Poland and the greater part of France under his iron heel, would occupy Rumania with Hungary in tow, with Italy and Japan as Axis partners, he would have been accounted guilty of 'midsummer madness'."

'Wish you all a good day,' called the master of the "abode of love" without fail, as he left, with Ed, at crack of dawn, waking Todge and driving Ooly mad. It was bitter cold; milk froze in bottles on the doorstep and the northeast wind whipped around the roof tops; the ground was hard as iron.

The *Daily Mirror* offered Patience Strong to its readers:
"Weary not upon the path, though rough the road ahead
Fix your eyes upon the goal. Keep on, and you'll be led—
To the Gateways of Tomorrow where the Sun's bright rays—
Shed the glory of God's promise o'er the future days."

Sid cut it out and pinned it up in the shop, on the shelf next to the tins of Dean's jam.

Doomandgloom Davies paused to read it: 'Some future days we've got to look forward to! Night after night daan into those ruddy stinkin' shelters – piles of shit, screamin' kids, freezin' cold. Ave you 'eard what its like in the Tilbury? that 'uge place daan the Commercial Road – old railway goods yard – said to be the safest 'ereabouts. My missus refuses to go anywhere else. But – my Gawd – its like going daan into the pit of hell – 20,000 people they say – they start queuin' up at dinner time to get in – tarts, negroes, Chinese, Jews, seamen on leave, all crammed into the filthy 'ole, stinkin' of excrement and fried fish. I've eard spivs are sellin' places in shelters for half a crown.'

'Yea,' chimed in Fanny Bastaple. 'And all them ruddy toffs sippin' cocktails in their fur lined bleedin' 'otel basements, all shored up with iron girders – safe as 'aases. And now these orders for us all to do the guardin' our bloomin' selves.'

Doomandgloom added: 'Mm – I can't see that this new rule about fire watchin's genna be of much use. What good's a bunch of old folk and women with buckets of sand and stirrup pumps against them monsters with their whizzo killing machines?'

Bert Gum had come in to get some fuse wire: 'Come on now, mate – we must all do our bit – every little 'elps. Our lads are up there are fightin' for us fit to bust; our guns are crackin' away – good old Winnie will pull us through, mark my word. Our only 'ope is stickin' together.'

Sid, emerging from the out-house with a tiny bottle of paraffin for Fanny Bastaple, proclaimed in his best chapel voice:

'"If a kingdom is divided against itself, that kingdom cannot stand." Mark 3;25.

Remember that, Mrs Bastaple when next you take advantage of another's distress to avail yourself of items for which you have not paid.'

He wrote the quotation out in his fine copperplate hand and pinned it to the front of the counter. Outside, on the shop door, he stuck another: "If you bite and devour one another, take care that ye be not consumed

150

one of another." (Galatians) It was torn off within the hour.

That afternoon poor old Dai Lewis, the dairyman, came in to the shop shaking and drawn.

'Got one of your soldered buckets, Sid?' he asked, his normally jolly sing-song voice reduced to a tremulous little air.

'Here you take this nice new one, brother – no charge.'

'Thank you, thank you – that's very good of you. They're like gold dust these days.'

'Least I can do, mate. You've had enough trouble.'

'Indeed to goodness I 'ave – my baby girl – oh my baby girl.' He put his head in his hands.

My Gwen's lost her reason, you know, after that night – they've taken 'er away. And my poor cows; they found my Blodwyn, the only one of my little 'erd left after the raid wanderin' around mooin' with misery up by Bow Road Station. I've got 'er safe now, mind, in my sister-in-law's backyard, in Armagh Road, that's where I'm livin' now – temporary, like – don't know 'ow long I can keep 'er there, mind. Thought about takin' 'er (she's all I've got now, see) and goin' 'ome to Cardiff, but there's no 'ome left since those bastards smashed it up last week and 'ow could I get 'er there, anyway?'

Lil wrote to Mog – it was a few days later:

Dad brought a cow home. him and old Dai Lewis walked it all the way from Bow on a rope in the blackout. It's in the shed in the orchard. Dot and Ooly are oppin mad. i larfed. dont know what the Spoons will say. Dad's rigged up a gate so it cant get out of the orchard. i suppose we might get some milk from it. Ed says he knows ow to get it out but hes too scared to get near it. Its poor old Dai's – he had to get it out of where hes stayin. He says its only for a little wile. i should coco. we're a proper farm now in't we?

just a few sweeteys i thought it will help you over the stile. i hope you will get them for the week end. Todge is doing grand. i wish you could see her. what about the blitts on Bristol – that's near to you, in't it? don't you get goin' anyway near that place. you keep yourself warm and safe. i miss you this rotten weather. i hope you are not too cold – it has been snowing nearly all this week. on Thursday evening we were going to the flicks, but it has been snowing hard so i did not go. i feeling so tired these days. I am sending your jumper – it is warm.

don't say nothing to Pan about the cow–she'll blow er top. she's in a bate because their char has given up. I say they can keep the house strait.

Mog wrote:

We could see the flames in the sky from Bristol. Don't worry –we rarely go there. If we do go on the razzle it's to Bath. Not that we do much. We get no warnings here – planes are fairly active, especially at night but they don't worry me much – I think our danger would only be a chance bomb if the raiders were chased from Wales or Bristol ... whats to be will be ... Don't worry about me old cockie, I expect you have enough to think about – what with the cow and everything. I'd love to see old Ed doing his milkmaid bit – hope you're getting him a frilly cap!

She wrote to Ooly:

We took the littluns tobogganing up on the hills yesterday – they loved it. We all rolled home under a leaden sky to tea and hot buttered toast round the log fire in the Great Hall. It's so pretty round here with cottages nestling in blankets of soft white. Freda and I went for a walk after blackout yesterday – it was like fairyland with moonbeams dancing on the glassy lakes and the Tillingham lions all capped with snow.

What about this cow? Has dad taken leave of his senses?

Ooly wrote back:

Well – you seem to be having a good time in your wonderland. All hell has broken lose here. Mrs Plunket, the rather naice young woman from number 27 came knocking on the door and said she'd seen a cow in our orchard. I was opening my mouth to try and explain it away when mum pops up and accuses Mrs P of being drunk!: 'I wonder 'ave you taken a drop of sherry waine, missus. A cow in our orchard! You'll be spotting pink elephants next.'

She was livid and next thing a bobby appears and then our friendly neighbourhood bossy-boots ARP warden, and, to cut a long story short, Blodwyn (that was her name) was removed. It was a happy ending, though – she was taken to a farm out Abridge way and they said they'd keep her until poor old Dai got himself sorted out. The whole affair has soured neighbourly relations, as you can imagine.

So what of your fancy man – or fancy lord, should I say? You haven't mentioned him lately.

Mog replied:

Edmund's been a bit funny since Sir Horace died. I suppose he was more attached to the old boy than he appeared to be. To tell you the truth, the gilt is wearing off the gingerbread a teeny bit. I occasionally find myself thinking about solemn Old Tom and even merry Old Morgan.

The day after Blodwyn's departure Merry Old Morgan, who now spent most of his time doing what he could for families down in the shelters, was hurled by bomb blast into the path of an on-coming train at Bank Station, 110 other people lost their lives in one of the worst disasters yet.

'Terrible thing,' said Sid, 'a man of God to have his life extinguished like that.'

'Man of God nothin,' said Lil, ''e was just a kid, really, bright as ninepence, like a ray of sunshine lightin' up the 'ouse – bounding up the stairs, two at a time, always larfin' and jokin', all warm and cuddly – bit like a puppy. And now what's left of 'im is stuck in a coffin' draped in a ruddy Union Jack …'

'Oh Mum, don't.'

'I always thought that he and Mog might make a match of it,' said Dot.

'Oh, I don't think there was ever any chance of that, mate.' said Sid 'He wasn't the marrying kind – he lived only for his flock.'

Ooly remembered Mog having to put a chair under the handle of the bedroom door on the couple of occasions when they had put Old Morgan up for the night. She said nothing.

Sid risked a rare phone call to New Hall. 'Hallo, mate – sorry to take up the phone there, but I thought you ought to know – old Morgan was killed in the Bank business.'

'Oh, Dad, how awful. I'm *so* sorry. Have you got his mother's address – I should write.'

Lil wrote to Pan:

I'm sending a bit of choc to help you keep your pecker up, duck. lots of people round here have got boils. Dad says you should try and stop frettin about everything and get your beauty sleep. He's taken Old Morgan's death very hard. it worries me and Aunty.

While I am writing this the guns are cracking like hell. Well Ooly, and Aunty were on fire duty last night. Dad and Ed had to stay up in Old Ford – there part of some rota the roman traders have got together.

Well I cant say any more about this rotten raids – we get fed up. you hear nothing else but war. give my love to Gif. Good night God bless you my Dear, Mum xxx.

Heavy bombing of London went on until the bad weather in February offered a few weeks respite.

On the evening of the ninth the Prime Minister spoke to the nation:

"All through these dark winter months the enemy has had the power to drop three or four tons of bombs upon us for every ton we could send to Germany in return. We are arranging so that presently this will be rather the other way round; but, meanwhile, London and our big cities have had to stand their pounding. They remind me of the British squares at Waterloo. They are not squares of soldiers; they do not wear scarlet coats. They are just ordinary English, Scottish and Welsh folk men, women and children – standing steadfastly together. But their spirit is the same, their glory is the same; and, in the end, their victory will be greater than far-famed Waterloo."

'Hurrah for old Winnie! Hurrah for us all!' rang out the cry in the blue drawing room at New Hall. 'The pater would have reminded us that the 7th baronet fought at Waterloo,' remarked Isabella.

Churchill continued: "All honour to the civil defence services of all kinds, emergency and regular, volunteer and professional, who have helped our people through this formidable ordeal, the like of which no civilized community has ever been called upon to undergo."

''E must 'ave been up Roman the other week and seen old Ed,' said Lil, 'dancin about like Hiawatha brandishing a dustbin lid fightin' off one of them insanitaries and shoutin, "Fire Bomb Fritz – Britain shall not burn".'

'Mum, do be quiet.'

"I left the greatest issue to the end. You will have seen that Sir John Dill, our principal military adviser, the Chief of the Imperial General Staff, has warned us all yesterday that Hitler may be forced by the strategic, economic and political stresses in Europe to try to invade these islands in the near future. OK, that is a warning which no one should disregard."

The Tillingham Parva Home Guard, sitting in solemn conclave in the rarely used saloon bar of the Tillingham Arms, proclaimed themselves at the ready.

The Prime Minister now addressed himself to the Americans: "Put your confidence in us. Give us your faith and your blessing, and under Providence all will be well. We shall not fail or falter; we shall not weaken or tire. Neither the sudden shock of battle nor the long-drawn

155

trials of vigilance and exertion will wear us down. Give us the tools and we will finish the job."

Pan stood to attention and sang 'God save the King'.

With the coming of March the bombardment started again. Whole streets in the East End were razed to the ground; 44 people were killed when several "maxes", huge, heavy bombs, landed on a shelter in Poplar.

Chalked on a wall near the shop was a new Sunday School hymn: Sid copied it out and pinned it up next to his rolls of wire netting:

"God is our refuge, be not afraid,

He will take care of you through the raid.

When bombs are dropping and danger is near,

He will be with you until the all clear."

Jam was put on the ration. Sid had a bit of stock – tinned stuff, not very good quality. He kept some of it "under the counter" for his regulars – charged them a few extra pence – those who could afford it – but that suited everyone.

Mum wrote to Pan:

we are enjoying ourselves – we are having Blitts every evening at regular. good isnt it? we get plenty of gun fire.

now about your birthday visit – i dont think it is worth it. dad and I think you need a rest. Do your garden then take it easy ... we shall all want what you will be growing ... it will not be long to Easter now will it ? then we can have a snak of whisky together.

Easter fell on 13th April. It had been decided that it really was time that Todge was christened and this might be a good day and would cheer everyone up. Major disagreements between the parties concerned as to who should be god parents had, so far, prevented Elizabeth Marlene's trip to the font.

'You simply must have Pan,' advised Dot, 'She'd be so upset if you didn't.'

'And Mog, of course,' said Lil.

'I can't see Mog abandoning her country paradise to come up here,' said Ooly.

'I've heard that it can by done by proxy, with someone standing in for her,' offered Dot.

'Only the quality do that, mate.' said her brother.

'She needs a godfather, too. What about Poor Old Tom?' suggested Lil. ''E goes to church a lot and 'e's only in Kent.'

'He's not family, duck. That wouldn't be right at all.' said Sid.

Ooly was riled: 'Johnny wants to have his cousin, the vet, with Norah as god mother,'

'Pan wouldn't like that, mate.' Sid was appalled.

'Look – this is my child, not hers.'

'She's never going to have a kiddie,' said Dot. 'It's only fair that she should have bit of a share of Todge.'

So no arrangements had been made – and where, in any case, would this momentous event take place?

No body fancied going up to the snooty church on the Green. Johnny proffered the RAF chaplain in Barking, Sid his chapel at Hermon Hill; both were rejected. But of late, St Alphege himself had, as it were, risen from the grave.

The February respite had allowed the battered East End to sit back, and minor repairs were done to some of the damaged properties. Teddy B and the loyal remnants of his depleted flock decided to make a little chapel in the vicarage basement. It was discussed in the shop.

'I thought the vicarage was a gonner – went up with the church that night when poor old Mrs. B met her end. Vicar's campin' out with some family out Purleigh way, I've 'eard.'

'Most of it went, but there was enough of the structure left for some sort of affair to be rigged up in the cellar.' said Sid.

Nell came in for some Lisol: 'Vicar's had it done it up rather nicely. Albie's been working there day and night. We were wondering if the baby might be christened there? It's time she was – she'll be a year old in no time at all.'

Sid bridled. 'You know Ooly doesn't like bringing her up here with all this going on. It's her decision, of course, but I would advise against it, Mrs W.'

He discussed the Great Matter with Dot and Lil that evening.

Dot was in favour: 'Pan would love it – Teddy B – her dear old church come to life again.'

Lil wrote to Mog:

Well it looks as if Todge is goin to be done, at last. They've all decided on the new make-shift chapel at Old Ford – Little St Alphege, they call it. Blinkin' madness if you ask me with all this bombin goin on. There still rowing about god parents. It's a rotten shame you can't make it.'

In the event Johnny's cousin was unable to come and Norah was brewing up for her annual bout of flu. That left Pan. Amun was, yet again, to be prepared for the perilous trip to Old Ford.

'I've got my grandmamma's christening robe tucked away – it'll need some attention, but it's beautiful Honiton lace. What d'you think?' Gif, was pleased with her plan.

'I can't see my bloody-minded sister accepting anything like that from us.'

'I'll drop her a line,' replied Gif. Ooly answered at once:

Dear Gif,

I was very touched by your offer, but as Todge is nearly one, I'm afraid there's no chance of your lovely gown fitting her.

She grumbled to Lil: 'I'm not having my daughter dressed up in some musty old Drayman cast-off.'

'No mate,' said her mother. 'Aunty and I will make her a nice new frock – I've got some luverly white satin put by and some good ribbon to trim it.'

'Oh, Mum really don't bother – she'll be fine in one of her romper suits.'

Dot looked up from the sock she was darning: 'Surely she should be properly dressed for the occasion. She would look so sweet in a gorgeous white gown.'

'She's fat and practically bald and she's not a doll for dressing up – she's a feisty, fighting human being – she's walking for goodness sake – not a tiny bundle to be wrapped up in a gossamer shawl and swathed in a mini wedding dress.'

Gif was not to be deterred:

Dear Ooly,
No problem about the size – I'm more than happy to get to work with my needle. Just send me her measurements.

Dear Gif,
I couldn't possibly put you to the trouble of altering your precious heirloom – but thanks for the thought – it was most generous of you.

'Miserable cow – I told you she wouldn't agree to the idea.' Pan took up her pen and started scribbling some abuse in her large, flowery hand.

Ooly opened the unaccustomed letter from her sister with some temerity: 'Oh God – Pan's in one of her rages about the wretched christening robe.'

'Best let her have her way, mate,' said her father. 'It won't do any harm.'

'That's not the point, Dad. Why should she always be allowed to

159

dictate to us? Johnny will be hopping mad.'

'Let's just try and keep the peace, mate.'

'Dad's right,' added Lil. 'We don't want Pan spoiling Todge's big day with 'er tantrums, do we Ool?'

So number 29 caved in and on Easter Sunday Todge was duly trussed up in antique lace. It was chilly and drizzling with rain as the christening party and the faithful of Teddy B's congregation gathered under their umbrellas at the vicarage gate, among the hollow eyed houses in the rubble of Church Road.

'Poor Old bloody Ford, just look at all this.' Lil had not been here since they left Selman Street.

Ooly, tight lipped, wore navy: a clinging silk jersey ruched dress, a boxy hat with a net, a fox fur draped over her shoulder. Johnny wore his uniform and a very sulky expression:

'Whose child is she, I'd like to know? I'm rather surprised my mother is permitted to attend the ceremony at all.'

Pan was hysterical: 'I can't go in! I can't go in!'

'Chin up, Piggo, you've been looking forward to this for weeks. It's your day. All your old friends are here – look – here comes Teddy B.'

'Pansy, my dear, how delightful to see you. Miss Drayman, Miss Smart, Mrs Smart, Mrs Walters, Albert, Mr Smart, Johnny, Mr Davids – welcome to our new place of worship. And welcome indeed to your latest addition – how charming she looks.'

'What the hell's the matter with your sister – she's got her way, as usual.' Johnny hissed in Ooly's ear.

'Oh, I expect it's just her claustrophobia. She'll be OK once Teddy B has worked his magic on her. Here take the baby for a minute, I need to adjust my veil.' Todge screamed at the transfer.

'Give 'er to me.' Lil tried to seize the child, but Johnny hung on. She continued to wail.

Little St Alphege braced himself for the onslaught.

It was a damp, spooky hole, Lil thought. There were two underground rooms linked by an unlit passage. One room was done up like a chapel, with a lot of curtains to disguise the crumbling plaster on the walls, a makeshift altar at one end, with a lamp that never went out hanging beside it and some carved wooden rails around the place, which Teddy B had procured from somewhere. There were wooden chairs to sit on with slots at the back to hold hymn books. A print of Holman Hunt's 'Light of the World' glimmered in sinister fashion in the corner. The other room had a table, some chairs and a fizzing tea urn.

The harmonium wheezed through the dim catacomb as the company filed along the dark corridor towards the holy of holies, heavy with the scent of Easter lilies. Pan gripped Gif's arm, her jaw set, looking warily around her, as if she expected some ghoul to come gliding out from the shadows.

Ooly cosied up to her mother-in-law: 'Albie has done so well – I gather he's spent hours down here making the chapel ready for today. And Vicar says he's carved a beautiful miniature wooden font especially for the occasion.'

'Yes,' said Nell tightly. 'We would like to see more of Elizabeth – but what with these terrible raids, I suppose you don't want to risk coming back to Bow too often.'

Everyone settled in their seats.

Lil spoke to her sister-in-law in a stage whisper: 'The kiddie is really uncomfortable in that rusty old lace – there's bits sticking into her poor little neck.

'Wish my Mog was 'ere.'

They belted out, 'Christ the Lord is risen today', written by Charles Wesley (Sid noted with satisfaction); it was, of course, the first time Little St Alphege had experienced the thunderous alleluias of Ooly *v* Pan – he *was* surprised. Teddy B floated in, led by Albie, large in a billowing white surplice and carrying a cross.

'We are gathered here today in our new chapel on this day of joy, this Easter Sunday, to welcome a new member into our little community,

161

but also to remember those who have left us. Foremost in *my* mind is my beloved wife, Beatrice, who did so much for our parish and whose loss is so hard to bear. But my personal sorrow is but a drop in the ocean of misery which has engulfed us all in the last year. May the baptism of our latest addition to the Smart clan (Nell and Johnny exchanged sour glances) bring with it a new dawn of hope, a healing of wounds and a path towards peace.

Dearly beloved, forasmuch as all men are conceived and born in sin, and that our Saviour Christ saith, none can enter into the kingdom of God except he be regenerate and born anew …'

Pan, white and tense, duly promised to renounce the devil and all his works on Todge's behalf. Teddy B took the squirming Todge in his arms and asked Pan how he should name her. Ooly intervened and whispered something in his ear.

'Oh, my dear, how thoughtful, how very kind.'

'I baptize thee in the name of the Father and of the Son and of the Holy Ghost, Elizabeth Marlene *Beatrice.*'

Murmurs of surprise all round. Pan blenched.

Afterwards there was to be tea in the other room and then back home before the siren went. Pan grabbed hold of Ooly's arm as they went along the passage way and growled in a hoarse whisper: 'What do you think you're playing at? Beatrice!!'

Ooly was truly astonished:

'I thought you'd be pleased. Your Vicar is delighted.'

She flung off angrily to charm some of the old chinas.

Lil had overheard:

'What the dickens is up with you, Pansy Smart? You were so fond of old Mrs B. And what abaat that time when you took your posh college chum to tea in the vicarage because you was ashamed of bringing 'er 'ome to us! What abaat that!'

Pan shook: 'She didn't care whether you were alive or dead.'

'What are you talkin' abaat?'

162

'Come on, mate,' her father admonished. 'That's no way to speak of the departed. Let's all go and have a good cup of tea.'

'None of our family names.' noted Nell tartly as she took charge of the urn.

'It's a luverly tribute for the Vicar, though, duck,' soothed her husband.

Scones were distributed, made with marge and thinly spread with precious butter; Nell had been saving up her rations.

'I thought they might come up with the top layer of the wedding cake – that's what's proper – but no sign of it.'

Pan was deeply engrossed in soft conversation with Teddy B.

'Pansy, my dear – do tell me how your gels at school are faring in these troubled times – I imagine you have a number of evacuees.'

'"Oh Yes, Vicar, No, Vicar, three bags full, Vicar. What an absolute delight your new chapel is – such an oasis of calm and serenity. Such a moving ceremony for my niece and what a splendid way of honouring dear Mrs Billington-Smythe." I can just hear her,' said Ooly to Johnny, *sotto voce*. 'She'll be kissing the hem of his surplice next.'

Johnny went out for a smoke and found Gif rootling around in the glove compartment of Amun, in search of some sweets.

'Pan seems rather upset,' he ventured. He never knew quite what to make of Gif. 'Ooly says she doesn't like enclosed spaces.'

'Billington-Smythe will undoubtedly bring her round.'

'Yes, that's what Ooly said. But what got her in such a bate about the names?'

'My dear good man, I really couldn't say.' She stuffed a couple of pear drops in her mouth and went back inside.

Chapter 14:

16 April to May 1941

With Pan firmly placed as guardian of Todge's soul, and the daffs, at last, putting in an appearance in the still chilly garden at number 29, bombing started again with renewed ferocity.

Three days after Easter, came the terrible night known to Londoners thereafter as "The Wednesday", followed, a few days later, by yet another onslaught on the East End: the Royal Docks, the East and West India Docks, granaries at Millwall Docks and St Peter's Hospital Stepney went up. This was the worst night since Black Saturday.

The Emporium was not doing too badly – regulars knew they could always get something "under the counter" from Sid's, and with gas unreliable the sale of paraffin was up. Looting was a worry for all the shopkeepers and Sid put up some strong wooden shutters and fixed new padlocks on the doors, back and front.

'One of them O'Brien boys was caught breakin' into some poor old duck's gas meter.' It was Harry Bastaple who spoke, Fanny's old man.

'Looters are more of a trouble than Jerry – that's what I say. The buggers wait till folk are tucked away safe in the shelters and then off they go, smashin' and grabbin' to their 'earts' content. My brother-in-law Frank had all 'is stock nicked on "The Wednesday" – 'es a furrier – fousands of pounds worth of stuff gorn. And that's not the worst of it.'

'What's the worst of it, then, brother?' asked Sid, remembering the theft of his sugar.

'The worst of it is, in my opinion, when they gets 'old of the corpses

164

– poor buggers what 'ave copp'd it good and proper –'and seize the bits of jewellery from their 'ands, their necks, their wrists. Even their clothes get torn off. My sister, Frank's missus, she copp'd it in a raid daan the Dogs, and before Frank could do anythin' abaat it, they was gorn – her diamond earrings, 'er fancy watch, even 'er gold band.'

Sid couldn't help wondering if there was just a touch of triumph in Harry's tale of the woes of his rich relatives.

'Bomb chasers they're callin' them. They gets wind of a bad raid and, before you can say Winston Churchill they're on their way. That O'Brien kid and all the rest of them should be strung up.'

'Yea – right,' said Vi Kerridge. 'Bloody micks.'

It was still bitter cold when May brought with it the introduction of double summer time and eerie interminable light evenings. After tea Ed would set about cementing the pond – it was the only thing he could do properly, according to Sid.

Sometimes he was out there until ten o'clock when it finally got dark. At least there was the Cup Final to look forward to, for him, if no one else at number 29. It was something to take your mind off the raids. Not that he ever went to the match, of course, but he was an Arsenal supporter and was hoping that they would give the northerners from Preston a good bashing. He wouldn't even be able to listen to it on the wireless as he would be busy with his paraffin at the shop.

In any event, the big match was a wash-out, the teams drew and there was going to have to be a replay. That night came the raid to end all raids – there was not much doubt who was the winner there. From Bow to Belgravia, north and south of the river – all London was set alight, burning as if its heart would burst. This capped even the Second Great Fire of London when Wax Chandlers' Hall had fallen victim to the enemy. News first reached number 29 via Mrs Spoon who had a phone call from her sister-in-law in Aldgate on Sunday morning. Lil was in the garden, checking on the pond and putting some nappies out on the line.

'Mrs. Smart – you can't imagine what a sight it is. Ethel says this is it – London's a gonner. Such a mess, such wreckage and fires everywhere. She says sightseers are coming in from all around to gawp.'

Lil hurried back inside. In no time she was done up in her Sunday best and itching to be off.

'Come on Dot, get yer titfer – let's go and see what's bin goin' on.'

'What are you talking about?'

'Old Ma Spoon was aat in the garden when I was puttin' the nappies aat – she says everyone's goin' to see the sights.'

'Lil, you really shouldn't hang the washing out on Sunday – not round here. What sights?'

'Lunnun Town burnt to ashes – them sights. Come on – let's go up west and 'ave a butcher's. 'Urry up or we'll miss all the fun.'

'For goodness sake – we shouldn't take pleasure in the sufferings of others, should we? Sid wouldn't care for it at all.'

'Well 'es not 'ere, is 'e? – 'e's gorn to 'is bloomin' chapel. Anyway – we've got a right to see what's 'appened to our Lunnun.'

Truth to tell, Dot was rather curious.

'Come on, mate, let's be up and doin.' Don't let Ooly know where we're goin' – she'll go mad.'

It was a chilly but sunny day; perhaps spring had come at last. They got on a bus up at the Green. 'Well, what a pickle we're in, ladies,' chirped the conductor as he clipped their tickets. 'That was some night! Aases of Parlyment 'it, Big Ben 'ad 'is face smashed in, the Abbey, Queen's 'All, Bow church, Old Bailey, all Fleet Street, stations, flames over 'Ackney Marshes five miles 'igh. Pandemonium up west naah – abaat a fousand roads closed off. Dunno 'ow far we're genner get.'

The bus, already quite full when they got on, was bursting at the seams by the time they got to Leytonstone – girls done up regardless in their best summer frocks, lads in boaters, chattering and laughing away, mums with excited children.

166

As they got nearer the city a curtain of smoke rose before them. Progress was slow the road was choked with vehicles; ambulances, fire engines, lorries, private cars.

As they inched by the ruins of Bow church, hunched up still smoking in the middle of the highway, a shiny dark green sports car drew alongside them.

'Just look at those toffs all piled up in that flash motor,' exclaimed Lil.

'I say, my man,' called one of them to their bus conductor, 'Which way do we go for the best sights?'

'Any way you like, mate. Any way you can get,' came the reply.

'Let's 'op off,' said Lil. 'We can walk quicker than this bleedin' bus is crawling.'

By the time they got to Whitechapel Dot was exhausted. 'Come on,' urged Lil, buoyed up with excitement, pushing her way through the crowds. 'Now we're 'ere we might as well make the most of it.'

They made the last lap to Aldgate and the entrance to the City.

'At least old St Botolph has got through it! But just look at Aldgit station!'

Sill they pressed on through the throng, over lumps of rubble and glass, hosepipes snaking under their feet, everyone jostling and pressing for a better view and all swathed in acrid smoke, curling and twirling, to the sound of ringing bells, the shriek of police whistles and shouts of 'Keep back! Keep back!'

'Bloody rubber-neckers – go home!' shouted a fireman lying limp and shattered on the pavement by the smouldering wreck of St Mary le Bow.

'No more Bow Bells – no more Cockneys!' shouted someone.

Sparks burst out in showers, fizzing about like fireflies among toppling walls. Flames licked around window frames. Shreds of torn clothing and scraps of blackened paper danced out from the jagged, sooty remains of office buildings.

On they all pressed making for the prize – the palace of Westminster – chattering and joking, kiddies held aloft on their father's shoulder so they could see the carnage.

'London was the greatest city in the world – until the Yanks overtook us as top dogs.' one dad proudly announce to his offspring.

'Yea – where are the bloody Yanks in all this?' called out another.

Someone was selling hot pies and calling out his wares. Someone else was selling souvenirs: 'Buy a bit of metal from Bow Bells – only a couple of bob to remember Olde London by.

'That's a tale of tub if ever there was one. Metal from the bells would be molten hot!' said Lil 'Gawd luv us – it's like a bloomin' fun fair.'

'More like the fall of the Roman Empire.' Dot was horrified.

They're sayin' Fleet Street's some spectacle.'

'We're not going all that way are we?' Dot was half dead.

'We must 'ave a gander at the best bits.'

'Lil, I can't go another step without a cuppa and a sit.'

'Right oh, duck – there's a café open over there.'

They queued up for half an hour, but by the time they got to the counter every bun, sandwich and rock cake had gone and there was no milk left for the tea and no chair free to have a sit.

'Blinkin' locusts! Oh my bleedin' Gawd, look at that dog over there – what's it got in its mouth?'

'It's a doll isn't it – oh no!' Dot blenched and reeled. Lil took her by the arm:

'Come on, mate. I think we've seen enough. Anyway my feet are killin' me.'

They didn't get home until late. Sid was frantic.

'Didn't they say where they were off to, Ooly?'

'Well no –Todge and I were out for a walk – we were gone some time – and when I got in Dot had left a note just saying they wouldn't be long.'

As night started to fall the two of them appeared, and collapsed into arm chairs.

'Where have you been? I've been worried sick.'

'Oh – we just went on the razzle. Went and 'ad tea with an old dame we met in the queue at Bumfords in the week.'

'Where?' Ooly was suspicious.

'Big 'aas up on the Green. Should 'ave seen the silver ware! What a palace.'

'You went for tea and now it's nearly black out!'

'Well we got chattin' – time flies.'

Lil was bursting to tell her tale of London burning, but they both managed to keep mum. Ooly was not convinced by the story of the long, posh tea party, but decided to pursue it no further.

Everyone had a bomb story. Doomandgloom Davies had a good one: ''Erd about what 'appened at Bethnal Green Woolies – it was all alight and a fireman sees someone inside. Takin' 'is life in 'is 'ands he dashes in and grabs the lifeless body – only to find out it's a dummy!'

Many wept over a special loss. For Old Winnie it was the chamber of the House of Commons, for Rabbi Hotzner it was the Great Synagogue in Duke's Place, for Sid it was the Queen's Hall, where he had thrilled to the sea shanties at many a promenade concert. For the Gums it was poor little Timmy Boy, cycling about his duties, finished off by a lump of flying shrapnel.

Five days later Churchill broadcast to the United States: "And now the old lion with her lion cubs at her side stands alone against hunters who are armed with deadly weapons and impelled by a desperate and destructive rage … United we stand divided we fall."

London waited with bated breath for the final smash, for invasion, for decimation. But none came. That May night turned out to be the finale, the last night of the Great Blitz. The monstrous Teutonic dragon had swung his mighty frame around and was going east towards Russia.

169

As the buds on the lilac in the front garden were struggling into bloom, after 243 sleepless terrified nights it was safe to go to bed and get your breath back, and time to attend to the vegetable garden.

But for for number 29 there would be a bombshell of a different kind – a far greater shock for the "abode of love" than any which might come from the air.

The letter came on Todge's birthday. A great pile of presents was piled up in the lounge; Lil and Sid had been scouring toy shops for weeks. Billy and Flo' were coming and Ooly had convinced the family that Nell and Albie should be invited; Johnny might manage an eight hour pass. Pan had been kept at bay; her last visit had caused such ructions. Lil was smearing some makeshift icing of marge and cocoa powder over a carrot cake when the postman arrived. There was a lovely hand-painted birthday card from Mog and inside it a letter. She usually wrote twice a week, but they hadn't heard from her since the Queen's Hall went up. Lil was relieved; she wiped her hands and sat down to tackle the missive – reading was still difficult – Mog had taught her to read and write when she was at Skoriers. She was such a good girl.

My Dear Old Maties,

I have some wonderful news to cheer you all up. I hope you won't be cross that I never told you anything about it before. It came as rather a surprise to me – I thought it best just to get on with it and not get you worried.

Edmund (Sir Edmund) proposed to me just a few weeks ago – it was so romantic – down on one knee in the arbour. And then – well – we just did it. It was only a small affair in the local church here, with Freda, a few old wurzels and Edmund's sister. I wore a pale blue silky costume with a hat decorated with tiny artificial forget-me-nots. The family lawyer gave me away and we had some champagne back at the Hall. There are a few snaps – I will send them when they are developed. We're not having a honeymoon, yet, anyway, what with war and everything. I gave Edmund a beautiful silver lighter; my wedding ring is a family heirloom.

I was sorry that you were not there, of course, but we thought it best to have a very quiet ceremony without any fuss and leave celebrating proper until the war is over.

You will love Edmund – he is so handsome and gentle. He's not particularly musical but loves poetry and books.

I keep pinching myself – it's so amazing – I am the Lady of the Manor – Lady Tillingham! What ever will all the old chinas say?

I was sorry to miss little Todge's big day – I would have loved to see her all done up in old Gif's heirloom!'

'Oh my bleedin' Gawd,' Lil whispered under her breath, tucking the letter into her overall pocket. 'This 'ad better keep until the party's over.'

When the guests had departed and Todge had been duly feted and her health drunk in a sip of sherry, Lil showed The letter to Dot and Sid.

'What are we genna do?' Lil was as near to tears as she ever got. 'I blame that Baggy – giving my girls ideas above their station.'

'Nothing we can do, duck. The deed is done. We'll just have to make the best of it.'

'Whatever will Pan say?' added Dot.

Sid wrote to Mog:

Your news came as rather a shock. We had no idea you were even keeping company with the young gent. Surely it would have been better to take a little longer to get to know one another, especially as he comes from such a different walk of life to ours? Of course, it is a great honour to be joined to the aristocracy, but their ways are not our ways, mate.

There's trouble with Maureen too – she's set her heart on young Mossy – the families are up in arms.

I wish you well and will pray for your happiness. Our best regards to the baronet.

171

Lil wrote:

Blimey O'Reilly. What 'ave you gorn and done? Up the duff i s'pose. And what about Poor Old Tom? I reckon we won't be seeing much of you from now on and, if we do, i s'pose we'll ave to curtsie.

She did, however, go speedily along to Maggots the stationer's *(recte* Baggots, re-christened by the Smarts because of the grumpiness of the assistants). There she enquired in a loud voice if they had a card suitable for conveying congratulations to a newly married lord – her son-in-law, Sir Edmund Tillingham.

Dot wrote:

I wish you every happiness, of course, but mum and I can't help wondering if it is really for the best. We could have brought the baby up here with no one any the wiser.'

Mog wrote to Pan:

Well you've been spared the torture of another bridesmaid's outfit!

I'm scatty with excitement! Freda doesn't seem to be very pleased and Isabella was a bit funny about it at first – she kept asking me if I knew what I was taking on – the responsibility of the estate, I suppose – and kept on about Edmund's "disability" and did I fully understand what sort of a man he was. Anyway – I told her I loved him to distraction and didn't give a hoot about his nerves or wonky leg. She still seemed unconvinced. I expect it's a class thing. I shall have to keep the old 'uns under wraps for a bit. I dare say she was hoping for an heiress to shore things up down here.

Pan was angry and cock-a-hoop by turns: 'How could she just go off and get herself married like that – without a word. Still it'll shut them up – the Others at School. No more allusions to my East End origins from that Oxendale woman – now that I'm a baronet's sister-in-law.

Puts you and your lot in the shade, doesn't it, Piggo!'

Gif looked grim. 'I presume she's got herself pregnant and he is doing the honourable thing. Pretty dollies have been nabbing unsuspecting members of the gentry since time began. I must say I never thought your Mog had it in her to pull in off!'

Rarely had Blacksmith's Cottage witnessed such uproar as followed this remark.

'My niece – Lady Tillingham, yer know, has often been compared to Greta Garbo,' proclaimed the family butcher to his fellows Wax Chandlers.' We always knew she would do well for herself. Didn't we Flo?'

'Oh, yes, Billy.'

To Ooly Mog wrote with immense care:

It wasn't a smashing do like yours, but really very chic.'

The news was an especially bitter blow for Ooly – her younger sister seizing the prize when hers had been so cruelly snatched away. She blamed her nose. Had hers been a neat protuberance like Mog's, it might have been St Margaret's Westminster and the Café Royal rather than pickled onions in the parish hall. It might have been gentle, sensitive, adoring Dougie.

She wrote to Mog:

I thought you said the gilt was wearing off the gingerbread! The old dames seem to think you're expecting. If you are carrying a Tillingham heir (or heiress) you'd be well advised to keep it away from the continual interference which goes on here.

You've probably heard that Maureen's getting married to Mossy Goldberg – rather a different affair from yours, I dare say. She would like you to come but I suppose that will not be on. There've been terrible ructions in the O'Brien family, as you can imagine – 'Mary, Mother of

173

God – not a Jew boy.' Ma Goldberg is tearing her hair out too – it looks as if neither set of parents is going to attend.

Poor Old Tom, by no means a drinking man, consumed a whole bottle of Scotch which had been put aside for peace celebration, and drove his army lorry into a brick wall. He was in hospital for three months.

When Mog's news got out in Bow, it was the general opinion of the Roman and among the old chinas from church, that she was, indeed, up the duff. St Mary the Virgin of Tillingham Magna knew different.

Chapter 15:
June to August 1941

On the evening of the 21st of June, Winnie spoke to the blue drawing room at New Hall, to the kitchen at number 29 and to the study at Blacksmith's Cottage: it was a Saturday and had been blisteringly hot:

"At four o'clock this morning Hitler attacked and invaded Russia. All his usual formalities of perfidy were observed with scrupulous technique. A non-aggression treaty had been solemnly signed and was in force between the two countries. No complaint had been made by Germany of its non-fulfilment. Under its cloak of false confidence, the German armies drew up in immense strength along a line which stretches from the White Sea to the Black Sea; and their air fleets and armoured divisions slowly and methodically took their stations. Then, suddenly without declaration of war, without even an ultimatum, German bombs rained down from the air upon the Russian cities, the German troops violated the frontiers."

Lil wrote to Pan:

we went to the flicks this week Thursday. we saw bitter sweet. it was good – dogs ain't we? what do you think of Russia? Good dont you think. what we should do is bash them jerries more & more. i could do it myself. i wish i was a man i be up in the air quick if i were young. i expect you laugh but i feel very bitter lately i could kill some of them myself. i dont what to do (sic) about the schelters – i don't think we shall get many more raids.

175

i have just ritten to Mog – or Lady Tillingham, i should say. i don't think shes going to come up for Maureens do. i think it is going to be retched turn out – Maureen says there will not be much – its at the Town Hall – she is suppose to of had some nice presents. i hope she will be happy – it is a big step for 'er – 'er mum's sworn on the sacred eart what shes got up over 'er sink, that she wont ever speak a word to 'er agin. Just as well Maureen ain't living at home any more. i sometimes wonder if i shall ever see my Mog agin – what with er being a lady now. she's 'oppin mad that we thought she was in the family way.
well now I must get old Dot some tea.

Good night God bless & keep you from harm ...

Maureen's "do" was indeed a wretched turn-out. The Goldbergs were quite determined to keep their distance, but, at least came up with a generous present. Mossy Jnr. begged his adored mother: 'Mum, it's not like I'm asking you to go to *Corpus Christi.* 'ow *can* you miss my wedding?'

Even Sid, at Ooly's instance, went over to Wanstead and put in a good word, without letting on to Lil, of course. Well – he owed a great debt of gratitude to the Goldbergs – without them there would be no new home in the leafy suburbs, no orchard, no almond tree. He also felt a bit responsible as he suspected Mossy and Maureen had got together at Ooly's wedding. But Edie, pleased as she was to see him, was adamant:

'With so many nice Jewish girls around – Oh Sidney – why did he have to choose a shiksa? My father must be turning in his grave.'

Sid wondered privately whether her plight was worse than having your darling blue-eyed girl given away by some legal man to a toff – and you not knowing anything about it.

'But, mate, we're all in this pickle together – all in the same boat. Now is not the time to cause anymore division than there is already.

Maureen's a respectable, kind girl – belongs to a very well thought of choir.'

'You're a good man Sidney Smart, but principles is principles, I sticks to mine and you sticks to yours.'

To make matters considerably worse, Poplar Town Hall, an extravagant and much criticised brand new building, very modern and not looking in the least like a town hall, had been christened "the bacon factory" by the locals.

Kathleen and Paddy O'Brien had rather surprisingly relented and agreed to put in an appearance at the nuptials. Ooly, who had always got on well with Kathleen, was put in charge of making sure she and Paddy stuck by their decision. Todge was entrusted to Nell (to Lil's horror), and Ooly went off to collect the parents of the bride from Selman Street.

The ceremony was scheduled for noon. Ooly arrived at eleven o'clock to be on the safe side even though the Town Hall was no distance away. Mossy had laid on a limousine to pick them up.

'C'min, c'min. Paddy's just getting' 'is finery on. Will you take a drop?'

'Oh no, Mrs O'Brien. I really think we should be getting off – the car's outside. Where are the children?'

'Oh for sure a registry office's no place for kiddies. My sister has dem.'

'Isn't she coming, then?'

'Oh – dey'll be joinin' us later.'

'C'mon now, just a drop to wet your whistle.'

She poured a large slug of Irish whisky. 'I've managed to get this special like – from 'ome. And I've just cut us some nice fresh sandwiches.'

Ooly tipped her drink surreptitiously into the aspidistra and tucked a ham sandwich up her sleeve: 'Mrs O'Brien, we must go.'

Still no sign of Paddy.

'The driver must 'ave a drop.'

'C'min, c'min,' she went to the front door and called to the chap at the wheel. 'You must drink my girl's health.'

'Thanks, mate, but it's time to be makin' tracks.'

'What – you won't 'ave a drink with me on my Maureen's weddin' day?'

'OK, mate, OK – just a splash.'

He joined them in the parlour and drank his whisky with relish.

'Good stuff, missus. Good stuff, 'aven't 'ad anyfing like this since before the war.'

'Take another drop – no – c'mon, c'mon.'

With just twenty minutes to go Paddy appeared in a tight and shiny suit.

'We must all 'ave a drop together, now,' he announced firmly.

'But, Mr O'Brien, we haven't got time.'

''Aven't the time to toast the father of the bride?'

He looked a bit threatening so more drinks were poured.

'Please drink up,' pleaded Ooly.

'Ah yes – we'll be takin' de bottle with us.'

She managed to get them into the car and they careered dangerously in the direction of Bow Road.

'Just stop 'ere, will yer, kindly.' said Kathleen, as they neared Gum's shop. 'I'll just pop in and get a carnation for Paddy's buttonhole.'

'But, Mrs O'Brien, Mossy has that all arranged at the Town Hall,' wailed Ooly.

'For sure – but Paddy had a special one in mind, a double one with them kinder speckles, didn't you now?' and she hopped out.

Minutes ticked by. She bundled back in, flower in hand and off they went. They had only driven a very short distance when Kathleen, yet again, called a halt.

'It's just a couple of minutes, I'll be.'

'Where's she off to this time?' asked the driver.

'Oh God,' groaned Ooly as she watched the mother of the bride hastily tie a head scarf on. 'Not *Corpus Christi*.'

'Ah – she'll just be poppin' in to 'ave a word with the Father.' Paddy took a swig.

It was a longer wait this time. Ooly, like Sid, anxious about punctuality at the best of times, was in despair.

'Right – off we go. Father O'Reilly wasn't dere. I had to speak to Father Jim.'

As they turned the corner she shrieked.

'Mary, Mother of God, Patrick O'Brien – you can't go to yer daughter's weddin' in dat tie! We must go back and get de proper one.'

The car was turned round, at which point Ooly gave up.

By the time they arrived at the Town Hall the ceremony was safely over. Kathleen crossed herself in gratitude and they proceeded to the reception.

Mog wrote home:

Dear Old Coves,

I was sorry to miss Maureen's wedding. I sent a telegram – I expect you heard it read out – and I thought of you all having a good old knees-up. I'd love to have seen dad leading the conga along Bow Road in his trilby! I must say I'm surprised mum let him attend – you know what she thinks about the O'Briens – and the Goldbergs, come to that. What a shame that neither of the families would come round. You would have thought that all this war horror would put things into proportion. It's the Germans we're supposed to be fighting, not our own nearest and dearest. At least the O'Briens made it to the reception, but poor old Mossy – he must have been so terribly sad that his mum didn't turn up at all.

I'm sitting at the desk in my bedroom – it overlooks the lakes and the drive. When I wake in the morning and draw the curtains I can hardly believe that as far as the eye can see is mine – well partly mine. The old wurzels even touch their forelocks to me!

Lil wrote:

*Dont you get above yourself. Just remember us old wurzels up ere –
dont exspect us to be touchin our forelocks WHEN we see you. I suppose
you are just lazin about eatin grapes and sippin out of gold goblets. you
know we went up to town to see lady hammilant [Hamilton]– i think
that is wrong way to spell it. well it was at the plaza last week. I thought
of you.*

Mog replied:

*I'm really very busy, as a matter of fact. There's a lot to be done
here. Strictly speaking I think now I'm a married woman I suppose I
ought to give up my job – but I shall carry on helping Freda as long as
the kiddies are kept here. Isabella says we could do with the money, but
Mrs P's very sniffy about the Lady of the Manor earning a living. She
said darkly, that Edmund's mother did, and that caused a very great
deal of trouble.*

July was hot and wet – good growing weather at last. Still no more
bombs. Old Ford took a well-earned breather and, at the shop, trade
picked up a bit now it seemed worthwhile doing out the wash house
again – if you had one left!

Sam from the chippie came in: 'I'll 'ave some of your nice light
stone Sid. And a couple of brushes.'

'You look a bit tired, mate. Been overdoing it?'

'It's 'ard doin' all the fryin' meself wiv me boys called up and young
Betty gorn daan that factory off Burdett Road where they makes parts
for fighters. Can't get the fat for the fryin'. Queues outside clamouring
for me fish and chips and no ruddy fat!'

'There's always paraffin wax and glycerine – I've got a good stock
of that. Your trade's good, brother – you should be thankful for that.'

'Oh, yeh – since the Eytie shop's gone – yer know the one daan the
other end. Old Renzo got interned and his missus couldn't cope and 'ad

180

to shut up shop. I've got no lack of customers, thank Gawd, but it's 'ard graft. And I've bin up since the crack, queueing up for fags. Then when I got to the counter they'd bloomin' well run out!'

'I've got a few loose Woodbines under the counter. You can have some of them – a penny each.

'Blimey, Sid. They're only fivepence for a packet of ten!'

'It's up to you, mate.'

'Oh – go on then – my missus can't do without 'er fags.'

'Got any tins of pease pudding out back, Mr Short?' asked Ethel Jiggins from Old Ford Wesleyan.'

'I think I've got a couple.'

'I'll take them both then. And a couple of bottles of vinegar – the cheap stuff will do – need something to give the food some sort of flavour.'

'There's some good tips to be had from the wireless about making good nourishing, tasty meals,' said Sid. 'You'd do well to listen to what Grandma Buggins has to say – it's very comical, too.'

'Blinkin' Grandma Buggins,' interjected Fanny Bastaple, 'With 'er creaky voice – makin' out she's one of us – tellin' 'ow to make sausages taste better with bits of liver and kidney stuck in. I'm fed up with 'earing about cocoa powder and carrot flour and them great pies of parsnips and oats with a mite of cheese to kid you you've got something tasty. "Fire Fighters' Pie" my arse – do they really think callin' porridge and pot'erbs something fancy will do any good?'

'Anyway,' chimed in Vi Kerridge, 'Don't these toffee nosed articles know we lived through worse times when there was no work and no money for sausages – let alone kidney and liver. There was no stuck up preachin' to us then as to 'ow we might make a delicious meal out of muck – we 'ad to make shift for ourselves. I was always tryin' to stretch a tiny bit of best end between the nine of us – and that was only a few years back. What d'they think Yorkshire puddin' and dumplins was all abaat? Abaat fillin' you up with cheap stuff and makin' the meat go further – that's what. Let Grandma Buggins try feedin' a family of nine on a docker's wages. Let 'er try that!'

'Well mate – the Home Service is doing its best to stop us from being starved into surrender.' said Sid. 'Not all folk have the experience of making do like us East Enders. I'm sure there's plenty of housewives who are grateful for the advice. Now, Mrs Bastaple, Mrs Kerridge, can I serve you with something or are you just here to sow discord?'

'Got any soap?'

'No, Mrs B – not a mite to be had. They're saying it'll be on the ration soon.'

'Not even any of your special Knight's Castile? I know its pricey but my 'Arry is beginning to stink sommat rotten.'

'Well – I might just have one bar out the back.'

'Thanks, mate. 'Ow long d'you reckon this let up from Jerry is genna last?'

Doomandgloom had just come in: ''E'll be back, you wait and see. You just wait and see. I said to my missus – when they've done with the Ruskies they'll be takin' revenge on us for what the RAF boys 'ave bin droppin' on them.'

Winnie was of a mind with the undertaker:

"In the last few weeks alone we have thrown upon Germany about half the tonnage of bombs thrown by the Germans upon our cities during the whole course of the war. But this is only the beginning, and we hope by next July to multiply our deliveries manifold.

It is for this reason that I must ask you to be prepared for vehement counter-action by the enemy."

August was wet and chilly – not good for the veg. Over Blacksmith's Cottage dark clouds were gathering across the wide East Anglian skies.

'For goodness sake, Pig – you're not listening to "Carrot Time" again.'

Kitchen Front, the food programme, which ran for five minutes every morning at 8.15am had been christened by Pan "Carrot Time" for obvious reasons.

'What is it this morning – carrot marmalade, carrot sausage roll, carrot and cream cheese, carrot cookies or carrot top and potato soup? – that was your most unsuccessful effort. Filthy! I don't know why you bother; we're all right here. Plenty of meat if you play your cards right with the local farmers. I can't say we lack anything much – except sugar, I suppose.'

'Not everyone has an arrangement like you appear to have with the Kilminster girl.'

'I still maintain all that carrot talk is for townies.'

'I thought I'd make some carrot flans for the church fete. What d'you think?'

'I shan't be here.'

'What?' You're supposed to be judging the chrysanthemums!'

'Well they'll have to manage without me. In any case, no one's bothering with flowers anymore: they've all turned their flower beds into vegetable gardens.'

'Good Lord Alive – you can't just abandon ship like that. You promised the Committee – and its next week. Where are you off to, anyway?'

'Jocasta is taking me to an hotel – she says I need a break.'

'You need a break !'

'I had three boils last term. She says I'm probably run down. I've been stuck here all summer. There's only a week of holiday left.'

'What about me?'

'What about you? You had a week with your God Almighty Archdeacon Pa at the end of July.'

'I will not have you speak of my father like that! In any case – you were invited and refused to come and my mother was in hospital.'

'I wasn't going to endure your father's thinly disguised contempt and your mother's probing questions.'

'In any case – they're my family. It's hardly the same as you taking off with that Meredith woman.'

'You know perfectly well that it was impossible for me to stay with my family over the summer hols. Dad made it clear that he felt it wasn't safe and would be bad for my nerves to be so close to London.'

'You managed it for the christening.'

'That was just one day, as you are well aware. You know how much I long to be with them – its so unfair of you to bring this up – so damned unfair.' she sobbed.

'No – I'm simply not having it. It's bad enough watching your sighs and simperings with that awful creature. I will not be treated like this.'

'I'll bring you back some nice sweeties! And perhaps there'll be some special treats for you when I come back – *really* special treats. Come on, Piggo – just think of that!'

'No. You are not going.'

'You can't stop me. You don't own me – I might as well be living with some bully of a man. A bloody Nazi – that's what you are. Carrot flan for the war effort does not alter the fact that you have friends in Munich. I know what's going on. I know which side you're on. Does anyone else, I wonder – perhaps it's time they did.' Pan's eyes were flashing dangerously.

'Don't be ridiculous.'

'I've listened to you – what a wonderful transformation Hitler has brought about in Germany. You were there in the bad times when a wheelbarrow of marks wouldn't buy a loaf of bread, when children were starving and all because of what the wicked allies had done, punishing of poor German folk for what Kaiser Bill and his posh cronies had inflicted on them. How different it became when the sainted Fuhrer took things in hand. What about your friend Helga, your dearest and best friend – you went and stayed with Helga, your dearest and best friend just before war broke out, didn't you …?'

'Look, I spent a couple of years in Munich as a student. I got friendly with the family I stayed with. That's all. That's it.'

'I'm not sure everyone would view it like that. The Others at School would be most interested in your Fascist proclivities.'

The ultimate threat of The Others at School saw Pan duly make off for a "rest cure". On Sunday Jocasta and Pan set off in the green Morris 8, making for The Ship, a cosy hostelry in Aldeburgh. It was raining and the great grey North Sea lashed in turmoil waiting for the enemy's approach while the Martello Towers, which had stood firm against Napoleon, were again on the watch.

Chapter 16:
24 August to October 1941

A solitary, deflated, miserable Gif, having lost all interest in devising a carrot flan settled down in her wing chair with some sugar almonds she had been keeping for an emergency. After a sniff or two she applied herself to the Hundred Years War – she enjoyed teaching her gels about the victories of Sluys, Crecy, Agincourt.

After an hour or so she turned on the wireless to listen to Churchill's broadcast about a meeting with President Roosevelt. First he spoke to Europe:

"Do not despair, brave Norwegians: your land shall be cleansed not only from the invader but from the filthy quislings who are his tools. Be sure of yourselves, Czechs: your independence shall be restored. Poles, the heroism of your people standing up to cruel oppressors, the courage of your soldiers, sailors and airmen, shall not be forgotten: your country shall live again and resume its rightful pan in the new organization of Europe. Lift up your heads, gallant Frenchmen: not all the infamies of Darlan and of Laval shall stand between you and the restoration of your birth-right. Tough, stout-hearted Dutch, Belgians, Luxembourgers, tormented, mishandled, shamefully cast-away peoples of Yugoslavia, glorious Greece, now subjected to the crowning insult of the rule of the Italian jackanapes: yield not an inch!"

He addressed Gif: 'Keep your souls clean from all contact with the Nazis; make them feel even in their fleeting hour of brutish triumph that they are the moral outcasts of mankind.'

Chesnut Avenue was listening too:

"We had a church parade on the Sunday in our Atlantic bay. The President came onto the quarterdeck of the *Prince of Wales* where there were mingled together many hundreds of American and British sailors and marines. The sun shone bright and warm while we all sang the old hymns which are our common inheritance and which we learned as children in our homes. We sang the hymn founded on the psalm which John Hampden's soldiers sang when they bore his body to the grave and in which the brief precarious span of human life is contrasted with the immutability of Him to whom a thousand ages past are but as yesterday and as a watch that is past in the night. We sang the sailors' hymn 'For Those in Peril', and there are very many in peril on the sea. We sang 'Onward, Christian Soldiers', and indeed I felt that this was no vain presumption, but that we had the right to feel that we were serving a cause for the sake of which a trumpet has sounded from on high."

'Well – what did Winnie have to say this time?' Ooly came in from the garden where she had left Todge asleep in her pram under the almond tree.

'Best bring the kiddie in, duck,' said Dot. 'It looks like rain is threatening again and it's chilly out there.'

Ooly ignored her and repeated:

'What did Winnie say? Are the Americans going to come in like they did last time. It's our only chance of survival. You do realize that. Johnny says we've not got a hope in hell without them.'

'It was all "chin up" and flag wavin',' growled Ed. 'Lot of stuff abaat 'istory and "let's all gang up and do the buggers down" – the usual. Load of baloney abaat them all singin' ymns together on some ship – wherever it was – and being pally pally with Roosifelt and the Yanks – and 'ow it'll be all right in the end. I should coco.'

'That's no way to speak,' snapped Sid, who had been mightily impressed by the lengthy talk of hymn singing.' It was a wonderful stirring message.'

'Anyway – what about the Americans?' Ooly asked again.

''E said sommat abaat "mighty forces arming",' said Lil. 'So I s'pose they might bestir themselves. Who's to blinkin' know?'

'We must trust in Old Winnie, duck,' said Sid. ' He'll sort it out if anyone can. Didn't you hear him say: "Help is coming … Have faith. Have hope. Deliverance is sure".'

'Darling, did you listen to Churchill?' called Mog, as she came into the drawing room at New Hall with an armful of lavender, bound for the Great Bowl in the Great Hall. She had heard the broadcast with Isabella and Freda in the conservatory:

Edmund (Sir Edmund) was lying on the faded blue brocade chaise longue, reading *Of Human Bondage:*

'Mm.'

'Well – what d'you think?'

'I suppose Roosevelt might come up trumps.'

'You don't seem very concerned.'

'Of course I'm damn well concerned!'

Mog was taken aback: 'Why don't we go into Bath tomorrow – we could do the bookshops, have some lunch – make a day of it. I want to try and find some curtain material for my bedroom – the ones hanging in there are a disgrace – must have been there since the Armada. I need some remnants for the puppets I'm making, too. I thought I'd to put on a show for the village children at the tenants' harvest party. And I promised the family at Keeper's Cottage that I'd look out some paints for the children. There's a lovely shop which sells artists' materials just near the Assembly Rooms; I should be able to get something to suit there – not too pricey.'

'You go with Bella – I've arranged to ride tomorrow.'

'Well what about Tuesday, then? We never do anything together,

Edmund. Old Bob can drive us and we could even take in a flic. It's an age since I saw a flic. It would be such fun.'

'Oh, I'm lunching with the Portmans over at Nether Tillingham on Tuesday.'

'I'm not invited?'

'Not your sort of thing, my dear girl. Harry Portman's got a few days leave – I haven't seen him since he joined the RAF – we'll just be chewing the fat about the old days. In any case, aren't you supposed to be with the vaccies?'

'I do wish you wouldn't call them that.'

'Would you prefer gutter snipes?'

'Don't be beastly.'

'Sorry. My leg's playing up today. Feeling a bit under the weather.'

She went over and put her arms round him.

'Mog, don't do that, you'll lose my place.'

She retreated and sat down.

'Look, Edmund, I know how you must be feeling, with all your pals doing their bit and you stuck here. Is there *anything* I can do to help?'

'Just sit there and let me gaze upon your beauty, my Rose of Tillingham.'

'Edmund, don't be silly.'

The baronet looked immeasurably sad: 'I'm not being silly.'

The long and bitter siege of Leningrad began and all eyes turned to the Eastern Front : "Come then," exhorted Minister of Supply Lord Beaverbrook, "in the foundries and forges of Britain, in the engine works and the assembly lines, to the task and duty of helping Russia to repel the savage invaders." In Old Ford, too, an invasion was underway. The first few days of September were very hot, and out they came, crawling, creeping, biting.

Sid was doing a brisk Saturday morning trade when Will Kerridge came in, scratching his mighty docker's biceps: 'Give us some of yer bug blinder, mate – the warm weather's bringin' the buggers aat.'

'Make sure you wash down all the walls and floors, not just the bedsteads. And take the backs off the pictures – you'll find them in there. You'll need a good big bottle, perhaps a couple.'

'O K I'll 'ave a couple. The itchin's givin' us the pip. We never 'ad it as bad as this when we was in our own place. Dirty cow – my sister-in-law. Dozens of 'em on the ruddy piller when yer wakes up – streamin' across the walls. Still, we're lucky to ave a bed to lay down on at all. S'pose the Jerries might leave us alone now they're taken up with the poor old Ruskies – wiv any luck. Bloody funny that agreement between them and 'Itler in the first place – like that Mosley had cosied up with the Whitechapel Jews!'

'Just did it to share out Poland between 'em, is my view,' said Doomandgloom who had come in for some fly papers.'

'At all events,' said Sid, 'Russia coming in with us should see an end to the Reds round here stirring things up against Winnie, now we're in cahoots with their chums.' He looked hard at the docker – he wasn't sure of his political affiliation, but he had a good idea.

The undertaker went on: 'Old Mackenzie reckons the war's genna go on for years unless the Yanks join in.'

'Who's 'e when 'e's at 'ome?' asked Will.

'The Canadian PM, 'e made some speech – talkin' of 'orrors still undreamt of, he repeats this'orrors still undreamt of'. Mark my words, we've seen nothin' yet.'

'Time the bleedin' Yanks started pullin' their weight,' went on Will. 'I've 'eard some of 'em are even moanin' abaat all the stuff they're sendin' over 'ere. Wouldn't mind if it was any good – 'ave you 'ad any of that bloody fat bacon they've sent? My missus put some in my sandwiches. Reckon they wouldn't eat it themselves – just pack it off to the Brits – they won't know any better!'

'Come on, now, brother.' Sid shook his head wisely. 'We'd be in a fine state without their tinned stuff, not to mention their guns and ships. My son-in-law's cousin's a pilot and he's been training over in America. They're doing their bit, as best they can. This Lend-Lease arrangement is doing us proud.'

'Lend-Lease my arse. Just a way of 'em keepin' aat of the war. Send us a few tins of beans and some guns and let us get on wiv it – sittin' smug in their ranches, with their refridges and cocktails, all safe and saand, dancin' abaat with top 'ats and canes ...'

'Old Roosevelt will see us right, brother.'

Ooly had been up to the Green blackberrying with Todge in the push chair. She found her mother sitting alone at the kitchen table, wrapping up apples for winter storage. There was a letter by her side.

'What's up, Mum? – you look fed up.'

She put Todge on her mother's lap.

'I'm feelin' a bit groggy – just tired. When's it genna stop – all this? I don't know 'ow the ruddy time goes down 'ere – it is so quiet some times. I get the 'ump with them all away. Woodford's a damp hole. I just put the wireless on and they started playin' this song – "I walk beside you" – I think they must know I've 'ad the blues this week – everywhere seems so miserable.'

Ooly, 'At least the bombs have stopped.'

'What abaat Newcastle ?'

'Well it's been all quiet down here. And you've got us – Todge and me.'

'I don't know what I'd do without the kiddie.'

'What's the letter?'

'Oh – it's from my Mog.'

'Is that what's upset you? It's not like you to get so down in the dumps.'

'I sometimes wonder if she's all right down there, playin' lady muck.'

'All right! She's living the life of Riley – no queueing up for meagre rations for that lot! Everyone kowtowing – "Yes, Lady Tillingham, no,

Lady Tillingham, may I kiss you arse, Lady Tillingham?" "May I have the honour of presenting you with this fine pineapple I've grown in my hot house. Perhaps you would do me the favour of accepting this gift of a side of beef. Darling – could you pop down to the cellar and find a bottle or two of champagne for this evening?"'

'Nan, Nan, syrup,' interposed Todge.

Lil went over to the dresser and got out a table spoon.

'Mum, I wish you would stop giving the child great spoon-fulls of golden syrup – it's hard enough to come by and she's fat enough as it is.'

'She's only a baby, duck, she needs something sweet.'

'More, Nan. More.'

'Mum, for goodness sake …'

'Oh, I suppose it will all come right some day, but I wish I could see my Mog. As it's quieter now, I thought she might come up. She's never even clapped eyes on Todge – and she loves kiddies so. She used to talk abaat comin' 'ome for a visit when she was first daan there.'

'Yes, but it's all rather different now,' said Ooly sharply. 'I can't see her putting up with what we have to put up with, now she's got used to the high life. Anyway – what's she got to say in her latest letter?'

Dear Maties, Moggo calling,

Autumn is lovely here – it's all "season of mists and mellow fruitfulness". The trees in the park are beginning to turn – all the tints of copper and gold – reminds me of old Baggy – Ooly, do you remember she was always saying: "Gels, the glory days of autumn far outshine the chilly spite of spring." We're busy stacking up fire wood and logs against the winter – we're using the stable block to store our fruit. It's a lovely old building, a bit away from the house. Bella and Mrs P and I spent absolutely hours wrapping up apples individually, making sure that any damaged ones were thrown out.

I did a puppet show for the children at the tenants' harvest do. They loved it – it had to be a bit more grown-up than I usually do, as we had big boys from Readers (the local posh school) helping out with the harvest. I made some new puppets and had a patriotic theme – a sort of pageant all about our great triumphs – I had Henry V at Agincourt, Wellington at Waterloo etc. I was really pleased with my Wellington puppet – I gave him an Ooly nose! Of course they were victories over the French – but I suppose it doesn't matter as long as it's "Rule Britannia".

Now, about Christmas. Of course I'd love to come; it's such an age since I saw you all and I'm longing to see your new home and, of course, little Todge. Does she look like Ooly or Johnny? You haven't told me. At this rate she'll be at school before I meet her. But I really think Bella needs me here. I've decided that the blue drawing room has really got to have some attention – I shouldn't think it's seen a paint brush since the Boer War. Freda and Bella are up for it and I thought I might even get some of my kids to help. Should be fun. We could do with some of your "nice light stone", Dad!

Then there's the kitchen! You should see the range – it looks as if it came out of the ark. There's no spare cash to do anything about that and, in any case Mrs P seems rather attached to it, but I've persuaded a couple of handy wurzels to get the old cracked sinks out and replace them with a couple of nice modern looking ones that I managed to find in a salvage place in Bath. Mrs P is dubious ("They sinks were good enough for old Lady T" etc. I seriously doubt if she ever actually saw them) but they'll smarten the place up a bit. Bella and I spent yesterday taking up the lino in the lobby – what a job that was. Still we had quite a lark. I shall be trying my hand at re-upholstery next.

So you can see there's a lot to do. And we are still told not to make unnecessary journeys – even though things have quietened down so much. Let's wait until this wretched war is over and then we can have a wonderful reunion.

'Poor old Mrs P, poor old Bella – when my Mog gets the wind in her tail there's no stopping her.'

'Hm. No mention of the baronet.'

Lil wrote to Pan:

My Dear Pan excuse the paper – we are working our old stuff up.

I was surprised when my parcels came on Friday afternoon. i was just getting ready to do my shoping – another ½ hour i should have brought my weekly vegetables. They were a lovely surprise – i have made nearly six pounds of plum jam.

nothing much is going on here –.little Todge is in the pink. it has been raining all the afternoon – a rotten day. some snooty dame from the WVS turned up and said there was some voluntry women offering to to our shoppin if we was late home from the factory and couldn't do it ourselves! missus, says i, i'm not havin no strange woman doin my chores – poking her nose into our business. And no one here works in a factory, i'm telling you that –my youngest, Lady Tillingham, you know, wuldn't here of it.

Ooly has jus been to Bow. they had their dinner with Nell. it was harvest there – it was full to good muster full of young men of the army. you would like to have been their – it is rotten being away from home – you miss all these shows. i had a quiet day it does one good to rest from it all. i get very tired sometimes.

Sid was worried about Lil. He wrote to Mog:

The Big Woman is very down in the mouth; nothing seems to buck her up. Aunty and I think it would be a lovely treat for her if you could just manage a short visit.

Don't go over doing it down there – you've got a lot on. You know how your appendix plays up if you strain yourself. Make sure you prepare the woodwork properly before you get down to the painting and have plenty of turps to hand in case any paint gets spilt.'

To his wife he offered what words of comfort he could: 'Come on, pecker up, duck. Mog will be home soon enough – just think what the neighbours will say when she rolls up in her glass coach! Things seem to be looking up on the war front; just listen to what old Winnie's saying.'

He read out from the paper: 'There will be better Christmas dinners … We are no longer alone … we have climbed from the pit of peril … He says there are devoted battle lines of the Russian armies to the East, and to the West. The majestic momentum of the US reserves and actions …'

Lil was unimpressed: 'What's 'e talkin' abaat – "majestic momentum" – dried egg, I suppose.'

Sid cut out Winnie's message of hope and pinned in up up in the shop, by the carpet beaters.

Mog rang up.

'Dad, I simply can't abandon ship now I've got everyone all geared up to get the Hall tarted up a bit.'

'No, mate, no, I can see that.'

'You see, there's the hot water business and the curtains to be made and I need to keep an eye on the wurzels – they need keeping at it. I'd *love* to come and see you all, you know that, but …'

'Yes, mate. I see.'

'Then there's the children; they can't be left to the tender mercies of Freda. She's a good old cove but a bit deficient in the caring quarter, if you see what I mean.'

'Have a word with mum.'

Lil took the receiver tentatively; she was uneasy with the new-fangled device.

'Hello, Mum. How are you? Dad says you're not feeling hundred percent.'

'Just got the pip a bit. We was 'opin' you might come 'ome for Christmas if 'is lordship can spare you!'

'It's not that, Mum. I'd *love* to come but there's so much I have to do here.'

'Sounds like you've bitten off a deal more than you can chew,' said her mother. 'If you keep at it like the clappers, like you're doin', you'll never get yerself in the family way.'

'No, Mum.'

Dad wrote to Pan:

Just a few words. The week has been much as usual. We have got on well for victuals – had some lovely fish. Mog rang – she keeps busy.

Went to pictures Thursday, up west, and saw Santa Fe Trail. It's a marvellous tale – a western-with Errol Flynn and Olivia de Havilland. Raymond Massey gave a wonderful performance as John Brown, the slave abolitionist. Makes you realise how the poor blacks suffered. You should try and see it when it comes up your way. Had a good repast at Jo Lyons afterwards, very reasonable, only 1s 6d each.

The new clock is going but gains rather. We went to choir Friday, and had a good practice. Aunty attended a fire guards meeting at 9.30 Sunday morning so we had to get up early. Todge is very saucy and full of beans. She talks quite a lot about you. I can imagine what you would give to see her sometimes. I said to mum and Ooly the other day I wonder what Pan would think if she saw us walking down her road. They all said in one voice you would think we had been bombed. Aunty has got her new glasses – they suit her well. We have not got the piano back yet. Aunty has gone in for an insurance sum at a given period. I think this is all for the present. We have just had supper and Ooly has had a bath, Remember me to Gif. All Love.

Lil wrote:

i have made you a cake with 2 real eggs – I had 10 in my order last week so i made one for home and one for you. i cant get on with that dried stuff. Mog rang – she seems to be turnin that ruddy mansion of hers upside down. We saw Erral Flinn in a film. dad thought it was very good – so did Aunty. they think I need to be bucked up. the piano is away bein put right so I get some peace. Aunty has got new specs.

Aunty and i had a bit of barny at the fish shop. they had a notice up sayin theyd be opening at ten o'clock. so we starts kewing at 9 to be on the safe side. by the time we gets to the counter theres only a couple of bits of moldy looking herrings left – and there's errand boys going off with parcels in there bike baskets. it turns out all the good stuff has been taken by rich women who've got accounts – they've phoned up before 10 o'clock and got the best pickings. i says to Aunty – i m not having this – and when one of the lads was not lookin, quick as a flash, i grab one of the parcels. Aunty seezes it out of my hand then the fishmonger comes up and what a to do. in the end he let us have it – we had to pay over the odds. luverly skate and 2 great long haddicks!. don't mention this to dad. he liked the fish. i cant think of moore ... bless and keep you safe. Mum xx.

There was a chill in the air now; the wind was in the east. Vera Lynn was on the wireless: 'Wishing will make it so'. The last of Lil's treasured potatoes were dug up from the vegetable patch as winter began its deathly sweep over the vast spaces of Russia and the Huns encircled Moscow. The national press and the News Exchange at 363 Roman Road deplored the government's seeming inactivity.

'Not much goin' on,' said Bert Gum. 'It's a bit like the phoney war. When are we goin' to get at them bastards agin? Pay 'em back for what they've done to us – takin my kid. When are we genna get to fight proper – smash them to bloody smithereens, instead of just waitin' for the poor sods of Ruskies to do it all?'

'Yea – and what abaat the ruddy Yanks?' said Will Kerridge, warming to his favourite theme. 'Just listen to what this bloke, a Yank 'imself, says in the paper':

"America gazes at the world with a fatuous smile – the smile of a village beauty watching through the window as boys turn cartwheels for her."

'Too bloody right, mate.'

'We must all take comfort from what they're saying brother,' said Sid 'I've heard that the Russian winter may be the finish of Jerry.'

But Bert and Will were not to be comforted: 'Take more than a few flakes of snow to put pay to that lot.'

'At least we've got some onions now,' said Sid.

'But at what a bleedin' price? My Vi says she can't stretch 'er 'aas keepin' that far.'

'A touch of onion, goes a long way,' went on the master of the Emporium. 'Just one in a stew makes all the difference.'

'We've been all right for onions,' said Bert, 'my missus 'as got some farmin' folk daan near the coast – they've bin sendin' us parcels.'

'Its all right for them out in the country – they don't know they're a bleedin' live!' was Will's riposte. 'Got any jam for us, Sid?'

'No mate. You've had your ration. Tell your Vi she can make some from carrots and golden syrup – good stuff. I've got a couple of tins of syrup and you can get carrots from the stall up by the Baths.'

'My missus won't 'ave any truck with that I'm tellin' yer.'

Fanny Bastaple bustled in and conversation turned to the murders up west, near Regents Park:

'What a terrible thing – four in a week. And that poor sod of a dog found shut in a cupboard. 'Course that Maple Church, she was just a Soho tart.'

Doomandgloom came in for some coffin nails: 'These days folk can be done away wiv and put in the rubble, dumped in a bombed aat 'aas, like that Maple Church – and no one any the wiser. I've 'ad a couple of dodgy corpses – bodies are found –a bit suspicious like and nuffin' done – can't tell whether it was fallin' masonry or someone smashin' someone's 'ead in wiv a "blunt instrument" like they say on the flics.'

Chapter 17:

November to December 1941

It was late November – a foggy day in London Town. Ooly wheeled Todge's push chair through the grimy, war-torn streets of Old Ford, passed the wreck of Bow Road Station, the ruins of St Alphege, the pile of rubble that was once The Dook, along the poor old Roman, once so gay and chirpy, now forlorn, with just a few pathetic stalls struggling on. Through the rusty iron gate she went, by the sumac tree, and tapped on the door with the heavy iron knocker.

'Come on in, me duck. What a lovely surprise! I've just made a little cake, a sponge, it'll do the two of us. It's very small, but nice and light. I'll put the kettle on and we can have a good chat. Little Lizzie is lookin' more and more like her beautiful mum.'

'Nell – you're such a wonder. Where did you learn to bake so professionally? You should taste some of the stuff mum and Aunty come up with, especially these days when they're experimenting with some recipe they've got from the wireless.'

'It was my aunt, Win, she taught me all I know. She was in service with the Rothschilds and the head cook took a bit of a shine to her, took her under her wing.'

'Was she the aunt you went to live with?'

'That's it. She was given a tidy sum when she had to leave them – poorly she was – they were generous folk – and she bought herself a cottage back home. I was only twelve when she took me on, as a sort of maid, more like a companion. Those were happy days.'

'Didn't you mind leaving your mum ?'

'Gracious no. There were so many of us at home I'm not sure she knew which one I was. With Aunty Win it was different. There was just the two of us. We used to have cosy times by her fireside, making bread in her great old oven, slicing it up, hot, and spreadin' it thick with butter we'd made in a churn and jam made from blackberries we'd picked ourselves. She told me how to make pastry light as a feather – always make sure your hands are cold. We went for walks along the river bank – I had to push her in a kind'a baath chair – and she would tell me tales of the old days – the wondrous balls they'd had, the silk gowns, the feathers, the diamonds, the piles of pineapples. It was on one of them walks that we met Charlie Bowyer – he was tall, fair, handsome as may be. That was me finished. I was only sixteen then.'

'So how old were you when you married Charlie?'

'Bless you, – Charlie was not Johnny's father.' We walked out for a bit and then – well he went off and his brother Jack was waiting in the wings. But it was never the same.'

'You mean …'

'Well – you just have to make the best of what's on offer, don't you, Ooly?'

She peered meaningfully over her specs.

'Jack was not an easy man, I tell you, grumpy, quiet, all in on himself. You know, Ooly. Still, he was a good provider until he went and passed away. Come on – let's make a fresh brew.'

Off she went down the kitchen passage and came back with a biscuit for Todge. She took a photograph out of her overall pocket, a faded, crumpled, brown thing.

'Here – this is my Charlie – well not my Charlie, Edith's.'

'Edith?'

'The one he took up with. She's a teacher like him. They live in Cricklewood. No children. They visit now and again, but Bow is a bit beneath them.'

'It must be awful for you.'

'Well, you get used to it. As a matter of fact just a glimpse of him keeps me goin' – that and my memories. He used to come on his own, sometimes. And Albie's a good man.'

'It's so sad. Nell.'

'Golden memories are treasures, me duck. You'll realise that when you get over the hill. Some afternoons, when the sun shines, I sit in my bay window and shut my eyes and just take meself back to the bridge over the mill pond where me and Charlie lingered of a summer's day.'

Ooly, depressed by the thought that all she had to look forward to was memories, changed the subject.

'Have you heard from Derek?' He was in Libya.

There was a large framed photograph of him on the mantelpiece, resplendent in his officer's uniform. None of Johnny, she noticed.

'Oh yes, but the letters don't tell you much about what's going on. My Derek has a way with words, of course, but he's not allowed to say anything really. He's in the thick of it out there – papers are full of it, look "Britain Attacks" at last. I think of him as a little lad, golden curls, cheeky grin. He won all hearts. I'll be glad when he's home safe and sound. Norah's always round here weepin' and wailin' – more about her troubles at home than what Derek's goin' through.'

'Poor Norah, she doesn't have it easy.'

'None of us do, chick. None of us do.'

'No, I suppose not.'

'Now – you must tell me all about your sister. You must all be so proud – being connected to the gentry. My mother used to say we were descended from the original Lord Leigh. Have you met your brother-in-law? What's the mansion like?

I remember when I once went with Aunty Win to visit her place – sweeping drive, footmen with powdered wigs, great stone basins full of geraniums.'

'I don't know much about Mog's life now. None of us have met *him* and no invitations have been issued from New Hall. Mum is pretty upset, so is dad. I think they're wondering if they're ever going to see Mog again.'

'Well – they're very lucky to have you, that's all I can say.'

'Mm.'

Ooly took her leave, having reapplied her lipstick and arranged her hair, promising to return soon. She pushed Todge along towards Bow Road and decided to take a turn round Tredegar Square, for old times' sake. The fog was thickening and it was difficult to make your way. She thought she saw him, hurrying along, his collar turned up – she was sure it was him – or was it just a phantom, an hallucination brought on by Nell's talk of Charlie and the old rustic bridge by the mill? No – it was him. She called his name. He turned and came towards her. As the fog blanket wrapped comfortingly around their long embrace, she thought: 'That's me finished.'

Christmas was approaching; Lil and Dot were busy making marzipan from mashed potato, crushing up the few almonds Sid's precious tree had produced. The news, born by an excited Mrs Spoon, broke in on their attempts to spread the crumbly paste over an eggless Christmas cake: 'Its old Roosevelt – he says they're coming in with us – the Americans!'

'So what's this Pearl 'Arbour place that's got bombed by the Japs and got the wind up the Yanks?' Lil asked Dot.

'It's in Hawaii. The Americans have got ships there and planes.'

'I thought that was all grass skirts and holiday whoopee – we saw old Bing in that film a few years back, didn't we? – "Wakky Weddin", wasn't it – d'you remember 'im singin' "Blue Hawaii"? Lovely.'

'The family don't approve of crooning. Pan says its not proper singing.'

'Well – I like old Bing. Anyway – so we're all at war now – Japs joined up with Jerry, us joined up with the Yanks? What's genna ''appen to all those Chinks daan Lime 'aas? They'll be for it!'

'Those are Chinese, Lil, not Japs. It's the Chinese that the Japs are fighting.'

'I thought it was the Yanks. I'm blowed if I understand what it's got to do with us. No more dried egg and spam I shouldn't wonder, now they've got their own war to fight.'

Ooly came in: 'What wonderful news! They're in with us at last. We'll be all right now!'

'You're dolled up. Where are you off to?'

'Nell's. Don't wait supper for us.'

'You really shouldn't be keeping the child out late in this cold weather.'

'Aunty, she'll be fine.' Off she went with a spring in her step.

'What's got into 'er – she's full of beans all of a sudden,' said Lil.

'Well – Johnny's been going on to her about the Yanks – how we'd never make it without them.'

'Mm. She's a terrible worrier, like 'er dad, but covers it up.'

'Yes – with snide remarks. She's spending too much time up in Bow, in my view.' said Dot. 'It's not good for the kiddie to be hawked around from pillar to post. Children need a good, stable routine. They were only at Nell's last week – and yet she complains that Ooly's visits are only fleeting.'

''Ow d'you know that?'

'Sid says she was in the shop, having a moan to that woman from Old Ford Wesleyan.'

'Bloomin' cheek. Sid never said nuffin' to me – reckon he knew I'd be riled.

D'you know I've 'eard that some girls are getting' themselves up the duff just to get out of war work, Deidre O'Brien for one – yer know Maureen's next down sister?'

'But she's not married!' Exclaimed Dot in horror.

'Will be soon.'

'Who's the father, then?'

'The favver is neither 'ere nor there, I ham reliably informed. There was some goin's-on in a shelter. Typical.'

'But, I thought you said she was getting wed?'

'And so she is – to that Doyle boy who used to work for poor old Lewis when 'e 'ad the dairy. Paddy O'Brien's got sommat on 'im.'

'How d'you know all this? Sounds like a lot of tittle tattle to me!'

'I 'ave my sources,' said Lil, tapping her nose.

'What sources?'

'Ooly, as a matter of fact. She got it from Kathleen O'Brien 'erself – when she was up Bow last week. Met 'er queuein' up for some fish and chips up near the Majestic.'

'Well, you would think that Nell might cook a proper meal for them. *And* I 've heard her say that she wouldn't be seen dead with fried fish in a newspaper sitting in her shopping basket.'

'That's why she sent Ooly, I s'pose.'

Fighting was fierce in Russia.

Lil wrote to Pan:

'what do you think of Russia? they've got the wind up jerry. now they are the people to look up to. they have bore the blunt of this war, the same as they did the last, only they have been trained better and I feel they are a much better nation than when they had the other ruler. Now, about Christmas. Dad and i think you would be better at home, safe and comfortable. but if you reely want to make the jurney we have plenty of room.'

Thousands were dying of cold and starvation in Leningrad; chairs and tables were burned as fuel, cats and dogs were killed for food. At Blacksmith's Cottage Gif was assembling her special Kitchen Front

Christmas pudding.

'Come on, Piggo, give it a stir.'

'What sort of a concoction have we got now, "eye of newt and toe of frog"?' Pan reluctantly took the wooden spoon.

'You're leaving it rather late, aren't you? Mum and Aunty used to make the pudding in September.'

'So did Ma's cook.'

'Oh, Ma's cook, is it. I dare say my sister has a head chef, not to mention a team of scullions!' She stirred vigorously.

'I understood that the family were in rather reduced circumstances.'

Pan ignored this comment and went on stirring. 'I shan't be here for Christmas.'

'W-what!'

'I said I shan't be here.'

'My sainted aunt! You're not going off with that Meredith woman again! Not for Christmas – you can't. I've invited some of the people from church in for drinks. You simply can't do this to me. Am I to be left alone here again – twiddling my thumbs while you – you.'

'I'm spending Christmas with my family. Elsa's coming.'

'Piggo – this is too much. I am not prepared to take any more humiliation. How dare you treat me like this!' She flung the pudding and its basin across the kitchen.

Pan smirked. 'Temper, temper. Come too, if you like. If you can get the petrol. I know you have your sources.'

The wind was taken out of Gif's sails, but there was a puff left: 'Why on earth didn't you tell me before?'

'My dear good woman, I didn't make my mind up until today.'

'You seem to have told the wretched Rush soon enough.'

Und so weiter.

Pan was high with excitement and anticipation; she sang carols at the top of her voice as Amun, crammed to the gunwales with parcels and potatoes, brussel sprouts and bottles of homemade wine, tinsel and tins of goodies, ducks and dripping, bowled through Colchester, Dunmow, Romford. He thought his carburettor might explode. Elsa was pinned down in the back with an enormous bunch of holly, but she was content.

Number 29 was prepared, primped and pristine. Beds were moved around and about so that Pan and Gif could have the grand big bedroom overlooking the garden. Ed's little room was fumigated and walls, floor and woodwork washed down with Lisol for Elsa's benefit. Ed was to sleep on the settee. Johnny could have the camp bed in the dining room and Ooly and Todge could go in with Dot. Taps were polished, skirting boards wiped, windows cleaned, every surface cleared of clutter, curtains washed, dish cloths boiled, lino scrubbed and cushions plumped.

Ooly muttered to herself as she moved yet another pile of bedding: 'If they make this fuss about Pan and her crew coming home, what will they do when and if Lady Muck Tillingham graces us with her presence?'

A triumphant toot announced the arrival in Chestnut Avenue; they were late – much too late to make it to Old Ford for the midnight service. Amun disgorged his bullying and bellowing load, plus Elsa, all elegant arbitration, if rather scratched.

'Mr S, delighted to see you.' Gif extended a chubby hand.

'May I offer you, one and all, the very warmest of the season's greetings,' replied the beaming patriarch.

Lil was fussing about: 'Come on, come on in – the fish'll be ruined if you don't get a move on.'

'What an absolutely charming house, Mrs Smart,' screamed Elsa in ecstasy, 'And just look at your granddaughter! What a darling, heavenly child – I have rarely seen such perfectly formed features. Oh – and she speaks – how advanced she is!'

Todge clung to her Nan's apron and scowled.

Pan suddenly felt awkward and almost shy. It had been so long and this was not the dear old home she knew: 'I'll unpack the car.'

'Come on, duck,' said Dot, giving her a hug. 'We can leave that until after supper. You wait till you see our lounge.'

'No. I'll unpack now.' Sid lent her a hand.

'Potatoes – we've got plenty of them, mate, and brussels – mum has grown them herself. Tinsel and holly! Don't know what Ooly will make of that – she's been busy decorating the house all week. She's got it looking really special – she's spent hours spraying ivy leaves with white paint – light stone actually – but they look well in the candle light.'

Pan felt the all too familiar sinking in her stomach. 'I brought you a couple of ducks for tomorrow from our neighbourhood farm.'

'Very nice too, mate, but we've got Billy's goose already stuffed and ready to go – Ooly's just finished doing it.'

'Perhaps you would rather I hadn't brought anything at all – perhaps you would rather I hadn't come.' She flung the rejected offerings into the street and fled into the house.

Dot gathered them up and followed her in. 'Don't mind your dad – he's been talking of nothing else but your homecoming.'

'Some bloody homecoming. Hello Ooly, I gather you've taken over the running of the festivities.'

'Happy Kissmus! Happy Kissmus!' Todge was jumping up and down.

'Isn't it time she was in bed?' snapped Johnny, who had just arrived and was cross about the camp bed.

'Come with me, Todge,' said Pan firmly, taking her hand. 'I've got something for you from Father Christmas. We met him and his reindeer on the way here.'

Todge looked wary.

'Look – you unwrap it. Well – p'raps we'll do it together. Careful, now.'

The brown paper was torn off and the string removed (Sid coiled it up and put in away safely for future use) and out came a soft, fluffy toy kitten.

'Puddy tat, puddy tat.' shouted the delighted Todge.

Pan grinned a great wide grin: 'Well, at least someone appreciates what I've brought them.'

Thus, to Ooly's dismay, and Johnny's horror, an enduring hoop of steel grappled Elizabeth Bowyer to her godmother. Henceforth Pan and Gif would call the child Pud or even Old Pud.

Sid read aloud to number 29 from *Pickwick*. They ate their haddock, drank a toast to Roosevelt and sang the old songs. All was relatively calm and by the time Pan issued her orders of marching for the morrow, everyone was sufficiently soothed by their celebratory tipple not to care very much.

"Here, in the midst of war, raging and roaring over all the lands and seas," proclaimed Winnie, "creeping nearer to our hearts and homes, here, amid all the tumult, we have tonight the peace of the spirit in each cottage home and in every generous heart."

Mog rang early on Christmas morning and spoke to everyone who was up.

'I was 'opin against 'ope that you might make it, after all,' said her mother.

'Oh, Mum – I just couldn't – what with things here and the ban on travel and everything …'

'Oh well, duck, raise a glass of champagne to us old 'uns when you sit down to your peasant – or whatever you're 'avin. I s'pose your dinner table's so long you can't 'ardly see your 'usband at the other end! You all right? – you sound a bit crock. 'Ere 'ave a word with Aunty.'

'Happy Christmas, Mog dear. I hope you are having a wonderful time.'

'Is mum all right, Aunty?'

'Well, she's rather upset that you aren't with us here, but I understand *just* why you feel the need to put your past behind you. Don't you worry – just enjoy your first Christmas as a lady – and I wish you many more.'

It was Sid's turn: 'Merry Christmas to yourself and the baronet,' said her father. 'I expect you're all having a high old time. Little Todge is wild with excitement – you should have seen her opening the present Old Pan brought!'

Ooly took the phone; she checked that her parents were out of earshot before she spoke:

'Hello Mog. Happy Blooming Christmas. Ructions here. You'd die! Pan brought a whole load of vegetables and other stuff and dad said we didn't need them! You can imagine! Potatoes and brussels rolling all over the road. God knows what today will bring – you're well out of it. Pan and her acolytes are still in bed – lazy devils – at least we'll have breakfast in peace.'

They didn't.

The tradition in the Smart household had always been presents at the crack of dawn for the clamouring children, followed by a feast of a breakfast and dinner towards evening. Pan had, however, decreed that in the best households (Drayman's) gifts were distributed after lunch, which should be served at two o'clock so that the King's speech might coincide with the lighting of the brandy on the pudding.

'Not very fair on Todge,' Lil grumbled, dishing out the measly toast spread thinly with margarine – so as to leave room for the banquet to come so soon.

'No,' said Sid. 'We can't expect the kiddie to wait for her toys until the afternoon.'

'Todge won't know any different,' said Dot.

'Oh – for goodness sake – anything for peace and quiet,' said Ooly.

'Bloody woman, charging in here and throwing her weight about,' thought Johnny. He said nothing, but scowled meaningfully at his wife.

The invading forces eventually swept down in brocade dressing gowns and took their places at the dining room table; it was nicely laid, with a sprig of Suffolk holly in a glass vase decorated with Pan's tinsel. Compliments of the season were exchanged and orders taken.

'You're not giving them our precious eggs, Aunty? Why can't they have toast like the rest of us? And why can't they eat in the kitchen like we did?' Ooly was angry.

'It's Christmas, duck. Don't begrudge them a little bit of a treat – Pan hasn't been home since the war started.'

No comment was made on the offering made at such cost; eggs were plentiful at Blacksmith's Cottage. Comment was, however, made on the burnt spoon which had been inadvertently laid at Gif's place, for her boiled egg: 'What's this we've got here – Cranmer I suppose?' (Hearty laugh.)

Elsa squeezed Pan's hand under the table, thus preventing an outburst.

Christmas Day moved with majestic momentum towards its climax. Sid had gone to chapel, Ooly was putting the finishing touches to her table decoration while Lil and Dot bustled around in the kitchen with Todge in tow. Johnny had offered to take charge of the cooking, but was told, kindly, to keep his nose out:

'You have a good rest; I'm sure you need it.'

The kitchen was no place for a man.

What he needed was a drink.

He wandered into the lounge where, Gif, reading, billowed out from the large armchair, Elsa perched prettily on the piano stool, her legs crossed, and Pan stood surveying the garden, smoking a tom thumb cigar and planning improvements.

'Who's for a Christmas tipple?' he ventured boldly. 'What about you, Pan – wet your whistle for the Yuletide concert?'

'What at this time of day!'

'Elsa?'

'Oh, not for me, thank you so much. I'll just have a small glass of Pan's delicious wine with my lunch.'

'Gif?'

'Never touch the stuff.'

'Mind if I do?' He poured himself a large gin.

'Good show about the Yanks – things are certainly looking up.'

'Oh, yes,' said Elsa. 'It is a great comfort.'

Gif looked up from her book: 'I'm not convinced that its going to be quite as plain sailing as all that. American resources will be stretched to the limit fighting the Japs. Our reliance on their munitions-ships has been crucial. If the Far East is top of their agenda – what happens to us?'

Pan turned to the company: 'You bloody misery, Piggo. Can't you just for once look on the bright side. As Winnie says, we've got four fifths of the population of the whole world on our side – which may, or may not, include you.'

Time for a change of subject.

Johnny offered: 'No church for anybody today then? No one going up to Bow to wish Little St Alphege the compliments of the season?'

'We're all *so* exhausted.' said Elsa.

Johnny, emboldened by the gin, stared over at his foe.

'Exhausted? Why?' Your holidays are long enough. Too exhausted to pay your respects to Teddy B?'

Pan turned, snarling:

'This term has been an absolute swine – we've been flat out, struggling with the refugee girls, the nativity play, the concert, fire watching – we've hardly had a moment to breath. You don't seem to have any idea how damned tiring our work is – jollifying with your RAF chums – Flying Officer – you've never even been up in a plane!'

Oh dear – it might have been better to stay with the war situation.

Johnny left the room and took himself off for a turn around the frosty avenues. He met Mr Spoon who invited him in for seasonal glass of whisky. They had several and a companionable chat. After an hour or so, rather the worse for wear, he returned to the fray.

Ooly opened the door:

'Where on earth have you been?' What ever's the matter with you?'

'Your bloody sister. That's what the matter with me. Have I really got to sit down to a meal with that vicious bitch?'

Ooly laughed: 'I've had to put up with her all my life – or most of it. Now you know what it's like.'

A voice called out from the kitchen: 'Dinner's up. Come on ladies and gents, please take your places for the feast!'

'Oh, God, Holy Joe's back, is he?'

Chapter 18:
Christmas Dinner 1941

Mog was a proud, plucky little body. No one would have guessed. She sat erect and stiff at one end of the long table, which stretched out interminably, in all its Christmas finery, towards Edmund, at the other end. Her head was held high, her powder was carefully applied, especially under the eyes, and a touch of rouge lifted her deathly pallor. The Tillingham amethyst choker covered her throat – the diamonds had been sold off to pay the young Horror's mess bills – or so it was said. She fingered the lavender stones which glimmered in the shafts of sunlight fighting their way through the stained glass windows.

It was a rare gathering of the clans: Bella was looking anxious, attired in her everyday tweeds, her only tweeds, rather threadbare. There was Bertie and Honor Portman (Harry's parents) from Nether Tillingham, the Venerable Freddy (a cousin of sorts), a shadowy widow from the other end of the county called Lady F (Mog never found out what the F stood for), a decrepit colonel, the Tollington-Thomases from Tollington St Mary and Hailshot, and the family lawyer from Midsummer Norton. Sitting next to Mog was a bronzed god from somewhere in the Rockies, now with the Canadian air force stationed over at Charmy Down. On her other side was someone they called Pooty; he was quite high up in the War Office and wore thick specs.

The burbling of "county set" noises filled the Great Hall: talk of the Boxing Day Meet, the shortage of soap, ruddy Japs, the impossibility of getting staff or oysters, the state of the cricket pavilion, Pearl Harbour and Woolton Pie. Lady Tillingham was silent, going over in her head the events of the night before.

They had come back from St Mary's midnight service in the early hours, just the three of them – Freda had gone home for Christmas, so had most of the children; the two that were left had been invited over to Keeper's Cottage. The stone lions stood at the ready under the frosty stars of Olde England as the dog cart swung by, driven by Bella, carrying Sir Edmund and Lady Tillingham.

'D'you think Bess (the pony) spoke while we were in church?' said Mog.

'What on earth d'you mean, Moggins,' asked her sister-in-law.

'You must know the old legend that the animals speak at midnight on Christmas Eve?'

'I expect she said, "Get a move on, you buggers. I want to get home to my nice warm stable",' said Edmund. 'Get a move on, Bella – *I* want to get back to my nice cold champagne.'

The yule log was smouldering in the Great Hearth in the Great Hall and the tall spruce spread out its arms in fragrant welcome. The Labradors, having just had a conversation about the shortage of decent bones, lumbered to their feet and wagged a greeting.

Mrs P had left two bottles of champagne sitting in an ice bucket and laid out three glasses.

'Two bottles!' exclaimed Bella. 'Does she think we're made of money! Tomorrow's party is costing the earth. Still – I suppose we have to try and keep our end up.'

'Come on, Bell – it's Christmas. Drink up. Here's to the ravishing Lady Tillingham and her first Christmas at New Hall.'

'I'm rather nervous about tomorrow,' said Mog.

'Good God, why?' said Bella. 'It's only a few old crumbs of county crust and a couple of Edmund's chums. You'll stun 'em – you always do.'

Formal entertaining at New Hall was a thing of the past; this would be her first performance. They finished the two bottles and went up to bed.

As soon as she was alone in her room Mog opened the parcels from home, not wanting to give her new family any opportunity to sneer at anything offered by her old one. The Tillinghams were very modest in their present giving: crystallized fruits or dates in a fancy box, if they could run to it. Dad had sent one of his kettles – quite useful actually – Mrs P's battered old black thing looked as if it had been around at least since the 4th baronet fought at Sedgemoor. Ooly and Aunty had clubbed together to buy a rather splendid needlework box – 'for your curtain making'. There was nothing from Pan – she was always weeks late with Christmas and birthday presents. Mum had sent some pretty high heeled velvet slippers and very fine silk negligee – it was like gossamer. Wherever did she get that from? Must have cost her a packet. Dear old mum. She took off her clothes and slid into it, twirling about and admiring herself in the long mirror. Perhaps it was her legs that did it. Her face was near perfect, her bosom was well shaped, though not as good as Ooly's, her waist was tiny. It must be her legs. Still – come on – let's give it a try – perhaps this magic night would work its wonders. He had drunk a quantity of champagne and she'd had just enough. Nothing ventured … she opened her door and stepped out.

About an hour later she returned, sobbing, bleeding and bruised. She stuffed the torn gossamer into the bottom of the armoire and lay on the bed, in a fitful sleep until the Christmas morning cock crowed.

The Canadian spoke, jolting Mog out of her nightmare:

'The Yanks are shocked to the core by the audacity of Pearl Harbour – it's a slap in the face for the Isolationists. You know a bunch of women threw rotten eggs at your ambassador a few weeks ago. So much for their damned notion that no power, however strong, would dare to strike at the mighty US of A. Don't you think, Lady Tillingham? Lady Tillingham?'

'I'm so sorry. I was miles away. You were saying ?'

'The Americans …'

'Oh, yes – it's a great relief that they're in with us, at last.'

'Sure – war production should be greatly speeded by their actually joining in, but, on the other hand, their own requirements for taking on the Japs will make big claims on their industrial output – and on their naval strength, I guess.'

'Quite so.'

'Of course, the Pearl Harbour business was very much a response to the oil embargo.'

'Naturally. My father's in oil.'

'Gee – I say – which company?

'Bread sauce, Sir?'

Mrs P had come to the rescue: she was dressed up in a make-shift maid's costume for the occasion and hovering around with the vast silver sauce boat (George III).

'Oh my! Whatever is this?' He gazed in horror at the porridge-like mixture.

'Bread sauce, Sir. We always have it with pheasant. Will you try some?'

'Sure, Sure.'

Mog eagerly turned the conversation from oil to the ingredients of bread sauce and then, hastily, to what they ate at Christmas in Canada, and then to enquiries about life at Charmy Down. She wanted to ask exactly how her companion had encountered Edmund, but thought better of it.

Honor Portman entertained the company with tales of Harry's exploits in the air – how he had brought his Spit home, looped the loop over the ha-ha and landed in the north field.

'Didn't he get into hot water?'

'Harry can talk himself out of anything.'

The Tollington-Thomases had just returned from a trip to town to see *Blithe Spirit.* 'Margaret Rutherford was an absolute scream as Madame Arcati! The Ritz was serving something they called *Ballotine De Jambon Valentinoise* – bloody spam, would you believe!'

Malaya, Moscow, black market, Luftwaffe, looting, Libya, Leningrad, Goering, Grandma Buggins, Mussolini (fat little upstart), ration books – on they buzzed.

'I've always maintained that the real threat to us was from the Commies.' muttered the decrepit colonel.

The stable boy, who had been commandeered to help Mrs P serve, whispered in Mog's ear: 'Mind you use the right knife and fork, milady.'

Pooty kept looking at Mog. She was used to that. But he kept on – staring very hard, as if he was trying to remember something.

'Lady T, may I compliment you on your absolutely stunning – er –get up. Not many people bother these days.'

Oh dear – was she over-dressed ?

'Thank you. One does ones best in these difficult times. I gather you're a neighbour of ours?'

'My folk have got a place near Wells – my Pa popped his clogs a few years back, so I spend some time down here with the mater. Old Tilly was my fag at Eton, as a matter of fact. You remind me of someone. I can't for the life of me think who it might be. It's almost as if I've met you before but … Where do you hail from?'

'Oh, London.'

'I mainly hang out in our pad overlooking Regent's Park – it's just a flat, only three or four bedrooms, but it suits me. Are your people anywhere near Regent's Park?'

'No.'

This time the King came to her rescue. The stable boy staggered in with the wireless set; knives and forks were put down and the colonel adjusted his hearing aid.

"Christmas is a festival of home, and it is right that we should remember those who this year must spend it away from home … I think of you, my people, as one great family, for that is how we are learning to live.

If the skies before us are still dark and threatening, there are stars to guide us on our way ... Never did heroism shine more brightly than it does now, nor fortitude, nor sacrifice, nor sympathy, nor neighbourly kindness. And with them the brightest of all stars – is our faith in God. These stars will we follow with His help until the light shall shine and the darkness will collapse. May God bless you, everyone."

'Tiny Tim,' said Mog to quietly to herself.

'Who?' asked the Canadian.

'You aren't familiar with Charles Dickens – *Christmas Carol*?'

'Oh yes, of course.'

'My dad loves Dickens.'

How desperately she suddenly missed home. What stars would guide her on her way?

At Chestnut Avenue the festive season bickered on. Crackers were pulled and the goose brought to the table. Johnny was withdrawn, only speaking to pointedly decline any of Pan's gooseberry wine. She grimaced and Sid produced a couple of bottles of pale ale.

Lil refused to wear her paper hat, as she always did, but objections were good natured, and conversation went on merrily enough: talk of the Boxing Day outing to the panto, the shortage of soap, ruddy Japs, the impossibility of getting petrol or decent fish, the state of Old Ford, Pearl Harbour, the Others at School.

Ooly drifted away: she was dreaming of the day before. Johnny had only got a 24 hour pass and had reluctantly agreed that it would be spent at Chestnut Avenue. He wouldn't be arriving until quite late in the evening so Ooly and Todge had set off early for a Christmas Eve visit to Nell.

'Would you mind if I left Todge with you for a few hours – I've got to go and deliver some presents to some of the old chinas?'

'No dear – that'll be all right. You won't be too long will you? I've got a few things to do still, not much, as it's only me and Albie sitting down to dinner tomorrow. Will she be all right – she doesn't know me that well, after all.'

'I've brought some of her toys. Keep her busy and she'll be fine. She likes washing-up!'

'You'll have some lunch before you go?'

'Oh, no thanks, Nell. I've promised to eat with an old school friend.'

'Oh.'

'I'll see you later. Give her whatever you're having now and she can have bread and marmite for her tea – she likes that.'

'Her tea!

'Well – I've got quite a lot of errands to run.' She put on some lipstick, dabbed some scent on her neck and rushed off.

They met outside the London.

'D-d-darling, you look wonderful. No Todge today?'

'She's getting a bit too chatty – I'm worried she's going to say something.'

'So we could go somewhere special instead of our usual fish and chips. I've got about three hours until I'm on call again. What about you?'

'Mm – me too, at a pinch.'

'I've got the motor – cabs are impossible these days – we could drive up to town if you like. I've got some p-petrol. What about the Savoy Grill?'

'Have we got time? … What if someone sees us?'

'We might all be d-d-dead tomorrow.'

They whizzed along in a flurry of gay abandon, talking nineteen to the dozen about nothing at all. Everyone looked so happy – last minute shoppers popping out from the office, typists with bunches of mistletoe, portly city gents with parcels under their arms. The sooty buildings smiled benevolently and St Paul's gave them the thumbs up.

'You usual table, sir?'

He splashed out on a bottle of *Veuve Cliquot* and they sat just gazing at one another, not heeding the menu or the holly decked world around them, hands clasped, as the pianist tinkled away.

'Your order, sir?'

'Oh – w-w-whatever you've got.'

'I know there's a war on, sir, but we still have quite an extensive menu. For our special customers, I would recommend the grouse.'

'Yes, yes. That'll be fine.'

He slid off.

Ooly was laughing: 'I thought the snotty devil was going to recommend Woolton Pie – their chef invented it didn't he?'

'I think so. Have you ever tried it? They serve it at the hospital – it is truly appalling – just a mess of turnips and other tasteless vegetables in an even more tasteless white sauce with hard-as-a rock pastry on top.'

'Is there anyone famous here? Any foreign royals?'

Ooly scanned the room, noticing a family party settling down excitedly at a nearby table: father (in RAF uniform), mother, a small girl and what she took to be a grandmother. A great lurch of guilt and misery took hold of her – what on earth was she doing?

'Dougie, I can't do this. I've left little Todge with my poor, unsuspecting mother-in-law on Christmas Eve, of all days.'

'B-b-but ...'

'I'm so sorry.'

'Okey doke, my darling girl. Off we go.'

They drove in silence back along the Strand, Fleet Street, by St Paul's, along Cheapside, into Aldgate and poor old Whitechapel. The festive gaiety had evaporated. He drew into a dim alley which lay between two bomb sites and stopped.

'Oh, Dougie.'

'Come here.'

By the time the ARP warden knocked on the windscreen and ticked them off, several hours had elapsed.

'Oh my God. look at the time! We might just as well have stayed for the grouse.'

'I'm glad we didn't.'

'So am I.'

A final tender kiss. A promise about the New Year. Presents exchanged.

'Oh yes – here's something for the little one. I love you, Lily Smart. You may think you belong to someone else, but you don't, you're mine. Keep safe. Keep safe.' He wiped a tear from his cheek and was gone.

Elsa was speaking. 'Ooly, Ooly, are you with us?'

'So sorry I was miles away.' said Ooly.

'I was just remarking on your simply gorgeous table decoration. How inspired to coat ivy leaves with cream paint and sprinkle them with soda to catch the candle light.'

'Yes. It's quite effective, isn't it.'

Pan snorted and tackled her father on the subject of the re-ordering of the garden.

Malaya, Moscow, black market, looting, Libya, Leningrad, Goering, Grandma Buggins, The Others at School, Mussolini (fat little Eytie), meat ration – on they buzzed until the King silenced them: 'God bless *us* everyone,' corrected Sid.

'Come on – present time,' announced Pan. The grown-up exchange was a mere preliminary to the big event – the showering of Todge with gifts.

Sid had made a dolls' pram from bits and bobs he had at the shop and Dot had spent weeks smocking a dear little bright red frock. Ed gave Ooly £20 to start a savings account. Lil had procured from somewhere a truly magnificent miniature tea set. There were tiny plates, cups and saucers, twelve of each, decorated with cornflowers, tea pot, milk jug, dinky spoons and knives, all nestling in tissue paper in a little wicker hamper.

Todge gasped with delight and made a grab: 'Cuppa tea! Cuppa tea!'

Ooly, unaware of her mother's extravagant purchase, had got a cheap tin tea set (four cups and saucers) decorated with mickey mouse, presented in a flat cardboard box. It was cast aside.

An unlabelled parcel brought forth a teddy bear.

'Good lord alive,' said Gif. 'That's got a button in its ear– it's a Steiff bear – they cost the earth – can't get 'em these days anyway – they're German.'

'Where the devil did it come from? asked Johnny.

'Oh, a buddy of mine gave it to me for Todge when I was up at your mother's.'

'Which buddy?

You don't know her – Phyllis Mottram – we used to sing together. Her family are well off.'

'And German, I suppose.'

'Don't be silly.'

Gif gave her *The Just So Stories* for when she was older, and Elsa produced a small packet of chalks.

Johnny was very proud of his gift for Mini Lizzie – he had managed to get hold of a doll – it cost him £5 – he'd bought it just before the introduction of price control on toys came in, just nine days before Christmas. He held on to it, rather than adding to the pile of presents, so that it would be the climax to the presentation.

'Don't want dat. Want puddy tat! Want teddy!' And off toddled Todge with puddy under one plump little arm, and Steiff under the other.

'Look at Daddy Johnny's lovely dolly – its got golden hair and such a pretty frock,' said Dot. 'You could put in her in your new bass …'

222

With a malevolent glance at her father Todge thrust puddy and Steiff into the pram and wheeled it off unsteadily into the kitchen.

By such slight happenings are hearts broken and lives changed.

Next came charades.

Gif performed Edward I's presentation of his baby son to the people of Wales – the first Prince of Wales – but Pan said that was no good as it wasn't a play or a book or a film. Gif said that when they played it at home historical events were acceptable. Pan said that when they had played it at the vicarage they were not. Gif said they were not in the vicarage now – und so weiter.

Ooly did a magnificent rendering of Anna Karenina (Greta Garbo) throwing herself under the train, pointing at the photo of Mog the while. Everyone immediately guessed that Sid's rather confusing enactment of eager anticipation, by clasping his hands together and raising his eyebrows, was *Great Expectations*. Pan was such a convincing "Cat that walked by Himself" that even Todge got that: 'Puddy Tat!'

Elsa chose "Old King Cole", doddering around with a paper hat on, and pointing at the fire. Gif guessed it, but said that as it was a nursery rhyme and it didn't count. Pan said nursery rhymes were OK. Gif said it wasn't fair that nursery rhymes were OK and historical events were not. Pan said that when they had played at the vicarage, songs and rhymes were acceptable. Gif said the Billington-Smythes knew nothing about anything. Und so weiter.

Dot foxed everyone by pointing at the photo of her cousin Jane in a group photograph on the mantelpiece and then opening the window (air – Eyre). Ooly said that was cheating because nobody, except Dot and Sid, knew she was called Jane, she had always been known as Old Grumpy Guts. Lil, after a whispered conversation with Ooly, beat her breast for ITMA (hit ma) and Ed danced about being Hiawatha. Sid said if Elsa couldn't have "Old King Cole" Ed couldn't have Hiawatha. Johnny refused to join in.

Several rounds of this were played; proceedings were called to a halt when Gif made a sour face, flapped around as if flying and held up Puddy Tat's tale, waving it around vigorously (Grimm's Fairy Tales). Todge screamed and Pan declared anything German was quite out of order.

'Let's have something for the kiddie,' said Sid. They decided on "Hunt the twinkly knob", this was the Smart variation of "Hunt the Thimble", using a cut glass paper weight which Pan had once bought for Lil. Someone is sent out of the room and the twinkly knob hidden. When the victim returns he/she sets about looking for it while everyone else has to sing 'How green you are, how green you are', softly, if the victim is a off the mark, getting louder and louder, as loud as you can get, as the knob is approached. The full force of the Smart clan and outliers shrieking to a crescendo of 'How green you are' scared Todge half to death. It was not a success.

Next came the musical entertainment, opened by Dot's annual performance of 'London's burning' with bells on her wrists. Roars of laughter and approval except from Johnny, who thought it was inappropriate to say the least. Then Ooly took her place and the concert proper began with Mendelsohn 's exquisite heart rending 'On Wings of Song', delivered by Pan, Elsa thought especially for her:

'Together we'll rest, beloved,
Praying the gods will send
A dream that knows no waking
A love that knows no end.'

There was a general call for carols. "Good King Wenceslas" was always a favourite: Sid sang the part of the king, of course:
"Hither page and stand by me."
'My Mog always used to be the page,' said Lil wistfully to Elsa.

Ooly sang the Virgin's Lullaby and Pan countered with "The angel Gabriel from heaven came …"

'Can't we 'ave some proper carols – not that boring posh stuff?' said Lil.

A rousing "Oh come all ye faithful" followed, "God rest you merry gentlemen", "While shepherds watched" and so on. Everyone joined in – even Johnny and Ed.

After an interval for drinks and paste sandwiches Sid took the floor with the endless verses of "If it wasn't for the 'ouses in between". Those who knew it joined in the chorus:

'Oh! it really is a wery pretty garden
And Chingford to the Eastward could be seen
Wiv a ladder and some glasses
You could see to 'Ackney Marshes
If it wasn't for the 'ouses in between.'

Pan sang "He shall feed his flock"; Ooly countered with "I know that my redeemer liveth."

After came a return to the old musical songs, culminating in the whole company belting out "My old man said follow the van."

And then, one last song before bed; Ooly sang "She was only a bird in a gilded cage."

' … she lives in a mansion grand.
She's only a bird in a gilded cage,
A beautiful sight to see.
You may think she's happy and free from care,
She's not, though she seems to be.'

225

Chapter 19:

January to June 1942

Mog, in her gilded cage, had been half expecting a grovelling apology – sobbing remorse – a bunch of flowers – even a fairly expensive piece of jewellery. That was what happened in the flics. None came. The baronet, indeed, behaved as if nothing had happened, and, if it had, somehow, she had been at fault. She even began to think she had been – 'Their ways are not our ways,' dad had told her. Nothing was said – the Christmas party was accounted a great success and it was business as usual at New Hall.

A lesser mortal might have packed their bags forthwith, but there could be no going back. What shame – how could she creep home, blood stained and battered, when they were expecting a triumphal entry? A lesser mortal might have flung themselves, sobbing on the nearest friendly bosom. She kept her own counsel and ploughed her own furrow. She was, after all, Lady Tillingham. There were her plans for the conservatory, her little charges to consider, the tenants who were growing to love their capable, caring Lady of the Manor, and good old Bella who had come to rely on her so much. Her boats were burnt. Cockneys, after all, are famed for "making the best of it all" and "putting on a brave front". Better keep calm and carry on.

It was a grim New Year all round; gone was the the euphoria which had accompanied the forging of the "Grand Alliance". All the news was of the Yellow Peril spreading its dastardly tentacles over the crumbling British Empire far away in the Pacific. At New Hall, the corridors whispered anxiously, the logs in the Great Fireplace smouldered and spat in anger, drawing draughts from all corners, the wind howled despairingly in the chimneys.

Freda and the children returned – thank God, and Mog set about refurbishing the conservatory. This would be some task – the panes of glass were cracked, the window frames were not in a good state, the floor tiles needed replacing. As to the walls, they were in dire need of re-plastering. Perhaps she would just paper over the cracks. Help was forthcoming from the village boys; they would do anything for Greta Garbo. Bella managed to find some cash for a glazier and Freda turned out to be quite handy at woodwork. Keep busy. What was her hurt and humiliation compared to the crushing of the little body of Pete O'Mally, compared to poor old Morgan, blown to bits, compared to all the death and destruction that raged around the whole world?

Not that the events of Christmas were ever very far from her mind. They hammered away relentlessly, day and night, crowding in as soon as she was alone. The lurch in her stomach when she woke was only stilled when she was in the classroom. Was there something terribly wrong with her? Perhaps if she hadn't lost her temper, said what she said, and provoked him … mum always said her rarely lost but violent temper would get her into trouble. She literally saw a red mist rising before her eyes when it struck.

'Bitch on heat,' he'd shrieked. 'Bitch on heat,' anger, terror and revulsion burning in his eyes. 'Get out.' Then came the attack, the punching, the slapping; he grabbed one of her pretty new slippers and smashed its pointy heel into her head with all his might. Blood poured down into her eyes. He went for her throat but she managed to kick him off. She could have sworn that as she fled from the room he was smiling.

She cried quite a lot, secretly, shutting herself in the Great Water Closet (installed by the 10th baronet). Keeping it all to herself made it worse, of course. It all just rolled round and round in her head, driving her frantic. What spell had been cast on that gentle creature, who so admired her beauty, her singing – who so loved poetry, the woods, the flowers, who was so reluctant for her to leave New Hall, even to see her dear old mum and dad? None of it made sense.

Why had it taken so many months for her to admit her marriage was a sham. What an idiot she had been, what an absolute idiot. Ooly would take her for some prize fool. Why had Bella not warned her more explicitly? Did he love her? Now she came to think about it, he'd never actually said he did – not using that word. He's said he adored her, worshipped her. He'd married her, for goodness sake. Often she caught him gazing at her with such a funny look on his face. The separate bedrooms she took to be a class thing, but, if she was honest, the slight chaste pecks on the cheek, the very occasional touch of the hand was all there had ever been. Perhaps, as he said, he was waiting for the right moment. One day the excuses might stop: his leg, migraine, the war, an early start; one day he would sweep her into his arms and into his bed. All would be well, perhaps, when the war was over, or so she told herself time and again.

What of the future as things stood now? No babies on the horizon. How she had longed for the time when she would tenderly lay her own little heir in the carved oak cradle in the nursery and sing to him as she rocked it with her foot. How she had dreamt of her very own Isabella dancing in the Great Hall at her coming of age. But it seemed likely she would go childless to her grave. "Here lies the body of Lady Rose Tillingham, beloved wife of Sir Edmund Tillingham, bart. Her life was one of unceasing devotion to New Hall and its tenants." Full stop.

She applied putty carefully around another window frame and strengthened her resolve. An East End oil and colourman's daughter made good, that's what she was. What did she expect? Perhaps, after all, "going all the way" was not everything it was cracked up to be; certainly she got that impression from mum – not that such matters were ever actually mentioned at home.

Towards the end of January snow started to fall, weighing down rooves, bringing a hushed darkness to rooms otherwise light. Mog had always loved snow, but this time the sheets of blank white spreading as far as the eye could see just looked cold and heartless. More came in February.

She wrote home:

My dear old coves,

Hope you haven't got as much snow as we have – I know how mum hates it. It's all heaped up here so you can hardly open the outside doors. The house is fr-fr-freezing. Logs don't throw out nearly so much heat as coal and we haven't got any of that. Have you got any? I keep thinking about the lovely glowing fires we had at home – us all sitting round for a feast of cockles and winkles on a Saturday night in our cosy little parlour. Can't do any work on the conservatory in this weather, so we're going to try our hands at paper hanging – the blue drawing room. One of the tenants came up with some rolls of pre-war stuff – it's not marvellous, but at least it's clean. None of us has done any before – I expect it'll be rather like "When father papered the parlour".

Dad wrote:

Just a few lines to let you know all's well. It is Sunday evening. Just going to have supper. We have had rather a hectic week. We have had the ceilings done. He has done them very well, but took a long time over them. Little Todge gets more saucy every day – we had a good game of snow balls. We went to a rehearsal of Hiawatha Friday evening. The lady conductor was a scream. She was throwing herself about like a contortionist. We are all well and trust you are the same ...

I am enclosing some good wallpaper paste – it may come in useful.'

Mum wrote:

We are still knocking about. Todge likes the snow – dad has been playing snow balls with her. we have been very bussie. we had the ceilings cleaned they were rotten. it has been a rotten job having them done – they can go blue befor i have them done again. i hate this bloomin wether. you just keep yourself warm and don't overtax your strength.

Dot wrote:

The man doing the ceilings has been here all week. They do look better, but it makes everything else look a bit shabby. When he finished we scuttled round and got our work done and then we mended the armchair. Mum and I went shopping. We borrowed The Woman Thou Gavest Me by Hall Caine – by the way I am very interested in it, so you may be sure it is merry and bright – still it seems to be holding mum; we take it in turns, one time she sews while I read and next time I sew while she reads. I borrowed a book for dad. After dinner Ooly collared it and read it through, then she passed it over to dad and he read it through: now tonight, wonder of wonders, Ed is devouring – you see it is rather a small book and big print, but they will have their 3d out of it won't they? we borrow them from two shops, 3d for seven days – we returned one I had got out for Pan over Christmas but had 1/6 to pay that was a nasty shock especially as we were on our way to the pictures Saturday afternoon and then the pictures were rotten – at least I thought so. Mum and Ooly laughed because I was fed up. I had wasted my money and my time.

February was a month of unrelieved gloom. At nine o'clock in the evening of the 15th, Winnie spoke to the nation:

"I speak to you all under the shadow of a heavy and far-reaching military defeat. It is a British and Imperial defeat. Singapore has fallen. All the Malay Peninsula has been overrun."

'Well – that's the British Empire on its way out, on its way out,' announced Doomandgloom to the company assembled in the

Emporium. 'What a shockin' waste of money – all those millions of pounds spent on fortifyin' the place and then in a flash the Japs take it – just like that and fousands of our poor lads taken prisoner – 73,000 they're sayin' in the papers.'

'And what abaat Winnie admittin' he didn't reckon the Japs would ever 'ave the face to take on us and the Yanks,' chimed in Bert Gum. 'Makes you start to wonder if 'e knows what 'es doin' at all. 'E's getting' some stick now.'

'You've changed your tune a bit, Mister ARP Warden,' said Fanny Bastaple. 'You were always talkin' 'im up – Good old Winnie – 'e'll see us through it.'

'Well – fings 'ave 'appened,' said Bert quietly.

'Yeah – sorry, mate – your Timmy Boy …'

'I'm not sure where Singapore is,' said Ethel Jiggins. 'I saw the '*Road to Singapore* –that was a comical film – Bob Hope and Bing Crosby larking about – everyone wearing garlands and dancing. It looked like some kind of paradise.'

'It's a great sort of fortified dockyard – way out east, on the way to Australia. Not much of a paradise now, more like a blood bath. It's really put the wind up the Ozzies,' said Bert.

'Well – I don't know anyfing' abaat them 'ot places in films,' huffed Vi Kerridge. 'If you ask me we ought to be more worried abaat them Jerry ships right on our door step the other day. Three of the buggers, great battleships steamin' up the Straits of Dover, right under our noses, right under the white cliffs, and no one spottin' them. Few decrepit old planes sent out to deal with them and all the poor sods shot to pieces. My Will says if they can do that the next thing is they'll be over 'ere and we'll all be under the ruddy jack boot.'

'That's right, Mrs K. That's right.' added Doomandgloom. 'Invasion is at hand, mark my words. I said to my missus – Singapore today, London tomorrow, London tomorrow.'

What with soap now on the ration now and the coal shortage which

231

brought increased dependence on paraffin, the Lord of the Emporium was a force to be reckoned with these days. He took the floor:

'Come on now, mates, Winnie reminded us of "The wonderful strength and power of Russia". Hitler is too busy with the Ruskies to be bothering with us and now the Americans are in with us … like he says …' (he read from the paper): 'We are in the midst of a great company. Three quarters of the human race are now moving with us. The whole future of mankind may depend upon our actions and upon our conduct. So far we have not failed. We shall not fail now. Let us move forward steadfastly together into the storm and through the storm.'

'Mr Smart's right,' said Ethel Jiggins. 'We must all support Mr Churchill – nothing is to be gained from expecting the worst and spreading frightening rumours round the place. We weathered the blitz, after all.'

Bert straightened himself up. 'Yeah – I s'pose yer right. I owe it to my Timmy Boy to do my bit to try and keep morale up in our little patch. 'E would never 'ave given up – bright, sparky little chap 'e was – all for 'elpin' out and forgin' on.'

'That's the spirit, brother.' Sid patted Bert's back and whispered in his ear: 'Have a bar of Sunlight – on me – no coupons.'

Spring was late in coming.

Mum wrote to Pan:

Thank you for the onions – don't bother with any moore – they are a fine lot – they must be a trouble with your schooling ... we have got a snowdrop out at last. Todge just loves it – she just touches it with her little hand and says "luvely snowdrop".'

With a final struggle, at the end of March, a few purple and yellow crocuses pushed their bright little heads up from the cold earth. Pan came in from the garden, triumphant:

'Have you seen the crocuses, Piggo – they're up at last.'

'Mm.' – Gif was deep in marmalade and toast and the newspaper.

'Come on – you've had quite enough fodder – we'll be late for school.'

'Haven't you heard the latest war news? The RAF have bombed Lubeck – smashed it to pieces. They're saying it's the biggest raid on Germany yet. What a crying shame. I went there once, in winter 1933. It was like walking into a Grimm's fairy tale with snow flakes twirling about above the deep pitched rooves. You expected the Goose Girl to appear round every corner. It's a medieval walled city on an island in the river – tiny narrow cobbled lanes, half-timbered houses, all jumbled up, funny green Gothic spires everywhere, fine merchants' houses, ancient warehouses, dating from its glory days. It was the "Queen of the Hanseatic League", you know, one of the "glories of the Holy Roman Empire" the "City of Seven Spires".' Tip top marzipan, too – never tasted anything so delicious in my life.'

Pan arranged some crocuses carefully in a blue glass vase: 'They said on the news that it's a big industrial port, supplying the Eastern Front … What's the Hanseatic League anyway?'

'An old trading association of Baltic merchants. There's some of their warehouses still standing in King's Lynn. They were a very powerful and wealthy lot – had a great fortress of a place in London just where Cannon Street station is. It was called the Steelyard. Queen Elizabeth chucked them out – too much competition.'

Pan's mind was elsewhere: 'It can hardly be just a quaint old picture postcard town if there are steel yards!'

'No – no, Piggo. The London headquarters was called "the Steelyard"; it's from an old Low German word, *Stalhof.*'

'Oh. Anyway, I hardly call in a "crying shame" that at last we're getting some of our own back at last.'

'How can you say that – the Germans have never deliberately targeted any of our pretty country towns.'

'I should keep your traitorous notions to yourself. No mention of marzipan or scrap metal yards in the staff room or you'll be for the chop. Heard from Helga recently?

Didn't you say her brother was in the Luftwaffe?'

The great raid on Lubeck was well received at the Emporium and a bright show of yellow daffodils in Mrs Gum's shop (pricey, mind) together with the bombing of Tokyo in April brought cheer all round.

'We're lettin' 'em 'ave it now good and proper,' announced Bert with satisfaction. 'It's that Bomber 'Arris what 'as taken over – 'es getting' fings on the go.'

'Yes – let the blighters suffer like we did,' said Dai Lewis.

'We have no quarrel with the German people, brother,' said Sid.

'That's what they say – but who's to blame for 'Itler if it's not the German people? just tell me that, boyo.'

Murmurs of agreement.

Doomandgloom was thoughtful. 'Tit for tat. Tit for tat,' he said solemnly. 'You wait and see, they'll be getting' their revenge soon enough.'

And so they did. First it was Exeter, then Bath, Norwich and York. Reports from the enemy threatened that every town in Britain which was marked with three stars in the Baedeker guide book was a target: "Should Britain continue their wanton and systematic destruction of our cultural treasures, we shall pay them back in coin."

Meanwhile the RAF smashed Rostock and the Heinkel aircraft factory in a raid which lasted four days.

Herbert Morrison spoke at Shoreditch of "Hitler's blow for blow – Bath, Norwich, York. A gem of Regency architecture for a U boat race, an ancient church for a ship yard, old and beautiful monuments for a Heinkel works … These are the frenzied blows of a mad lout."

A week after Rostock Exeter was bombed again – this time it was a much heavier raid – 10,000 incendiaries and 75 tons of high explosive. Its heart was burned out; lathe and plaster houses went up like firewood.

'Piggo – did you get through to your parents?' Pan wandered, bleary eyed into the hall; she had just got up. Gif was standing by the phone.

'Did they tell you all about the Exeter raid?'

'Yes.'

For Gif, Exeter had always been a special place – a place for childhood outings and treats, for high days and holidays. Pa's rectory was in a village just a few miles away and she remembered the excitement of piling into the dog cart, all decked out in her best Sunday-go-to-meeting garb, bound for the big city. Colson's in the High Street had been hit – the grand old department store, a cavern of delights. She recalled her first visit – going there with Ma when she was just three, to buy embroidery silks. She could see the skeins now, laid out on the counter, all the colours of the rainbow. She stood on a stool to see them. Funny the things you remember. Ma had a dressmaker who lived in the maze of tiny, cobbled alleys behind the High Street, in a dear little cottage with tubs of flowers outside, deep blue grape hyacinths in the spring, red and yellow nasturtiums in late summer.'

'Swine, Damnable swine.'

'Well – that's change of heart,' said Pan. 'Turned against Jerry at last, have we?'

'We have no quarrel with the German people.'

'And who's to blame for Hitler if it's not the German people? just tell me that, Piggo.'

It went on – Norwich again, Hull, Poole, Grimsby and at the end of the month, Canterbury, coinciding with the the biggest air raid the world had ever known – over 1000 bombers dropped their wares on Cologne. Canterbury for Cologne – Cologne for Canterbury. Tit for tat.

Lil wrote to Pan:

Thankyou for the luvely lily of the valie it was luvely it scented the room out. you keep away from Norwich and any of those oldee worldee places that itlers got aat of that guide book. there is not much to talk

235

about here. Todge is getting big and saucey. i put my beens in today it is tireing old job –Ed dug the earth – i sow. now I am going to bed ...

Sid wrote:

We are all sitting listening to the half-hour hymn singing. Wonder if you are doing same. Went to service this morning at the Union Chapel on the green, to hear a special man, but he was not preaching. But I enjoyed the service. It's marvellous how these men can find the beauty in simple things. He took the line of the hymn: "Nothing in my hand I bring, simply to thy cross I cling". I took Todge for a walk today but had to exercise a great deal of patience, as we took her bass. We all consider it's no less than a miracle that the cathedrals have been spared with all those other wonderful old buildings, burnt and smashed. Mog says Bath is a wreck.

While the British Empire in the East was crashing down, the glories of Olde England going up in flames and even dedicated non-believers crept to church before work, the ladies of the Emporium were much concerned with the National Loaf.

'As if we 'adn't got enough to put up with,' moaned Fanny Bastaple. 'Dingy, grey muck – sour and sticky inside, wiv crust like rubber. My 'Arry 'as had the runs ever since we was forced to eat it.'

'Well – my boils have come back in the last couple of months. I put that down to the bread.' said Ethel Jiggins.

'What's it all abaat, anyway?' asked Vi Kerridge.

'Saving space on the cargo ships, mate,' said Sid. 'The flour the new loaf's baked from of is made from all of the wheat, so the cereal goes farther and we can make out with less of it.'

'What – stalks and all? No wonder the bloody stuff's makin' us ill. They'll be makin' us eat grass next!.'

'Harry Grocer down at the baker's says it's more than his life's worth to bake any proper white bread.' said Ethel.

'Grocer nuffin,' guffawed Fanny. 'Is dad was a Jerry – *Groscocel*. When I was a kid, before the last war, Roman was full of Jerries – landlady of the Rose of Denmark – she were a Jerry.'

'Jews, I s'pose.'

'Not all of 'em – I remember Fred Ehninger the pork butcher – 'e can't 'ardly 'ave bin a Jew.'

'So d'you reckon 'Arry Whatever-' es-called is a Jerry spy?' said Vi. 'They're sayin' the National Bloody Loaf is 'Itler's secret weapon, yer know.'

'Don't be so bloomin' daft,' snorted Fanny.

'Anyway – I've 'eard that 'e – 'Arry Grocer, or whatever 'es called, 'as some flour stashed away and is bakin' luvely rolls, white as snow, for special customers.'

'At some special prices, no doubt. Interjected Kathleen O'Brien, who had just come in.

Fanny swung round: 'You'd do well to keep your opinions to yerself, Mrs O'Brien until your lot 'ave the decency to step into this war and back us up.'

'I'll have yer know. Mrs Bastaple, our Denny is fightin' for King and county – an lots of good Irish lads beside.'

'So does your Denny bein' in the army make up for your Liam nicking the cash aat of gas meters?'

Kathleen's blood was up now: 'Different from you takin' a bag of sugar from this very shop, I'm thinkin.'

'And what abaat them Nazi U boats dockin' in Dublin?' chimed in Vi, 'If it weren't for them U boats sinking our ships we'd still be eatin' nice white bread. Just think abaat that next time yer get yer gnashers stuck in that 'orrible stuff.'

Before Sid could stop her Kathleen O'Brien seized a carpet beater that was hanging up by the door and took a swipe at her persecutors. Ed seized it from her grasp and the Lord of the Emporium took charge.

'Any more of this behaviour and none of you gets any of my flour.

Mrs K, Mrs B, just you be aware that Mrs O'Brien has, as she says, a son fighting in this war, which is more than either of you have. It's probably all tittle tattle about U boats in Dublin. Now Mrs O'Brien –you are well advised to refrain from violence. And I expect remuneration for damage done to that carpet beater. Now – let us at least attempt a modicum of good order.'

'What flour?' Fanny was all ears.

'If there are apologies all round I may be able to sell you each a couple of bags of white flour.'

The bargain was struck.

Pan and Gif spent Whit weekend at Chestnut Avenue. Shortly after their return home the Luftwaffe took on Ipswich; the docks were set ablaze.

Mum wrote :

You mind you keep away from them docks. i can not find your nicks – they all swear you have got them some wear dirty. All theirs have got no seat in them so I went out and got you a pair in case you fall off your bike with know draws on and show your bottle and glass. We had some lovely strawberries this week. Ooly and Aunty and Todge has gorn to Old Ford to a plecial service. Oolys always at Bow these days – at Nells. she doesn't take Todge much – aunty and I are glad. they are marching from Selman Street to the Ruins and holding their service in the ruins – rathur nice don't you think so. Me and dad are alone – it is a change.

Aunty has just come home – she says it is the 84th Anniversary of the Church – they collected £10 17s 2d – grand was it ? it was packed – all the old members – she saw Nell.

Dot wrote:

The anniversary service at St Alphege was very moving – I wish you had been able to be there. All the old chinas turned up and we made grand parade, led by Vicar with Albie Walters carrying the cross, walking through the streets to the ruins. It was rather wet, but the singing was hearty and nobody seemed put off by the weather.

Nell was there. She was pleased to see Todge and reproved Ooly for neglecting her – in quite a nice way, though. mum and I thought it was very strange as Ooly has been going up to Bow at least once a week, sometimes twice, since last Christmas. Mum says Nell is probably just disappointed that Todge is left with us, and meant that.'

Dot's suspicions were aroused, however, and, a few days later, when Ooly announced she was off to Bow the following day, she determined to investigate.

'I'll come with you, Ooly – there's something I need to do at the shop.'

Although no longer serving at the Emporium, she was still involved and made the occasional foray to Bow to check stock and pass her eagle eye over the accounts.

'Oh – yes – OK. But I shan't be setting off until after dinner – won't that be a bit late for you?'

'No, not at all. I only need an hour or so there.'

They parted company in the market; Ooly said she was going to buy some flowers for Nell. As soon as Dot was safely out of sight she ran, hell-for-leather in the direction of the London.

Sid was surprised, and a little put out to see his sister unexpectedly. 'What you doing in here, Dot? You never mentioned you were coming in today?'

'Oh – I just wanted to pick up something for Mrs Spoon.'

'I could have done that, mate.'

'She needs a colander and can't get one anywhere round our way with this chronic shortage of pots and pans. I said I'd get it for her myself – she's very particular, you know.'

'Oh. I see.' He didn't really, but thought they might be able to charge Mrs Spoon a little over the odds.

'And, I thought I'd call in on Nell.'

'Whatever for?'

Ever since the wedding and the offending photograph, relations between Dot and Nell had been less than cordial.

'Just – to be friendly.'

They rummaged around out back and found a colander. Dot popped in for a chat with Mrs Gum, strolled down among the stalls to see if she could find any fruit to take home for Lil, and the set off for her destination. She tapped with the heavy iron knocker.

Ooly opened the door. 'Why, Aunty – you didn't say you would call in! Nell will be pleased. We've just made a fresh pot of tea.'

'Well – this is quite a party,' said Nell. 'Come and sit down. I'm sure a cup of tea would be welcome and would you like a piece of cake?'

'Thank you. How nice. I won't stop long, but, as Ooly is such a regular visitor these days, I suppose you haven't got much news to exchange. After all, she was only here a couple of days ago, wasn't she?'

Ooly froze. Nell looked slightly puzzled: 'More tea, Dot?'

'Oh, yes, that would be most acceptable. As I was saying – it must be a great comfort to you to have Ooly here so often, with both your lads in the forces.'

'I see Johnny now and again, of course, but my Derek hasn't had any leave for some time. There he is up on the mantle – doesn't he look handsome in his uniform. He's a second lieutenant, you know – and so young.'

'It must be such a worry, but you must be very proud of him.'

'Oh, my goodness, yes I am. I'm praying that he'll be home for a

240

few days this summer.'

'I suppose you see Norah – not as often as Ooly, I don't suppose.'

Nell glanced at her daughter-in-law and noted a look of helpless pleading.

'Well – no. But she pops in for a moan now and again.'

They all laughed.

'I must be off,' said Dot

Ooly breathed a sigh of relief: 'I'll stay for a bit, Aunty, and say hello to Albie. See you later.'

As the inquisitor scuttled disconsolately down the path, colander in hand, Nell poured out two thimblesful of whisky.

'Well, chick. Get that down you. I won't ask what's going on, but you take care.'

Chapter 20:
June to October 1942

June brought the good news of the American victory over the Japanese at Midway in the Pacific, bad news of the fall of Tobruk. July brought the cherry harvest at home – some fruit at last. Gif was tucking in to a large bowl:

'What about going down to Devon for a bit in the vac? I would like to see Exeter for myself and there's Ma and Pa.'

'I'm simply not prepared to stay with your parents. That house gives me the heebie-jeebies – tiny little windows, so dark and oppressive and your wretched Pa looking over his pince nez at me as if I was something the cat had sicked up.'

'Piggo, must you be so offensive? Suppose we stay in Exeter – we could splash out and book into the Clarence – my treat. You could show off your new suit, but we must at least pay a visit home.'

'D'you really want to go and stay in that bombed-out wreck of a place? What's the Clarence?'

'Top-hole hotel –used to be the Assembly Rooms – famous for its cocktails – there's one invented for the war called a "gloom chaser".'

'Cocktails are hardly going to be of any interest to you, or me, come to that. Is it still there?'

'Yes – I think it is. Thomas Hardy stayed there one time. Wrote a poem about a prehistoric bird he'd seen in the museum.'

'Well, clever clogs – here's something I happen to know about. It was an archaeopteryx.'

She threw her head back and declaimed in her best theatrical listen-to-my-beautifully-rounded-vowels-voice:

'Here's the mould of a musical bird long passed from light,
Which over the earth before man came was winging;
There's a contralto voice I heard last night,
That lodges in me still with its sweet singing.
　　Such a dream is Time that the coo of this ancient bird
Has perished not, but is blent, or will be blending
Mid visionless wilds of space with the voice that I heard,
In the full-fugued song of the universe unending.'

'You do recite wonderfully, Piggo.'
　'Well perhaps just a few days …'
Pan capitulated completely and agreed to a week, once she was assured that the windows of the Royal Clarence were large and its rooms airy. After a tedious and grumpy journey on the train (no petrol for Amun) their taxi drew up outside its stately portals.

The sight of the city horrified Gif; it was one thing to hear about it, but to actually see the ruination of her beloved home town was heart breaking. Pan, the while, overawed by the grandeur of the hotel, was more concerned with exactly how she should conduct herself towards the doormen, receptionists, chamber maids, waiters et al.

'You can't stand mushrooms, Piggo! What possessed you to eat them?'
　'We mustn't leave anything – it's so rude? You've not drunk all your tea!'
　'I've had enough.'
　'They'll think you don't like it.'
　'Don't be ridiculous.'
　'Drain that cup – and keep your voice down – if you don't, I'm leaving, now.'

Elsa's first letter arrived promptly:

My dearest little love,

Thank you for your wire which relieved me considerably. It came about 6.30 so you must have arrived nice and early and had time to settle in comfortably. I suppose you didn't have a walk round because Aelgifu is not very keen on exercise, is she? Tell me about everything but I don't expect lots of letters my darling. Have a lovely, restful time. Have you created a sensation in your new suit yet? ...

Does Aelgifu mind me writing to you – no kisses on the paper because someone might see when you open the letter. Il y a longtemps ...

She wrote every day.

Off they set to explore the town. Gif looked sadly the remnants of Colson's where they had bought the silks. The lanes and courtyards where she had visited Ma's dressmaker were no more, and at least half of the picturesque High Street had gone – tall half-timbered Tudor, elegant Georgian, imposing Victorian and Edwardian – blown out, burnt out; just rubble now.

'Look, Pig – where those demolition men are at work on that building – that's Deller's Café – we used to take afternoon tea there – scrummy cakes and a little orchestra playing. My sisters and I thought it was heaven.'

'Have we really got to stay for a week – isn't a bit ghoulish, wallowing in the destruction of this fine place?'

'The King and Queen came – so did Winnie.'

'That is entirely different. We are hardly leaders of the nation. And there's nothing to see except rubble and ruins.'

'As a matter of fact there is. And you can use your imagination.'

Not usually much of a one for walking, as Elsa had noted, on this trip Gif was indefatigable. On she ploughed, providing a running commentary of Exeter's history: the legions in Isca Dumnoniorum (Isca is Celtic for river – the word Exeter is derived from it), Bishop Leofric and William the Conqueror, the Exeter Domesday, monasteries (endlessly), Sir Francis Drake's favourite inn, Charles II's favourite sister, Minette, christened in the cathedral. They inspected the ancient and venerable Guildhall, (Judge Jeffreys presiding over the Bloody Assizes), the custom house (Exeter's wool wealth), Rougemont Castle (William the Conqueror again).

'Piggo, give it a rest! I'm not your history club.'

Pan cheered up a bit when they went to see the plaster cast of the bird fossil. She cheered up a lot, in fact, and when no one was looking, took several photographs, to take back and show to her girls. At lunch that day she spoke of archaeopteryx a good deal, moving on to dinosaurs in general at tea. Dead bishops and other Exeter luminaries were kept at bay, at least for a time.

They poked about in what shops were left, bought a few pieces of Honiton lace and found a little antique and bric-a-brac shop down among the venerable old wool warehouses on the Quay.

'Oh just look at that – it's a Bellarmine jug. I've always wanted one of those.' Gif picked up the quaint bulbous pot with a grotesque bearded face on it and inspected the price.

'Mm. A bit too much. It's probably a nineteenth century copy anyway. But I would love it.'

'What is it, for goodness sake? Who's that horrible looking fellow?'

'It's Cardinal Bellarmine – he was a vicious persecutor of German protestants in the late sixteenth century.'

'Not more history, and German at that!'

'Well – you asked.'

She pushed the face at Pan, her eyes popping: 'They're also called "witch bottles" – so watch out.'

'Ugh – take it away.'

'You had to put some hair and some wee and some other things into

245

it – to trap a witch! It would protect you if you had fallen under a curse or had a run of bad luck – and do your enemies down!'

'Did it work?'

'Who's to know? There was a woman in our village, an intelligent old bird, well read, feet on the ground –s he used one, she swore, to great effect!'

'That's rather fascinating.' Pan took the jug and looked at it closely.

On the fifth day they took the bus, the wandering, occasional, bumbly, country bus, to the Drayman village and spent an hour or two over a meagre repast, beneath the beady eye of the archdeacon and his tight-lipped lady. The archdeacon did have a fairly amusing tale of a couple who had recently brought their child to him for baptism. When asked what he should name the little girl, the father replied firmly "Urine". Apart from that it was a chilly visit and Pan was very glad to get back to the anonymous luxury of the Clarence and to Elsa's letter of the day:

My darling,
Just to say that if anything happened to you or if you went away I should be quite desolate.'

Two days left. Gif took herself off to visit some people she knew in Topsham – Pan refused to go and was left to her own devices. The last day was spent in packing and tidying up their room, on Pan's insistence that it should be left exactly as they had found it.

'Give me that brown paper bag, Pig,' said Gif, 'there's room in my holdall. What is it, anyway?'

Gif opened the bag and exclaimed with delight:

'Oh – Piggo – how absolutely splendid – how thoughtful of you – how generous – you've bought me the Bellarmine jug! Is it a thank-you present for the holiday?'

'I got it for Jocasta.'

Collapse of stout party.

Back to school they went, back to daily squabbling, to heartbreak at Blacksmith's Cottage.

At number 29 the garden was put to bed for the winter, Lil ordered logs from Romford, Sid's choir performed "Maunder's Song of Thanksgiving for Harvest", Ed was put to applying draught excluder to the French windows and Dot started knitting a good warm scarf for Pan. Ooly's twice weekly visits to Bow continued and Todge, infant prodigy that she was, continued to delight her grandparents

Lil wrote to Mog:

Little Todge has written a letter to you, in her way (two pages of inky scribbles were enclosed). will write to Mog she says. I show her your photo. you should have seen our marrows this year – they were up to the apple trees, the carrots were like worms and the celery you should have seen it ... i think the spuds are a success the taps were about 1 ½ yards long. I spose you dont get to do much gardening yourself.

Aunty's hert her leg – she fell over over the bleedin conkers which litter our street.

Mog wrote:

Dear Maties,

I long to meet Todge – she sounds such a card! I'm sorry about Aunty's leg – I suppose you would have conkers in Chestnut Avenue! We have a lot of horse chestnuts in the park here – everyone in the village is busy polishing their conkers for some great match which seems to be very important. They only have it every five years, apparently. The excitement is palpable. Bella says it's a serious business – not just for the kiddies. She says grown men take part and the rivalry is intense.

Mog had not ventured near the Tillingham Arms since the fancy stuff did for her on New Year's Eve – that was nearly two years ago now.

247

But this Saturday, the first in October, she would have to, for the Great Conker Match. This was Tillingham Parva's finest hour, not to be called off because of any world-wide conflict. From far and wide came participants and on-lookers, from high and low, from the heights of Mendip, from Tillingham Magna, from Nether Tillingham, from Midsomer Norton, from Bruton, Radstock, Warminster, Mells, Wells, Evercreech, even from Bath.

The rector, who was co-umpire with Edmund, and chairman of the Conker Committee, called at the Hall to discuss arrangements with Mog and Bella; Edmund was out riding.

'The Arms will organise the food and drink, as usual, with help from the village women and the Pony Club. The Home Guard chaps reckon they can rustle up some sort of brass band and Miss Scott Dickins will deal with the paper work – booking in the teams – that sort of thing. She's been doing it since before the Great War. My lady wife is in charge of the stalls – bottled fruit, home made fare, knitted items – that sort of thing. I assume Lord T will help me umpire – its traditional, and I wonder if you might be gracious enough to preside at the feast, Lady T, start off the circulation of the loving cup?'

'Of course – whatever that might be. I should be honoured. I could put on a puppet show if you like?'

'That would be delightful, delightful,' said the rector doubtfully. 'It's not traditional, of course.'

'Well – never mind, then. I'm sure there's something else I could do. What about organising some games for the children?'

'Well – the the school mistress at Nether Tillingham has that in hand – but …'

'OK, put Bella and me down for a stall – it's not too late is it? We'll bring our own table and organise some bric-a-brac – there's masses of stuff that we've cleared out of the conservatory and the west wing (her latest project).'

'It's not usual for anyone from the Hall to …'

'Come, come, Basil,' interposed Bella. 'We simply won't take no for an answer. Now tell her ladyship all about the conker match.'

'Its roots are very ancient indeed, very ancient indeed. A Tractarian predecessor of mine traced the origins of the festival back to early medieval times – the Oxford Movement was strong in these parts. He claimed it was held in honour of St Bruno of Cologne, founder of the Carthusian Order – his feast day is in October – the 6th I believe – the monastery at Witham Friary is said to have been the first Carthusian house in England. It was somehow linked to an age old dispute over a water mill which features in the Domesday Book.'

'Where's Witham Friary?' asked Mog.

'It doesn't exist any more – at some stage it became known as Tillingham Parva. Anyway – in the early days of its Victorian revival the festival was a fairly low key affair – a procession from the church, bearing a bottle of Chartreuse, followed by the combat, a meal at the Arms with some mouse racing after. Edmund's grandfather had it turned over to conkers and scrumpy, and made a great "do" of it – a funfair, dog show, brass band, vegetable show. It was a great day, especially for the miners from Radstock and Midsomer. During the Great War, St Bruno, being of Cologne, was replaced by a local saint, St Guthlac of Glastonbury. His feast day was actually on 11th April – but this didn't seem to matter. The team from Tillingham Parva still call themselves the "Brunies" – although none of them appear to know why. Our team from Magna are the "Guths" of course.'

'So, what is the order of events these days and whatever is this combat?'

'The teams process from the church and the conker match starts at eleven sharp, outside the Arms – it usually lasts about two or three hours, followed by the combat – the rest of the day is given over to feasting, drinking, mouse racing.'

'But – what is this "combat"?'

'Well, two of the members of the teams who have reached the final in the conker have a fight.'

'What – fisticuffs?'

'Yes – no weapons are allowed – not recently. There was an incident way back …'

'I assume its not a real fight – a mock affair, I suppose.'

'Well … er … er.'

'And the prize? I suppose there is a prize.'

'The Stert.'

'What – that useless bit of soggy marsh down where the willows grow by the stream at the end of Mill Lane?'

'Yes – that's apparently where the water mill was. The monks of Witham and the rector of Tillingham both laid claim to it.'

'The winner of the conker match gets the Stert?'

'Only for five years.'

'Then what?'

'There's another conker match.'

A mild, damp October day dawned. By nine o'clock, the sun had broken though and was illuminating the red, white and blue bunting strung across the proud chest of the Tillingham Arms. Over at St Mary the Virgin Miss Scott Dickins was running around with a whistle marshalling the troops as best she could and ticking off names. No entrants under fifteen and absolutely no women or girls had always been the rule, but, with many of the young men away and women getting into everything, it had to be relaxed. Boys and girls (over 12) were allowed to enter, and women, although, the line was drawn at wives. Widows were permissible.

The band (one trombone, a penny whistle and a comb and paper) struck up "Onward Christian Soldiers" (it was traditional) and the Grand Procession, led by the Home Guard started out, banners fluttering, conkers swinging. Mog and Bella, from their post at the bric-a-brac outside the Arms watched their approach.

250

'Good gracious me – there's so many of them! Are there usually as many as this?' asked Mog.

'Oh, yes, more usually. One year we had to hire two marquees for the feast.'

Behind the Home Guard marched a team of boys from Readers' School, bearing their banner, a book rampant. There followed the contingent from the Hall: the stable boy, old Bob, Freda and one of the more senior vaccies with the two teams of miners from the Midsomer pits close behind. Then came St Edmund of Vobster, St Adhelm of Doulting, St Andrew of Mells, St Giles of Leigh on Mendip with the numerous Virgins close behind: St Mary the Virgin, Bruton, Compton Pauncefoot, Frome, Bathwick, North Petherton, Batcombe and finally the team from St Mary the Virgin Tillingham Magna, better known as the Guths. Behind the saints were the sinners: old boys and farm hands from the George at Nunney, the White Hart at Truddox Hill, the Bell at Evercreech, the Red Lion at West Pennard and so on and so forth. There was an all-ladies team from the co-op at Radstock and from the dairy in Frome. Two sets of men caused a stir – a bunch of chemistry teachers seconded to the Royal Ordnance factory over at Woolavington and four muscular Canadian airmen. The Brunies from Parva brought up the rear, martial in their ferocity. They were, of course, the incumbent champions: this year its combatants were Grumpy Face from the Arms, two wurzels and the pot boy.

The procession came to a halt outside the pub and the competitors, one by one, proffered their conkers to the rector and his aides.

'What's going on now?' Mog was mystified.

'This is the inspection. It takes an age,' replied Bella. 'Where's Edmund got to – he's supposed to be involved in this.'

'He's in conclave with our team – bit the worse for wear. What's the inspection?'

'Some people cheat and bake their conkers in the oven to harden them. They are eliminated. I've no idea how you can tell, but Basil says you can spot them at a glance.'

With a blast from the trombone the match began, at last. The initial heats comprised furious smashing and swiping in twelve different spots, representing the twelve apostles. The ladies of the Frome dairy had been eliminated wholesale for "baking", as had the chemistry teachers; the teams from St Mary the Virgin, West Petherton and St Adhelm were disqualified for including married women in their number. The umpires had agreed to waive the "no foreigners" rule and let the Canadians participate. By the time the quarter finals were in progress much scrumpy had been consumed by all concerned, there were minor skirmishes around about and several casualties; someone from the Red Lion lost an eye. An outsider might have opined that all was chaos. Not so. By four o'clock the finalists had clearly emerged: Radco and the Hall. Everyone was astonished – the Brunies and the Guths ousted – for the first time in decades.

In the final Bob lost, as did the vaccie and the stable boy. Freda won her match, to the whooping delight of Mog and Bella. The Radco ladies reigned triumphant. Now for the combat which would, of course, be between Freda and the manageress of Radco, a fearsome opponent.

'I don't understand,' said Mog. 'If the Radco team have won, why is there a combat?'

'It's traditional,' said Bella.

'What would have happened if Freda had lost her match?'

'There would be a replay.'

'And what if all one team still lost their match?'

'Then the umpires have to decide who was most likely to have won from the losing team.'

'How?'

'I don't know.'

'Where's everyone going now?'

'Down to the Stert. That's where the combat happens.'

Now Freda was a conker player of great experience; she had been three-times champion at college, but wrestling in mud – which this particular combat turned out to be – was, by no means, her forte. Perhaps it was just as well – what would she have done with the Stert? What did anyone do with the Stert? At all events she was given a thorough mauling by the buxom manageress, who was duly proclaimed "Lord of the Stert" for five years, at least. The first woman ever.

Mog wrote to Pan:

Dear Pancake,

We have had the most extraordinary thing here – a conker match fought furiously over a bit of ground that nobody wants – half the county turned up. I would have loved you to have seen it. Feelings ran very high – all over nothing really. Anyway you will be pleased to know the winner was an all woman team. Poor old Freda got a black eye and two ribs broken in sort of duel with a battleaxe of a local shop keeper. Bella says it sometimes takes years for everyone to get over the trouble caused.'

In Egypt too, the conflict was bitter. Just a month after the conker match, on Wednesday Nov 4th, in Chestnut Avenue, Ed was sitting through the late music, waiting for the midnight news. At 11pm the programme was interrupted – the announcer told listeners to wait for a news bulletin "And it will be a cracking good one," he said. "Good news from Cairo."

'Monty's beaten Rommel! Monty's beaten Rommel.' Ed shouted, jumping up and down doing his famous Hiawatha war dance.

Dot appeared at the top of the stairs in her dressing gown and roared down: 'Stop that noise – you'll wake the kiddie – you stupid old fool!'

Thus was the news of the victory at El Alamein, the turning point of the war (said some) received in Chestnut Avenue.

In New Hall, Mog had retired early and was drifting off when a light tap came on the bedroom door. She started up – could it possibly be …

253

no surely not! Perhaps she had imagined it. It came again.

'Who's there?'

'It's Edmund. May I come in?'

'Ye-s.' Her heart leapt.

'I thought you might like to know I've just heard on the wireless, looks like we're winning a resounding victory over Rommel and the Italians in the desert. The tide is turning at last.'

'Oh, good.'

'Well – I'll leave you in peace.'

'Yes.'

Thus was the news of El Alamein received at New Hall.

After a series of defeats, from Dunkirk to Singapore, Churchill could finally announce a great victory: "General Alexander, with his brilliant comrade and lieutenant, General Montgomery, has gained a glorious and decisive victory in what I think should be called the battle of Egypt. Rommel's army has been defeated. It has been routed. It has been very largely destroyed as a fighting force ...

Now this is not the end. It is not even the beginning of the end. but it is, perhaps, the end of the beginning ... We mean to hold our own. I have not become the King's First Minister in order to preside over the liquidation of the British Empire ... I am proud to be a member of that vast commonwealth and society of nations and communities gathered in and around the ancient British monarchy, without which the good cause might well have perished from the face of the earth. Here we are, and here we stand, a veritable rock of salvation in this drifting world ..."

On Sunday Nov 15th, church bells all over the country rang out for the first time since war began, giving St Mary the Virgin of Tillingham Magna an opportunity to rejoice openly over the success of a ladies' team at the conker match.

Chapter 21:
End of November to December 1942

Preparations were underway for the fourth Christmas of the war; Christmas Day would be on a Friday – according to legend that meant a better year ahead, good harvest, peace and prosperity. Certainly there was much to celebrate. The press was exultant as news rolled in of American advances in North West Africa, British tanks roaring across the desert, allied triumphs in the Pacific and "Russia's Great Week":

"Cheers lasting ten minutes rang from very front-line radio transmitter when the news was flashed that Stalingrad had been relieved. All Russia was electrified by the rolling waves of mighty 'Hurrahs' which came from the men who had held out against the mightiest onslaught of history."

With Nazi Germany, Fascist Italy and Imperialist Japan at bay, thoughts at home, in the run up to Christmas, were on the shortage of currants, raisins and sultanas; plenty of prunes, though. The Mother of Parliaments, the while, turned her attention to the "brave new world", the golden dawn envisaged by the Beveridge Report, which offered protection from want from the "cradle to the grave".

Ooly and Dougie had snatched a couple of hours and were strolling arm in arm along Bow Road. Tuesday was their regular day now.

'What are you up to for Christmas? Will h-h-he be home?'

'No, he says he thinks his leave is going to be cancelled. We're all off to my sister's in the country – God help us.'

'What – the one who's married into the gentry?'

'Blimey, no. No invitations are forthcoming from that quarter. We're going to my sister in Suffolk, Blacksmith's Cottage, in a village called Radswick.'

'That'll be delightful – snow piled onto the cottage rooves, village church bells ringing out into the frosty air – you know they're saying that church bells are going to be set free to ring out their El Alamein victory peal on Christmas Day?'

'Snow is about as likely as meeting Hitler at a Ba Mitzvah – there's only a few weeks to go and its still like summer – roses and pansies are still in full bloom in mum's garden.'

'Well – you'll all be tucked up cosily together, having fun and games. You can't imagine what Christmas is like at B-b-barrington Gardens – not that they're there – gone off to California for the duration, thank the Lord. I shall be working – I rather envy you your close, loving family, you know.'

'You haven't met my sister Pan.'

'I can't imagine any sister of yours being other than enchanting.' He kissed her cheek. 'She's the biology teacher, isn't she? What's wrong with her? You've never said anything before!'

'Well – family's family, but – well actually she's a basket case, and she has no time for men, if you get my drift. Everyone kow-tows to her because she's clever and a bully – especially my dad. No one wants to go to her's for Christmas, but nobody dares say "no". No one ever says no to Pan, never have. And now Todge has taken to her in a big way.'

'Oh dear. Why?'

'She's got a way with kids, they all have – her, dad, Mog …'

'Mog?'

'That's my lady-of-the-manor sister. She's really called Rose, I've told you.'

'What's she like?'

'Greta Garbo.'

'What d'you mean?'

''She's very, very beautiful – fat legs though. And she's very nice. And my mum's favourite.'

'Darling girl – darling girl – come here. Can't you escape – just for once – come and share a tinned turkey – probably rather disgusting – just you and me in Tredegar Square.'

'Of course I can't. What on earth could I tell them? And what about Todge?'

'I suppose it's not on. One day perhaps, when the war is over …'

'Oh, Dougie, I'm sorry to be so maggoty when we've got so little time together.'

'Dear girl, you be whatever you like. If I hadn't been such a sp-sp-spineless wimp, letting the Pater drag me off, letting the H-h-hawk put you through that awful business, letting Vron convince me that you were f-f-fast and a g-g-gold-digger ...'

'I think Veronica Brackenthorpe had her own agenda.'

'Mm –maybe. I shall never forgive myself for all that. Don't know how you can ever trust me.'

'I'm hardly whiter than white – going through that pantomime with poor old Johnny at St Alphege. I couldn't bear looking at the place afterwards – and then it got bombed out – a direct hit.'

'All your family go to church, do they?'

'Not dad, of course, and mum only goes on high days and holidays.'

'Oh, I see. Actually, I was the incident doctor when St Alphege got its packet. That was a fishy business – parson's wife. She had a sinister blow to the head – didn't look like the result of falling masonry to me – more like someone had taken a swipe at her with something heavy. I suppose I should have got the police involved, but with all that chaos … and I was never quite sure.'

'Mrs B – good heavens. You know Todge has her name?'

'Whatever do you mean?'

'Well – when we had her christened it just seemed to me it would be a nice gesture to cheer old Teddy B up – to give Todge his dead wife's name – Beatrice – as her third name, of course.'

'Teddy B?'

'Yes – Edward Billington-Smythe – he's the vicar – you probably met him. Pan's got a thing about him. We call him Teddy B. He's a good, kind man, but the thing with Pan gets on my wick.'

'I thought you said she didn't have any time for men?'

'She doesn't usually. She's got three women in tow currently – the way they fawn on her! It was the same at school. Johnny can't stand her.'

'Well – we'll have our own private celebration before you go down to Sappho's hideaway. I'll get a little tree and some champagne and we'll draw the curtains and have a good fire and pretend its snowing outside. My cousin will be away and our housekeeper will keep mum if I bribe her with the tin of butter I've got from my chum in South Africa.'

'That'll be lovely, Dougie – lovely.'

'And next year – who knows?'

'D'you think everything might be over by then?'

'I suppose it's possible – if the powers that be can waste time devising a post-war Utopia, as they are now doing – planning to put us doctors under the iron g-g-grip of some Ministry of Something-or-other with nasty little b-b-bureaucrats telling us what we can and can't do.'

'You're not too keen on Beveridge's report, then?' Ooly laughed.

'He admits himself it's half way to Moscow! Half way to B-b-berlin more like it!'

'My uncle Billy, whose always been bit of a fascist up till now, says the state will become like a slave owner – he says we'll all just be looked after like prize cattle (he's a butcher) – give up all our freedom in return for security. Johnny reckons what he's really worried about is the minimum wage business. He says men won't work for a wage which is less than their benefit and out of the window goes Billy paying his shop hands a miserable pittance.'

'Well – I'm sure the Flying Officer knows what he's talking about.'

In the Emporium the mood was joyful.

'Blimey O'Reilly,' exclaimed Fanny, ''ave you 'eard? Twenty quid for a funeral! I've bin payin' a penny a week to some graspin' geezer who came round knockin' regular as clockwork every Tuesday evenin' since time began. Well you 'ave to ave a decent send off. And wot abaat eight bob a week for every kiddie (except the first) – good news for the likes of Ma O'Brien.'

'Dole up and no more ruddy means test,' said Vi.' I've 'ad them comin' raand –sell this, sell that – all you was allowed to keep was table, beddin', knives and forks. We was told to sell the jo but no one had enough cash to buy it – no one in our street had thirty bob. Know wot I mean?'

'That'll be the finish of uncle.' Went on Fanny. 'No more poppin' stuff to keep you goin' through the week. My dad had been dead for years and every Monday, like clockwork, mum took his boots to be pawned. Won't be no more trade for the likes of them – serves the bleeders right.'

'We could never afford five bob for a doctor,' added Vi, ' – or the bit you 'ad to pay to get on the panel, so – any sign of a fever, mum would go daan Lime'aas and get a pinch of some powder from a Chink she knew there – that put us right.'

Doomandgloom was, as ever, dubious:

'There'll be 'uge war debts to be paid off – how can they think they're goin' to finance doles ad lib and all the rest of it. Our prices will go up – no one from abroad will be able to buy from us.

Anyway – I doubt it'll come to anything – it'll be whacked down soon enough by those who pull the strings in the old puppet show. Insurance companies are up in arms –they'll be ruined, and the Friendly

Societies. Remember what happened after the last war – all that stuff about a land fit for heroes – promises, promises. And what happened, what happened? Poor old soldiers, crippled with wooden legs and shattered nerves beggin' around the place.'

'Yeah,' agreed Mrs Gum. 'My aunt Doris – 'er old man come home from the Somme with no arms and no wits: she used to push him round in a bass, beggin'.'

Sid, not wishing to add to the undertaker's despondency, said 'Winnie's in favour – he'll see it through.' Privately, he thought the offering of blanket benefits was a mistake. So little difference between relief offered and a working man's pay was surely an invitation to idleness!

Rabbi Hotzner came in for some wax candles for Hanukkah – Sid always kept him a small stock.

'What do you think about Beveridge, Reverend?' asked Sid.

'It's a wonderful utopian dream, but Britain's brave new world must wait until Hitler's slave new world has been wiped out. Skipping along the primrose path of day dreams is not what is needed at present.'

'It's all right for you lot,' piped up Fanny. 'The Jewish board of Guardians see you all right.'

'I think, Mrs Bastaple, it is hardly "all right for us lot", as you put it. I assume you are not unaware of the news that the Germans plan to exterminate the whole of European Jewry? Have you heard what's been happening to our brothers and sisters in Poland? Thousands upon thousands put to death – innocent children, women – sent off to slaughter houses, to be electrocuted and gassed – babies and toddlers thrown into lorries and driven away – few of these little ones survive even the journey to the stations, so brutally are they handled. Their mothers are driven insane by the sight – as many go mad as are shot. In the Warsaw ghetto the authorities have ordered all chemist shops to be closed so that poison cannot be purchased – the streets are strewn with the bodies of women who have thrown themselves from windows

260

in their terrible despair.'

'My bleedin' gawd! We've 'eard rumours, o'course – but – well – there are some as reckons that it's exaggerated – stuff put abaat to make Jerry appear even worse than what 'e is.'

'I can assure you, Mrs Bastaple, that what I tell you is God's truth.'

Silence. The company dispersed.

Over at Westminster, Eleanor Rathbone, that tough old fighter for the underdog, suggested to her fellow MPs that it was a mockery to have the church bells rung on Christmas Day when the children of the nation that gave us the bible were being massacred.

Liverpool Street was heaving with anxious, excited, festive travellers: soldiers, sailors, airmen, American, Canadian and home grown, mums and kids, nans and granddads, uncles and aunts. Sid was bearing a roll of wire netting and several packets of soap flakes; round his neck hung a frying pan; stuck into his trousers was his carving knife and tucked under his left arm was his fiddle.

'They'll take you for a bleedin' tinker,' grumbled Lil, who was struggling with string bags of cakes in tins, jam, and some packets of nice white flour.

"God rest you merry gentlemen," rang out hopefully from a hospital choir and the end of platform two. "Let nothing you dismay!"

Ooly had charge of the pushchair, loaded with Todge and her equipment, which, of course, included Puddy Tat. In addition two stone hot water bottles were tied to the handle and some rubber bands for kilner jars were stuffed behind the pillow. The child was bellowing with terror at the shrieking of whistles and the deafening blasts of steam and her mother, usually in such a light and happy frame of mind these days, was disconsolate:

'Honestly, there's no need to take all this stuff; they're doing perfectly all right for supplies out in the countryside.'

'Nobody can get hold of rubber hot water bottles, mate and all metal items are, as you know, like gold dust,' replied her father.

"Tidings of comfort and joy of co-o-omfort and joy!"

Dot, hobbling because of a bad leg, could only manage the bags of presents, all expertly wrapped, while Ed brought up the rear with four bulging suitcases, a fag hanging out of his mouth.

Sid, of course, had them all at the station in plenty of time and they bundled into the Ipswich train and settled down to the sandwiches Lil had made for the journey.

'How are we going to get to Radswick?' asked Ooly. 'Are they going to collect us in the car – there wouldn't be room for us all.'

'Dad told them not to waste their petrol. Pan says there are a few buses,' said Dot. 'She says there's usually one to Highbridge that meets the London trains. Apparently we can get a taxi to Radswick from there.'

'Well, I hope we don't have to hang about for too long. Todge will get frantic.'

They had been waiting for only a short time outside Ipswich station when a voice called from a lorry:

'Hey, you guys. Wanna lift somewhere?'

'They're Yankee airmen,' whispered Ooly to her father.

'That's very kind of you, brother. Going anywhere near Radswick?'

Dot was wary – a lift from the American air force didn't seem quite nice. She was, however, overruled and the family were soon ensconced and rattling along the Suffolk lanes in the company of several very large GIs, one of whom seemed to be rather important; the others called him "sir".

'How are you finding it over here?' Ooly asked the driver.

'Well, ma'am,' came the reply. 'It sure is different from home. No ice for drinks, no central heating, not enough grub. Would your kid like some candy? I've got a littl'un back home like her, look.' He produced a snap.

'British girls are pretty swell, though,' called a voice from the back, 'pretty swell. May I compliment you on your hat, ma'am – sets off those bea-utiful black eyes.'

Ooly laughed coquettishly.

The colonel intervened in a loud, authoritative voice: 'We just love your quaint old villages, churches, cathedrals, cottages –like something out of a fairy tale. There's nothing in my home town older than my grand pappy. Are you from these parts?'

'Oh, no, brother. We're from London.' Sid said proudly.

'You've been going through hell, then.'

'We struggle on and try and make the best of it.'

'I take it from the luggage you're carrying that you're moving house.'

'Oh, no, we're just off to my daughter's for Christmas. I'm taking her a few bits – the shortages, you know ...'

'Well, I'm sure the little lady will be more than grateful.'

Giggles from the Smarts.

'What's the joke?' asked the colonel, good humouredly.

'It's just you calling my sister a "little lady", said Ooly. 'She's very tall and ...'

'My niece is a biology teacher,' interrupted Dot hastily. 'She went to University.'

'That's quite something,' said the colonel. ' You must be very proud of her.'

Lil spoke loudly, in her best voice: 'I've got another girl who's a real lady – Lady Tillingham – married to a lord.'

'Gee! Is that so?' The colonel sounded doubtful and could hardly wait to write to his folks and tell them that they'd given a lift to a bunch of little Cockney clowns who claimed a connection to the aristocracy.

'Yes. She was 'vacuated daan Somerset and they was billeted in 'is 'aas (stately 'ome I should say) and – well – 'e took up wiv 'er. She's quite a looker – they take 'er for Greta Garbo raand our way.'

'Takes after her mum, I guess.'

Lil was delighted but felt she should put him right, nevertheless:

'No, ducks, She ain't nuffin' like me. Great big blue eyes – she's more like 'er dad.'

'Strange things happen in war time,' Sid said, rather sadly. 'Have you got children, brother?'

'No – no – I'm not married, Mr er … Er …'

'Smart. Sidney Smart, Pleased to make your acquaintance, colonel?'

'Ed Muslow.'

They shook hands.

'My daughter, Lily – my sister, Dorothy, my wife and my granddaughter, Elizabeth.'

'And the other gentleman?'

'Oh, he's my brother-in-law.'

'So you've got three daughters. Any sons?'

'Lily, Pansy and Rose are quite enough for us.'

'A garden of flowers! How charming. One teaches, one's a Lady and our delightful companion here?'

'I'm just a mother,' said Ooly.

'Lily has been a pianist of some renown,' said her father firmly. 'And she has also won numerous awards for her singing. My girls are all very talented musically – I am very fortunate.'

'And yourself? – I see you have a violin.'

'We are quite a musical family, brother.'

The colonel made a mental note for his letter home: musical clowns.

A hip flask of some rather odd tasting whisky was passed round; Sid refused, of course, but, fearing he might jeopardise Anglo-American relations if he persisted, eventually submitted to quite a few swigs. The voice from the back suggested they might sing some carols, which they did.

Radswick village was all a-twinkle with Christmas Eve anticipation as they sped along, and arrived, a very jolly party, at Blacksmith's Cottage.

'My sainted aunt!' exclaimed Pan, who was watching from the window. 'That's an American lorry they're in, with some wretched GIs. And just look at dad – you might take him for a one man band! I hope no one in the village spotted them coming in this direction.'

'They must have got a lift from the station. I suppose we'd better ask them all in for a drink,' said Gif.

'Over my dead body!' said Pan. 'I'm not having damned predatory Yanks in my house with their swaggering, wads of cash, their vulgar ways.'

'Come on, Piggo,' coaxed Gif. 'It's Christmas and they have done your family a favour.'

Elsa added, 'Pan, dear, we are told to be welcoming to our transatlantic saviours.'

Anyway – they were all at the door.

'Dear Old Pud!' Pan swept Todge up in her arms.

'May I introduce Colonel Muslow,' slurred Sid. 'And some of his very fine airmen – my daughter, Pansy, Aelgifu Drayman, Elsa Rush.'

Thus was Sappho's hideaway invaded by some large chunks of American bully beef. Everyone wished everyone else the compliments of the season – that is to say, everyone except Pan, who took Todge off to inspect the Christmas tree. Elsa poured out elderflower wine and Gif offered round her mince pies – unable to get any dried fruit to make mince meat she had filled the grey, leaden potato pastry cases with prunes.

'Mm.'

One of the airmen produced a bottle of Bourbon and more was consumed. Elsa took a surprising shine to the handsome colonel and, unused to such strong liquor, found herself fluttering her elegant fingers along his mighty arm: 'We're all so immensely grateful for the strong arm of the American forces,' she cooed. Gif was more than startled at this display, but could not help feeling gratified – even without benefit of alcohol – by the colonel's complimentary (and informed) remarks about her Napoleon III clock. Pan was incandescent.

The driver played balloons with Todge, the "voice from the back" made up to Ooly while the other two men, only boys, really, sat with Lil and Dot and talked about their mums and Christmas at home. Pan stood, fuming, apart, while Sid settled himself in a wing chair and took a snooze; Ed hopped about uncomfortably, not sure whether he should sit down or not.

Eventually the invaders left, wondering what the wire netting was for.

Pan slammed the door with relief: 'God – what a crew!'

'I thought the colonel was quite charming,' said Elsa.

'We noticed,' growled Pan with menace.

Gif was in a flap on Christmas morning; they would be fourteen for lunch and she was unused to entertaining on this scale. The Kilminsters – farmer and farmer's wife, Jenny and her little brother – had been invited by Pan, in spite of Gif's protests – they had, after all, supplied the birds. Dom Sci. would be in attendance (with a number of cakes); Pan worship would be in full flood – thank the lord Meredith was spending the holidays with her people. Elsa was, of course, a guest, cringing with shame at her performance of the previous evening. At least she was out of favour.

A couple of trestle tables borrowed from the village hall were manoeuvred into the drawing room – the only room big enough for them – and Ed was ordered to take the arm chairs into the study, without knocking anything on his way.

'Who's for a tale of Dingley Dell?' offered Sid.

'For heaven's sake, Dad, not now.' Pan snapped, and then turned to her aunt she to admonish her for laying the table with the every-day cutlery and folding the linen napkins in the wrong way.

'Not those glasses, Mum – the ones from the dresser – and they need polishing.'

266

'Come on, Piggo, get a move on,' called Gif from the steamy chaos of the kitchen, 'Rush is about to come out with the veg – *achtung strasenbahn*!'

'I wish you wouldn't use that dreadful German expression.'

The board groaned with ducks. Having little meat on them, it took a good number to feed such a large party, and a long time to carve them. Good job Sid had brought his specially sharpened carving knife with him. By the time the meat was dished up everything else had got cold and Pan was in a serious paddy.

'It would have been so much more sensible to have a big bird – a turkey or a goose. I told you that, Piggo.' She hissed in a stage whisper, so as not to seem ungrateful to the Kilminsters.

Lil couldn't bear cold food. More than that, she couldn't bear cold plates. She whispered to Dot, 'Shouldn't we offer to go and 'ot the plates up – they're stone bloomin' cold.'

'No, leave it be, duck. We don't want to offend.'

'The brussels are like rocks and they're cold too.'

'Shush! Put some nice hot gravy on the – that'll do the trick.'

The gravy was chilly.

'Can we pull Pan's absolutely amazing crackers?' asked Elsa. These were Pan's contribution to Christmas dinner. She had spent hours, days, weeks assembling them, using old scraps of coloured crepe paper, something from the chemistry lab to make them go "bang", clever little jokes, devised by herself, and in each a home made paper hat and a novelty. Never mind ducks slaved over by Gif, never mind the mounds of vegetables, stuffing, sauces, puddings, marzipan treats, etc. etc. the crackers were to be the star of the show.

'Come on then, Jenny – I'll pull mine with you,' said Pan graciously. The girl blushed with pleasure and took hold of her cracker. Pan pulled hard at the other end.

The explosion was not as bad as it might have been. No windows were blown out and although the food was covered in a slight sooty deposit, Gif declared it still quite edible, after a wipe down. No one was seriously hurt, although Jenny had a bit of a burn on her arm and Mrs K was given a sedative when the doctor arrived. The Smarts, not unaccustomed to bombs, were made of sterner stuff. Todge, after her initial shriek, was delighted with the whole proceeding and thereafter always called her aunt "Bang".

The rest of the day was something of an anti-climax. After the King they played "Family Coach", always a favourite in the Drayman household at festival times. Pan explained the rules:

'Someone tells the story: a family – mother, father, children, nurse – set off for a picnic in the family coach and have various adventures. Each member of the party is assigned a role: mother, father, etc. coach springs, coachman's whip, family crest, wheels etc. When ever the story teller mentions their character/item the individual concerned has to get up and twirl round. When the "family coach" itself is mentioned everyone gets up and spins round. If you fail to turn round when you should you have to pay a forfeit – some silly task thought up by the narrator.'

'Is that it?' Lil was puzzled. 'Who wins?'

'Well – no one, really. It's just fun.'

'Is it?'

Elsa, eager to please, immediately opted for the springs – they wouldn't be mentioned much, she hoped, having eaten much more than she normally allowed herself, she would have welcomed a nap.

Gif was usually the narrator, but Pan decided she would take the role on this occasion, and seized the opportunity to embark on a long and complicated tale which featured the coach springs at every breath:

'It was a fine summer morning and mother instructed the coachman to oil the springs of the family coach; the springs had got rusty during the winter months – it was an elderly family coach and the springs were really past it – the coachman had been complaining about the springs for years, etc. etc.'

Fifteen minutes into the story and Elsa had paid two unpleasant forfeits, involving putting her head in a bucket of water and removing her false teeth, and was purple with exhaustion. Pan ploughed on, relentlessly. The Kilminster boy, not nearly as intelligent as his sister, didn't quite get the hang of it, neither did Todge; they just kept on spinning round and round regardless. The game proceeded – horrible in its ferocity – until Elsa fainted; the Kilminster boy and Todge were both violently sick soon after.

In its aftermath, a nice quiet game of Happy Families, Ooly sneaked out to the village phone box to ring Dougie, pleading slight nausea – she felt like a breath of fresh air. Sid warned that she should take a torch (dimmed) and not be long. Dot was suspicious: 'I've never heard you express any interest in fresh air in your entire life!' Exhausted from her exertions at Family Coach (she had been the coachman) she forbore to accompany her niece, however.

The phone box was dank and full of fag ends. After a few false starts she managed to get through to the hospital and Dougie was located:

'Just ringing to say hello and wish you Happy Christmas ... I'm wearing your brooch – I keep touching it to remind me you're real ...'

Yes – of course I do, I do. It's pretty grim here – we had an explosion ...

No – everyone's fine. I keep thinking of our peaceful, heavenly little Christmas together – the tinned turkey was ambrosia to me ...'

'Oh – we ate sooty duck with cold gravy followed by prune trifle.'

She hadn't been back at the cottage more than a few minutes when Johnny rang. Whew!

'Hello. Oh – did you. Mm – were you? Well you seem to have had a pretty fun day, then.

Todge is absolutely loaded up with toys ...

Well, yes – I suppose you could say that we are having a good time.

269

The best bit so far was yesterday – we had a jolly party with some GIs who gave us a lift from the station. One of them was a *very* senior officer in the American air force – a colonel …'

Boxing Day brought an energetic walk across the fields and a full-scale battle about the number of potatoes which should be left to bake in the oven before they set off.

Chapter 22:

3 December 1942 to February 1943

The Tillingham Christmas was a low key affair this year; most of the vaccies and Freda had gone home and Mog was feeling bereft. About eight o'clock on Christmas Eve she had telephoned Blacksmith's Cottage.

'How were your family when you spoke to them?' enquired Bella.

'To be honest with you, they sounded rather funny. My sister Pan was in a rage; she kept muttering about "bloody Yanks", and, if I didn't know it couldn't be so, I would say that my father was slightly tipsy. Mum was odd, too. She kept saying the same thing over and over again and then they all came on the phone and roared together "We wish you a merry Christmas", and then the line went went dead.'

'Oh, I'm sure they're all right. I expect they were just having a riotous time.'

'I do miss them, Bella.'

'Why on earth don't you just sneak off and pay them a visit? It's been over two years.'

'Edmund would go mad – you know he would. He'd probably go into one of his terrible sulks, probably for weeks, and I can't bear the thought of that.'

'Well – you may be right, but I don't see that a couple of days would do any harm. Why don't you pop off for New Year; I dare say Edmund will be taken up with Harry Portman – he's got some long leave, I gather. Just go and I'll tell him you're mother's ill and you'll be back in no time at all.'

'I couldn't deceive him, Bella, I don't believe in that sort of thing –dad was always such a stickler for honesty. He was always coming out with: "Lying lips *are* abomination to the Lord: but they that deal truly *are* his delight." (Proverbs 12:22) In his shop, just near the bottles of bug blinder, he had another quote pinned up : (Ephesians 4:25) "Wherefore put away lying, speak every man truth with his neighbour: for we are members one of another".'

Bella was always rather fond of Blake's "A truth that's told with bad intent

Beats all the lies you can invent." But she passed no comment.

So Mog decided to tackle the baronet; he was in the blue drawing room (now a rather alarming shade of turquoise) reading Keats.

'Have you got any plans for New Year, Edmund?'

'No, not really.'

'Oh.'

'Why?'

'Well – it's so long since I've seen my family, I thought I might just take a short trip to London.'

A cloud passed over Edmund's face and he left the room without a word.

'You've done it now,' said Bella, who was busy with bills in the library. 'He's gone off riding in a thunderous mood. No doubt he'll have one of his turns. Why don't we ask your people to come down here for a day or two?'

'Dad can't get away from the shop and mum doesn't like long train journeys, neither does Aunty.' ("Lying lips are abomination to the Lord.")

Heaven forbid that Miss Scott-Dickens or the stable boy should spot their approach – the dog cart loaded up with tins of nice light stone and God knows what else. Knowing the lady of the manor was from humble origins (they usually were at New Hall) was one thing, but seeing the actuality of the humility was another. She imagined her father addressing Edmund as "brother" and taking him aside for a quiet word, her mother dropping her aitches and hints about the nursery. Heaven forbid that Aunty's eagle eyes should be allowed to spy out the sleeping arrangements at New Hall.

'What about you making a day trip, then – he wouldn't even notice you'd gone! Tell him you've changed your mind about going for New Year and just hop off for a few hours. No need for any fibs at all.'

'Yes – but I'd better leave it for a few weeks – otherwise he might be suspicious.'

Mog wrote a careful letter:

Dear Maties,

Moggo calling. Prepare yourselves for a flying visit! We're in the middle of things here and I don't like leaving the kiddies over night ("Speak every man truth with his neighbour"). The train gets in to Paddington at 11.44 – next Saturday, Jan. the 30th – we could have a few hours together – catch up and everything, then I'm afraid it'll have to be the 4.20 back.'

'Blimey O'Reilly – Mog's coming next week! Look at this, Ool.'

Lil handed the letter over. Ooly was annoyed, very annoyed:

'The royal command goes forth and we all jump to. Why on earth can't she at least stay overnight? I suppose our accommodation isn't regarded as suitable!'

'Now, now,' said her father. 'We must be grateful that she's coming at all. I wonder if the baronet will accompany her.'

Lil was excited but, just a little disappointed. She had dreamt of Mog's homecoming so often, placing it in the early summer. What a grand welcome they would lay on. She imagined the Spoons, peeping out through their net curtains – and that stuck-up Plunkett woman, how she would gawp as the chauffeur driven limousine drew up outside

273

number 29. There would be some new furniture for the lounge, if any was to be got – Billy would know of a source. Perhaps they could find some pretty forget-me-not wallpaper for the bedroom she would use. The table would be laid with a lace cloth, Mog's favourite cockles and winkles, a cold, roast fowl, an iced cake. How she would admire the garden, the lilies full out, the rambler over the arch with its pink roses bigger than ever before, the syringa is in full blow. This year the garden had begun to pay for the work put into it. How impressed she would be with the rows of beans and cabbages, onions, carrots, with Sid's scarlet geraniums in pots on the terrace and Ed's pond, with its floating lily.

'Oh dear there won't even be time to bring 'er 'ome. I did want er to see my vegetable patch. Never mind – I'll make some sandwiches and we can take a thermos of tea and something for the kiddie – make a nice outing of it.'

Billy was at Chestnut Avenue when the letter arrived – he had brought the family a leg of lamb:

'Lilian, I think you are forgetting that your daughter is a member of the gentry now. It is incumbent upon us, her family, to provide a suitable reception, something which befits her station in life.'

'What have you in mind, mate?' asked his brother.

'It just so happens that I have a little business arrangement with the Great Western Hotel at Paddington, with regard to beef – fillet, rump, chateaubriand – you name it. A table in the restaurant can be arranged and a generous discount, I'm sure.'

'Oh, my bleedin' gawd,' gasped Lil, wondering what on earth she might be expected to wear, how she should address the waiters, and what her brother-in-law was up to.

Sid was dubious: 'I really can't run to anything too fancy – even with the five shilling limit it'll cost – there'll be you and Flo', Dot and Lil and me, Ooly and the kiddie – seven or eight of us.'

'Come, come,' said Billy 'You can hardly welcome the wife of a baronet with spam sandwiches on a station forecourt! And just think how much you saved, not having to cough up for the wedding.'

Actually the party was much larger than seven or eight. When Lady Rose Tillingham nervously tip tapped along platform one, a tiny figure, svelte in her moleskin hat and cape, there they all were, waiting agog: mum, dad, Aunty, Ooly and Todge, Billy and Flo', Ed, an elderly couple she didn't recognise (Mr and Mrs Spoon), the Gums, Doomandgloom Davies (Mrs Davies rarely emerged from the funeral parlour), Dai Lewis, Rabbi Hotzner, Maureen (great with child) and Mossy (with his camera), Teddy B, Nell and Albie, Norah, Old Matthews and some others (from the choir). Every one of them was done up in their Sunday best; Lil had been forced into the hat she wore for Ooly's wedding and Sid was sporting his diamond tie pin.

'Here she comes, and here we go,' said Sid'

At her approach, Old Matthews raised his baton and she heard her father's fine tenor voice ring out, making itself heard over the whistling, bustling roar:

'Grown in one land alone
Where proud winds have blown
There's not a flower born of the shower
Braver than England's own
Though gales of winter blow
Piercing hail and snow
Shining she stays bright as in days of yore
Old England's pride still blossoms
Fresh on England's shore.'

They then all joined in, lustily, heartily, especially Lil, reading from the sheets Sid had supplied:

'*Rose* of England thou shall fade not here
Proud and bright from growing year to year

Red shall thy petals be as rich wine untold
Shared by thy warriors who served thee of old.
Rose of England breathing England's air
Flower of chivalry beyond compare
While hand and heart endure to cherish thy prime
Thou shalt blossom to the end of time.

Rose of England breathing England's air
Flower of liberty beyond compare
While hand and heart endure to cherish thy prime
Thou shalt blossom to the end of time.'

Mog thought her heart would break.

Dad did a funny little bow and kissed her hand; Dot bobbed a curtsey.

'Oh, Dad, Aunty – stop it for goodness sake,' she laughed through her tears.

Lil was embarrassed and dumb struck when it came to it. This longed for moment was so different from all that she had imagined – why had Sid let all this lot turn up? –She would have liked Mog to herself. She clung to Todge and then pushed her forward;

''Ere – say hello to your Aunty Mog.'

'Dear, dear Todge – at last! Oh Mum, Mum ...' Mother and daughter hugged briefly.

'I'm so sorry, so sorry, Mum.'

'Sorry for what?'

'You know ...'

'Come on, duck, never mind about all that. Yer Uncle Billy has got us all into some posh hotel for our dinner. You're lookin' thin as a stick – let's get some food inter yer.'

Ooly came up and gave her sister a peck. 'I must say, you look the part! Where's Sir Edmund?'

'Oh – he though I'd prefer a reunion just on my own.'

Led by Billy they all proceeded towards the Great Western: 'Private lunch party for Lady Tillingham,' he announced to the commissionaire who looked doubtfully at the motley crew before him. They were hastily hustled up the Grand Staircase, but not before identity cards had been produced.

Lil had never seen anything quite like it – except at the flics, neither had Dai, Doomandgloom, the Gums, Albie, Norah, Old Matthews or most of the choir members. Ed had, of course – he was among the "good old East End Commies" who had marched into the Savoy, back in the Blitz – but nobody knew about that.

It was the curtains that struck Lil most – all looped up with gold cords, against the high, wide windows. An enormous, long table was laid with goodness knows what, certainly nothing she recognised as food, silver platters, serviettes made into flower shapes, sparkling glasses, bowls of out-of-season roses. At each corner stood massive silver buckets on stands, holding bottles of champagne.

'Strike me pink – who's payin' for this lot, Sid? And what about coupons?'

'Dad, you can't possibly afford all this!' Ooly whispered in horrified tones.

'I'm not paying, mate.'

'Who is? Mog?'

'No.'

'Who then? Uncle Billy might be a good fixer, but he's not known for putting his hand into his pocket.'

'No, mate. Not Billy.'

'Oh, Dad, who is it then?'

'Never you mind.'

Near to tears, most of the time, Mog managed to dispense ladylike charm, first offering her most sincere condolences to Teddy B, Dai and the Gums for their appalling losses.

'May I present Mr and Mrs Spoon, our neighbours in Chestnut Avenue – my daughter, Lady Tillingham.' Sid beamed with pride.

'How kind of you all to come! Why Rabbi – how nice of you – what absolutely ghastly news about your people in Poland! Mr Davies, Nell, Albie, Norah – have you heard from Derek? I didn't expect such a welcome. Mr Matthews – I was so touched by the singing – Mossy and Maureen – I was so sorry to miss your wedding and so happy for you both. Uncle Ed – how have you been getting on? Still doing the pools? Won anything?'

Ed smiled a knowing smile. He missed Mog, more than most, if the truth be known, she was the only one of the family who seemed to have any time for him. He was just about to reply when Billy pushed himself forward and put his arm round her in a proprietorial fashion:

'Well, my old Mog, how does life among the landed gentry suit?'

'Lost a deal of weight, dear?' said Dot. 'Never mind, I'm sure there'll soon be a reason for putting it on.'

Mossy clicked away, Doomandgloom regaled Mog with the horrors of the Blitz, Old Matthews hoped she was keeping up with her singing, Teddy B enquired about St Mary the Virgin, Nell asked how many servants they had at New Hall, Dai Lewis wondered if they had a dairy herd, Sid asked how the refurbishment of the house was proceeding (he had brought her some of his finest paint brushes), Norah asked if she wore a tiara often. Mr and Mrs Spoon sat quietly on the tiny gilt chairs, rather overawed.

'Are you happy, Mog?' asked Ooly.

'Are you?' responded her sister.

Lil was hoping for a quiet chat, but in the twinkling of an eye four o'clock struck and the star of the show was off at the run.

'Goodbye everyone. See you soon. Thank you *so* much for coming.'

'Don't forget your paint brushes, mate,' called Sid, as she flew down the Grand Staircase. She did.

Sid wrote to Pan:

Mog came for a fleeting visit. It was a fine occasion. Old Matthews and I organised a bit of a choral tribute for her and we all had a meal at the Great Western Hotel, thanks to Uncle Billy. She's looking very glamorous these days, but rather thin. I hope you're not upset that we didn't mention anything before – mum thought it was best not to get you worrying that you ought to be here – with all your school work and everything.

Lil wrote:

Mog called in – we had to meet her at the station. i didn't really get any chance to talk to her proper. she is very thin. she talks very posh. Her husband didn't come. she liked Todge.

Dot wrote:

I expect dad has told you about our visitation from Lady Tillingham. It was a very grand affair – I'm sorry you weren't there. Billy arranged a private room at the Great Western Hotel – he's involved in some dealing, I'm afraid. There was champagne and lobster and all sorts of fare – five-shilling limit how are you? Goodness knows where the money came from – dad was very funny about it. Mog hasn't changed much, but she is quite skinny now and her voice is different – rather poshed-up. The baronet didn't come, which I thought strange; I shouldn't be surprised if she's ashamed of us – don't say anything about this to mum!

You had better burn this – we don't want Billy getting arrested! I enclose a cutting of the piece about it that he got into the Old Ford Examiner. The photograph was one of Mossy's.

"Roman Road trader's daughter is married to baronet. William Smart, butcher of Green Street, hosted a party in a West End hotel to celebrate the elevation of his niece, Lady Rose Tillingham, daughter of Sidney

Smart, oil and colourman of Roman Road. Her marriage, to Sir Edmund Tillingham bart. of Tillingham Newall in Somerset, took place in May 1941, but the bride's family were unable to attend because of the war. Lady Rose has often been compared to Greta Garbo and is well known in Old Ford for her fine soprano voice."

Pan was very angry indeed – angry that no one had seen fit to tell her about the visit, angry that Mog might, indeed, be ashamed of her family, angry that the fatted calf had been killed, that she (and Gif) had spent a good deal of last month's hard earned salary on providing a Christmas to be remembered for them all – and now, off they go and have the blow out of all blow outs without even telling her.

'Choral tribute, indeed! I wonder if they sang "She's only a bird in a gilded cage"?'

'She hardly married for an old man's gold, as it says in the song – Edmund's not much older than her and she professed great devotion to him in her letters, I seem to remember.' Elsa had rather taken to Mog.

'Mm,' said Gif. 'I'm not so sure about the gold, either. The Tillinghams are as poor as church mice.'

'Not, I think, by any ordinary standards,' snorted Pan.

'No, I suppose not, 1,000 acres of land, farms, tenants, a mansion with 20 bedrooms hardly constitutes poverty.'

'How d'you know all that?' asked Pan.

'Pa had some dealings with the Tillinghams – years ago – over the living of Tillingham Magna.'

'Oh really – and, why, may we know, had this not been mentioned before?'

'You never asked.'

'I never asked!!! You deceitful creature! You ...'

Und so weiter.

'Trust old Butcher Short to get 'imself in the local rag.' remarked Vi Kerridge. 'Anybody'd think that Rose was 'is girl.' Sid was out the

280

back getting some paraffin.

'It was a very good do, we 'ad,' said Dai Lewis. 'All sorts – silver forks, silver champagne buckets – you should 'ave seen it!'

'Opportunity would 'ave bin a fine thing!' replied Vi.

'That Funny One seemed rather out of sorts. Got the 'ump, I reckon, with her sister gettin' all the fuss,' went on Dai.

'Nothin' much funny abaat 'er since she got spliced *and* I've 'eard rumours …' Fanny Bastaple said darkly, tapping the side of her nose.

'Shush! 'ere comes old Sid.'

'We was just talkin' abaat your do, Sid. Some fancy party! Shame none of you got to the weddin' though.' Vi got out her purse. 'Got any grease for us?' [*margarine*].

'No, mate. I have not.' Sid was riled.

'Dai was just sayin' your eldest girl wasn't best pleased.'

'I never said that Mrs K. I never said that. I was just remarkin' that she didn't look too well.'

'Lily's in good spirits,' snapped Sid. 'She's got the kiddie.'

''ow's 'er old man?' asked Fanny. 'In the RAF ain't 'e? I s'pose she don't see much of 'im.'

'He's stationed not far away so he's with us quite often.'

'That's a mercy – such trouble 'appens to couples in war time, don't it?' Fanny smiled knowingly.

At that point Bert Gum came in. 'Read about the party 'ave we?'

'We was just talkin' about it,' said Dai. 'I've never seen anything like that marvelous spread since before the war!'

'It was some do – but I was speakin' of the other party – the one in Berlin. Old Fatso Goering blown off the air by the RAF. We're givin' the Krauts a good blast of their own medicine these days. Paper says a "roaring laugh rang round the world" when our boys turned up for That Man's anniversary party with their Mosquitos.'

'What'yer talkin' abaat, Bert?' Fanny hadn't heard the story and was, in any case, rather more interested in gossip about the Smart girls.

281

'Well, Fatso's due to make this big speech on their radio, it bein' the 10th anniversary of 'itler puttin' 'imself in charge. It was just about the time we was all larkin' abaat at that posh 'otel – Fatso's abaat to start, when over'ead comes our bombers and bomp– and the kibosh is put on *that* performance.'

'Well – not the complete kibosh,' added Doomandgloom sagely. ''e did speak later on and 'ad the bloomin' cheek to say this – listen; "England never appeared on the scene in Europe to shed her own blood."'

'I reckon 'es taken leave of 'is senses,' said Dai.

'Hardly the time for celebration in Berlin,' said Sid. 'Now the Russians have come up trumps. That was some mistake Hitler made – going all out for Stalingrad. They're saying he's lost a million men and … well I'm blowed, what you doing here, brother?'

'I just came in to see how you all were – I've got a few days leave.'

Tom Tittler, talk, dark and uneasy, stood there in his uniform, shifting from foot to foot.

'I saw Mog's photo in the *Examiner*. She looks well.'

'Yes, mate. She's well.' Sid was rather flummoxed. 'And how's your Mother?'

Mrs Tittler's health was always a fruitful (and safe) topic of conversation.

'She's suffering a good deal with boils I'm afraid and she's crippled with arthritis. How's Mrs Smart – and Aunty?'

'Bearing up, bearing up.'

'You've settled in at your new home by now, I imagine.'

'Oh yes, we're quite settled.'

'Good news from Russia isn't it?'

'Indeed it is.'

'And Ooly – how's marriage suiting her?'

'Well – we've got our little Todge now. She'll be three in May. I suppose she was only a titch when you came to see us that time. You should see her now – and hear her. She never stops chattering away ...'

'Well – remember me to Mrs S and the others. I'd better be off.'

'Yes – good to see you, brother. My best regards to your mother.'

Poor Old Tom.

That evening, rehearsing the day's events at home, as was his wont, Sid was undecided as to whether or not he should mention his unexpected visitor; he thought it might set Lil off. Matters were taken out of his hands by Ed:

'That Tom cum into the shop today – that soldier who was sweet on Mog before she went away. Well 'e weren't a soldier then, of course, but 'e is naah.'

'Why didn't you say nuffin, Sid?' Lil was hopping mad.

Sid looked pained; 'Well, I ... er ...'

'Come on – what's 'e bin up to, is 'e wounded or sommat? Did you ask 'im over – I'd love to see 'im agin – such a nice boy and with that old cow of a muvver.'

'He seemed all right – he was on leave – I didn't ask him much, to be honest. If was all a bit difficult, with him being so fond of Mog and her married now.'

'What d'you mean "difficult"? Friends is friends, Sid Smart and you don't just push them orf because you find it difficult.'

'Come on now, mate. Mog wouldn't like it if she knew we had been entertaining her old beau.'

'Sid's right,' said Dot. 'It wouldn't be proper for Tom Tittler to come here. We don't want to upset the Tillingham galleon now, do we?' She giggled.

'Poor Old Tom's loomed up again, has he?' said Ooly, coming into the kitchen.

'Yeah, and your dad won't be doin' with 'im. I consider it's a rotten shame, 'e was like a son to me. The nearest I'll ever get to avin' a boy of my own.'

'What about Johnny?' Ooly asked bitterly.

'Well – yeah – Johnny's my proper son-in-law, but well 'es …'

'He's what?'

'Well – 'e keeps to 'imself, like. Tom used to come into my kitchen and we'd 'ave a bit of a larf together.'

'When Johnny tried to come into the kitchen to help with the Christmas dinner last year, you saw him off.'

'Oh, Ool – you know what I mean. Anyway, Johnny's got his own mum – you should know – you see enough of 'er!'

With that final rejoinder she got out the cheese and pickled onions for supper and firmly announced that she was disgusted with the lot of them, and that there was not enough cheese to go round so they would have to make do with brawn she'd made from a pig's head (supplied by Billy).

Chapter 23:
March 1943

February drizzled on into March – the Paddington Party seemed a long-ago dream. The wind of victory was blowing hard now. Russia, the ally, was triumphant; Italy, now christened the "soft underbelly of the axis", its colonies all but gone, shattered by aerial bombardment and losses on the eastern front, "trembled before the impact of the coming blow".' The RAF began its rain of terror over Germany.

But all was far from well at home. As the comradeship of war was receding, the old cracks reappeared. Sir Stafford Cripps warned: "The days of defeat, the compulsion of war once removed, the old differences between classes or sections of the community have come back to destroy the unity and purpose of the people."

In the East End all was very far from well.

On early closing day, Thursday the 4th of March, the traders of Old Ford were setting about their morning tasks as black news from Bethnal Green fluttered towards them like a satanic crow. It darted among the shops, pubs and houses in Green Street, along to Roman Road, settling on the Emporium just as Sid and Ed were sitting down on their orange boxes for elevenses.

It was Billy who was the first bearer of the tidings. Sid had never seen his brother like that before – he seemed to have shrunk.

'Not opening up today, mate?'

'I shut up shop after I heard what had happened.' He sat down on the rickety chair by the counter and put his head in his hands.

'What's up? What's happened?'

'Hundreds killed in the shelter at the tube. Hundreds. One of my regulars, name of Elsie Bartholomew, lost her little boy, Charlie – six he was – down there in the shelter with his Nan.

They're saying it was a direct hit – revenge for our raid on Berlin on Monday. It was strange, though, when I passed by there was no sign of anything – just a couple of bobbies standing outside the entrance.'

Mrs Gum came in from next door:

'Oh Sid, Mr Smart – 'ave you 'eard what's 'appened? Some bloke just cum into the shop for some flowers for 'is wife – she's in 'ospital – was in the shelter at Bethnal Green last night. Trapped for hours they were – masses of kiddies killed and maimed, thousands dead – they're sayin'.'

Dougie and Ooly met outside the London at noon. It was her birthday and they had planned an afternoon at Tredegar Square.

'Darling, I can't make it. We've got a panic on.'

'What's happened?'

'Well, we've all been told to keep quiet about it, but there was a fearful calamity at Bethnal Green last night.'

'A bomb?'

'Well... no ...'

'Well, what?'

'Keep this to yourself, Ooly – there was a some sort of a panic crush down the stairs of the tube shelter and numbers of people lost their lives and were injured. Nearly a hundred children, I gather.'

'Oh my God. Oh my God. Will it never end! Why is it to be kept secret?'

'If it's negligence on the part of the wardens, or in any way the fault of the authorities just imagine the effect on morale: Bethnal Green Council kills hundreds of innocent inhabitants; "it wasn't Jerry that took my family – it was the council". There's talk of the stairs not being

286

properly lit.'

'Why did the siren go off if there was no raid?'

'Lord knows. Look – I must go … perhaps we could do something next week – my cousins off for a couple of days at a conference and I've got a few days owing to me.'

As the day progressed, all around, the usual clatter was stilled: no errand boy whistled; no coster called out his wares. Despair gave way to anger as people started gathering in and around St John on Bethnal Green, demanding to know what had happened. Rumours were scurrying like mice, swooping like house martins: ''ave you 'eard …? it was a gas leak, a fascist plot, a gas attack; all down to the ruddy Yids panicking; there was no proper light – the bulb was smashed, the light was too dim, no hand rail – wardens not doin' their bloody job. I blame to council. Old So-and-so's lost his whole family – he's genna sue. And why do we 'ave to keep mum – that's what I'd like to knows? Kiddies are not turnin' up at school and no one knows who's dead and who's alive. If 'undreds had copped it in Kensington tube there'd 'ave bin be some to-do. Don't matter abaat us poor sods of East Enders as 'ave born the brunt of this bleedin' war.'

Hundreds packed into the small coroner's court for the inquest on the following day. They stood on the stairs and queued along the road; the mood was angry – a scapegoat must be found – the Jews would do – they always did. Witnesses were examined in two and threes, simply stating the identity of the corpses, one by one.

The papers announced that 178 people had been killed, a woman with a baby and a parcel had stumbled and fallen down the steps, followed by an old man. There were various eye witness reports. There had been no bomb and there was, or so it said, no panic.

Fanny Bastaple disagreed; she told an eager audience in the Emporium:

'We was 'avin' a bit of a night of it at the Salmon and Ball. Raand

287

abaat eight orf goes the siren and we all proceeds over to the shelter in the chube station – nice and orderly like. We was all expectin' Jerry to come and get his own back after what our lads 'ave been droppin' on Berlin – just like they did after Lubeck. Anyway – I was just waitin' for my 'Arry at the entrance – he'd gorn orf onto the allotments on the Green to 'ave a slash – then –blimey – there's this great noise like bombs whistlin', searchlights are wheelin' araand and daahn the shelter steps rush a whole load of passengers orf a couple of number eights what 'ave just arrived. They're all in a blind panic – shoutin' "There's bombs! There's bombs!" They're pushin' and shovin' and shoutin' – it was a right stampede – I turn raand and I says to 'Arry we're not goin' in there. Next thing there's ambulances – scores of 'em, hundreds of coppers, wardens, home guard – terrible screams, terrible screams – I shall never forget them screams. Turns aat there's hundreds of poor buggers all squashed up in a great pile – all crushed to death – kiddies an' all, masses of dead kiddies.'

Bert Gum had some more information:

'Bloody cock-up it was – I've 'eard they was practicing with the new rocket guns in Vicky Park, sounded like bombs and they 'ad the search lights out – makin' us think there was a raid. Old Dick Corbett the boxer copped it – and some of the lads from the boxing club.'

'I suppose we'd better not tell Pan abaat them terrible goin's-on at Bethnal Green.'

Lil and Sid were writing their Sunday evening letter. 'It'll set orf 'er boils what wiv 'er claustrophobia and 'er nerves.'

'Oh no, mate.' Replied Sid. 'Anyway we've all been told to keep it under wraps.'

'Bugger that. I dare say she might 'ave seen something in the papers.'

'But – it doesn't say where it was.'

'Well then – better keep schtum.'

Dad from the abode of love.

Dear Pan,

Dad penning a few words prior to mum adding a little to this epistle. This week with us as been about as usual – much to be thankful for. Lots of people I know are having boils, Mr Spoon included. He is having inoculation same as you've had. Old Bert Gum in Old Ford also. Maureen has had her baby, a boy. Ooly's going over to Chigwell tomorrow for a couple of days to help out. Mum has promised to look after our Todge. She didn't like the thought of leaving her, but I'm sure she'll be very good indeed.

All love to you both. God Bless You. Dad.

Two whole days and two whole nights. It would be the longest they had ever had together. It was a bit of a risk, confiding in Maureen, but she had taken enough advantage of Nell. Her trusted old friend was not as sympathetic as she might have hoped. Ooly rang her from a phone box:

'Not that toff that did the dirty on you before the war! You must be out of your mind. Are you really expecting something to come of it? Just because Mog …'

'It's nothing to do with Mog, absolutely nothing, and I expect nothing.' Ooly was livid, but needed Maureen's cooperation.

'Your dad and mum would go spare!'

'You're hardly in a position to judge me on that score, Mrs Goldberg.'

'Oh, Ooly, for heaven's sake – of course I'll cover for you – I'll have to let Mossy in on it. We don't have secrets. Now, don't go getting yourself hurt again. What excuses has yer man got for what happened before?'

'His parents.'

'What d'you mean?'

'Well that Brackenthorpe woman – I've told you about her – she'd had here eye on him for years and when she saw that Dougie and I were well …'

'In love. Go on.'

'She told the Mitchell parents that I was East End trash, after his money, but worse than that, I was a Jewess.'

'But you're not.'

'Actually, I'm often taken for one – this great hooter, brown eyes, East End – you know.'

'Well my Mossy hasn't got a big nose, neither have any of his family.'

'But you know what funny ideas people have got – Fagin, Shylock – all that.'

'I suppose. But it's no big deal, is it?'

'No big deal! Not what your mum and dad thought. Not what Hitler, Musso and the rest think!'

'My parents weren't against my marriage on anti-Semitic grounds. They just wanted me to hitch up with a good Catholic boy.'

'And Dougie's parents wanted him to hitch up with a good Gentile girl.'

'I doubt if they would have objected to a Rothschild.'

'They are fascists, you know.'

'So his awful, Nazi parents told him to back off – and he just did?'

'They're terrible bullies, apparently, – well his mother is – and he had a sort of breakdown.'

'Surely he could have written or something?'

'He swears he did – but I never got any letters.'

'Well – what a despicable wimp! If Mossy and I had given in to our folks, there would be no adorable little Aaron Patrick here in my arms. When are you really going to come over to Chigwell? I'm dying for Todge to see him.'

'I'll come the week after next, I promise.'

'You better had. Now you haven't mentioned poor old Johnny or his mum that you're so fond of. Wish I could get on that well, or at all, with Edie Goldberg.'

'Mm.'

'Well?'

'No. I haven't said anything about Johnny or Nell.'

'OK, OK.'

The deal was struck.

With Dougie's cousin out of the way and the housekeeper gone off to stay with her sick mum, with little likelihood of returning, they would have the house to themselves. Ooly felt rather nervous, if she was honest, but heady with excitement.

He met her at the station, looking drawn and exhausted from a night's unremitting attendance on the injured and dying.

After frenetic almost angry love making he lay motionless, smoking and staring at the ceiling.

'Shall we go out somewhere tonight?' suggested Ooly. 'A flic perhaps? Or would you rather we stayed here and cosy up to the wireless? I could try my hand at some carrot concoction – though cooking is hardly my forte.'

'Oh, darling – I'm all in –' and light entertainment hardly seems the thing with all those poor little bodies, blue with asphyxiation piled up nearly on our doorstep.

Would you like a noggin?'

He took a bottle out from his bedside cabinet.

'Not for me, thanks.'

Poor Ooly – it was not that she was being insensitive, suggesting a film – quite the reverse. Of all the Smart clan she was the one perhaps least able to bear the sorrows of the world, to confront them face on.

Dougie took a slug or two and drifted off into a fitful slumber.

Hours passed. The clock ticked the morning into afternoon. He was snoring and starting by turns. Ooly wandered around the room, fingering the silver backed hair brushes on the dressing table, the box of studs and cuff links; she opened the wardrobe and stroked the

291

garments, lovingly, lifted his pullover from the chair and sniffed it. On the top of the tallboy she noticed a framed photograph of his mother and a man she took to be his father; she shuddered, remembering the Humiliation, vividly. Behind it were some others, a wedding photo caught her eye; there was a vast group of people – blimey – there was even the old King with Queen Mary! She recognised a very young Dougie tucked between his parents, looking shy and uncomfortable in a tail coat. The bride was spectacular, but, Ooly noted with satisfaction, her sheaf of lilies was not nearly so large as her own wedding bouquet had been. What a gorgeous handsome groom! She took it down to have a closer look. He looked familiar – oh my God – it couldn't be –but – yes – it was that awful Mosley man!

She was half inclined to wake Dougie and ask him about it, but he seemed quite peaceful now and, pocketing a tiny snap of him, she decided to leave it and have a look around the house. The top floor housed three smallish bedrooms, one of which had the appearance of having been recently abandoned – must be the housekeeper's room. On the floor beneath Dougie's bedroom was a large double room, with folding doors dividing it, and long sash windows at either end. Books and papers littered the tables and chairs, ash trays overflowed, the carpet was muddied in colour and threadbare, the two sofas looked rickety and saggy. An ornate china clock on the marble mantelpiece struck five, with a tinkley voice; time for Todge's tea. Ooly felt sick. She closed the door and made her way down the staircase and looked for a kitchen. At least she could make something for Dougie to eat.

The kitchen, which was in the basement, was in some disarray, with piles of washing up in the sink and a litter of burnt saucepans, but she was able to locate some dried egg, potatoes and flour. Underneath a mesh cover in the pantry, on a tin plate, was a small hard, reddish lump. She nicked a tiny bit off and tasted it – it was bacon. OK – she had seen mum and Aunty put a reasonable egg and bacon pie together, using potato pastry. She would have a go.

After a struggle with a sticky mess and a fight with the recalcitrant ancient Kitchener stove, she left the pie to cook while she took a peep into the rooms on the ground floor. At the back, overlooking the long, bedraggled garden with the rusty remains of a rose arbour, was what she took to be the cousin's room; obviously another medical man occupied it – there was a skeleton sprawled on top of the wardrobe and a stethoscope thrown over a chair. The room at the front was lined with books and there was a grand piano at the window overlooking the square. It was just like the room where she had her music lessons – it seemed so long ago now. She sat on the stool and started playing Brahms' lullaby – ever so softly, and singing as she did to Todge. 'What on earth am I doing here?' As the thought came Dougie appeared at the door, in a grey silk dressing gown, his black hair flopping over his aristocratic brow.

'I was frightened you'd gone. Don't leave me yet, Ooly. I need you so much.'

He put his arms round her – the pie was burnt to cinders (probably just as well); Mosley was forgotten and so, I regret to say was Todge.

Blackout was at nine. All in the March evening, soft, damp and as delightful as everything is to those in the spring of passion, Ooly, having reapplied her lipstick, set out for the fish and chip shop, nursing a reverie along the way – Todge's push chair standing in the hall, herself in a gown of crimson shantung at the piano, Dougie, darling Dougie, pouring cocktails for their guests and the maid dispensing lobster patties. One day perhaps the grand old square would be restored, its garden graced with lilac and azaleas, its lawn trimmed. One day she would post her Christmas cards into that pillar box on the corner – it would be capped with snow, while a ten foot spruce glittered in her grand drawing room. How mum would beam with pride when the family all came for Christmas dinner, and how she would love Dougie.

When she got back to the house and tapped lightly with the brass knocker, Dougie, opened the door immediately; his eyes were popping

293

out of his head – there was someone standing just behind him.

'Th-th-this is Lily B-b-bowyer. She's applied for the job as h-h-housekeeper. May I introduce my cousin, Archie.'

'Wow! I say! Good show. Mind if we call you Jessie – our housekeepers are always called Jessie. Not that you resemble your predecessors in any way, I hasten to add.'

Ooly was struck dumb.

Archie took his eyes off her, just for a second or two, to address Dougie:

'Uncle Mitch and the Hawk are back in Blighty – they're coming over to visit tomorrow. We'd better get the place a bit ship-shape. Can you start straight away, Miss B?'

'I don't see why not,' said Ooly, catching Dougie's eye. ' Dr Mitchell has shown me my accommodation. It will suit me quite well, but I should make it clear that I am not prepared to clean, clear out the hearth, lay the fire, wash up or do any of the duties normally undertaken by a house or scullery maid. I will give you a 24 hour trial. Now – in the absence of any other servants I suggest you two gentlemen set to work, as we appear to have an emergency on our hands. Dr Mitchell can clean, sweep, dust and polish the public rooms, set the fires for tomorrow and Dr ?'

'Mosley.'

'Dr Mosley can change the bedding, turn the mattresses, clean the kitchen and offices. In the meantime I shall settle in, decide on the menus for tomorrow and take a bath. I take it there is hot water? At midnight I will inspect the work you have done. Here, gentlemen, is your supper – I'm not sure if it's whale meat or barracuda.'

She thrust the vinegary newspaper parcel into Dougie's hands and swept up the stairs.

'Struth, Doug, where on earth did you find her? I'm not sure I'm going to be able to cope with a glamour puss ordering us around. And who's going to do the heavy stuff if she's not prepared to? Why isn't she doing war work, anyway?'

'I th-think she's got a t-toddler.'

'Is there a Mr Bowyer – I suppose not? No better than she ought to be, I dare say. She's not bringing her bastard here!'

'I th-think there's a grandmother. But I shouldn't worry – she's never going to take us on. You heard what she said about 24 hours probation!'

'Well – if we don't do what we've been told to do she'll certainly bugger off. But, on the other hand, it's well nigh impossible to get anyone at all to do domestic work at the moment, perhaps we had better try and hang on to her.'

'Whatever happens we've got to get the place straight before Pater and the Hawk put in an appearance, so we might as well make a start.'

'I've never changed a bed in my life – let alone turned a mattress – whatever that means.'

As the clock struck twelve, Ooly, attired in an ivory silk and satin peignoir, trimmed with lace, descended and declared the work satisfactory. She then retired to the housekeeper's room and locked the door.

Soon enough came a little tap and a whispered, 'Ooly c-c-can I come in?'

'She opened the door a crack and hissed at him, 'No you can't.'

'Ooly, come on. Let me in.'

'If I'm going to be passed off to your wretched fascist family as a housekeeper that's what I shall be – at least till I go home tomorrow. Last time it was a hired musician; this time a servant.'

'D-d-darling – it was the first thing that came into my head when Archie turned up out of the blue like that. You are a married woman now, remember. If the coz blabbed then all hell would be let loose. I must say you were absolutely sp-splendid!'

'And what's this Mosley business? I see you attended that monster's wedding – and your cousin, Dr Mosley?'

'The Hawk's remotely related to Oswald, that's all.'

'Can't be that remote if you went to his wedding.'

'Oh – my mother's always hanging round the upper echelons of the family. At least we didn't join Hitler and Goebbels at Oswald's second wedding. Come on, Ooly – you know perfectly well I have absolutely no tr-tr-truck with fascism and all its ghastly works. Neither does old Archie – he's considered changing his name, poor blighter. Even the Pater has changed horses. Anyway – I recall you telling me your uncle Billy had blackshirt sympathies.'

'That's different – and hasn't any more, not since Jerry destroyed his livery company's hall.'

'Ooly, open the door – you look so delicious in that lacy thing – you can't banish me for the only night we've got together!'

'You've been asleep most of the day.'

'I know. I'm hopeless …'

The door was opened and Dr Mitchell did an exaggerated goose-step across the room and collapsed, laughing, into the housekeeper's narrow bed:

'Come on, Jessie, I always did fancy a bit of rough trade.'

'You are a sod!'

They laughed and cried, tumbled and cuddled until the morning light squeezed through the blackout curtains and reminded them that there was a cruel, bitter world out there where the march of mourners moved slowly along Bow Road, following coffin after coffin into the cemetery nearby.

Ooly left early.

'Is she coming back?' asked Archie doubtfully.

'Lord knows,' replied his cousin sadly, 'I think she was expecting something rather different.'

Ooly queued up for a bus which arrived after a few moments, crammed full of girls off to work in the factories and at the docks, chattering away, smoking and swapping stories about the tube disaster.

'My mum and aunty were down there in the main bit of the shelter, be'ind that great metal door – they never knew anyfing abaat what 'appened at the entrance until the all-clear let them aat and by then all the bodies were gorn.'

'Our neighbour's a warden. 'E saw the corpses – all purple and blue, big and small, laid out in rows along the pavement then stashed onto carts and lorries. And word down from 'on 'igh that no one's to breave a word – not a bleedin' word, abaat what they've seen.'

'My dad's like a madman – 'es no good wivout my mum, 'e got the shell shock in the first lot. Now she's copped it daan in that ruddy shelter, Gawd knows who's genna get 'is porridge and wipe 'is bum, I've got my work to do. 'E says 'es goin' to sue the council. 'E says that if there 'ad bin a handrail down the middle of them steps it would never 'ave 'appened. Sue – he can't even piss straight into 'is pot!'

'My nan was in it – Gawd rest 'er. She were a luverly nan – we always 'ad our tea at 'ers – mum was out at business, if you know what I mean. Nan 'ad my little bruvver wiv 'er, too. We're buryin' them dinner time – my boss said I could take the day orf but I can put in a couple of hours – we 'ave to do our bit, don't we?'

'What is my contribution to the war effort?' thought Ooly. 'What is my contribution towards anything.' Adultery was not a reserved occupation.

On the 11th March the press reported that there would be an enquiry into the shelter disaster. Now there would be some answers. Eighty witnesses were called; it seemed to be a thorough affair, but when all was accomplished, the powers that be decided the findings of the report should be kept secret. A short statement simply announced that no one had been negligent, there was no fascist plot and it was not the fault of

297

the Jews.

Vi Kerridge, along with all Sid's customers and practically the whole seething boroughs of Poplar and Bethnal Green was up in arms.

'Bleedin' disgustin. Why are we all gagged.? Why aren't they genna tell us what 'appened? National security, my arse. Bloody fishy if you ask me. Would 'ave been a different case if all them poor perishers were in some place up west, you can be sure of that. And you would 'ave thought the King or Winnie might 'ave come down 'ere to offer their condolences.'

Over at Westminster, Sir Percy Harris Liberal MP for Bethnal Green South West had words for Herbert Morrison, the Home Secretary:

"Does the Right Honourable Gentleman realise what deep resentment will be felt by the hundreds of relatives of the persons who were victims of this unfortunate disaster? Does he realise the bad effect there will be on the morale of the people if a suspicion arises that he wants to conceal the facts that have been stated to the magistrate who made the inquiry?"

Sid did his best as self-appointed Government Spokesman for Roman Road, Keeper of Winnie's Conscience for Old Ford, Morale Booster in Chief – but this time it was very hard – all those kiddies. He pinned up an extract from Psalm 25 on the door of the Emporium:

"Turn thee unto me, and have mercy upon me; for I am desolate and afflicted.

The troubles of my heart are enlarged: O bring thou me out of my distresses."

Elsie Bartholomew, continued to go to the school gate every afternoon, regular as clockwork, to meet her little Charlie.

'The other mothers are very kind,' Billy told Sid.

Chapter 24:
March to June 1943

When Ooly got back to Chestnut Avenue Lil and Dot were turning out the kitchen cupboards, with Todge's assistance.

'Has she been all right?'

'We've 'ad a fine time,' said Lil. 'There was no need for you to come back early, you know. I thought you were genna be away till tomorrow?'

'Edie Goldberg suddenly announced that she was coming for an inaugural visit, would you believe? – so I thought I'd make myself scarce before she noticed the sacred heart over the kitchen sink and all hell broke loose.'

What a tangled web we weave, especially if we have a lively imagination.

Dot was mildly suspicious: 'What brought Edie round? I thought the rift in that family would be there for all time.'

'A grandson, I suppose – a boy. What Jewish mum could resist?'

'And how is Maureen coping? Of course she always was quite a domestic body – I suppose she might make a natural mother, unlike some people who find it hard to adjust.' Dot smiled to herself and picked up her knitting.

'Maureen's really soppy about the baby. I find it rather sickening. I'll take Todge next time I go – I've promised to visit again soon.'

'There's no need for that,' said her mother quickly. 'She's quite 'appy ere wiv us, in't you, mate?'

Ooly seized her daughter : 'Come on, Todge, let's go and feed the ducks up on the Green – you can bring your pram with Puddy Tat in it.'

Todge expressed her desire to stay with her Nan in no uncertain terms and Ooly said, in that case, she would go and change the library books.

'We haven't finished ours yet, duck.'

'Oh, I'll make a start on the dinner, then.'

'Mum's got a stew on.'

'For goodness sake!' muttered Ooly and she flung out of the kitchen.

Lil was perplexed: 'She's in a funny mood. Missin' Johnny, may be.' She called out:

'Ooly, mate – Johnny rang. 'e's got a few days' leave coming up.'

'When?'

'I'm not sure. 'E's talking about just the two of you going off for a couple of nights at some 'otel or other in a few weeks. Bit funny, I thought.'

'Oh.'

So one sunny Sunday – it was the warmest spring for 50 years – they set off on Johnny's surprise spree. A friend of his had lent him a car, quite a smart one, and the RAF (unwittingly) supplied a modicum of petrol. As they sped through Epping Forest, banks of daffodils were grinning along the way. Cheer up, Ooly.

'Where are we going? I hope it's not too far away!'

'Only about a quarter of an hour's drive. In no time at all we'll be there, downing some wallop in front of a log fire.'

'In this weather! Better to be out in the garden.'

'OK – sitting under the shade of an old oak tree, then.'

'Will there be a phone? – I wouldn't like to be out of contact for too long.'

'Of course there'll be a damned phone – we're only going to be there for two nights and it's only a hop and a skip away from Chestnut

Avenue, in any case. You were happy enough to leave the nipper to gallivant off to Maureen's.'

Ooly examined the pearly buttons on her fine kid gloves and remarked on the daffodils.

'Here we are. Impressive joint!'

The massive chimneys and towering gables of a grand old coaching inn rose before them; 'The King's Head, Chigwell.'

Chigwell. Oh God.

'The King's Head – how wonderful.'

'You know it? Been here with Maureen and Mossy, I suppose?'

'Oh, no. Dad used to bring us here on some of our Sunday outings on his push bike. It's called the Maypole in one of Dickens's books – can't remember which one. Dad was always quoting something about it being "an old inn with more gable ends than a lazy man would care to count on a sunny day".'

'You mean Holy Joe actually took you girls into a pub?'

'No, don't be daft. We just looked at it from the outside.'

'Well – now we're going inside.'

A four poster hung with heavy curtains, a bar to warm the human breast (as Dickens said of another hostelry), pewter mugs with "beaded bubbles winking at the brim", food with a pre-war country taste – what a waste. Such a game pie! Johnny tucked in with a will. Ooly picked at hers.

'What's up, Missus. Not hungry?'

'Not very.'

'What shall we do this afternoon? A nap, perhaps, and then a stroll in the forest? I feel like a good health-giving walk.'

'If you like.'

'The landlord says the bluebells are really early this year.'

'OK.'

The "nap" was not a success. After some sulky tea downstairs, in the not-unwelcome company of two jolly WAAFs, they set off for their walk.

'You knew those girls?'

'Yes, slightly – we're being taken over by WAAFs these days – I must admit, they're a terrific crew. We've got a base here in Chigwell.'

'What – balloons?'

'Yes.'

'You never said.'

'I didn't think you would be interested.'

She wasn't.

'Todge loves bluebells. She loves all flowers actually, you should have seen her stroking the first snowdrops when they appeared. The only flowers she doesn't like are pansies; she says they look like cross little witches peeping out.'

'What a canny kid. But I thought she liked Pan.'

'She does. I don't think she knows that her name's really Pansy. Oh, look, Johnny – they are quite breath-taking:

"…Like a skylit water stood

The bluebells in the azured wood".'

'What's that?'

'Houseman, I think. It was one of Baggy's favourites.'

'Who?'

'You know – Miss Bagwell, our art mistress at Skoriers. I must have told you about her.'

'Oh, her. What would you like to do tomorrow? We could drive around a bit – might as well make the most of my shiny chum and what petrol I've managed to procure.'

'Why not? And this evening? We passed a cinema showing the Great Waltz – I've seen it before, of course – but it's a lovely flic, wonderful music – its all about Strauss and the Blue Danube – so romantic – old Vienna.'

'Oh – I thought we might just stay in, after dinner, and … catch up. That Viennese stuff is not really up my street.'

'I wouldn't have had you down as a bluebell man either.'

Ooly, determined to avoid any more catching up than was strictly necessary, decided on the green chartreuse option; she had noticed a bottle of it behind the bar. It was a favourite of Johnny's. Long before any catching up was in play, he was out for the count.

The following morning he had a bad head and a mood to match.

Over scrambled egg (dried,) he asked: 'Where is the ruddy Goldberg residence?'

'I can't quite remember.'

'You can't remember. You really are hopeless, Missus ...'

'Maureen met me at the station and we were so busy chatting I didn't notice where we were going.'

'I suppose it's rather grand – Mossy's done very well for himself. The first thing a chap wants when he gets his uniform is a photo for his mother or his wife. Ozzies and Canadians are especially keen to have photos to send home. Why hasn't he been called up?'

'I really don't know,' replied Ooly, and, anxious to get off the subject of the Goldbergs, asked brightly, 'So – where are we off to today? I wouldn't mind having a look at ...'

She stopped, startled – what should she see out of the window but a magnificent perambulator, springing along on enormous shiny wheels. Pushing it with elegant pride was Maureen – little Maureen O'Brien from Bow, togged up to the nines.

'What ever are you staring at – oh it's your chum.' Johnny knocked on the window and called out to her. She manoeuvred the carriage, with some difficulty, through the entrance and into the dining room.

'Well, good gracious me – what are you two doing here? Meet Aaron Patrick, isn't he gorgeous – we call him AP. Would you like to hold him, Ooly?'

'Well – I've held him before, *haven't* I, Maureen ?'

'Oh ... oh ... yes ... of course you have. Well. How is everyone? Fancy you two slipping away on your own. How are your balloons,

303

Johnny? Where's Todge? With your mum, I suppose. What a glorious day – why don't you come over this evening? You will still be here, I suppose. Mossy would love to see you – and I'm dying to show you round our house. The lounge is like a ball room and we've got five bedrooms and you ought to see the kitchen! When I think of mum's scruffy old scullery in Bow I can hardly believe it.'

'Ooly's already seen it,' said Johnny.

Ooly dug her heel into Maureen's foot, hard.

'Oh, yes, but you haven't, Johnny.'

'It would be lovely, Maureen, but we're going home this afternoon, *aren't we* Johnny?'

'You could call in for a cuppa, after AP's three o'clock feed. Mossy won't be back, of course, but you could see the house – er – er, Johnny. We're only a few minutes away – you remember, Ooly, The Bower, in Manor Road, detached, big monkey puzzle tree at the front, near the golf course.'

Any further objections might seem rude, or suspicious, so it was agreed.

'Christ Almighty!' Johnny growled in the privacy of their room. 'Can't we be left alone for more than two seconds? Detached, monkey puzzle tree, golf course – we've got our own perfectly good semi – if I'd taken to snapping clots of servicemen and charging them what Mossy charges, we could have been detached.'

"The Bower" was all it promised to be.

'Struth,' whispered Johnny, 'Kitchen looks like a bedroom full of fitted wardrobes.'

There was no sacred heart over the sink, but, in pride of place on the endless, sleek sideboard in the vast panelled dining room (with its French windows overlooking the golf course) was a menorah.

Unexpectedly, Mossy turned up.

''Allo, 'allo,' he called from the hall, 'I'm 'ome early – picked up 12 luverly tins of salmon – no points. 'Ow's my lovely Colleen and my darlin' little boychick. Look, girl, I've managed to get you a lipstick! 'ope it's the right shade.'

Hugs and kisses. AP was seized from his fur lined cradle and squeezed half to death.

'And who 'ave we got 'ere? Ooly 'erself, good old Ooly, as luscious as ever, and 'er lawful wedded. Well, well, well. What a treat!'

'Johnny and Ooly are having a bit of a break at the King's Head. I wanted to show them the house – well, show it to Johnny that is – Ooly's seen it before, of course.' Maureen winked at her husband.

'Oh – yeah – so she 'as. So she 'as.'

'What d'you think of our gaff? All right init? Bit of a change from Selman Street, eh? 'ave you shown our guests the gold taps, Mo?'

'Very impressive,' said Johnny.

'Mossy – stop showing off and get everyone a drink.'

'Right oh, boss – shall we 'ave a snifter? What's your poison? I've got most things stashed away – contacts, yer know. Mo and I don't drink much – quack's warned me off it – me ticker, yer know – what's kept me out of the forces – but I like to 'ave a stock in for visitors.'

'Oh, no, thanks, we really must be off, Mossy.' Ooly was really scared now.

'Come on – just one little drinkie to warm the cockles.' And off he went and returned with some glasses:

'Waterford crystal – nothing like it. Irish whiskey do yer? Girls rather have sherry?' He settled himself in an outsized arm chair.

'Well – we're certainly dishin' it out to the Krauts now – Cologne, Essen, poundin' away at the Eyties, Rommel bein' kicked out of Tunisia. Whole show'll be over soon, wiv any luck.'

'What about the terrible thing in Bethnal Green?' said Maureen.

'Oy – yoy – yoy,' wailed Mossy. 'And they're blamin' it on us! As if we 'adn't got enough troubles. 6,000 poor blighters dyin' everyday in Poland, they're sayin'.

Nuffin' like a baby boy to cheer you up – when are you two genna

305

get yourselves a bruvver for old Todge?'

Johnny blew his nose: 'I think one nipper's quite enough for us – for the time being. When the war's over perhaps ...'

'How's Pan? 'aven't seen 'er since before the war. We 'ad such times together when we was kids – we shared spit for our slates at Malmesbury Road, yer know. And what about Lady Tillingham – that was a good do at Paddington. Who'd 'ave thought old Mog would land 'erself a nob. She always was a looker, of course, but, blimey – a baronet! Some 'ouse she's got, I s'pose?'

'None of us have been privileged to view it,' said Ooly. 'Neither have we been allowed to meet the baronet. Mum's really upset; so is dad, though he pretends not to be.'

'Well – when the war's over ... it'll all come right. We've got our family troubles 'ere, too – our mums, yer know. We miss our mums, don't we, girl? Still – come on, drink up – 'ere's to our AP and to Todge's little bruvver!' Wink, wink.

Johnny stood up: 'We really must get weaving. Good to see you.'

'When it's all over we must get together,' said Mossy. 'Your 'ouse in Buckhurst Hill is only a couple of miles from 'ere, after all. In the meantime if you're short of anything – well – yer know what I mean. Just let me know. 'Appy to oblige our mates.'

As the front door closed Maureen turned anxiously to her husband.

'Oh, crumbs. We've done it now. I'm sure he suspects. He's so quiet and ...'

'Sullen, I'd call it. No wonder she's 'avin' a fling Poor old Ooly – she used to be such a laugh.'

The Come-Latelys spent a quiet evening at the King's Head. There was some desultory catching up; they were going home tomorrow, Tuesday.

'Back to the fray,' announced Johnny, as he drew up outside number 29. 'How's mother? Dot said you usually see her on Tuesdays. I really should try and get up to Bow and say hallo before I go back.'

'Give her my love.'

'Any news of Derek?'

'She gets a letter now and again, but it doesn't say much, of course.'

'Well – I'll be off.'

'Aren't you coming in to see Todge?'

'She'll only shriek at me. I'll try and get a pass for her birthday. Good bye, missus. Chin up. It'll all be over soon.'

Dot was deep in ration books and shopping lists. Todge was eating bread and syrup. Lil was darning a sock.

''Allo, mate. 'Ave a good time?'

'Oh, yes.'

'Where's Johnny? Not coming in to say hallo.'

'No. He's got to get back.'

'No Daddy Johnny today then,' said Dot.

'No, Aunty, no Daddy Johnny today. Mum, I do wish you wouldn't give her so much syrup. Come and help me unpack, Todge. I've got something for you.'

She produced a bunch of rather sad looking bluebells.

'Say thank you to your mummy,' said Dot.

She did and went on munching away.

Ooly left the kitchen.

Lil put down her sock: ' She's got the 'ump agin.'

'Funny he didn't even bother to come in,' said Dot 'Perhaps they've had a falling out.'

'Never 'ad much of a fallin' in, if you ask me. I reckon she could do with sommat to occupy herself – stop 'er moonin' about all day long. The only time we get a smile out of 'er is when she's orf to see Nell. War work – that's what she needs.'

'I can't see her in turban and overall, serving in a canteen, making

307

spam sandwiches and doing fry ups for the lads.'

'But, Dot, mate, she could get on the jo and lead some sing songs.'

'I imagine she regards herself as being a cut above that sort of thing.'

'Come to that she could join ENSA – Lily Smart, the Fabulous Forces Favourite – put that Vera Lynn in 'er place. She'd go daahn a storm singin' "The White Cliffs of Dover".'

'Sid would never hear of her joining ENSA. The WVS do visits to old people. She'd be good at that – all the practice she's had with Nell.'

May came blustering in, blowing the blossom from the trees, and bringing with it reports of successes in north Africa and of "one of the most spectacular raids of the war", the busting of the great German dams and the flooding of Ruhr and its arms factories. Winnie said that it was like the Seven Years War, back in the eighteenth century, when every morning one had to get up early to enquire for victories in case of missing one.

When Ooly and Dougie went up west to see *Gone with the Wind*, London seemed to be *en fête*. American jeeps wheeled around and uniforms from all corners of the earth jostled together – some soldiers wore labels: Poland, Canada, USA. Souvenir sellers wove among the crowds and girls with platinum blond hair and bright lipstick offered their wares. Yanks paid well.

'Did you call in on your mother-in-law today?' asked Dougie, as they joined the queue at the Empire Leicester Square.

'No – I couldn't face it. She knows, you know.'

'What!'

'She knows something's going on.'

'How, for goodness sake? You didn't tell her, I assume.'

'She kind of guessed.'

'Isn't she livid?'

'No. She's sad. I sometimes think she likes me better than Johnny.'

'How extraordinary.'

'Oh, thank you …'

'D-d-darling, I didn't m-m-mean … Obviously you're adorable, but it is unusual for a woman to prefer her daughter-in-law to her son.'

'Mm. She doesn't like poor Norah.'

'No?'

'I suppose it's because she's Derek's wife and Derek's her blue-eyed boy, her favourite. He always was and now, what with him fighting in the thick of it – and Johnny just in balloons and not even far from home – a "ground wallah" they call it, don't they? He's never even been up in a plane, you see.'

Dougie smiled.

It was nearly a month before she went to visit Nell again.

'Come in, chick. I missed you the last few weeks. Something up?'

'No. Not really. I'm sorry I …'

'Never you mind. How long have you got today?'

'I should go at about twelve.'

'Mm. Well let's have some tea and you can tell me your news.'

'Yours first. How is Derek getting on?'

'I haven't heard for a while. Neither has Norah – mind you I'm not surprised at that – when she writes to him, he says, it's all about whether or not to have a sweet pea design on their china when they finally get their own place.'

'Well, I suppose it's something to look forward to, to take his mind off the daily horrors.'

'Yes. It is such a worry. How was your weekend with Johnny?'

'He seemed rather low. Nell, I do worry about the way he is with Todge. He doesn't seem very interested in her – it's got worse. It breaks my heart when I see other dads all over their little ones. You ought to see Mossy Goldberg with his baby!'

'Mm – in my opinion he'd get the top brick off the chimney for that child. You mustn't take too much notice of his manner – that's the way

309

he is. He might just be a bit jealous of her, of course.'

'Jealous of his own daughter!'

'It's not unusual you know, especially when wives are – well – don't show their feelings much, shall we say, for whatever reason.'

Ooly blushed.

'And – I don't know if I should say this, but your family are all for kiddies, aren't they?'

'Oh yes. They are.'

'I dare say he feels rather pushed out, what with one thing and another.'

'Poor Daddy Johnny, I suppose he does.'

'As to the other matter – I'm not saying a word. I'll just say this: I know Johnny's not an easy man, same as Jack, not the sort to make a girl feel special, if you see what I mean. I suppose I was always a bit chilly with him. But I can tell you he worships the ground you tread on.'

Ooly looked doubtful.

'Are you doing anything with your music these days – it would do you good.'

'I sang at Stoke Newington last Saturday and I'm booked for some accompanying over at Ilford quite soon.'

'They're crying out for pianists and singers at the Red Cross places you know.'

'They don't want my sort of stuff, Nell. I can't croon.'

'Anybody would be thrilled to listen to your lovely voice.'

As she walked over to Tredegar Square she shivered and her umbrella blew inside out as the wind veered round into the east.

Chapter 25:

June to September 1943

'Bloody weather. Call this summer?' June was a damply disappointing month, not least for the customers at the Emporium.

'Still – it cleared up for the Queen.' Ethel Jiggins was ecstatic: she had been among the small crowd of observers at the royal visit to the plots of the Bethnal Green Bombed Sites Allotment Association. 'She did look nice, all in soft lavendery shades, with one of them hats with a great feather curled round and the diamonds – you should have seen them sparkling in the sunlight.'

'Fanlight Bloody Fanny. No clothin' coupons for 'er,' said Vi Kerridge. 'You should 'ave 'eard 'er squeakin': It does not seem possible ... Whey peas are in bloom and everything looks sew lovely. Didn't look *sew* lovely last 3rd of March with all them bodies lyin' on the pavement. Where was she then, I'd like to know.'

'What was you doin' gawpin' at 'er, if you think she's such rubbish, Vi Kerridge,' said Bert Gum.

'I just 'appened to be passin.'

'I should coco.'

Ethel thought it advisable to change the subject:

'Poor Leslie Howard – shot down on his way here from Portugal. Did you see him as Ashley in Gone with the Wind? – what a gent. he was! When the Americans want the best for their flics they turn to us – no one has actors like we do.'

'They're sayin that the plane 'e was in was shot daan because Jerry thought Winnie was in it,' added Bert.

'Pity 'e wasn't if you ask me.' Vi was on a roll.

'I will not have that talk in my shop,' announced Sid firmly, as he came through from the back room, bearing a large paraffin lamp. He plonked it on the counter with pride:

'This, Mrs Jiggins, is the very best, a Number Eight Round Kosmos Burner, I've got just one left. It's a bit pricey, but gives out an excellent light and will last you for years, as long as you look after the wick.'

'That's German made, Sid. I wouldn't 'ave a Jerry lamp lightin' my aas – rather sit in the dark if the power goes off.' said Bert.

'Pre-war stock, mate.'

'It's a beautiful thing,' said Ethel stroking it.

'Solid brass, mate. Polishes up a treat. You'd best take some Brasso, too.'

'Spend your money on that and the Squanderbug'll[2] get yer!' cackled Vi, unimpressed by the expensive fascist lamp. But she had not yet finished her political tirade: 'Will and I reckon we'd be better orf without them royal leeches. Look at the Ruskies, good old Joe Stalin, 'es just an ordinary bloke, no fancy crowns for him and his lot. That's what its like over there – ordinary folk runnin' the country for ordinary folk. And we'd be in a fair old pickle without that Red Army. Stuff Alamein and Monty, it's Stalingrad what turned this war raand.'

Profits from the annual charity cricket match and dance at Tillingham Parva would, this year, inevitably, go to Mrs Churchill's Aid to Russia Fund. In the last week of June the temperature rose and brought steam rising from the damp pitch, as excitement mounted in the villages around. The day dawned; it was a peaseblossom, cobweb, of a summer day, a wild thyme and nodding violets day, with a heat haze hanging over the pavilion, blurring the outline of the cottages around the green

---

2 *Squanderbug: cartoon character used to urge people not to spend money on luxury items.*

and obscuring the face of the Tillingham Arms. Mog floated around in diaphanous pale mint green, organising the all-important tea. Edmund, glorious in his white flannels, greeted his team members with self-effacing charm; he would, as usual, be leading the batting for the home team with the stable boy taking his runs for him.

Pooty from the War Office was one of the first to arrive, mopping his brow: 'Wonderful day for it, Lady T. Can I carry anything for you?'

'Oh, no thanks. I've got a whole crew of helpers. Are you playing?'

'They've roped me into the Evercreech team – I'm not much use but with the war and everything – they're desperate I suppose.'

'Aren't the Canadians joining in?'

'Well – they've moved away from Charmy Down, and the squadron is off in North Africa, I think, but that chap we met at your Christmas dinner party is coming – sick leave. I think he was shot down – he's OK now and off to the fray again soon. I must say you look terrific in that floaty thing.'

'D'you like my hat?'

She took up a wide straw hat and fixed it with a long pin, pulling the brim down fetchingly over her beautifully arched brows.

'It's a cracker, Lady T. May I book you for the first dance – that is if I can still move my creaking limbs after my efforts on behalf of Evercreech?'

Edmund came over with the Bronzed God from the fateful Christmas dinner table. He had a very becoming scar down one side of his handsome face.

'Pooty, old cheappe. Splendid show! I've got to make a fool of myself out on the pitch, as usual – still, needs must. You remember Jake Campbell. He was with us at Christmas in '41? One of our stalwart defenders from Canada. Been doing great things in the Desert. Darling, you remember Jake?'

'Oh yes,' said Mog. 'Delighted to see you again, Flight Lieutenant. Do you bat or bowl?'

'Anything that's required of me, ma'am, anything at all for the honour of the house of Tillingham and for the beautiful Lady of the Manor.'

'You're not batting for the other side then?'

'Gee, no, ma'am, whatever gave you that idea?'

'Oh – nothing, nothing at all. I look forward to watching you all in action. Now I must get back to my ladies.'

'I guess you will be at this evening's affair ? I would be honoured if you would allow me a dance, or two?'

Edmund gave a creditable performance, swiping away, and rendering the stable boy quite breathless. The day drifted lazily on – the soft thud of leather on willow, discreet showers of applause, strawberries and scones for tea. Only the occasional whine of a plane in the cloudless sky disturbed that English idyll.

Bella, in a cotton frock, sat in a deck chair next to the rector. 'What d'you think of the Russians, Basil? The whole world seems to have gone mad for them – it only seems two blinks ago when we were regarding them as the devil incarnate – you should have heard pa on the subject of the Bogey of Bolshevism! And now – what about this wretched sword?'

'Russo mania can't last, me dear – this – oh well done, sir, well done indeed (old Bertie Portman had hit a six) – You were saying?'

'The sword – the Sword of Stalingrad, ordered by the King, to be presented to the people of Stalingrad. Apparently it's going on a grand tour of the country, ending up with a sort of lying in state at Westminster Abbey – before its given to them. Seems rather bizarre to me as they were in cahoots with Jerry only a couple of years ago.

'Indeed, indeed. Godless animals who massacred their royal family – purges, labour camps, unimagined horrors. God help Europe if they get to Berlin before we do, which seems more than likely at present.'

'But, on the other hand,' said Bella. 'They are winning the war for us, no doubt about that. A bit of fancy steel is a small price to pay, I

314

suppose – rather cheaper in terms of cash and lives than a western front.'

'Well – things are building up in the Med. or the "soft underbelly of the Axis" as we are now to call it. Shame! Shame!' bellowed the rector as his churchwarden was called out LBW. 'Young Laurence doesn't know what he's doing.' The umpire was one of the erstwhile chemistry teachers from the Ordnance at Woolavington.

Evercreech were batting now and it turned out that Jake was a serious whizz of a fast bowler. He cut a magnificent figure, with his rippling muscles, a fine head of crisp curly hair, his hero's scar, a neat moustache, and a most engaging grin – Clark Gable-ish, thought Mog.

He bowled poor Pooty clean out.

As the shadows lengthened across the green, stumps were pulled up and victory declared for the home team. It was pronounced a good match; preparations got underway for the dance and the company dispersed to change into their evening finery. As the party from the Hall strolled home along the warm summer evening lane, the hedgerows spangled with Queen Anne's Lace and fragrant with honeysuckle, Lady Tillingham was in romantic mood. She quoted Elizabeth Barret Browning:

".... hedgerows all alive
With birds and gnats and large white butterflies
Which look as if the Mayflower had caught life
And palpitated forth upon the wind ..."

Edmund finished off:

"Hills, vales, woods, netted in a silver mist,
Farm, granges, doubled up among the hills,
And cattle grazing in the watered vales,
And cottage chimneys smoking from the woods,
And cottage gardens smelling everywhere,
Confused with smell of orchards."

315

She touched his hand, fleetingly: 'Darling, it is heavenly here. We're so lucky.'

'I can scarcely join with you in your to your claim of good fortune – stuck in this damn backwater, too feeble to be allowed to fight for King and Country.'

'You did terrifically well, batting.'

'Considering my disability, you mean.'

'No, I didn't mean that at all.'

'Here comes the hero of the hour,' said Edmund, as Jake drew up in his jeep.

'Can't have the ladies from the manor hoofing it. Lady Tillingham, Miss Tillingham, Miss Lovell, guys and gals, may I offer you a lift? Edmund – you sure could do with a leg up.'

'Everybody walks everywhere these days,' said Bella. 'It'll be terrific to have a ride.'

Jake got out and helped Mog and Bella into the vehicle. Edmund said he was fine with his stick and would welcome the walk, Pooty felt obliged to keep him company and Freda said the children could do with the exercise.

The jeep rattled along at an alarming pace.

'You certainly excelled yourself, Flight Lieutenant.' said Mog, adopting an admiring gaze.' I didn't know Canadians went in for cricket.'

'Well – we're hardly on a par with the Ozzies, but we have a go. D'you play any sport, Lady T?'

'Only a bit of tennis, when I was at college.'

'Miss Joan Hunter Dunn!'

'Oh – you like poetry?'

'I suppose you thought Canadians didn't go in for poetry either?' He laughed. 'Betjeman's something of a passion of mine. I'm very versatile, you know.'

'Yes,' said Mog, carefully.

'You ladies care for a lift down to the village hall later?'

'I'm not much of a one for dances,' said Bella. 'And, of course Edmund won't be going. But I'm sure her ladyship will take up your offer.'

When they got to the Hall he lifted Mog down from the jeep. Bella clambered out unassisted.

Mog wore a dress of dove grey georgette with a diamante trim, and the Tillingham amethysts.

'Wow,' said Freda. 'You look glam.'

'You don't think it's a bit too much for war time in the village hall?'

'Certainly not – Greta Garbo to the life.' said Bella.

'You should get Bob to take you down in the pony and trap or you'll ruin that beautiful dress,' said Freda.

'Well, actually the Flight Lieutenant is picking me up – I'm sure you can come too.'

'I don't think so, Mog.'

Bella and Freda exchanged glances.

'Why not?'

'Well, as a matter of fact Bob asked if I would go with him. He likes a jig, apparently, but didn't want to turn up on his own.'

'Oh, I see,' said Mog, checking, with immense satisfaction, her reflection in the Great Mirror.

As the band struck up, Pooty advanced for his promised dance. But that was that. Thereafter, Greta Garbo and Clark Gable, gorgeous in his blue and gold uniform, took to the floor, again and again; wurzels and maidens, servicemen and spinsters, matrons and miners – all were agog at the glittering display. The last waltz saw them entwined in what Miss Scott-Dickins regarded as a most unseemly embrace. Pooty had left. Before God Save the King finished the evening off, the couple had slipped away.

Sunrise over the Mendips, heralding another fine summer day, found the Flight Lieutenant speeding joyously back to base. Anyone up at that Godless hour might have heard him, chanting at the top of his voice, over and over again:

'We lay in the hay barn till long after one
And I have deflowered Miss Joan Hunter Dunn.'

'Jake gone?'

Edmund was irritable at lunch the next day – he had not appeared for breakfast.

'I believe so,' said Bella. 'Mrs P was turning out his bedroom earlier.'

Mog tucked silently into her faggots; they had never tasted so good.

'"I am half-sick of shadows,' said the Lady of Shalott."

Mog wrote home:

My Dearest Old Maties,

We've had the loveliest day imaginable here. There was a special cricket match, with lots of visiting players, and a dance to raise money for Mrs Churchill's Aid to Russia Fund – mum will be pleased to hear. It was glorious weather and everybody enjoyed themselves no end. Freda and Bella and I organised a pretty good tea, with cucumber sandwiches (really tiny ones), masses of scones, wild strawberries and real cream. Mrs P was in charge of the urn. We even brought the china over from the Hall – not the best stuff, of course, but the plates and things have our crest on them, in dark blue. Our littlies were brilliant, helping dish out the food – our eldest boy even took part in the match and turned out to be quite good.

The evening was such fun. I did myself up to the nines and danced into a state of euphoria. I've never felt so wonderful – ever. I got chatting to some really nice people, one of them was a Canadian air force chap, I had met him before – quite a hero – he'd come miles

especially to play for us – can you imagine. I can't tell you what a truly
amazing night it was! Freda thought he looked just like Clark Gable.'
Hope you are all well.

'Mm. She seems very full of herself,' said Lil as she read the letter.
'Fancy my Mog 'avin' her own crest.'
'Let's see,' said Ooly, snatching the letter.
She scanned it quickly: 'Mm. I'd say the wind was in the east.'

Winnie promised "heavy fighting in the Mediterranean before the
leaves of autumn fall", but no one knew any details. At the end of the
first week of July news came of the bombing of the Sicilian airfields,
preparatory to the Allied invasion of the island. Lil and Sid were
celebrating their wedding anniversary – it was fine day for it.

Dot was reading the paper; 'Listen to this, Lil. Apparently a gunner
in the American air force shot down seven enemy planes over Sicily
yesterday, or the day before – and it was *his* wedding anniversary. It
says he's the tallest man they've got – a six-foot-six, sixteen-stone
giant of a bloke. I wouldn't mind meeting him in the blackout.'

Lil and Ooly looked at each other in total astonishment. Sid was
appalled, and also hoped no one expected him to shoot down seven
enemy planes today, or any other day.

Lil wrote to Pan:
Thank you for the telegram. Todge pickd us a lovely bunch of
flowers. i thought you had a lot of boming last week so i heard – it
is just talk. have you started your exams – i should get the pip of that
work. Mog seems on top of the world. she does not have the work that
you do. Aunty seems to have taken a fancy to some Yank she read about
in the papers – would you credit it.

Old Mrs Spoon keeps throwing me over cabbages & lettice. we are
going to have chats like. well i feel tired this weather. our roses are

lovely they have been twice the size this year. the sunflowers are a foot high. some of my beens are coming up – my spinach my goodness you should see it, the onions you should see them and the tulips have been lovely.

Dad wrote:

Your telegram was well received. We had a good, restful day. Todge was in fine form and presented us with some flowers. The gardens round here are simply gorgeous. You would be amused – we had a circus in our village. A lady went home and told her brother she had seen an elephant in Woodford. He asked her what she had had to drink. Mr Spoon came in one day this week (evening time) to borrow some bread. He stayed some time, and had a drink with us.

Dot wrote :

We had a nice day yesterday, with the exception that you and Mog were missing. Dad said 'I bet old Pan has forgotten our wedding day' and a few minutes after, the telegram arrived. I tried to get them a few roses but I couldn't get any ... All the shops in Woodford opened but dad said he wanted a rest, so I was glad it was fine, because he sat in the garden and he really did look well for the rest in the sun. You will be pleased to know we had tea in the garden but had to swamp the lounge steps with paraffin because Mrs S and Ooly was stung to bits with flying ants.

While the inhabitants of Chestnut Avenue battled with flying ants, the Hun was treated to a round the clock blitz; the press exulted: "Details were given last night of the trail of fire and devastation that has been blazed through Germany's greatest war-making zones – Krupp's (Essen), Hamburg, Hanover." Over in the Med. the fall of the Roman Empire commenced. Monty and the Eighth Army, along with American and Canadian forces, pounded up the coast of Sicily on their Odyssey from El Alamein. The invasion had gone like clockwork.

On 26 July the headlines were: "Mussolini sacked." "The keystone of the Fascist Arch has crumbled," proclaimed Winnie, "The first of the aggressor war-lords cast down."

'Musso's 'ad it, then,' Bert Gum announced to the Emporium. 'Yer know I feel quite sorry for those poor old Wops. Not that fat bastard, I don't mean. Angelo the ice cream bloke, Renzo at the chippie – they were such kindly, gentle sort of coves, always laughin.' I've 'eard they're all really scared of their Jerry allies – 'ate 'em, by all accounts.'

Doomandgloom was, as usual, wary of good news : 'It's all very well gettin' a toe 'old in Italy; Eyties might be a bit of walk-over, soft underbelly and all that, but that King of theirs and the new bloke what's taken over – Bad Dolly, [Badoglio] or whatever 'e's called – they're stickin' fast with Jerry – too scared not too, maybe. Jerry will be zoomin' in full force, mark my words, mark my words.'

Fanny Bastaple was more interested in Lana Turner's baby who's birth was announced the same day as Musso's downfall. ''Ere, just listen to this,' she read out from the *Mirror*: "Last January she filed a suit for annulment and custody of her unborn child when it was disclosed that her husband's divorce (some rich business man) from his previous wife had not been made absolute. They remarried in March." 'Ow these people carry on!'

'Got a packet of Lux, Sid?' asked Doomandgloom, anxiously. 'My missus says there's nothing like them soapflakes for washin' 'er woollies.'

'Been withdrawn, brother. Lever Brothers have announced that they've stopped producing them – can't get the proper ingredients these days. You'll have to make do with Oxydol.'

'Blinkin' war. My missus won't touch that – she'll go mad – anything sets 'er orf.' Mrs Davies was said to be "difficult", though no one had first hand knowledge of this, as she was rarely seen.

'Well, brother, I've got a couple of packets put by – but I'll have to

321

charge a bit extra – scarcity value.'

'Anything to keep 'er 'appy.' And off he went with the very pricey packet of soapflakes.

'Reckon 'es as scared of 'er in the funeral parlour as the Eyties are of Jerry!' remarked Fanny.

By the end of August the Axis had been driven out of Sicily and on the fourth anniversary of the outbreak of war Allied forces invaded mainland Italy. Monty spoke on the wireless: "There can only be one end to this next battle, and that is another success. Forward to victory! Let us knock Italy out of the war." In only five days the invasion was well underway and General Eisenhower, Commander in chief of Allied forces in the Mediterranean, announced the good news to the kitchen at Chestnut Avenue, the study at Blacksmith's Cottage, the Blue Drawing Room at New Hall and to Sid's customers: "The surrender was signed five days ago in secret by a representative of Marshal Pietro Badoglio, Italy's prime minister since the downfall of Benito Mussolini in July."

'Is that it? Are the Eyties on our side now, Sid?' asked Dai Lewis.

'Well, no – not all of them. Not yet, anyway.' The Lord of Roman Road wasn't really quite clear what was going on.

'Paper says that Bad Dolly has urged them to fight for us.' said Bert Gum. ' And they're all crying with joy and doin' a lot of 'uggin.'

'That's Wops for you.' said Fanny Bastaple.

'How things change – I can't keep up with it.' Ethel Jiggins was puzzled. 'First the Russians are our enemies and now they're our best friends. Now the papers are talking about the Italian "years of war, suffering and degradation" and how the Nazis always was their real enemies. Whatever will happen next?'

'P'raps Fatso Goering will pal up with Roosifelt and Winnie will get together with that Tojo [Prime Minister of Japan]' Fanny chuckled.

'Wouldn't make a lot of difference to us lot,' said Dai Lewis. 'There'll always be some buggers smashin' up our 'ouses, killin' our kiddies, drivin' our cows away and forcin' that brown stodgy muck down our throats.'

'My Will,' said Vi Kerridge, 'says now the Wops are done for, we should go for Jerry good and proper, get into a second front and fight alongside the Ruskies for all we're worth. 'E says, Winnie and 'is lot won't be doin' wiv it, though.'

'And where did he get that from? The *Worker*, I suppose,' said Sid. 'Or maybe he had a private audience at number 10?'

'Well, the Axis is cracking,' announced Lord Tillingham as he smashed very hard at the shell of his breakfast egg with a silver spoon. 'And no doubt our good friend Flight Lieutenant Campbell is doing his bit.'

'The Italian army was a broken reed if ever there was one,' said Bella. 'Mussolini was never going to make those jolly little chaps into decent soldiers. Surely it can't be long now. Italy out of the war, incessant bombing of Germany, the sweeping successes of the Red Army. How are we going to celebrate? Mog, you could put on a victory puppet show – a sort of Punch and Judy – Punch can be a sort of "John Bull" character, perhaps Winnie – it would be easy to do a likeness of him. He can give Hitler and Musso a good old pasting.'

'I suppose I could.'

'Come on, Moggins, cheer up. The end is in sight.'

'Puppet shows better wait,' said Edmund. 'We haven't got there yet. Rommel is well entrenched in northern Italy – it's going to be the devil's own job to get him out. I gather Hitler has screeched some panicky nonsense into the microphone. Only when we get into Berlin and topple that hysterical upstart from the Austrian slums will the war be over; then Tillingham will fly the flag and all shall be well.'

Mog dipped a soldier into her egg and tried to eat it. She thought sadly of the promised post-war honeymoon:

"Jack shall have Jill.

Nought shall go ill.

The man shall have his mare again, and all shall be well."

Mrs P came in with the morning post; a letter for Mog from home, bills for Bella and a letter for Edmund.

He read it, crumpled it up and left the table hurriedly.

Mog and Bella exchanged glances.

'Oh dear. What's up now?'

St Mary the Virgin hosted a Thanksgiving service for the surrender (of Italy). Mog and Edmund sat in their pew, ashen and rigid; Jake had been shot down; this time it was the works.

Chapter 26:

Mid-September to October 1943

Mog went to the phone box outside the Tillingham Arms and made a call home:

'Hello, Aunty, it's me, Mog.

Yes – I'll talk to mum in a minute, but is Ooly there?'

Dot called out: 'Ooly, your sister's on the phone – wants to talk to you particular.'

'I'm not here – not to be on the receiving end of some abuse from Pan.'

'No – it's Mog.'

'Blimey.' She took the receiver. 'Well, Lady Tillingham, to what do I owe the honour of this call?'

'Ooly, do shut up. I need to talk to you – daren't write it down. I'm in a phone box. Something awful has happened and there's no one here I can possibly confide in. Promise you won't tell anyone, not even mum.'

'All right.'

'You do promise?'

'Yes – come on – what is it? Edmund?'

'Well – yes and no. It's not mainly about Edmund – but I suppose it is really. There's rather a lot to say.'

'Well – write then.'

'I can't bear to.'

'Has he got another woman or something.'

'No.'

'Well – what, for goodness sake?'

'I met this Canadian airman. It was wonderful,' she sobbed. 'And now he's dead – killed over Italy.'

'Did you …?'

'Oh yes, Ooly. I did. Only once, but he was so … so … and now I shall never see him again and I have to pretend there's nothing wrong and just carry on as usual being Lady Muck and jollying everyone here along. What will they think if they catch me in tears?'

'Why don't you come home for a bit – then we can have a proper talk and you can have a good old cry. Mum would be so pleased – you know how she misses you.'

'I can hardly tell her and dad what's happened! They'd certainly turn my face to the wall. And Edmund gets really funny if I ever suggest coming home.'

'Can't you talk to Freda, or Bella, then?'

More sobbing. 'No – I daren't say a dicky to anyone down here.'

'Why on earth did you get involved with this chap? Are things not right with Edmund?'

'Oh – it's not that. It was just a heavenly, hot summer night and I'd had some punch – he was so dashing in his uniform, so manly and gorgeous. He liked poetry too – and now he's gone for ever and …'

'It was just once, Mog. You didn't really know him, duck.'

'I feel as if I did. It's just as if I'd known him all my life. And anyway – it was special for me, it was my first time and …'

'You mean you and Edmund …?'

'Oh, no, no. I just meant it was the first time I had done anything sort of wild and romantic. The first time I'd broken the rules, I suppose.'

'Oh, yes,' said her sister. 'Well – you'd better tell them that you're upset because someone in the family has bought it. Make someone up – a cousin you were very fond of when we were kids.'

'Ooly, you know I don't like deceit and anyway …'

'Mog, absolutely nothing is to be gained from blowing the gaff. It'll just cause upset all round. Are you sure everything's OK with Edmund?'

'Oh, yes. Look, I've run out of change – I'll have to go now.' And she rang off.

'That was a long chat,' said Dot. 'Didn't she want to talk to mum?'

'Oh, yes, but she was in a phone box and ran out of cash.'

'So what were you two talking about?'

'She's got involved in organising some sort of concert to celebrate the Italian business and she wanted some advice about the programme.'

'Unlike Mog to want your advice,' said her Aunt.

So Cousin Arthur, a first cousin once removed actually, lost his life in Sicily. Mog didn't know any details. She thought he might have been a paratrooper. As a matter of fact Edmund was so withdrawn and strange that he didn't appear to notice Mog's distress. Bella did, of course, and was not altogether convinced by "Cousin Arthur".' Neither was Freda. Mog wiped her eyes and soldiered on, of course, rather regretting her outburst on the phone; she decided to take the pink drawing room (now the school room) in hand.

But this time her usual high spirits could not be summoned up. She found herself dreaming of that summer night as she wielded the paint brush. The smell of paint made her feel sick and it was weary, back breaking work. Her heart was not in it. Her erstwhile beloved mansion had become like a mausoleum, a prison, a grey monument to decline – there was no future here, no passion, no hope. This was no place to bring a new life into the world. In the event she didn't have to – she fell off the ladder and the foetus made its own speedy exit from New Hall down the Great Water Closet. Nobody knew.

Ooly wrote:

Just a quick line to let you know that I told the old 'uns you were organising a concert and that's why we were talking on the phone for so long. Just in case they mention it to you.

I'm so sorry about everything. It's awful having to keep intense misery to yourself. I can't say I blame you for grabbing any bit of joy you can – it's all we can do with the world crashing down about our ears. Though I was surprised – I thought you and the baronet were still in the first flush. At least you're relatively safe and quite comfortable down there – we had a terrifying raid the other night, the longest there's been in London for months and the first serious one in Woodford. I'm in a continual state of terror, and have been every single minute since the war started. Mum makes it worse – she seems to revel in the excitement. I could slosh her one sometimes. When Bow was getting its terrible pasting she used to make dad regale us with all the most gruesome details as soon as he got in from the shop. And the there's the insufferable Todge worship – it's driving me mad. I've never come across a family so dotty about kids.

Dot wrote to Pan:

Mog rang and had a long talk with Ooly, apparently about music for some concert she's got involved in down there. I thought it odd – Mog consulting Ooly about music, I mean. She didn't even have a word with mum. I hope nothing is wrong.

We had a bad raid here on Thursday – you probably know – the papers said that the planes flew over East Anglia and we heard that there was some bombs dropped your way.

Sid wrote:

Just a few words. Had a bit of a raid on Thursday night which scared little Todge out of her wits. Apart from that the week has been much as usual. We are feeling sorry for you, because we believe you are not having much peace at the moment. The best thing is to keep the mind fully occupied and not dwell on these things. We are rehearsing Bach's

Christmas Oratorio at choir. I am singing the Evangelist – a heavy load. Mog rang. She is organising a concert down there. I suppose you don't get much time for your music these days? I dare say there's a choir locally you could join – but I expect you have quite enough to do without fitting that in. There is some excellent stuff to listen to on the wireless – I was listening to Myra Hess play this afternoon.

Lil wrote:

What a firework display we had this week – our very own blitts, right here in Woodford – worst raid weev had. Moanin' Minnie starts up and then searchlights fill the sky – bomps and cracks, shells bursting Jerry planes coming in as ours are zoomin off to smash the buggers up. i hope you are not having these rotten raids – the barrage was so heavy, our doors and windows shook. little Todge slept on the couch – i held a pillow over her ears to stop the noise but in the end it woke her up but it was nearing the end. i then took her under the schelter – the plains was twirling round and round – it sounded right over the house. a lot of people were out in the street watching. Mog rang she only spoke to Ooly – something about music. aunty is sitting doing knitting dad doing his books – me writing – so we are a lively set.

The bombing of London went on intermittently through a damp and foggy October. "Bad Dolly" declared war on Germany as Monty and his band of heroes pressed on up through Italy. Meanwhile, on the Eastern Front, avalanches of Russian tanks were, according to the press, "overwhelming the Hun". Lil, Sid and Dot went to see the American film, *Battle of Britain.*

'My Gawd,' commented Lil as they walked back home, 'That car'oon of the Nazi monster with 'is great jaw open ready to gobble us up, like 'e'd just gobbled up the rest of Europe – what abaaht that! Gives you the bleedin' shivers rememberin' what it was like back in '40 – expectin' them Jerries to come marchin' along our road any day.

Bit different now thanks to the Russians, I'd say.'

'It's far from all over yet, mate,' said Sid. 'And I don't think we should forget the part played by our lads, by Winnie and Monty, and the Americans.

'But it's the poor buggers of Russians wot 'ave 'ad it worse and wot 'ave fought 'ardest and longest. Even the King knows that – look at that sword 'es givin' them.'

Pooty had popped into the Abbey during his lunch hour; he joined the throng with his sandwiches.

Typists and clerks, service men and civilians, nurses and nannies, Londoners and folk up from the country were filing silently past the Sword of Stalingrad, awed by the mysterious gloom and mindful of what they had seen at the flics: the German Sixth Army laying down their arms as the ragged, emaciated Russians emerged from their dug-outs to set about the rebuilding of the shattered city.

As he pushed through the crowds, he spotted someone he knew, still queuing up.

'Dougie Mitchell! How goes it – it's been an absolute age!'

'Pooty, old cheappe – still in civvy street?'

'I'm stuck in Whitehall. And you?'

'Whitechapel – London Hospital.'

'Come on – let's go and have a spot of lunch – my club's not too bad. The housekeeper has given me filthy spam and national loaf sandwiches today – I shall be delighted to chuck them away.'

'Darling?' Dougie turned uncertainly to Ooly. 'Oh – so sorry – Pooty th-th-this is …'

'The beauteous lady from that riotous evening at Claridges! What a delightful surprise!'

'So glad to meet you again,' said Ooly, not meaning it at all, not that she disliked Pooty – she had taken quite a shine to him, as a matter of fact – but, oh dear!

330

'Lunch would be lovely,' she said. 'But we haven't seen the sword yet and from the length of the queue it's going to be ages before we do.'

'What about an early supper?'

'Not possible, dear boy,' said Dougie. 'I've got to get back to the grindstone. Let's get together soon – this weekend any good?'

'Have to be the one after. I'm committed to Tilly.'

'And who, may we know, is Tilly? Is it serious? Wedding bells?'

Pooty roared with laughter.

'Nothing like that, I regret to say. You don't remember Tilly, Edmund Tillingham, from Eton? No – I suppose you'd probably left by the time he turned up. Odd ball – he's a baronet these days – but his wife's a smasher, a real smasher, not exactly out of the top drawer, but gorgeous looking – rather like Greta Garbo – and lots of fun. She's quite transformed their ghastly old tomb of a place – it's near the Mater's in the Mendips. We were all dumbfounded when he got married – not his cup of tea, if you see what I mean.'

Dougie and Ooly were all ears.

'So, if I read you right, it is Lady Tillingham to whom you are committed for the weekend?'

'Nothing like that either, I regret even more. No chance for poor old pen-pushing, bespectacled Pooty there. Lady T is a bit of a mystery, actually. She's a teacher – evacuated to New Hall in 1940. No one's met her people – none of them attended the wedding.

'Evidently not his lordship's cup of tea,' said Ooly sourly.

'Oh no – I didn't mean that. I meant marriage was not his cup of tea – a confirmed bachelor – don't you know.'

She wasn't sure she did.

Pooty took off, promising to take Dougie (and the lady if she was free) to the Ritz the Saturday after next. She would not be, of course.

'Oh my God,' said Ooly, as soon as he was out of ear shot. 'That's done it!'

'I d-d-don't see why; he doesn't know your name, unless he remembers it from Claridges, of course.'

'Look – Mog – Rose knows *your* name and he might just mention to her that he's seen you with a mysterious long-term female companion (possibly called Lily), and that will be that. She knows all about what happened in '37. We've had it. In no time at all we will be the talk of the town.'

'I'm not convinced that the town would care. It has other things on its mind at present. I suppose I could ask him to keep mum.'

'Yes – d'you think he will?'

'Pooty's a good chap. Seems to think a lot of your sister.'

He took her hand as they drew near to the Sword. In this still and hallowed place, in the dim light of two flickering candles, there it lay, the Sword of Honour, on an oak table in the nave. The blade was inscribed with the words "To the steel hearted citizens of Stalingrad, the gift of King George VI in token of the homage of the British people." The pommel was of rock crystal surmounted by a gold rose of England.

Sid was of the opinion that the Stalingrad Sword was a wonderful gesture, and suggested to Lil and Dot that they might go and view it, as it was early closing day.

'We can't very well go – we've got Todge – Ooly's goin' orf to Nell's agin. You and Dot go – we can't drag the kiddie up west and queue up for hours. I'm feelin' a bit tired these days, in any case.'

'No, Lil', that's not on,' said Dot. 'We're not going without you. You'd really like to see it, I know you would. I don't see why we shouldn't take the kiddie. Sid, we'll meet you at Bow Road station and we'll get the bus from there – you could shut up a bit early and we'll have tea at Lyons Corner House after. We won't mention it to Ooly – you know how funny she can be.'

Ed was determined to go too; he wasn't going to miss this, and after some debate it was agreed that he might join the party, even take the morning off from the shop, as he might be useful lifting the push-chair on and off the bus.

So off they set, all arrayed in their Sunday best, with a push chair piled high with paraphernalia and an excited Todge telling Puddy Tat that they were going to see the King's bootiful sword and he'd better behave himself and not shout out because it was going to be in a very quiet and important church.

By the time they got to Westminster the crowd was seething.

'Stick tight together, mates,' said Sid. 'We don't want anyone getting lost.'

Todge was getting restive and refused to stay in the push chair. An enormous, jolly GI offered to lift her up on his shoulders so she could see what was going on.

'That's all right, brother,' said Sid anxiously. 'We can manage.'

'Puddy Tat wants to see, Puddy Tat wants to see,' shouted Todge, holding her arms out to the giant.'

And so Todge was lifted aloft to survey the scene. As they entered the portals of the great cathedral, a shriek of delight thrilled through the hushed shadows:

'Mummee! Mummee! I can see my Mummee!'

'Ssh! Ssh! You's mummy's not here, mate.' Sid lifted her down from the American shoulders

'She is here. Mummee! Mummee!'

'Todge, you must be quiet,' said Dot. 'Your mummy has gone to see Nanna Bow.'

'Naughty, silly Puddy Tat' said Todge.

Ooly heard the cry and spotted her daughter and dad's trilby; she pulled her hat down, put her collar up and ran for it, scrambling and pushing her way out through the throng.

'Ooly – wait! Whatever is the matter?' Dougie fought his way after her as she ran, hell for leather, away from the Sword of Honour.

'They're here – dad and Todge – and the others I expect.'

'Well, what a party we're having today! Who will we see next? The mater, I shouldn't wonder. That would be a turn up for the book!'

That evening, back in Chestnut Avenue, over a mite of cheese, pickled onions and just a drop of ale, the day was discussed.

'I gather from Todge that you took her to see the Sword,' said Ooly tartly. 'I do wish you had at least mentioned it to me.'

'We only decided to go at the last minute,' said her mother.

Ooly knew this to be untrue as they must have made arrangements with dad before he left for the shop in the morning. She decided, however, that it was unwise to pursue it.

'She thought she saw you there,' said Dot, 'I suppose there was someone that looked like you, we couldn't see in all the crowds. You weren't there, I suppose? Hardly Nell's sort of thing, I wouldn't have thought.'

'Oh no,' replied Ooly. 'We just had tea and a chat, as usual. Derek's out in Italy. She's heard from him, but the letter doesn't say much. It must be so worrying for her – thank goodness Johnny's not in any firing line. She's had quite a difficult time, you know – she was telling me today about how awful it was when Johnny's father died and she was on her own with two boys and not a penny piece. That's why she had to send Johnny off to the Masonic School, where he was kept, fed and clothed and everything. She said it was the worst day of her life, waving him off at the station ...'

'So you didn't go and see the Sword, then?' persisted Dot.

'No, Aunty, I would like to see it. Was it magnificent?'

'Very impressive,' said her father, 'a touching and appropriate tribute.'

'It's on display tomorrow as well. You could go and see it then.' Dot was not to be put off. 'I think the Spoons are going – you could go with them.'

334

'I'll think about it,' said Ooly. 'But I have a feeling Johnny might have a day's leave.'

'Has he, now,' said Dot, collecting up the dishes and taking them into the scullery.

Sid wrote to Pan:

We went up to the Abbey to see the Sword of Stalingrad. Todge created a bit of a stir – poor kid saw someone who looked like Ooly and shouted out at the top of her voice.

I suppose the Sword hasn't been on show near you, has it? What exquisite workmanship, hand-forged of the finest Sheffield steel, what a fitting honour for the Russians! The hand grip is gold, with leopards' heads on either side, the pommel is crystal with gold roses on it, the scabbard is red leather, decorated with the Royal Coat of Arms with three rubies mounted on golden stars. I would like you to have seen it.

Pan had more on her mind than ornamental long swords or, indeed, events in Russia, Italy, the Pacific, or anywhere else, she was producing the staff Christmas play at school. She had selected *Toad of Toad Hall*. Those in the anti-Pan camp objected and plumped for a religious theme. Dom Sci. attempted a compromise by suggesting that the river bank story might be somehow adapted to incorporate the story of Moses in the bull rushes. This was dismissed out of hand and Art, who fancied herself as the Madonna alias Lady Diana Cooper, argued for *The Miracle* while Harriet Oxendale (Eng.) was all for something martial and topical like *The Trojan Women*. Jocasta, whose decision was, of course, final, opted for *Toad*. Pan always got her way.

Gif was to play the part of Mr Toad, while the mild, timorous Mole would suit Dom Sci. Whiskery Maths would do for the ponderous Badger and the Others (with the exception of Harriet Oxendale, who declined) would be the Wild Wooders. In the part of the gallant, charming water vole, Ratty, Pan had cast herself, in response to popular demand. Elsa would, as usual, take charge of the costumes. Jocasta was in too elevated a position to participate; she would introduce the production and say some complimentary things at the end.

Rehearsals went well. Pan couldn't fault Gif's blustering, bombastic Toad – it has to be said that play-acting together was something which gave both women satisfaction; they had fun and slipped happily into their roles even when at home in Blacksmith's Cottage or "poop pooping" along the Suffolk lanes in Amun. Gif was happy: Elsa was nicely marginalized and Jocasta was well out of the way.

'How's Rush doing with the costumes? She's usually flapping about and getting us to try things months before the performance.' Gif was concerned.

'I haven't seen much of her recently. She's hugely conscientious, I'm sure it'll be all right.'

Jocasta, while taking some interest in the play, was preoccupied with another matter; she called a council of war in the staff room.

Gif was put out: 'We've got a rehearsal; what's Meredith doing having a meeting this afternoon? Damn nuisance – I've a good mind not to go.'

'Pig, don't be ridiculous. You must put in an appearance – she is the head, after all.'

'Colleagues and friends,' Jocasta began, smiling her most superior and authoritative smile. 'Thank you for sparing your valuable time to attend this meeting. We are all confronted, I regret to say, with a problem of a grave and momentous nature.'

'Oh God – not more evacuees!' 'School closing down?' Murmurs flew around the room. 'Amalgamation with the boys' school?'

'A problem of great magnitude; the safety and well-being of our charges is threatened, not to mention the reputation of Harpisfield itself.'

'My sainted aunt, get on with it, woman,' muttered Gif, eager to be off to the river bank.

'A parent came to see me last week. I shall name no names and I must ask you all, most earnestly, to maintain the strictest silence about what I am about the tell you. One of our gels, a pupil of no more than seventeen years, is with child.'

Gasps all round, except from Art who was in on the secret and had started knitting.

'That is not all. The father, if he can be graced with that title, is an American airman. I have seen with my own eyes gels from this school in the town, some even wearing their school uniform, consorting with these dreadful men. They are, by all accounts, seduced by bulging wallets, brash behaviour, nylon stockings, chewing gum, chocolates, something they call "candy" and other unmentionable inducements. My school is in uproar. This must be stopped.'

'Obviously we're all aware of what's going on,' said Maths, who was bolder than most of her colleagues. 'But, honestly, Headmistress, I fail to see what can be done about it. Obviously the GIs. are swarming in here by the thousand, jitterbugging, throwing their weight about and making a damned nuisance of themselves – Pa says it's a built up of troops for the invasion of Europe – there's talk of a western front. Ruskies are fed up with going it alone. Can't blame them. Short of locking the girls up, I don't see how we can prevent them mixing, and, in all conscience, the Americans are over here to help us defeat the Hun. We should be making them welcome, surely.'

'There's hospitality and hospitality,' responded the Head 'I am sure your father knows a good deal more than we do about the conduct of the war, but this does not alter the fact that our gels are in moral peril from the "Yankee craze". I have decided that any gel seen in the company of an American serviceman will be expelled. There will be no appeal and no guarantee of her getting a place anywhere else. That will be the end of her education. I urge you all to be vigilant and encourage the gels themselves to keep a wary eye open for any transgressors. I shall address the school on the subject at assembly tomorrow.'

'With respect, Headmistress, I really doubt if that will do much good.' Dom Sci. was tentative. 'Most of the sixth formers – it is the sixth form we're talking about, I suppose? – are raring to be off and earn a mint at war work. Might I suggest a gentler approach? Perhaps a serious talk with them about the dangers of er – well – walking out with these rapacious, flashy individuals.'

'Good God, woman, it's no part of our duty to offer sex education,' boomed Gif. 'You'll be suggesting some sort of Marie Stopes outfit next.'

'Thank you, Miss Drayman,' warned Jocasta.

Pan was in quandary. Her special relationship with Jocasta, made it very difficult for her to make any sort of public stand against her, but, much as she deplored the Yanks and all their works, she did feel strongly that it was an atrocious thing to set the girls spying on one another. She spoke:

'While I thoroughly approve of the Headmistress's expulsion plan – we need to take a firm line with these flibbertigibbets – I am not entirely happy about encouraging the girls to tell tales.'

Murmurs of agreement.

'Well, we will leave the matter for now,' said Jocasta firmly. 'I am sure Miss Rush (Elsa was the upper sixth's form mistress) will offer some words of advice to her charges on the subject of modesty and self control, but I stand by my decision to expel.'

She scanned the room: 'And where, pray, *is* Miss Rush?'

Chapter 27:

November to December 1943

The nip in the air at the end of November, which usually brought with it the tremor of pre-Christmas thrill, found Harpisfield in deep turmoil; the Chairman of the Governors recommended that any girl found in possession of nylon stockings or (God – forbid) American cigarettes should be suspended for at least a week and, of course, have their ill-gotten gains confiscated.

Art was horrified. 'They'll be issuing chastity belts next and we'll have to add them to the wretched knicker inspection.' (Girls at Harpisfield were inspected every Monday morning to make sure they were wearing the regulation dark green bloomers and nothing more scanty or fancy).

Roman Road, too, was in uproar. Sir Oswald Mosley, fascist rabble rouser, of Battle of Cable Street fame, and relative of Dougie Mitchell, had been released from prison, where he had been interned as a threat to public safety in 1940. The reason given was that he was suffering from thrombophlebitis or inflamed varicose veins.

A shudder went through the East End, through London, through the country at large.

Rabbi Hotzner was grave: 'Many people who kept their anti-Semitic views underground have come out into the open as the result of the Home Secretary's action. This is a very serious misfortune.'

Dan Chater, that good old union man, MP for Bethnal Green North East, told his fellow members:

'Only on Monday night I had the testimony of several of my constituents that Fascism is already raising its head again in Bethnal Green. Only this last week the doors of Jews have had chalked upon them during the night "PJ", which means … "Perish Judah" or "Pig Jew". The blackshirts, when they go around see the "PJ' on the door, and that is the dwelling which gets the punching blow, as it were of the Fascists – a door broken, a window smashed."

'Oy-yoy-yoy,' wailed old Sarah Posnanski to the company in the Emporium. 'I have seen dese marks on de doors, "PJ". Vere vill it all end?'

'Yeah,' said Bert Gum. 'Release of that bastard has got them Bethnal Green blackshirt types all worked up agin. The man is a traitor to his country, should be treated as a war criminal, can't understand what Morrison's playin' at. You should 'ave seen the crowds protestin' in Trafalgar Square on Sunday – twenty fousand of 'em, all shoutin and wavin' banners. Some of 'em lifted up a Tommy from the Eighth Army who'd 'ad 'is leg shot off in the Desert.'

Will Kerridge was up in arms: 'What's Winnie and his crew up to? Foistin' them fascists Bad Dolly and that little sawn-off king[3] on the Wops and now, this Mosley business. Which bloody side are they on?'

'Paper says Mosley's bin livin' the life of Riley, life of Riley, anyway,' said Doomandgloom. 'Prison, my arse – own house in the grounds, central 'eatin', servants. At this rate, when the war is over, ruddy 'itler will be put in a luxury residence in Windsor Great Park, with truffles to eat – whatever they are.'

'Bert has varicose veins, don't you Bert?' said his wife. 'Never stopped you doin' your warden stuff, did it?'

'One law for the rich, one for the poor,' said Bert. 'Just because 'es a bloody baronet … no offence, Sid – I'm sure your son-in-law's a

---

3 *Victor Emmanuel III.*

decent bloke.'

'Oh, yes, brother.' Sid, having no notion what his son-in-law was like, and being in two minds about the whole business said no more. Harry Bastaple, who had a black shirt in his top drawer, kept his own counsel.

Ooly met Dougie outside the London; they had not seen each other for two whole weeks; first Johnny had some leave, then Todge went down with something, then Lil was laid up.

'Ooly, I simply can't bear these separations. When the war is over …' He looked at her pleadingly, weary and strained.

'Whatever's the matter? You look as if you'd seen a ghost.'

'We've had some tr-tr-trouble at Tredegar Square. Bunch of thugs broke all the windows, smashed in the front door and threw muck all over the house. Word has got round that we're related to Oswald.'

'Oh my God.'

'It is a scandal. A damn stupid thing to do – letting him out. Hundreds of elderly office cleaners have varicose veins, ulcers and attacks of phlebitis – so do fire watchers, blokes in the National Fire Service, Civil Defence and the Home Guard … I treat them all the time. It's not even as if the Mosleys were living in any discomfort at Holloway; their accommodation was quite luxurious; the Hawk went to visit one time.'

'So – what will you do?'

'Archie reckons we ought to move, now they know where we are. He's found some pokey little council flat in a block not far from here – hospital has laid it on for us – ironically the block's occupied mainly by Jewish families. It's appallingly basic but will do *pro tem* I suppose.'

'I hope the blackshirts aren't on the rampage there. That would be ironic. Can't you park yourselves in Barrington Gardens for the time being?'

'God forbid. Not now they're back.'

They linked arms and walked along, cuddled closely together in the kindly fog.

'How did you get on with Pooty, by the way? You said nothing about it on the phone.'

'Fine. He was gobsmacked to find out that you and his "Lady T" were sisters.'

'You didn't tell him!'

'Well – I had to – otherwise what reason could I give for asking him to keep his mouth shut? Anyway – he was tickled pink. He's got a real thing for your Rose, you know, thinks she's the bee's knees.'

'Couldn't you just have said that you didn't want *anyone* to know that we were seeing each other again.'

'I could have done, but … Ooly, I'm so fed up with all this subterfuge. Why don't we just face the music? D-d-divorce is not so unusual these days. Your husband would do the d-d-decent thing, surely?'

'What – pretend to take the blame! Divorce might be current in your elevated circles – look at Diana Mosley – but it is most certainly not in mine.'

'Come on – couples are coming a cr-cr-cropper all the time since the war started. Surely it has crossed your mind?'

Dreams she had dreamed and impossible, delicious longings had been her constant companion since that day two years ago, but the practicalities of how her desires might be achieved had not entered into them.

'Divorce. It's such a terrible word. My family would go absolutely mad – they think I'm a bit wayward as it is. And what about yours? I wasn't anywhere good enough for them when I was a single East End oil and colourman's daughter. How are they going to feel about a married one? – I've still got a hooked nose, too. And what about Todge? How can I take Todge away from him?'

'My d-d-dear, good girl – you're always saying he has no time for the child.'

'Nell seems to think I've got it all wrong.'

'Oh, I s-s-see. So what do you pr-pr-propose ? – Every Tuesday or Thursday, or every other Tuesday or Thursday, unless something crops up, of course, until Domesday, or until Johnny gets wind of it, or your family finds out, and then kaput! Goodbye to all that. Nice to have known you, Dr Mitchell, I'll be getting on with my proper life now.'

'Dougie, that's not fair. Once upon a time you kidded me that you really wanted to be with me for ever, until your parents clapped their hands and that was that; I was out of the window. You didn't write, you didn't explain – a bit of East End rubbish put aside. Now you seem to have decided that a legal union would not be so bad, after all – I suppose your chum, Pooty, has given you the green light.'

'Ooly, Ooly – I know I've d-d-done it all wrong, but can't we have a go? Pooty *is* all for it.'

'You've certainly changed your tune – only a few months ago we had to get up to all those ridiculous hi-jinks, just to stop your cousin finding out about us. And now you're actually discussing me with an old friend. Just because Pooty has assured you that I am respectable enough for you – linked with the great house of Tillingham – now it's OK for me to put aside my marriage to Johnny – never mind his feelings, Nell's feelings, my family's feelings, my child, my self respect.'

'Ooly, my d-d-darling, beautiful girl, every minute you spend with that wretched ground wallah I am driven to distraction. We've got some top notch lawyers in the family – it could be managed quickly and quietly – no shortage of funds, either. This time next year, when the war is over, we could all be off to C-c-caxton Hall – Todge in a little ermine cape – I picture you wrapped in silver fox with an armful of roses.'

'Roses? Why roses?' And she was gone, lost in the foggy depth of Bow Road.

Dot wrote to Pan:
No more raids this week, thank the Lord. No Christmas fare to be got

343

round here – nothing at all in the shops. Of course we'd love to come and see your play, and quite understand how you need family support, but mum is not too good and dad can't possibly leave the shop, not to mention the rehearsal for his Christmas concert at Hermon Hill. We wish you all the best for it, I'm sure it will do you credit. Ooly's being really odd – she's as sour and grumpy as may be, mooning around like a wet week. Mum says she's probably starting a stye. She seems to have given up her regular visits to Nell, for which mum and I are thankful.

Dad wrote:

Of course we would all love to come and see your play, and thank you and Gif for the kind invite, but I really can't leave the shop and mum and Aunty are beginning to feel their age, or so they say. We realise that you would like family support and it would, of course, be a wonderful experience for little Todge to see it, but I don't know if it would be wise for Ooly to take the trip on her own, without any help, I mean.

Mum wrote:

Sorry we carnt cum to your play. aunty and i would love to see you all careering about being animals. weeve told little Todge all about it and shes wildly exited. ooly can manage on her own on the train. dad is worried.

Ooly did not want to go at all.

'You can't disappoint Todge,' said her mother.

'If you hadn't told her all about it she wouldn't have known it was happening!'

'Pan needs family support,' said her aunt.

'I'm only staying one night, and that's that,' said Ooly. Oh well, it was something to do, to fill the empty, miserable days. She had decided that it was over; quite finished – no more lies, no more deception, no more guilt. Divorce was unthinkable. If that was what he wanted, then it must a clean break. She would not see him again, no, not even once to say goodbye.

So the trip to Suffolk was arranged.

Two weeks to go until the opening night. There would be three performances on Thursday, Friday and Saturday. Pan had done well – rehearsals were relatively calm, with few explosions. Nearly everyone acknowledged Pan's authority and her skill at drawing out the best in her cast; bullying was kept at a minimum. Gif and Maths were really very good actresses, but Dom Sci. needed some nursing and the Wildwooders got somewhat restive from time to time, having little to do. As for Pan herself, she loved rolling her perfectly articulated consonants and showing off her handsome profile and long, strong limbs. She had ordered from Elsa a red silk spotted cravat, a fine leather waistcoat and some suede breeches. Gif would be attired in plus fours, a tweed cap and some motoring goggles. On their heads they would all wear balaclava helmets with ears attached, appropriate to their species.

'Morning, Drayman,' said Elsa, cheerily, when she encountered Gif in the corridor. 'I just passed the history room and heard you telling the girls: "They changed their pointed bottoms for rounded ones." –Or was it the other way round? What on earth were you teaching them?'

'Canals. Industrial Revolution. How are the costumes getting on? I've got an old frock coat of my grandpapa's – would do for Badger.'

'Oh – yes – splendid, just the job.'

Just four days before the opening night the company of river bank folk gathered for the dress rehearsal, after school.

'Pan, darling. I'm so sorry,' Elsa was late. 'I have been so snowed under – I haven't had time to get everything together. Look, I've got the balaclava helmets – they just need some ears sewn on.'

'And where, may we know, are the actual costumes?' Pan was fuming, purple, and near to boiling point. 'Where, I said, are the costumes?' She strode towards Elsa with menace and caught hold of her by the lapels of her Harris tweed jacket and shook her, like a rat. 'You incompetent, thoughtless bitch. Where is my waistcoat, my cravat? You've had weeks ...'

Gif, alarmed, intervened and pulled her off. 'Come on, Piggo. Calm down.'

'I'm sure Rush will have everything ready by tomorrow,' intervened Dom Sci.

'Will you, Rush?' asked Gif.

'Well – er – I'm not sure.'

Pan struggled free and lunged at Elsa, landing her with a mighty punch. She fell to the ground, groaning.

'Oh dear.' Said Dom Sci. 'Whatever shall we do now?'

The Wildwooders dispersed, twittering; Gif and Maths carted Rush off to the sanatorium while Dom Sci. attempted to soothe Pan.

Dad insisted that he would accompany Ooly and Todge to Liverpool Street.

'Honestly, Dad, there is no need. I'm perfectly capable of looking after one three-year-old.'

'I'd feel happier if I saw you both safe on the train, mate.'

They arrived late in the afternoon before the big night. Nobody was there to meet them at the station, but they managed to cadge a lift. No one was at home when they arrived at Blacksmith's Cottage. They sat on the doorstep and waited. Puddy Tat was getting very agitated when two cyclists hove into view.

Spluttering noisily the occupants flung themselves off the bikes and, with much roaring they started unloading their baskets and saddle bags.

'Oh, my good God,' shrieked Pan. 'Ooly and Pud – you might have let us know you were going to be here so early! Ooly you are hopeless!'

Ooly looked sour, recalling that a letter had been sent clearly giving the time their train was scheduled to arrive. She decided it was inadvisable to point this out and changed the subject.

'What on earth have you got there – have you been raiding a furriers?'

'It's a long and ugly story,' said Pan. 'Come on let's go inside and get Old Pud warmed up; she must be frozen half to death.' She scooped the child up and hugged her hard.

Todge was overcome with shyness, not having seen her aunt for some time, and was surprised and disappointed to see a human face leering at her, expecting her to have become transmogrified into a furry animal, as Nan had said. The fire was lit, the table laid with a ham big enough to feed the Eighth Army and a "Wind in the Willows" cake prepared with loving care by Dom Sci.; it was decorated with darling little angelica trees and sugar mice.

'So what's going on?' asked Ooly.

'Damned woman let us down. Rush was meant to be doing the costumes for the play and she appears not to have lifted a finger.' Gif carved the ham with vigour and venom.

'Couldn't you hire something?'

'I tried that but they didn't have anything remotely suitable. Most of us are furry animals so one of the Others suggested that we collect what we can in the way of fur coats from parents and so forth. I've got grandpapa's frock coat – that'll have to do.'

'It's not like Elsa,' said Ooly who had always thought that the French mistress would have walked through fire for Pan. 'Is she cracking up or something?'

'Not much sign of that,' said Gif. '*Au contraire*, she appears to be on top of the world.'

She produced a bag of felt. 'Ooly, you can help me with the ears? Just cut them out and sew them on to these balaclava helmets.'

'What!' Ooly was well known for her inability to thread a needle, let alone wield one.

'There's weasels and ferrets, stoats, field mice, rabbits and, of course, a water rat, mole and badger.'

'But I don't know what they look like.'

'Here's a book. I'm Toad – some sort of nobs will do for me.'

They set to work while Pan read *The Wind in the Willows* to Todge, in preparation for the morrow and then practiced her songs.

It was four o'clock in the morning before they turned in. Ooly's fingers were bleeding and she dreamt of mice - they terrified her.

The Great Day dawned. Jocasta was at her desk, bright and early, writing yet another letter to the parent of an errant gel when there was a faint tap on the door.

'Come in.'

'Please, miss ...'

'Miss *Meredith* – how many times have you been told!'

'Please Miss Meredith ...'

'Yes, Audrey – it is Audrey, isn't it? Audrey Catchpole? Upper third?'

'Yes, miss.'

'Miss Meredith.'

'Yes, Miss Meredith.'

'Well?'

'You know what you said about GIs and girls and everything?'

'Yes, Audrey. I do know what I said.'

'Well, miss ...'

'Miss Meredith.'

'Well, Miss Meredith, is it the same for teachers?'

'What on earth are you talking about? Explain yourself, gel.'

'Well, me and my friend were in town last Wednesday. We went to see that Lassie film – ooh it was lovely, miss.'

'Yes, yes, go on.'

'Well – who should we see but Miss Rush.'

'What! *Lassie Come Home* is hardly to Miss Rush's taste.'

Oh, no, miss – Miss Meredith – she were walkin' along the street as

348

we come out.'

'And?'

'Well, Miss – she were arm in arm with a GI; 'e was quite an old man, as old as my dad, I'd say. 'E 'ad sort of brooches and ribbons on 'im.'

'Thank you, Audrey. You may go.'

Elsa, with only a faint black eye to show for her encounter, was summoned to The Presence; it took some time to locate her as she no longer dared enter the staff room. A severe dressing down was administered, with many references to "example", "discredit", "shock", "shame", "disgrace", etc.

The miscreant listened calmly, unabashed and untouched by the onslaught.

'You will be delighted to hear, Miss Meredith, that you not be troubled by my presence for much longer.'

She proffered her left hand; twinkling on her fourth finger was a diamond of vast proportions.

Case dismissed.

Jocasta was all shock-horror, but, on reflection, became rather pleased with the turn of events. She would be ridding herself of the super-intelligent, popular, elegant Rush who was, of course, a serious rival in the matter of Pan worship.

When the curtain went up that evening the audience was baffled by the sight of the stately school ma'ams of Harpisfield Grange capering around the stage attired in fur coats and balaclava helmets, adorned with an array of indeterminate ears. Pan's masterly rendering of 'Messing about on the river' was greeted with howls of delight from the girls; the production was talked about for many years to come.

Jocasta spoke at the end, thanking everyone for their efforts, particularly, with heavy irony, 'Miss Rush who will, sadly, be leaving us at the end of term to marry Colonel Muslow of the United States Airforce.'

Blacksmith's Cottage shook with Pan's wrathful sobs that evening: 'She promised me a spotted cravat, a leather waistcoat. She promised me undying love. If you hadn't insisted on inviting that bloody bastard of a colonel in at Christmas none of this would ever have happened.'

Poor Gif.

'What's the matter with Bang?' asked Todge. 'I s'pose she's crying because they didn't get the proper clothes to wear for the play and had to wear fur coats and funny hats and everybody laughed at them, really loud.'

Out of the mouths of babes.

'How did it go?'– Chestnut Avenue was all agog.

'There was a bit of a disaster with the costumes. Elsa was meant to be doing them but she's got herself mixed up with a Yank – she's going to marry him, apparently – it's that colonel we met at Christmas – you know he gave us a lift from the station. Anyway, she was too taken up with him – getting engaged and everything – to bother with the costumes.'

'Oh my lor – I bet Pan was in a taking! Who got it in the neck?' asked Lil.

'Why, Gif, of course.'

'I thought it might 'ave bin you!' He mother laughed.

'Even my crazy sister couldn't possibly link me to Elsa's betrayal.'

'Did you like the animals, Todge? ... Todge?' asked Dot.

'She won't answer to Todge any more. She says she's Pud, like Bang says.'

'OK. Did you like the animals, Pud?'

'Weren't animals. Just ladies in fur coats.'

So Elsa planned her wedding and prepared to dance off to a new life, where she would exchange her neat scrimping for a row of perky little cocktail hats and a handbag to match every outfit, while Blacksmith Cottage returned to what passed for normality.

'One down, one to go,' thought Gif and set about her Christmas preparations.

For the Flower Garden, nursing their respective wounds, it was a grim festival to be got through, rather than celebrated. Mog set about organising a Christmas dinner in the Great Barn for local pensioners and servicemen's families. Pan seethed, and applied herself to hand painting 26 calendars. Ooly decided to do her best to make a go of it with Johnny and managed to find him a very expensive silk tie, it would be his present from Todge – they had chosen it together.

Sid cut out the day's Patience Strong poem and pinned it up on the shop door:

"They came that night to Bethlehem, the simple and the wise.
The shepherd and the scholar saw the glory in the skies ...
The greatest men who walk the earth can offer us today
No dimmer revelation. This then is the way ...
Though to knowledge high and vast the human mind may soar
Every man must come at last unto the stable door."

Christmas Eve at Chestnut Avenue had none of its usual atmosphere of anticipation – no one was coming – well only Johnny, just for two days. They had a tree "for the kiddie", just a small one, and Ooly had helped Todge make some sticky paper chains. After she had gone to bed they were to gather around the wireless to listen to *A Christmas Carol*, on Sid's insistence, but Johnny dragged Ooly off to the pub on the Green, where she sipped some sherry and tried to make an effort.

The family had agreed, for once, to accept Billy's invitation to sample the delights of Forest Gate on Christmas Day. Lil was feeling rather under the weather and was grateful not to have to make the tremendous effort required for celebrations at home. Pan had been kept at bay and Billy had even somehow managed to get a taxi to convey them to his abode. It would pick them up at one o'clock.

There was, as usual, an enormous mound of presents for Todge, and it was decided that the exchange of gifts would be done before they left. Todge was very excited about giving her father his special gift. She had wrapped it up herself, after a fashion, and she thrust the mangled bundle at him with eager anticipation, helping him to disentangle the string.

'D'you like tie, Daddy Johnny?'

He was in a bad mood – he hated being called that; it sounded as if there were other daddies around from whom he had to be distinguished.

'It's a bit too bright for me.'

Todge hung her head.

Dot intervened: 'I expect Daddy Johnny will wear it for Christmas dinner at Uncle Billy's.'

'You must be joking.'

Todge held tight to Puddy Tat. She was a brave little body.

Oh, Johnny.

At that moment the telephone rang.

'Ooly, mate,' called Sid 'It's some one on the phone for you – says he's a doctor – is everything all right?'

Hanging around in the hall, he heard Ooly say: 'Tuesday will be fine, fine. Charing Cross will be fine.'

'What's that, mate – is there something up? Sid was alarmed.

'No, absolutely nothing is up, Dad – in fact all is very, very well.'

'Why is the doctor ringing you up on Christmas Day?'

'Oh, he's not a that sort of doctor – he's a doctor of music. It's just about a concert up west next week.'

Chapter 28:

28 December 1943 to May 1944

It had been nearly five weeks – as long as the interminable summer holidays when she was at school. Sid had tickets to take everyone to Peter Pan at the Cambridge Theatre, but Ooly pleaded an upset stomach – she needed to prepare for tomorrow. No time to go for a hair do to Frances and Betty in the Broadway – Monday was Boxing Day and they wouldn't be open.

She washed her hair and had a go with the curling tongs, stole a precious egg and mixed it with flour for a make-shift face pack, soaked her hands in very hot water and rubbed them with lard. On Tuesday morning, early, she laid out her heathery tweed suit, suede wedge heels and pearls, had a bath, slicked her eyebrows with Vaseline, and carefully painted her lips – plush red or carmine? She chose the former and painted her nails to match. With a generous dab of "Evening in Paris", a stylish black velvet hat with a bow on it, her fox fur slung over her shoulder, off she set. Why Charing Cross? she wondered.

They were to meet at 11.30. She was early, like Sid, she usually was. What a jostling and hustling of kit-bags there was, and what a racket – bellowing of steam engines, hubbub of busy, anxious humanity, the twang of American voices, the creaky tones of an accordion. She had some coffee and looked at the bookstall and at the clock. Down she went down into the ladies' room and checked her appearance in the mirror and ran back up again. She looked at the clock. It was time. She sat down and stood up and looked at the clock again. She walked round and round, not daring to go too far from the appointed spot, and looked at the clock. It was 11.42. She opened her compact and dabbed some powder on her cheeks, and checked the clock. An elderly, flustered woman asked her where the cafeteria was and engaged her in conversation about the national loaf. She bought a paper and tried to read it: the great Jerry battle ship, the *Scharnhorst* sunk, Monty says the Eighth Army has the best soldiers in the world, Eisenhower appointed Supreme Allied Commander for the liberation of Europe, more stuff about the wonderful war work done by women with homes to look after as well as their jobs. She looked up at the clock. It was noon. He was always on time. The throbbing in her chest got stronger and her palms started to sweat.

'Waiting for your beau, dearie? Have a bunch of heather to see you along. I expect he'll be here soon.'

'Oh – no thanks.'

'Stood you up has he? Perhaps he's had a better offer.' The disappointed gipsy cackled nastily.

Someone caught her arm: 'It is Mrs Bowyer, isn't it? Remember me – Archie Mosley.'

'Oh yes.'

'There's an emergency at the hospital – so I've come instead of Dougie. Can I buy you a drink? There's an American place near here where you can get whatever you want.'

He took her arm and led her off, firmly

Her heart was thumping away now. What was this all about? So Archie was in the know.

They sat down with martinis.

'Well, Mrs Bowyer, Lily, it's good to meet you properly, at last. Is this place all right? I think Dougie had the Savoy Grill in mind.'

'Please call me Ooly. No one ever uses my proper name.'

'Okey doke. So sorry about that stupid business – Jessie and everything.'

'No need to apologise.' she said rather huffily.

Some small talk followed: the *Scharnhorst*, the invasion of Europe, the invasion of Yanks.

'Another?'

'No thank you. I must be getting home.'

'Oh dear, must you – I'm enjoying myself in the company of the best looking woman in the bar! Just one more?'

They had another. Was he trying it on with her? Was this some sort of test or was he just going to warn her off.

'So did you ever get a new housekeeper? Or are you turning the mattresses yourselves?'

They both collapsed in laughter

'No – we couldn't get anyone and now we've moved to this little place …'

'I thought that was going to be a temporary measure until the fuss died down.'

'Well – it suits us – much nearer the hospital and my uncle's talking about getting rid of Tredegar Square. We've got a daily who comes in twice a week – she used to work at St Alphege vicarage.'

'That's where I got married – St Alphege.' Ooly was suddenly overcome with embarrassment.

'She's a nice girl, a bit of a gossip – never stops talking. There's nothing I don't know about goings-on in the locality these days. She's told me all about your pa and his shop.'

'W-what! But how did you know she was talking about my dad?'

'She said there was this wonderful oil shop in Roman Road, a real Aladdin's cave, selling everything you can name, run by a very kind old gent – the only gent in Bow, she said – who was like a saint – couldn't do enough for his customers, crazy about children. She said he kept a light shining in that little place, like a beacon of hope in the darkest days.'

'How did you know he was my dad?'

'Put two and two together. She said he had three girls, all called after flowers, two of them real stunners, the other one a bit of a case. All known for their singing. The youngest, she said, was married to a lord in the west country. Now – there aren't many of them in the East End.'

'So, Dougie told you about my sister did he?'

'He told me everything. Let's have another.'

He returned from the bar with two more martinis.

'So what's going on, Ooly?'

'Have you been sent to interrogate me?'

'Of course not. The poor blighter was out of his mind with worry that you would think he'd stood you up and I offered to come.'

'Oh – is that all?'

'That's all.'

'Now – are you going to tell me what's going on?' He twiddled the stem of his glass: 'You aren't – em – stringing him along, are you?'

'That's rich, I must say. I take it you know what happened back in '37?'

'Of course, of course, but … well – he's a lovely chap, but has always been a bit easily influenced by others. I've never seen him so determined about anything as he is about hanging on to you now. Are you really set on finishing with him?'

'I was, I really was, but, oh dear, I simply can't bear the thought of not seeing him again. Didn't he send a message?'

'Just this.' He took a handkerchief out of his pocket and unwrapped it slowly, revealing an exquisitely wrought gold ring set with a large opal surrounded by rubies. 'He says please wear it on your right hand until it can be transferred to your left. It was grandmamma's.'

'She wasn't a Mosley was she?'

''Fraid so.'

They both giggled.

She slipped the ring on her finger: 'Oh God,' she thought. 'That's me finished.'

When she got home she hung the opal ring on a long thin gold chain and wore it, unseen. In the days that followed she practiced writing what might be her new name and spent many hours anguishing at the piano as to how, when the time came, she would break the news to Johnny, to Nell, to mum and dad, to Mog, to Pan. Todge would not be such a problem – after all, she had never lived with Daddy Johnny. Nineteen forty-four, she thought, would be her "year of destiny", as it would be for much of the world.

"Help us God to strike the blow to set the nations free", ran Patience Strong's New Year message. The Old Lion and her cubs stood at the ready, with the great American Eagle poised for flight. Victory was in the air; talk of the Allied invasion of Europe on every tongue and, with it, an apprehension that the worst was yet to come, before Winnie's "broad sunlit uplands" might be trod. He now promised: "Victory may not be so far away, and it will certainly not be denied us in the end." Goebbels warned "The British people will have to get accustomed to bombing as we are being bombed now."

Heavy raids on London started at the end of January, revenge for the on-going onslaught on Berlin.

Lil and Dot both had February birthdays. They wrote to Pan:

Mum wrote:
My Dear just a line to thank you for the lovely glass – it looks lovely on my table. i had some lovely presents. Ooly gave me a table cloth – it is a beauty. i think of you a lot these days. it will be a blessing when it is all over. not long now. I hope you are better – I meen your Back – it must be rotten having to go to school. i have been doing the garden today – i was not out long – it was bitter cold and I get tired. Aunty went to fire drill this morning – it was like dan leano [Dan Leno comedian d. 1904] turn out. then we went out to bye a hat with our birthday presents and aunty bought such a nice one nearly one pound. I of cause bought 2, one for days with Mog, if she ever comes. good

357

warent it? i hope you have not had any raids – they have made a mess of Leytonstone Station. try to get some milk down your neck. they said it was going to be moor plentiful. johnnie came Sunday afternoon. he had some tea – I cut him some sandwich to take with him i have put Todges little note what she scribbled. she gave it to me to put in mine. i cant think of moore ... bless and keep you safe. Mum xx.

Dot wrote:

Dear Pan,

Thank you for my birthday money – it is very generous of you. Mum and I went on a shopping expedition and I bought a lovely hat from Bearman's – you should see the bomb damage to the station in Leytonstone. Mum, dad and Ooly gave me money, too – they say I'm too fussy to buy presents for! Ed came up with a five pound note – I was surprised; he must have had a win on the pools. Mog sent a lovely card, hand painted by herself, and a pretty scarf. I went to fire drill – what a disorganised affair it was – the man instructing us broke his stirrup pump! We are very pleased to hear that you are going to bed early, if your spine shows wear and tear of a person of 60, you must need the rest of a woman of 60. Dad got an estimate for mending your watch £3 5s! Needless to say he didn't leave it, but Johnny took it to a friend of his and he is doing it for 12s 6s. He seems to be wangling a lot of leave recently, but we've heard all leave will be cancelled soon.'

And so it was. The country was alive with armed men awaiting the order to attack. After nearly five years, the war was building up to a terrifying crescendo. "This second front will be the biggest show ever," warned the press. "It is going to be warfare of the most severe and bloody character." American and British bombers roared off on their daily trips to smash aircraft factories, bridges, railway lines and anything which might allow Jerry to repel the great invasion which was to come.

On Tuesdays Ooly and Dougie made love in the little flat near the hospital and talked of their plans for a life together: a fine house, up on the Green, perhaps, to be near mum and dad. They would have a sweeping, gravel drive, lawns and flower beds, sunlight would stream through the tall sash windows, across the high gloss of a concert grand. Todge would attend the small private school nearby where the girls wore boaters, brown blazers and brown and white check dresses. When the waiting was over, when the war was over ...

'You'd think from the papers that the bleedin' war was already over,' remarked Doomandgloom. 'Papers is full of 'ow we're goin' to treat Jerry when its all finished, 'ow we're genna parcel up the continong, all the continong, when us and the Yanks and the Ruskies are in charge.'

'Just the Yanks and the Ruskies, shouldn't wonder,' said Bert Gum. It's all abaat them these days – Eisenhower in charge – the great saviours, what about us standing all alone and fightin' our corner in '40? what about the Blitz? the Battle of Britain, Alamein? And, as Winnie said, "The honour of bombing Berlin has fallen almost entirely on us".'

Doomandgloom went on: 'Country's in a shockin' state, shockin state, these days – no 'ouses, no teachers, union men swearin' they're not going back to the pre-war slavery. Some outlook. Look at the miners' carry-on – and the dockers. All these ruddy strikes ... Shouldn't be surprised if the whole thing blew up – no second front, no invasion and, what's more ...'

'But its terrible, dangerous work, minin',' interrupted Dai Lewis – 'My cousin Emrys, 'e were blown to bits back in '32. I feel for those poor lads who've been sent down the pits by Ernie Bevin[4] with no choice about it. The regular men 'ate 'em. I 'eard story from my old Da – some Bevin Boys, posh chaps from England, only kiddies, really,

---

4 Minister of Labour.

were put in charge of the pit ponies who only take notice of commands given to them in Welsh.'

'Boss classes are doin' well out of this war, make no mistake, Mr Undertaker,' said Will Kerridge threateningly. 'And d'you know 'ow much they're sayin' this war is costin'? Eighteen million a day! And they reckon the invasion's genna gonna put another two hundred and fifty million on top of that! And who's payin'?'

'That's as maybe,' said Bert, 'But now's not the time to be striking for more pay with this big show comin' up and the lads in the forces are riskin' their lives for us. Your ordinary soldier has only five or six bob a day (Yanks get ten bob), miners get five quid a week. Not so bad is it? My lad lost 'is life doin' 'is bit for king and country.'

'Come, come, brothers,' said Sid. 'We must all pull together at this time of crisis. Let's try and find the bright side – lemons are back, back in plenty, brought over from Sicily just in time for our pancakes.'

He pinned up Patience Strong's latest:

"If we must wait – then let us wait with patience. If we must work, then let it be with zest … If we must suffer, let it be in silence. If we must give – give only of the best. If we must march, then let it be like brothers, close in the kinship of our common ties. If we must strike, then let us strike to vanquish evil and tyranny in every guise."

The raids on London went on. Rumours flew around, convoys of military vehicles rumbled along the roads, forces were assembling, tension mounted, the thunder clouds were gathering.

'Is Johnny involved in all this?' asked Dot.

'How should I know. Nobody knows anything about anything,' snapped Ooly.

They were on their way to the shops; Mrs Spoon had called in to let them know the good news that oranges were to be had at the greengrocer's in the Broadway. Chestnut Avenue was touched with gold, daffs and forsythia blazing out from fresh green lawns, white bursts of creamy magnolia and the palest pink filigree of almond blossom, all putting on a brave front, while regiments of vegetables stood at the ready at the back.

'Are you off to Bow again this week?'

'Yes.' Ooly tapped crossly along the pavement. 'I hope Todge likes oranges – she's never tasted one. I'm not sure that I can remember what they're like. I was never that keen – such a business peeling them.'

'How is Nell?'

'She's bearing up, but she hasn't heard from Derek for some weeks. I gather they're having a terrible time slogging it out in Italy. She read somewhere that it's a bit like the first war, a slow, grinding war of attrition, every yard contested, barbed wire, minefields. Only six months ago we thought Italy was in the bag. So much for Winnie's "soft underbelly".'

'What about Johnny. I expect she's worried he'll be part of this second front business?'

'I've told you, Aunty, we know nothing about his movements.'

'I suppose he won't be home for a bit.'

'I suppose not.'

'Never mind.'

They joined the orange queue and then proceeded to the fishmongers where they were for some time.

April brought a ban on travel in a ten-mile coastal strip from the Wash to Lands End. Over Easter sea side resorts were dead, the beaches empty, the dance bands silenced; police manned the stations. Mr and Mrs Spoon had to cancel their trip to visit their daughter in Southend. There were dire warnings of much more severe restrictions on movement to come, intended to sabotage enemy paratrooper/rs when they turned up. Whole districts, the papers threatened, would be cut off from one another. No phone calls might be made or telegrams sent. There would be no post for weeks on end.

Sid wrote to Pan:

Just a hasty line I expect you've seen the reports in the paper about the mail being stopped, so I thought I'd get a letter in quickly, in case it does come to pass, to assure you that all is well with us, and to make sure that if you don't hear from us for a while it doesn't mean we are neglecting you or we are in any trouble. Mum is sending a cake and some lemons – we've got a plentiful supply here and don't know if you've got any yet.

The week has been much as usual. We have got on well for victuals. Little Jane is in the pink ... Johnny was due home for a few days but had his leave cancelled. Went to pictures Thursday but did not care much for them. We went to choir as usual on Friday; it was a good practice – Mrs Belcher and Mrs Fordham asked after you ... '

The papers were still only hinting at the coming crisis, as May tripped in on a tiptoe of expectancy: the German navy is being massed – subs and gun boats are accumulating in the French ports; the Gestapo will arrest all known members of the French resistance and send them to labour camps. The Allied bombers set off on the daily round, but now the destination was northern France. At home there was a rash of imprisonments of miners under a new rule that made incitement to strike an offence. 'What 'ave we bin fightin' for?' asked Will Kerridge. 'Bloody Bevin is trying to stop our union rights.'

At New Hall, Edmund was exercised about the mines: 'What a nonsensical measure, sending these so-called Bevin Boys, educated and intelligent boys, down the pits. Old Raglan Fitzroy has got a good letter in the [Western] Mail: "It is as though the men of Syracuse had sent their best warriors to the quarries, or the Athenians had insisted on their best oarsmen going to the silver mines at Laurium."

Mog, not having the benefit of a classical education, was not sure of the significance of the comparisons and had no idea who "old Raglan" might be.

'Who's he?'

'Old soldier, Lord Lieutenant of Monmouth – writes about Gods and Heroes. His great grandfather was commander of our troops in the Crimea – Charge of the Light Brigade and all that.'

'Into the valley of death …'

'I must say, I'm sickened by this rash of strikes,' he went on. 'Wouldn't be surprised if the whole invasion is stymied by the good old British working man who reckons he's been conned all in the name of the war effort.'

'Good Heavens, Edmund, you sound like your father. Have you any idea what terrible conditions these poor men have to endure in the pits?' Mog's blood was up.

'And have you any idea what it's like to face a barrage of hot metal, to be given the order to charge, shitting yourself, to fly, blind, into a black sky, to almost certain death?'

'No, but then neither do you.'

Sir Edmund Tillingham, bart. flung out of the room and shut himself away.

Mog wrote to Pan:

My dear old cocky,

I hope you're staggering along all right and your boils and back aren't giving you too much gip.

Sorry not to have written for such an age. I can't seem to get down to anything at the moment – I decide to do something and then – well – I just don't.

What do you think about the miners? And what about Winnie putting the kibosh on equal pay for women teachers. I only get about three quid a week – I suppose you get more. I know you're all for Winnie – I always have been too – but this seems too bad. Edmund says it would bring all sorts of ramifications and would end up with all women, civil servants and everybody wanting the same as men. He says that when a woman goes to work she will either stay single all her life, so have no dependants, or she will, quickly, creep under the protecting shoulder of some man who will bring home the bacon for the whole family. I suppose he's right – but it seems very unfair to me – we work as hard as them, harder, often. We've had quite a few words about it, and the miners, as a matter of fact.'

Pan was planting out some seedlings when the post arrived. The garden at Blacksmith's cottage was sumptuous, its pergola decked with mauve wisteria, its beds crammed with brilliant red and yellow tulips, dark blue ceanothus, froths of London Pride with its tiny pink flowers on spindly dark red stems, its tubs packed with purple and yellow pansies, splashed with scarlet geraniums, its borders high with irises of many hues, orange and yellow wallflowers, dark purple lilac. The village gardens, with their proud battalions of cabbages, onions, potatoes and carrots looked askance at what their owners called "the alarming garden up at Blacksmith's".' Pan's vegetables were tucked behind a high beech hedge.

She skimmed Mog's letter and moved quickly on to the next item, a thick white important looking envelope. She recognised Elsa's hand writing.

'My sainted bloody aunt, she's only had the damned cheek to invite us to her wedding!' Pan rushed, shouting, into the dining room, where Gif was deep in the paper.

'Who?'

'Rush, of course.'

'Hope she'll be wearing a bullet-proof vest,' said Gif. 'When is it?'

'Next Saturday.'

'Getting it in before the great expedition sallies forth, I shouldn't wonder. I suppose she thinks it unlikely that we will put in an appearance, but I think we should.'

'You think we should – you do, do you? Well I can tell you that I have absolutely no intention of turning up for that charade.'

Gif laughed: 'I suppose we could go in our *Toad* headgear. Anything else in the post?'

'A letter from Mog. She's asking what we think about Winnie and the equal pay business.'

'Well, much as I deplore the whole thing – now is hardly the time to have the government toppled and the Prime Minister resigning, with our forces about to hurl themselves into the final battle against the enemy.' She was not a brigadier general's granddaughter for nothing.

'Good God Almighty, Piggo! How can you be so dismissive. How can you calmly accept a blow like this. We work ourselves to the bone and paid nearly a quarter less than the wretched men for no reason at all except our gender.'

Und so weiter

There was another letter, as a matter of fact; it, too, was from Elsa. Pan opened it when she was alone.

My darling Pan,

I shall never forget you – I shall never stop loving you and remembering the heavenly times we were together. There will always be a place in my heart for you. Edward is a wonderful man and it would mean everything to me if you could bring yourself to come to our wedding and complete my happiness. '.

Pan tore it into tiny fragments and flung them into the waste paper basket. She then went down to her study and penned a gracious acceptance to the invitation.

On Saturday the stage was set. Candles glittered on the mosaics in the gloom of St Silas. Elsa wore a dark-green silk suit with a peacock feather in a dainty hat. They were all there: the Others from School, a host of gels, Jocasta, a smattering of Rushes, a good number of GIs, the groom resplendent in his decorations, his best man, also in uniform.

Pan and Gif were late – the first hymn was in progress as they took their places in a back pew. The diminutive curate, looking like a pixie beside the two giant Americans, had to stand in for Father Jessop at the last minute. The priest was nowhere to be found. Later he was discovered in the presbytery, bound and gagged with a red spotted cravat. Nothing was stolen.

Chapter 29:
D Day, June 1944

All eyes were on southern England as June stole in, bringing a fearful excitement. The incessant rumble of military might spoke of the great battle to come; lorry loads of guns, tanks, cranes and jeeps choked the highways. The crowds of GIs which had filled London disappeared like snow in summer, to be locked behind the barbed wire of their camps, awaiting the fateful order. The papers said nothing, the wireless said nothing – there was a hushed dread abroad. No one knew when or where it would happen – they just knew that D Day was at hand.

'Got any of them Dr Cassell's Nerve Tablets, Sid? It's the ruddy waitin', ruddy waitin', my missus can't take it.' Doomandgloom was all of a tremor.

Vi Kerridge was commanding a good audience with her tales of the mysterious goings on down in the Docks: 'My Will says there's these 'normous great concrete box type things they've bin makin' for months down the East India and the Royals – 'uge they are – size of Bow Baths – or more. And then they chuck them into the river – 'es seen 'em floatin' daahn stream.'

'Get away!' said Fanny Bastaple.

Vi went on: 'I says to Will, I says, I reckon they're planning to build some ruddy great wall of China to keep the Hun out.'

'I thought we was supposed to be goin' over there, at last, not buildin' a barricade over 'ere. 'Aven't you noticed all them troop ships lyin' along daahn the river? More like they're makin' a 'uge great prison to shut all the Jerries in when we've won.' Fanny cackled.

'Don't be so bloody daft,' said Vi.

'Well, ladies,' asked Sid 'What can I do for you – or are you just here to pass the time of day?'

'Mary, Mother of God,' shrieked Kathleen O'Brien, rushing through the door. 'It's startin' up for sure now and on the very day they've rescued the Holy Father! [The fall of Rome was announced in the press on the 5th June.]. I've seen dem with my own eyes in Wappin' – GIs on the march, stridin' along with a fierce gleam in their eyes, makin' for the West India. Girls were throwin' packets of fags and offerin' dem cups of tea.'

'I dare say that's not all they was offerin',' said Fanny.

The next day, at nine o'clock in the morning the BBC broke its silence. Ed was out the back of the shop, pouring out paraffin. He switched on the news and caught "paratroopers landing in the Seine estuary."

''ere, Sid, it's 'appenin'! It's started.'

'Mind what you're doing with that can, you'll have the place on fire!'

'But 'es just said German ships are fighting invasion barges in the Channel.'

'Before we have a celebratory bonfire, I suggest we wait for some official report.'

That came soon enough: at 9.33am a news bulletin told everyone that a communiqué from Supreme Headquarters Allied Expeditionary Force had announced: "Allied Naval Forces supported by strong Air Forces began landing Allied Armies this morning on the Northern Coast of France."

Ooly was having a lie in; it was a Tuesday, but Dougie was on call. Lil was making a patty of dried egg for Todge's breakfast. Dot was hanging out some sheets, hoping the rain would hold off. Mr Spoon called over the fence, shouting at the top of his frail old voice: 'Miss

Smart, Mrs Smart, Mrs Bowyer have you heard the news? They're on their way, our lads are on their way.'

Ooly scrambled into her beige silk dressing gown and rushed down stairs. 'Mum, is it true?'

'Must be. I missed the news – Todge was fiddlin' abaat wiv the knobs. Look, I've made 'er a poached egg out of the dried stuff – good eh?'

Pan was with the upper fifth, preparing to dissect frogs and Gif was deep in the War of the Spanish Succession, when the school bell rang out, summoning everyone to the hall: 'But miss, we've had assembly.'

'Miss Meredith wants to make a special announcement.'

'Gels, the liberation of Europe has begun. This morning "fair stood the wind for France" – a second Armada left these shores, in the early hours of this morning, a vast fleet of vessels set sail for France and thousands of planes roared out; already Hitler's fortress has been breached. I ask you to raise a cheer for the brave soldiers, sailors and airmen of Great Britain who, along with a large contingent of men from Canada and the United States, have, this day, at terrible risk to life and limb, launched themselves in the final blow against the forces of evil.'

'She's enjoying this no end,' hissed Gif at Pan as the hall burst into an explosion of cheers.

At New Hall, Bella was out in the vegetable garden, thinning out the carrots, no sign of Edmund yet, Mog, had just settled her charges down to a spelling test, when the thunderous sound of the Great Knocker made them all jump.

'Gracious, Rector, whatever's up?'

'Didn't any of you hear the news bulletin?'

'I've been busy with the children. Bella's up to something with the veg. Edmund's not an early riser and Mrs P's gone into town, I think – she said something about it yesterday and Freda's gone with her to get some …'

'My dear lady, D Day is upon us. I'm having an Invasion Day service at eleven – I do hope you can all attend.'

That evening they all listened to the King on the wireless at 9pm: "At this historic moment surely not one of us is too busy, too young, or too old to play a part in a nationwide, a worldwide vigil of prayer as the great Crusade sets forth."

The following day [7th]Bayeux was liberated; Gif wondered where the tapestry was. At home lorries were rushing down to the coast to collect casualties; the Red Cross was on call.

"Enormous exertions lie before us." Winnie told the House on Thursday [8th].

Sid got in some union jacks and did a good trade.

Kathleen O'Brien was in high spirits: 'Sure, it's a victory street party we'll be 'avin' in no time at all! My Denny will be back, safe and sound. Got any balloons, Sid?'

'I've got a few out the back – you'd better take them now before I run out.'

'We're payin' them back good and proper now – Dunkirk reversed,' announced Bert Gum.

'Early days yet, early days,' warned Doomandgloom. 'They 'aven't finished with us yet, mark my words, mark my words.'

Exactly one week after the first Normandy landings, the undertaker's prophecy was fulfilled.

''Eard what 'appened in Grove Road this morning, Sid – ruddy funny business?' Bert Gum was in the shop first-thing, after some lino for his back kitchen.

'Can't get any for love nor money,' said Sid. 'I've just got a couple of strips left of pre-war stock. Good stuff – bit pricey, of course. So what happened in Grove Road?'

'Well – I 'eard it from Sam the Chippie's girl – she and 'er mates were all in a gaggle outside the baths, talkin' abaaht it as I passed.'

'Go on, brother.'

'Well, she were comin' 'ome after doin' a night shift, it was just getting' light and she was walkin' daahn Grove Road when she 'ears this chugging noise overhead – sort of put- put-put like a motor bike goin' across the sky, quite low down. Then it stops – dead silence, she said, and next thing a thunderous crash, the railway bridge cut clean in half, aahses around fallen like a pack of cards, 'uge crater – screamin' sirens. Worse than anything she'd seen in the blitz, she said.'

'Taking their revenge for the invasion, I suppose we should expect more raids, God help us.'

'But this wasn't no ordinary bomber. It came right low, made this funny sound, and some of the girls were sayin' there was no pilot found.'

'Something must have gone wrong with the engine – plane crashed, bomb exploded, pilot blown to nothing – no trace.'

'Yeah – I reckon.'

But there was no pilot; it was a flying bomb, a buzz bomb, a doodelbug, a robot – thousands would come thick and fast, more deadly than anything that had come before, Hitler's *Vergeltungsswaffe*, his vengeance weapon. Any celebration of the Normandy landings was put on hold, as London and the south of England cowered beneath the avalanche. They flew very low, at immense speed. When the spluttering noise stopped it meant the creature had run out of fuel and the dread descent began; whole terraces of houses were blown into the ether. In Forest Gate, Flo' stopped hoovering, afraid that she would not hear the buzz of the approaching robot.

'Gawd Almighty,' declaimed Fanny Bastaple. 'Nearly five years of this bloody war and us all expectin' the end was in sight and now up he comes wiv 'is secret weapon. Press keepin' schtum as usual, I note. Old Morrison said in Saturday's *Mirror* that the damage done by the flying bombs was "relatively small".' 'Relatively small – load of baloney. I've 'eard nearly 200 people were made homeless by that one robot in

Grove Road [*recte* 166].

And – 'ave you seen the price of carrots? Four bob a bunch! Would you credit it. Peas and beans not much cheaper. So much for Grandma Buggins and 'er delicious carrot recipes.'

'Never mind the bleedin' carrots. This lot is worse than the blitz if you ask me,' said Vi Kerridge. 'Doodles all day every day – at least back in '40 there was a bit of warnin' so you could get into the shelter. These days Moanin' Minnie's at it all bloody day long. You just 'ave a few minutes to pop aat to the shops and off she goes again. That Jiggins woman 'as buggered orf. Gorn to 'er sister in Grimsby. It's all right for some.'

What had started off as the summer of liberation, of triumph, for Londoners turned into perhaps the most terrifying months of all. Streets were all but deserted as those that could fled to the countryside, buses rattled along without passengers, the flags were put away. The heavens raged in that chilly, damp grey summer, as the robots snarled in there were storms the worst anyone could remember. Sid saw a notice pinned up near his chapel in Hermon Hill: "When the 'Doodle' dallies don't dawdle – DIVE!!" 'At least,' he told his family, 'With so many folk leaving London there's more food to go round – more fish, more milk.'

'Let's go and 'ave a gander at the newsreels – they're showin' the landin's – cheer us all up.' Lil was all for an expedition up west to join the queues at the cinemas.

'It'll be shown soon enough round here, mate, bits of it, anyway,' said Sid. 'Save us trekking all the way up there and dodging the doodles. You know how easily you tire these days.'

And so when D Day came to South Woodford, a trip was planned one Thursday afternoon – best hats and all, must show respect.

'Who's going to look after Todge?' asked Dot.

'I don't see why we shouldn't take her with us,' said Ooly. 'She's been to the flics before.'

'Oh, no, mate,' warned Sid. 'It's not right to expose the kiddie to this sort of thing.'

'They won't be showing us any gore – it'll be all triumphant flag-waving rushing about. In any case, she can't be shielded from the realties of life for ever.'

'Ooly – she's only four. I don't mind staying at home with her. I can always see it another time.' Dot was often ready with a spot of self-sacrifice.

'No, Aunty, I know you want to go. We'll take her and if she gets really maggoty I can always bring her out. There'll be a cartoon on, I expect.'

So the company at Chesnut Avenue (not Ed, of course) set off.

Todge was bewildered and rather scared of all the crashing and cracking, the rumbling and roars emanating from the big flickering screen, until: 'Look, Nan, there's Daddy Johnny's balloons, floating over the ships.'

Ooly touched the opal betrayer that hung secretly round her neck.

'Is Daddy Johnny in the film?'

The great adventure may have got off to a flying start, but there was a long way to go yet and a great battle yet to come.

Ooly, to her lasting shame, had not really given a second thought to the matter of Johnny's whereabouts in the last few tumultuous weeks. Since the war began, every Monday she had got a letter from him, as regular as clockwork. To be honest she didn't really read the contents – in the early days she just scanned the beginning and the end, hoping there might be some sign that these were love letters. There wasn't – 'Dear Missus,' they began, and ended with a terse 'take care of yourself' and (after she arrived) 'Minnie Lizzie'. These days she just checked if he was expecting some leave. It hadn't seriously occurred to her that he might be actually involved in the invasion, might be in danger. She hadn't heard from him this week, or last, come to that. Sick with anxiety, sick that she was so anxious, when she was planning to do the dirty on him, she started a stye.

When dad suggested that she and Todge should join the general evacuation – go to Pan's just until the worst was over, to her father's surprise she agreed readily. The doodlebugs filled her with terror and, until she knew Johnny was safe, she was disinclined to spend time with Dougie – this was the obvious excuse – awful though the prospect was of prolonged exposure to her sister.

Lil wrote to Pan:.

> *My dear Pan,*
>
> *It is evening in the twilight – two old crocks siting reading – the bread winners gorne fire watch. it is very quiet up till now.*
>
> *I hope your Boils are not very bad – why are you having them again? why don't you stop worrying about these things – they will soon stop – they cant last long, then you can come home with comfort ... I except your old mop has grown long ... I should not like you up heare – sometimes you would not like it. Dad thinks it would be good if Ooly and Todge came to you for a bit until these things stop. Aunty and I cant leave dad and dad cant leave the shop or weel all be on the parish.*
>
> *I have just been listening to the news – they seem good. Mr and Mrs Spoon has gorn to there son's so dad went over his garden and cut some of his cars (carnations). they are lovely – they are dark red – they smell lovely. a few minnets after, that old sally from munkums (Monkhams) avenu came strutting in – but her cars were gorn.*
>
> *now dont forget soon as it gets quiet come home ... you would hate it – I would not have told you about it but it is getting better than it was last week, so they must be nocking them out – then you can come home as soon as you like, but not yet. Dad says wait a little longer. dad send his love give my love to Gif. God bless and keep you safe.'*

Ooly dropped a note to Dougie:

My Dear,

Just a quick line to let you know that I'm not going to be able to make it on Tuesday or for a little while to come. Dad is insisting that I take Todge to my sister Pan's in Suffolk until the doodlebugs stop – we've had a number round here. We're going on Sunday. Naturally I don't want to go at all, but it does seem for the best. I shall miss you terribly, but let's hope it's not for long. The address is Blacksmith's Cottage, Radswick, but please don't write – it's too dangerous – I will phone you from the village phone box when I can. With all my love.'

She wrote to Johnny at the only address she had for him, asking him to get in touch, and enclosing Pan's address. Loaded up with the usual paraphernalia, this time adamantly refusing to accept offers of help from the family, she set off for Liverpool Street with an excited Todge in tow.

'You'll never manage all that luggage on your own, mate.'

'I'm not completely useless, Dad.'

They arrived at the busy station; the crush was terrible – Todge was high with excitement.

After queueing up for an hour, Ooly stowed their cases in the left luggage and announced to that they were going to see Nanna Bow.

'You said we were going to see Bang!'

'We are. But we're just going to see Nanna Bow first.'

'I want to go and see Bang. You said we were going to Bang's house and you said we were going to go to the seaside when we got there. I don't want to go to Nanna Bow's, its boring.'

'Come on – let's climb up to the top of the bus. You can show Puddy Tat all the people walking about.'

'He can't see anything. He's not real, you know, Mummy.'

'Well, me duck. What a surprise – you haven't been for so long. And Todge, too.'

'Dad is insisting that we go to Pan's until things calm down. We're off this afternoon. Have you heard from Johnny?'

'No – not for a couple of weeks, but with all this going on, I expect he's tied up. We mustn't get ourselves into a stew. Don't worry, chick. He'll be back soon enough.'

'D'you think he's – over there?'

'Could be. Albie says a good number of balloon command went over on D Day.'

'Yes – we saw the balloons floating over the invasion ships in the newsreels.'

'Daddy Johnny's balloons were in the film,' added Todge. 'They keep the bombs off.'

Pan was, of course, delighted to see her niece, and all went well for an hour or so. They would go to the beach, fly a kite, make sand castles and take a scrumptious picnic of cold soup in a thermos and delicious ham sandwiches.

'My Nan makes me syrup sandwiches,' said Todge.

'Good farm ham will make you big and strong,' said Pan. 'Surely you don't let mum feed her such rubbish, Ooly?'

'I do try and stop her,' said Ooly through gritted teeth.

Gif announced the house rules – no smoking upstairs or in the morning, absolutely no food to be taken into the bedrooms, except a biscuit with the morning tea, served in the yellow cups to be found hanging on hooks in the pantry and not the china in or on the dresser. Breakfast (porridge and fruit) was served on weekdays at 8am sharp. If the guests ventured out during the day, whilst Pan and Gif were at school, they must make sure that all three locks on the front door were secured, the back door bolted (twice) and the windows closed. The telephone was only to be used if strictly necessary. Bedding would be changed once a fortnight and soiled clothing and other items would be put in the linen basket on the landing for Mrs. Digby to take away and wash on Thursdays.

'Oh – don't worry about our washing,' said Ooly 'I'll do Todge's stuff and my smalls myself.'

'Not a good idea,' said Gif. 'We don't have a line.'

Ooly's heart sank. She hadn't brought nearly enough clothing for Todge's things to be washed only once a week. She determined to wash when they were out of the way and hang the things out on the bushes.

Todge was put in the tiny, chintzy spare room, in a dear little bed, with her very own small wardrobe and chest of drawers. She liked that, but would rather have been with her mother. Ooly was to share Gif's room, where there were two very high, lumpy divans. She didn't like that at all; Gif snored and was inordinately particular about the neat folding of clothes and bed making. At home Ooly tended to fling her garments anywhere and mum or Dot always hung them up and made the beds.

The first week brought nothing from Johnny and Ooly didn't ring Dougie. There were some minor incidents; marmite smeared on the Drayman wing chair in the sitting room, a wet towel left on the bathroom floor, use of the wrong rag for wiping up some spilt milk, a saucepan inadequately scoured, the willow pattern bowls used for the morning porridge:

'My Nan usually makes me a special poached egg out of powder for breakfast.'

Ooly had a letter from Dot:

When I went to get your emergency cards this morning, they said you ought to get them where you were staying, anyhow, they would issue them for this week: they wouldn't give anybody more than one week. If this is going to cause any controversy, or is likely to get you turned out, send your books back and we will get the things at Mumfords (grocer's shop in Woodford Broadway) and send them on every week. Don't run the risk of getting sent back, it is no trouble to us, only it does you out of your meat ration, but just for the time being you will have to manage with tin stuff. The bacon ration is 6 oz. now so that is a help. Let us know how long the parcels take to get to you. I did get two bottles of orange juice. We will send one in the next parcel. I do hope Pan's boils will soon be better. Love to you all including Todge. xxxxxxxxxxxx

Ooly wrote back:

Thank you for offering to send our groceries – if you don't mind, it would save trouble here and I don't know how long we will be staying. Pan says meat is not a problem, with the local farms and everything. Please forward any post for me directly.'

As was her way, she had not mentioned her worries at home. Always her deepest feelings were kept safely locked up – she couldn't bear the fussing and prodding. Certainly nothing would be said to the company at Blacksmith's Cottage, though, she did tell a complete stranger in the village shop that her husband was in the RAF and she hadn't heard from him for several weeks. With her famous smile and willingness to listen she was an immediate hit with the locals and her frequent outings to the shop were a welcome break from the chilly disapproval at the cottage. 'We don't mix with the village,' she was told.

Gif had managed to procure some petrol and they decided to risk an expedition to the sea side on Saturday – it wasn't far, after all and if they stuck to the country lanes and avoided road blocks, all should be well. The day dawned – fair, to begin with. Todge was all set, bucket and spade at the ready by seven o'clock. The morning ticked on, monitored by George, the grandfather clock in the hall and the cuckoo clock in the study. Nothing came in the post, no sign of Pan or Gif. At ten, Ooly, who had been attempting some secret washing, ventured upstairs to wake the sleepers.

'For Goodness sake, Ooly,' moaned her sister. 'We only have a chance for a lie in at weekends – it's all very well for ladies of leisure like you.'

'When are we going, when are we going, Mummy when are we absolutely going?' Todge was hopping up and down. 'Can't we go without them?'

'Don't be daft – I can't drive!'

'Can't we go on the train?'

'There aren't any trains.'

'Can't we walk?'

'It's too far.'

By eleven o'clock it had clouded over – still no sign of Pan and Gif. Eventually they drifted down and began the morning row – today it was about the venue for the picnic. At least they agreed that Felixtowe was out of the question – the police would stop them. Gif favoured Dunwich, wind swept and half eaten by the sea, where you could, it was said, hear the church bells ringing beneath the waves when a storm blew up, and collect coffin nails on the beach. Pan dismissed that as being too gloomy and proposed Southwold. Gif said the beach was sandier at Walberswick. Pan said Aldeburgh was more interesting. By the time Southwold was voted in, it had started to rain.

'Never mind,' said Pan 'It'll take us at least half an hour to get there – the rain will have passed over by then, and, if it hasn't we can have our picnic in Amun and go to the pottery.'

'The pottery's in Walberswick?' Said Gif.

'Don't be a fool – of course it's not.'

Und so weiter.

Gif set about preparing the picnic. Ooly's offer of help was declined. By now Todge was frantic – rushing around the cottage pretending to be driving a horse and cart, she crashed into the dresser and knocked down the string dispenser, smashing it to pieces.

Now, for some, the summer of 1944 was the summer of D Day, of the doodlebugs, of the liberation of France; for Ooly, however, it was

379

the summer of the string dispenser. This item was of brown and white china, fashioned in the shape of a dog, a fox terrier named Toaster – Gif's dog when she was a little girl at home. You lifted the head off, put the ball of string inside the body and threaded it through the mouth. It was a very prized possession.

'Oh, my God, not Toaster!' Pan was livid, not with Todge, of course, but with her sister.

'You blithering idiot – how could you let her break that!'

Gif burst into tears, and so did Todge.

Ooly was mortified, horrified, and, when the raging and sobbing had died down, tentatively suggested that they might go the disputed pottery and she would buy a replacement. Nothing, of course, could replace poor old Toaster, but she would find as nice a one as she could.

And so, after an uncomfortable and very, very late lunch in Amun, watching the rain pour down into the North Sea, they proceeded to the pottery. Todge was disappointed but her spirits lifted when her aunt bought her a dear little china Mrs Tiggywinkle. She would have preferred the mouse from the *Tailor of Gloucester*, but Pan seemed set on the fat lady hedgehog in the lace cap.

'Be careful you don't drop her, Pud. I'll keep her Blacksmith's Cottage for you – you can see her whenever you come.'

'Can't I just take her home and show her to Nan?'

'No. I'll keep her safe here for you. Nan can see it when she visits. Mrs Tiggywinkle can sit on my mantelpiece where she'll have my Peter Rabbit and the little crystal swan for company.'

That, thought Todge, was worse than not having a present at all. Mindful of the fate of the string dispenser, however, she said nothing.

Nothing even remotely resembling Toaster was available.

'Oh dear,' said Ooly. 'I'll go into Highbridge on the bus on Monday and see what I can find.'

Various unsuccessful expeditions to the market towns in the locality filled the coming week. Todge was fed up, being dragged from shop to shop, waiting around for the occasional country buses:

'Why is Toaster so important, anyway?'

'He was a present from Bang.'

'Bang and Gif like things, don't they, Mummy? You don't, do you? Well not much – only things like lipsticks.'

Ooly wrote home:

We are getting on all right. Todge rather threw a spanner in the works by smashing a string dispenser that Gif thought a lot of. Our trip to the beach was a bit of a damp squib – I wish the weather would cheer up. Pan insisted we all go to church on Sunday – I think she wanted to show Todge off. I did her up in that white frock with the red French knots that Mog sent, much to her disgust – you know what a tomboy she is. Laundry is only undertaken here on a weekly basis, so I need some more clothes for her – I wonder if you could send a couple of changes with the next food parcel? You will forward any letters for me as soon as they come, won't you? Hope the old doodles are leaving you in peace.

On Tuesday evening, Todge was happily listening to Gif's tale of how Queen Elizabeth (then just a princess) sat down in the mud at the Tower of London, refusing to enter at Traitor's Gate, as she "was no traitor".' This and the story of how Lady Nithsdale effected the escape of her condemned husband from the Tower, were Gif's favourites. Ooly took a walk into the village to phone Dougie. He was not as sympathetic as he might have been, she thought.

'My darling lovely girl, a fuss over a br-broken ch-china fox terrier is a small price to pay for safety from the wretched robots. But if it brings you back sooner, I hope Todge smashes the whole house up, I have to say. And, if you have to d-d-desert me like this, please just keep in touch – write if it's difficult to ring …

'It's not that. It's …' Her eyes fell on the mossy war memorial which stood just outside the phone box. 'Oh, Dougie – I can't talk any more. I'll ring next week.'

'N-n-nothing's changed has it?'

'No, no, nothing. I'll ring you next week.'

The only thing for Ooly in the post next morning was a parcel with a note from dad: "I thought this might help out – I put it together myself." Todge unwrapped the parcel eagerly – it was a tin with a hole in the lid with a paper wrapped round it bearing the inscription "string" in a very fine copperplate hand. Good old dad.

Ooly decided, however, it was unwise to present this object to Gif; she had, in any case, determined on a trip to Ipswich and, to that end, brought her charm to bear on Harry Kilminster who was going into the town to make some deliveries. They could get the one bus back. She promised Todge that they would have a very special tea with ice cream and Tizer; she promised herself a decent hair-do. It was a long tiresome day trudging round the department stores and china shops; Ooly was just giving up hope when, lo and lo! in the window of a funny little dusty antique shop Todge spotted a rather chipped Scottie with string coming out of its mouth. 'Look, Mum – there's one! It's not the right sort of dog, but it's much nicer than Toaster!'

The purchase was duly made and they set off back to Radswick, arriving, at last, to find the senior occupant in dangerous mood.

'May we know who left the bathroom window open?' Came a cry from the kitchen.

There was a telegram for Ooly on the hall table. She tore it open and read the contents. Taking a deep breath she spoke steadily to her daughter: 'Give them the dog. I'm just going upstairs to change.'

Todge wrestled with the brown paper bag: 'Look what we got you. It's not quite like Toaster, but it is a dog, and it's got string in it. I found it in a shop in Switch.'

'That's lovely, Pud, isn't it, Pig?' said Pan, fixing Gif with a threatening stare.

382

'Oh, yes, top hole.'

They heard the front door bang. 'Where's her ladyship gone?' asked Gif. 'It really is too bad of her, leaving the house unsecured. Did she see her telegram? Nothing untoward, I trust.'

Chapter 30:
July to September 1944

Ooly felt a sort of numb confusion; she just knew she must phone and talk to her mother-in-law, in private – Nell's neighbour and landlady, was willing for her instrument to be used in a real emergency. Fumbling frantically for the number and some change she set off in the direction of the village. Blacksmith's Lane wandered aimlessly through the damp July evening, flanked by high, honeysuckle wrapped hedgerows; just before it came upon the village green a few brick built workaday cottages gathered around, a petrol pump, a shop, a pond full of weeds. "Four ducks on a pond" – there *were* four – they flew up in a cloud as she passed. An old man was mowing the grass bank beyond – what a little thing to remember for years. There was the phone box and the war memorial behind it.

No answer. She tried again and again. Perhaps Miss Martin had joined the general escape from the doodlebugs, or perhaps she was in her shelter, perhaps she was just out. She would leave it for half and hour and then try again.

She took a turn round the village. Radswick was no picturesque chocolate box place, it worked for its living, especially hard these days when everyone was digging for victory. An ugly, square, squat Methodist chapel, stood on guard next to the shop, staring defiantly over towards the other side of the green where, ancient of days and sturdy of tower, stood St Mary the Virgin of Radswick, who had been comforting the distressed since the battle of Hastings. She beckoned.

The ancient door creaked as Ooly pushed it open and went into the gentle gloom, heavy with the scent of dying roses left over from Sunday. She sat down in the choir stalls.

Religion had never taken a hold with her as it had with her sister; Pan's piety got up her nose – all those holy notes stuck up round the place – like dad's in the Emporium, but at least he seemed to be trying to practice what he preached ... while Pan! Like mum, Ooly regarded the whole business with some cynicism. The social aspect was fine, the music, the flowers, the ceremonies marking rites of passage and the passing of the seasons, were a good idea, giving shape and form to life. So was sitting quietly for an hour or so a week, being reminded of the benefits of good behaviour, of compassion and forgiveness, not that it did Pan much good – but the magic at the top, what about that? She stumbled at the old man in the sky bit, the young man dying for our sins, the holy ghost flitting around everywhere, and all three somehow the same. She recalled Teddy B's predecessor trying to explain the Trinity to her confirmation class. And what about the power of prayer? Good old Roosevelt and the King evidently set a good deal of store by it – or were these days of public prayers for peace/victory just a sort of rallying call? Then there was heaven and hell, though no one spoke much of the fires of damnation these days. Worst was the problem of suffering and a supposedly all-powerful and compassionate creator over-seeing the slaughter of millions of innocents. Even Pan said that she thought she would have lost her faith if she had been in the trenches.

But, sitting here, alone, guarded by the stiff little angels, sprouting out from the roof beams, – homely looking medieval Suffolk lasses (Gif said they were lads) clinging tight to their shields and trumpets, her turbulence stilled. A thousand years of prayer and song and hope, of companionship and shared dreams, of trust and love, washed over her and brought an unexpected repose.

She sang softly, ever so softly:

'Ah! wake not yet from thy repose,
A fair dream spirit hovers near thee,
Weaving a web of gold and rose,
Through dream land's happy isles to bear thee!
Sleep, love, it is not yet the dawn,
Angels guard thee, sweet love, til morn!'

Her eyes fell on the brass lectern, polished weekly with such care, and she recalled Johnny reading the lesson – that first time – with the sunlight on his golden hair.

As a girl she had often dreamt of being a war widow – when she was growing up it was the height of romance – the pinnacle of her fancies. She had pictured her last agonising farewell on a station, getting the news, devoting herself to his memory – sitting at a grand piano with his photo in uniform in a silver frame and a bowl of dark, velvety Ena Harkness. She was, in her day dream, in a low built Jane Austen sort of house, on the edge of a small market town. There would be a few years, or months, of loneliness, long enough to become known as the beautiful, immaculately attired, very sad lady, who sat at the piano, weeping until *he* came along. He was a doctor, handsome and clever, perhaps, or a lawyer, in fine tweeds, with a briefcase shiny like a conker. Tentatively and sensitively he would woo her out of her pain …

She fingered the opal ring round her neck and touched the platinum band and the tiny diamond on her left hand.

My God. Had she really been wishing Johnny dead?

Her hands clasped tight, she repeated the familiar words of the General Confession. Worth a try.

"Almighty and most merciful Father; We have erred, and strayed from thy ways like lost sheep. We have followed too much the devices and desires of our own hearts. We have offended against thy holy laws. We have left undone those things which we ought to have done; And we have done those things which we ought not to have done; And there is no health in us. But thou, O Lord, have mercy upon us, miserable offenders. Spare thou those, O God, who confess their faults. Restore thou those who are penitent; According to thy promises declared unto mankind in Christ Jesus our Lord. And grant, O most merciful Father, for his sake; That we may hereafter live a godly, righteous, and sober life, To the glory of thy holy Name. Amen."

The church clock struck eight. She ran back to the phone box. This time the line was engaged – better get back – Todge would be wondering where she was. She'd just have to brave the phone at Blacksmith's Cottage.

'Where the dickens have you been?' asked her sister. 'You might have the courtesy to indicate what your movements are while you are staying under our roof. Pud has been out of her mind and you've missed two phone calls. I do wish you wouldn't hand out phone number out to all and sundry!'

'Who rang?'

'Old Mrs Walters – says your wretched husband is coming here, if you please. He's only arriving tomorrow.'

'Oh, yes, I know,' said Ooly. 'That's what the telegram was.'

'And the other call?'

'Some doctor. Said he needed to contact you urgently – something about a singing engagement. Dad had the cheek to give him our number.'

The next morning Johnny, bandaged and limping, arrived.

'And how's my Minnie Lizzie?'

He caught Todge up in his arms; she struggled free, protesting that her name was Pud.

'My God, what ever's happened to you. Were you over there?' said Ooly.

'We saw your balloons at the pictures,' shouted Todge. 'They were floating over the boats.'

'Shush!' urged her mother. 'You'll wake Bang and Gif.' It was Saturday.

'Nothing so glamorous as wounded in action, I'm afraid. There was a bit of an accident back at the base – I've been out for the count – sorry there were no letters. I suppose it's OK for me to stay a couple of days? I got a lift with some GIs.'

'Well ... er ... yes, but you know what Pan's like.'

'I do – that's why I didn't ring, but surely your benighted sister can put up with a man in the house for a night or two. There's war on, you know.'

'Yes, but ...'

'Ooly, for crying out loud! I haven't seen you for weeks.'

'I know, but ...'

Todge went flying upstairs: 'Bang! Bang! Daddy Johnny's here!'

Ooly put her head in her hands. There was a knock on the door: 'Special delivery for Bowyer.'

Gif lumbered down, all floral dressing gown and fury.

'What's going on here? Well – if it isn't the war hero!'

Todge flew at the large parcel and tore off the wrappings. The brown paper was thrown on the floor and there emerged a shiny box with Harrods written on it. Off came the lid and out of layers of tissue paper came an immaculate, smart new Toaster, Toaster to the life, with some string hanging out of his mouth.

'What the devil?' exclaimed Johnny.

'Oh – Todge broke Gif's string dispenser – this is a replacement,' fumbled Ooly.

'Struth, missus – you ordered this from Harrods at their prices!'

'Well – no. Someone bought it for me – I suppose.'

'Who on earth do you know who shops at Harrods? Look there's a note with it.'

At the bottom of the box was a sheet of stiff white paper with a monogram "M" at the top; it bore the simple message: "With love".

'Phyllis Mottram, I suppose,' said Johnny slowly.

'Who?'

'That "buddy" of yours who came up with the flash German teddy bear for Minnie Liz at Christmas a year or so ago.'

'Oh, yes, yes.' said Ooly.

Dot wrote to Ooly:

I hope dad's string tin came in useful. We are sorry Johnny has been in the wars. What a shame he could only stay with you for one night – I expect he found the camp bed rather uncomfortable – he seems to be in a deal of pain. He called in here and had his dinner with us. Mum and I thought he seemed very low, upset about that friend of his who was shot down, I dare say. I am enclosing your victuals for this week. Dad and I think it would be for the best if you stay in Suffolk for a little longer as we are not getting much peace here.

Lil wrote to Pan:

I sent a hot water lid – you press the white button then up it pops. I hope you are getting on all right for food. I just cooking some tripe. Poor Old Tom Tittler was hier again – brought me a lovely fowl he'd got from somewear – wasn't it good of him. He had his dinner hier and Johnnie was hier too so we were quite a party. we had a drop of gin in lime – I was going to send you a pice of cake but it all went so I made another one to send you to have some with a snack of wiskey. Auntys leg has been wonkey this week, rotten old age creeping on. i am just going to bed i feel tired. give Todge x for me I miss her.

Dad wrote:

The hot water lid is a clever device – I think you will find it comes in handy. You seem to be having a high old time with Todge. Terrible thing about Johnny's pal. I expect he was very pleased to see Ooly and

The end of term came; the residents of Blacksmiths Cottage collapsed from exhaustion, as they usually did at the end of term, and breakfast was moved from 8am to 11am. Todge rose with the lark and pulled her mother out of bed. They ate syrup sandwiches in secret, stole down to the village to visit a bunch of kittens who had arrived at the Kilminster's farm or took to the meadows, where Todge would amuse herself making daisy chains or digging for worms, while Ooly read Agatha Christie. At least the weather had perked up.

One fresh, dewy morning they were sitting on a tussock down by the stream near the Old Oak; Todge was pulling a daisy apart: 'Bang keeps telling me 'bout setals and pepals and other flower things. She says you told her all 'bout them when she was very little.'

'Did I?'

'She says so. I wish she wouldn't.'

'Wouldn't what?'

'Wouldn't keep on telling me bout flowers. It's really boring. I like Gif's stories bout the olden times much better.'

'Well, don't, for goodness sake, tell Bang that!'

'Why? Gif says this oak tree was here a long, long time ago, when there was a king who had his head chopped off and another man called Oliver Crumble was the ruler. Do you remember that, Mummy?'

'Bit before my time,' Ooly laughed. 'Wouldn't you like to go home and see Nan?'

'Yes. When the kittens have grown up.'

'That'll be ages.'

'Cats grow up quicker than us.'

'Yes, I know. But it'll still be a long time.'

'I s'pect you're missing Nanna Bow, aren't you? You went to see

390

her lots and lots. She's your sort of Nan isn't she?'

'Oh Todge,' sighed her mother, limply. 'Oh Todge. Whatever am I going to do?'

They walked back to the cottage where a full scale row was in progress. Gif's thunder could be heard as they opened the garden gate.

'My dear good woman, you simply can't expect me to put up with …'

'Oh God,' moaned Ooly 'What have we done now?'

But this time it was not the guests that had offended. Jocasta had invited them all to tea.

'Don't you think you're rather over reacting?' came Pan's reply. 'It's only tea.'

'I have to put up with that nonsense all term time – you two closeted for hours in her wretched study, the special smile for you when she's taking assembly, the little trips in that pathetic Morris supposedly to buy supplies for your lab. an't we at least have a break during the hols?'

'You're being ridiculous and down right offensive. I have never heard such nonsense. Am I not supposed to have any friends? And you're in no position to talk – don't imagine everyone hasn't noticed you ogling that fancy item you're coaching for Oxford.'

'How dare you! How dare you! I've had enough. I'm off to Devon – you can look after your bothersome evacuees yourself.'

'You selfish cow! And don't you ever speak of my family like that again!'

Slap. Sobbing. Banging of doors.

'Come on, Todge,' whispered Ooly. 'Let's go down to the orchard and see if there are any plums ripe.'

To be honest, it wasn't the furious exchanges which disgusted Ooly so much as the making up sessions, in the bathroom.

She wrote to Dougie:

391

I love our talks but I thought I'd write for a change and I think Pan and Gif are getting rather suspicious of my evening strolls. I keep thinking how thoughtful it was of you to send the china dog – hope the Squanderbug doesn't get you! I honestly don't think I can stand any more of this exile – though. I must say, we are having quite a nice time at the sea today. It's lovely and warm and relatively peaceful – Pan and Gif are usually going at it hammer and tongs. Todge and Pan are making a huge sand castle and I'm sitting in a deck chair, eating a Mars Bar, wearing rather a fetching turban, and writing to you, trying to make sure Gif doesn't see my letter. She's terribly nosey – for goodness sake don't write to me.

This weekend we are scheduled to have tea with their head mistress – that has caused a right old rumpus. Gif evidently doesn't care for the head but Pan seems to think she's God Almighty. You cannot imagine the song and dance about it all. Todge has got to wear her best dress and I'm to make sure she has clean white socks. I've not to wear red nail varnish or "too much" lipstick – would you credit it! I'm not to smoke when we're there and Todge has been told only to speak when spoken to. I'm so angry I just has to write it down – sorry – it seems rather petty when London is being doodled to death and everything.

I won't put any kisses on this as Gif might spot them – I've told her I'm writing a (rather late) thank you letter to the girl friend who sent the dog! Hope she doesn't offer to post it for me. She won't. I'll ring on Sunday at eight o'clock – we should be back from the royal audience by then.'

The drive to the Meredith residence was tense, peppered with outbursts: 'My good man!' (Gif) 'Pig, for God's sake keep your eyes on the road.' (Pan) Ooly and Todge sat in silence in the back, hot and all arrayed in their Sunday best.

It was surprisingly modest, for a palace. In fact, it bore quite a striking resemblance to Uncle Billy's three bedroomed semi in Forest

Gate, Ooly thought. The garden was August-dry with some tired looking blueish hydrangeas standing on guard, one each side of the porch; a few exhausted, papery roses drooped in a neat round bed. Two thin fair girls with plaits – they were rather older than Todge – stood at the front door, behind the beaming Jocasta.

'Welcome, one and all. These are my nieces, Cressida and Sybil.'

They were led into a small sitting room which was overwhelmed by large pieces of furniture more suited to Uncle George's Goodmayes residence.

'And this must be Elizabeth, or should we call you Pud?'

'Pud,' said Todge, almost inaudibly, looking warily at her aunt.

Cress and Syb giggled: 'Does she think she's a rice pudding or something?'

'More like jam roly poly. Ha! Ha!'

'Well, Pud,' said Jocasta, with a stern and reproving glance at her nieces. 'I thought we might play some games before tea.'

'Sardines! Sardines!' cried Sybil, who was the younger of the two Swallows and Amazons.

'My Nan makes me sardines on toast,' said Pud, puzzled.

Gales of laughter from the two Meredith appurtenances.

'Sardines is a game, everyone knows that. We play it at home,' said Cress in a superior fashion. 'Someone hides and everyone else has to try and find them. When they do they creep into the hiding place so that, in the end, everyone (except the last person left) is crammed into the hiding place – like sardines packed together in a tin. The last person is the next one to hide. It's ever such fun!'

Pan blenched. The thought of being crammed into a small space was truly terrifying to her – but there was no way she was going to admit to claustrophobia in this company, or spoil the party.

Gif, anxious to be seen to be joining in with enthusiasm, for fear of the ticking off to come if any sulking was detected, said it was a jolly good idea and volunteered to hide first. It was not easy to find a good place in the little semi; Cress and Syb, as they pointed out, were used to a large, rambling house with masses of hidey holes. The company gathered in the sitting room and counted to fifty while Gif roamed around, finally squeezing her huge bulk into the cupboard under the stairs, where she crouched, as quiet as a mouse.

Cress found her almost immediately, followed shortly after by Syb, then Ooly, Jocasta and last Pan with Todge just peeped into the cupboard. Shouts and squeals of delight. 'Pud you're next! You're next!'

Everyone clambered out, everyone except Gif.

'Come on Gif,' called Pan. 'Out you come.'

'I can't. Oh, Pig, I'm stuck. I'm stuck.'

'Nonsense. Just make an effort for once!' Pan hissed angrily.

'I'm wedged – I can't move.'

Pan was scared, really scared. Her heart started to pound and beads of sweat appeared on her forehead.

'Don't be so damn silly. Come on out, now!'

Ooly pulled off her white court shoes and scrambled back into the cupboard, tugging at Gif's mighty legs. Cress took hold of Ooly round the waist and pulled. Syb and Pud joined in. It was no good.

'Oh, dear,' said Jocasta. 'What a calamity. And you two gels stop laughing.'

Pan was shaking with terror, from head to foot. She rushed out into the garden calling for help.

Someone wearing a flowered overall crept humbly out of the kitchen into the hall, bearing a large silver teapot: 'What seems to be the trouble Miss M?'

'Oh, Mrs Crater, it's one of my guests,' said Jocasta. 'She appears to have rather foolishly got herself stuck in the cupboard under the stairs. I suppose we should call the fire brigade.'

'I reckon they've got better things to do. I'll get 'old of my Reg, 'es as strong as 'orse.'

So Reg came with his farmer mate and some calving chains, and the unfortunate Gif was eventually heaved, in a most undignified fashion, out into the daylight. Men had their uses.

Jocasta produced some brandy for Pan and everyone else tucked into cucumber sandwiches and cake. After tea, Gif, though shaken and bruised, was recovered enough to lead charades, she was not a brigadier general's granddaughter for nothing. The game kept everyone amused for some time until Jocasta absolutely insisted that Pan sing for them. She graciously acquiesced.

'Can anyone play the pianoforte? I learnt but nothing came of it, I regret to say, although my sisters are most proficient.'

'*My* sister is a prize winning pianist,' said Pan proudly, to Ooly's stupefaction. 'Come on Ooly, do you stuff.'

And she did, and she sang, and Pan sang; the girls were excused the performance and left to their own devices in the dining room with snakes and ladders and large bowl of cherries. Excluded from the game Todge ate all the cherries and, with care and precision spat the stones out of the open window, one by one.

By the time they got back to Blacksmith's Cottage it was too late for Ooly to ring Dougie, so she wrote instead:

Sorry I didn't ring; we didn't get back till nearly ten. Well – what a to-do! The tea at the palace, I mean. It turned out to be pokey little house and her Maj.'s horrid little nieces had us playing sardines. Poor old Gif got quite stuck in the cupboard under the stairs and had to be rescued by some old boys who pulled her out with chains! Pan was ansolutely furious with her, needless to say. Todge blotted her copybook by spitting a lot of cherry stones out of the window. We didn't witness this as the girls escaped to the dining room whilst we had a music session, but the two nasty little brats came rushing in to tell us what had happened, just as I was attempting the top note at the end of 'One Fine Day'. Jocasta (Her Maj.) was horrified, but, to my surprise, Pan was tickled to death and, on the way home, kept on about how ghastly the two girls were – "ill-bred bullies", etc.

You must be thinking my sister is the most awful person – she is a lot of the time, but then she'll suddenly do something nice that makes me feel bad about the way I keep slating her. She actually seemed rather proud of my prowess at the piano when we were at Jocasta's. She can be an absolute swine but when the chips are down, family comes first with her. Todge can do absolutely no wrong in her eyes.'

Paris was liberated to great rejoicing – when the news came Ooly bashed out the Marseillaise as loud as she could on the upright and the company at Blacksmith's Cottage threw back their heads and sang fit to bust. Only Gif really knew the words; Todge made up some of her own; Pan struggled with a few, while Ooly simply lah lah'd – at Skoriers she had achieved the all time low mark for one English/French test – minus seven out of a hundred – failing even to find the French word for train – which was, of course, train. They all managed a shout of "*Vive la France*" (Todge was coached) and drank a toast in elderflower wine. Pan said Pud could have just one tiny sip.

The weather cooled, the doodlebugs all but stopped and, as the Allies cut a swathe through France and tanks roared towards the German borders, victory was surely in sight. Londoners started drifting back from their exile. It was time for Ooly and Todge to go home.

Off they set, loaded up with plums and apples, butter and eggs from the Kilminsters, and a fine tabby she- kitten mewing in a basket.

'Don't forget to write and tell me how Mrs Tiggywinkle Cat gets on in Chestnut Avenue.' Tears were streaming down Pan's face as they clambered into the train.

'She's a funny old bundle,' thought Ooly.

'As soon as the war's over, Pud, I'll take you to the Tower of London,' bellowed Gif, as the steam shrilled the departure. 'And show you where Queen Elizabeth sat down in the mud.'

'Goodbye! Goodbye!'

Huff, puff, huff puff, huff puff, jigetty jig, jigetty jig ...

'What are you doing, Todge?' She was standing tiptoe on the seat trying to get at one of the suitcases.

'I'm just getting something out to sit on.'

'Why?'

'Bang says there may be Germans on the seat.'

'Germans! What are you talking about?'

'Bang says Germans get everywhere, they're specially in lavs.'

'Oh, germs, you mean. I shouldn't worry about that.'

'But Bang says ...'

'Look, come on, pay attention to Mrs Tigg. she's meowing. Perhaps, we could get her out? But hang on to her tight.'

'Yes! Yes!'

And so they did and by the time they got to Colchester she was fast asleep on Todge's lap, so was her mistress.

Funny how travelling on a train, speeding through the countryside, rushing past other people's lives, other people's back gardens, made you reflect on your own lot, more intensely than you otherwise might. For so long Ooly had been dying to get away from the cottage with its alarming bathroom, the lumpy, stiff single bed, the silly rules, the bickering, the explosions of rage, the creeping around for fear of causing offence. For so long she had craved the warmth and strength of Dougie's body – how she had missed manliness, closeted in that world of women. Even the touch of Johnny's rough uniform was welcome, the smell of his "Players" and sweat better than that faint/ indefinable aroma of Bakelite, moth balls and eau de cologne. But now, as Blacksmith's Cottage receded, put in its place by the LNER, out of sight, she felt unaccountably sad.

She would miss her mornings with Todge, being Todge's proper mum; the companionable times in the Kilminster's farmhouse kitchen, watching the furry bundles tumble about on the flagstones, the strolls through the fields, chats in the village shop, singing her heart out in church on Sundays – the glamorous grass widow from Blacksmith's – she would even miss those funny little angels in the rafters. And, after all, Pan hadn't been so bad – not nearly as bad as she was at home when mum and dad were around. Gif might have her rules, but at least no one was watching her every move to make sure she looked after her child properly.

And then there were those walks along the fragrant lane to the phone box as it was starting to get dimpsy, and listening to his whispered words of adoration and pleading: 'Darling, are you never going to come home? Darling, come back to me.'

Todge woke with a start as they stopped at Chelmsford.

'Why don't Bang and Gif have husbands?'

'They don't like men very much.'

'Do you like men, Mum?'

'Why on earth do you ask that?'

'You don't like Daddy Johnny much.'

'Of course, I do. What d'you mean?'

'You don't smile at him or laugh with him.'

'Don't I? Oh dear …'

Chapter 31:
October to December 1944

The summer of the triumphant Allied invasion seemed so far away as the sixth winter of the war closed in; Lil managed to get some logs from Romford – there were warnings of a severe coal shortage and people were queuing up along the Roman for Sid's precious paraffin. The war news was not good – thousands of wounded troops were brought back from the disastrous battle at Arnhem; victory might be trumpeted in the press, but when would it come? Sam the Chippie said at his girl's factory there was a rage for crystal balls and Vi Kerridge took herself off to a fortune teller in a bungalow in Ilford. And when the peace did come – what then? London, for so long in the front line, lay wrecked and bleeding, its faces grey and pinched, its nerves torn to shreds from doodle dodging. Half a million of its inhabitants were homeless, many living in shelters and rest centres, while some made do behind boarded up windows with tarpaulin for a roof. Even Cupid was said to be in for a rough ride – experts, said the *Mirror,* expect a rash of post-war divorces. The Ministry of Food tried to cheer everyone up by announcing massive imports of sage, thyme and marjoram – that would to pep up the taste of sausages. The Emporium was not impressed:

'Still, can't all be bad, the doodles have buggered orf and we're goin' to 'ave some luverly 'erbs in our sausages – never mind no bloody coal, never mind nowhere to live, 'erby sausages – yum yum!'

The robots might have stopped but there were whispers of a new sinister danger at home.

Lil wrote to Mog:

I hope your alright – how much longer is it going to last do you think it will be over by Christmas – i would stand on my head. Some high-up said that there wont be no more doodles no more raids but theres bin some funny goins on raand here. i say no more.

I am glad to have Todge back. they brought a kitten from Pan's – did I tell you? – I could do without a cat – we int got no mice here. Todge loves it. she calls it Mrs Tigwinkle from a story book Pan has got. she was surprised when the street lights cum on – shes never seen them before. How are you getting along witht this ruddy dim-out. Wardens here are still on the rampage if your light is too bright. Mrs Spoon got into hot water over it. Dad says its best to keep our blackouts up until we can have a proper victory lumination when its all over, just to be on the safe side.

Maureen brought her new baby over on Sunday – it is a nice baby ... I wish you had been their – she is quite motherly – she handled him quite well. Shes had practice with the other one of corse. he has a tit with gripe water in it – he wont sleep without it. Todge loved it –it is like a doll. Ooly said he and the other one had a lot of war savings given them. theyre lucky. Ooly says its alright now with there families. funny how babies make everything alright in't is? i think some couples are waiting until the war is over.'

Mog screwed the letter up. 'What's up?' asked Bella.

They were sitting over breakfast in the conservatory.

'Oh it's just mum ... er ... er hinting about "goings-on" – air raids or something.'

'That'll be the V2s, the supersonic rockets,' said Edmund.

Bella kicked her brother under the table.

'Well – she knows now,' said Edmund. 'What's the point in keeping mum?'

Mog was puzzled; 'I thought all that talk in the press earlier in the

400

year about the new secret weapon was just idle rumour, some sort of alarmist myth. D'you mean to say they're actually firing these things?'

'They're very hush hush, being passed off as gas explosions, according to Pooty, but everyone in London knows what's going on.'

'Why didn't anyone mention it to me?'

'Well, Pooty didn't want to get you all steamed up. You see the suburbs of London are getting the worst of it – Jerry hasn't got it quite right yet.'

He scanned the paper: 'Wretched press full of post war reconstruction – prefabricated housing and all the Beveridge stuff again. If things go on like this we'll all be blown to pieces before the flags can come out – what's the good of cradle to the grave security for the masses if they're all dead. The range of these monster rockets is terrific – anything might happen – in no time at all technology will allow these damned comets to destroy us all – London could be wiped out in a trice. Some people are saying they're powerful enough to reach America.'

'Don't be hysterical, Edmund,' said his sister. 'We've taken Paris, Brussels, we're in Holland, we've reached the Rhine. Our troops will be in Berlin before you can say knife and it'll all be over.'

'You are, dear girl, aware of the Arnhem debacle? – hardly a roaring success.'

'These rockets,' asked Mog, 'are they much more of a terror than the doodlebugs, then?'

'They're much more powerful,' said Edmund. 'Travel at the speed of sound, diving down from a tremendous height. Pooty says you just get a fleeting glimpse as the thing flashes across the sky in a half circle and then there's a terrifically loud explosion – it can be heard as far as 50 miles away [*recte* 30 miles] and then another. In the immediate neighbourhood the people hear nothing, apparently, they just see their homes begin to disintegrate before their eyes – whole streets are just wiped out. There's absolutely no warning and our fighters are helpless against them.'

'Why are they going for London so much – they are, aren't they?' Mog's eyes were huge. Her head whirled with jet propelled monsters chasing her mum and dad. In the Blitz, she had felt they were protected by a cloud of spitfires – now, apparently, there was nothing to shield them.

'The bastard's trying to break our will to win, as Morrison said: "make London squeal to such a pitch that the government will be forced to call off the war."'

'Come on now, Edmund,' said Bella. 'There have only been a few of these mysterious explosions. The doodles have practically stopped and we'll soon be smashing up the rocket bases in Holland and wiping the Hun out completely. Now, Moggins, time you and I planned a shopping expedition to Bath, take our minds off all this. We might take in a flic.'

In the event, what with jobs to be done around the estate, preparations for the children's nativity play and the painting of the dairy windows, it was nearing Christmas before they got round to their shopping trip.

No petrol was to be had and they set off in the dog cart, spanking through the frosty lanes wrapped up warm. Bella loved driving and Mog wore her moleskin to good effect. Bess was soon clip-clopping through the streets she knew so well, the golden Georgian facades grimy with soot and interspersed with piles of rubble. As they turned into the grand, wide boulevard of Great Pulteney Street the sun came out and for Mog the vista danced momentarily with bobbing bonnets, fluttering muslin, fans and parasols, with swaggering uniforms of navy blue and scarlet, sedan chairs and sporty gigs. She was the lady of the 7th baronet – he who fought at Waterloo – or perhaps Anne Elliot about to fall into the arms of Captain Wentworth. They drew up at the Cleveland: 'Miss Tillingham, Lady Tillingham –luncheon?'

'Struth no – not at your prices,' said Bella. 'Some coffee and and buns will do us – in the lounge.'

Sitting over by the window was Honor Portman, with Edith

Tollington-Thomas from Tollington St Mary, sipping some precious pre-prandial sherry.

'Better pay our respects to the old biddies,' whispered Bella.

Honor was on a roll: 'Christmas shopping is such a trial these days – just nothing to be had, and the prices! Have you seen what they're is asking for turkeys? Iniquitous. And toys! I've been looking for some little items for our brood – we've got five grandchildren now, you know? – a new one put in an appearance last month. There's simply not one decent thing in the shops. Bertie says we should give the festive season a miss this year – but he's a bit of an old misery.'

'It's such a wonderful time for the children,' added Edith. 'I love watching their faces as they open their stockings. Have you tried Cyril Howe in Cheap Street – I've managed to get a train set for our little Peregrine. Can't compete with you, Honor, we've only got one so far but I live in hope! I think my daughter is waiting until the war is over – so many women are, aren't they?'

'Well – can't get the staff; nurse maids and nannies are like snow in summer.' Honor, who was a plain woman with even plainer daughters, turned to Mog, 'Of course, you don't have to worry about any of this up at New Hall.'

'No aren't we the lucky ones,' said Bella brightly. 'No time for chat – we're just orf to get our Moggins measured up for something glam to wear at the Lord Lieutenant's bash. That's not something you usually attend I think?'

She swept out, hustling the white-faced Mog across the busy lounge, and made for Barrets the iron mongers in search of some lino. Jane Austen's world had gone now – giving way to sad shadows in dingy felt hats carrying string bags, to dull workaday hues of grey and khaki, heavy trucks and jeeps.

Barrets had no lino at all in stock.

'There's another place, up near the Little Theatre, run by an old boy called Crabtree – it's a funny little hole but he sometimes has stuff you can't get anywhere else. You try that and I'll just pop down to the saddler's. I'll meet you at the bookshop in about an hour – Edmund's got something on order.'

Crabtree's was tucked away between a shabby looking bespoke tailor's and a shop selling fishing gear; it was a pokey, ramshackle oil shop, dark and grimy, smelling of paraffin and soap, its shelves overflowing, every nook and cranny crammed with wares, all higgledy piggledy. On top of a roll of wire netting stood a tiny wobbly spruce, hung with tinsel and baubles. A bent old man in a brown overall emerged from the shadows: 'Can I help you, ma'am?

Mog was overcome. 'Oh ... er ... I'm so sorry, your shop reminds me of one I knew in London. I'd like some lino, if you have any.'

'Certainly, ma'am. I've got a few rolls out the back. Terrible time they're 'aving of it up Lunnun – they rockets!'

'My family are in London – I'm so worried about them. As a matter of fact it's my dad's shop that is like yours.'

The old man looked at his elegant, well dressed customer in surprise. 'Local yourself?'

'Oh, yes. – Tillingham. I was evacuated at the beginning of the war with some of the children I was teaching.'

'Still here, then?'

'Still here.'

'Be glad to get 'ome when it's all over, I suppose.'

She took a can of paraffin – just out of sentiment.

A cut glass vase for mum, a box of paints for Todge, a woollen scarf for Aunty, a book for dad, Woodbines for Ed, an enamel brooch for Ooly, paint brushes for Pan, crystallised fruits for Bella, some special cigars for Edmund, gloves for Freda, handkerchiefs for Mrs P, some niceties for the few remaining vaccies – all these were stowed away in the dog cart. It was bitter cold now and a thick fog had descended; they decided to forgo the cinema and off they set back to the Hall.

They would be home earlier than anticipated. As they passed through Tillingham Magna their pace slackened – Bess didn't like fog.

'Come on, old girl. Nearly there. Nearly home.'

There was a light on in the stable block.

'Just pop into the stable and get the boy to deal with Bess and the cart,' said Bella. 'I'll take the shopping in.'

'Okey doke. I'll put the paraffin in there.'

'Yes. Oh no, wait,' Bella called out in sudden alarm. 'I'll go. You take the shopping in.'

But it was too late; Mog had opened the stable door.

The boy was there – well, she took it to be him – a tangle of naked limbs, his and someone else's, on a filthy old mattress. Edmund's jodhpurs were flung over the back of a chair, his riding boots stood nearby, and the silver lighter she had given him on their wedding day lay glinting in the straw.

She picked it up, put it in her pocket and returned to the house. Walking steadily, she mounted the Great Staircase, calling out to Bella to tell her that the stable boy was not to be found. Pearl Harbour.

That familiar red mist rose before her eyes. Her jaw set firm, she laid the Tillingham amethysts out on her dressing table, with her wedding ring, on top of the volumes of poetry Edmund had given her. She took out the pigskin writing case which dad had sent for her birthday last year and, grasping the fountain pen mum had bought her when she went away to college, she applied herself to writing a note. Again and again she started: 'Dear Edmund, I need to go home and be with my family in these dangerous times.' 'Dear Edmund, It has been an honour and privilege to act as your consort, but I need something more.' 'Dear Edmund, I quite understand that your needs are not as I might have expected.' 'Dear Edmund, I think it better if we call a halt to this charade of a marriage.' 'Dear Edmund, I can no longer endure the shame and humiliation you have inflicted on me.' 'Dear Edmund,

I cannot live this appalling lie any more.' 'Dear Edmund, How could you have done this cruel and terrible thing to me.' 'Edmund – I'm leaving – you despicable apology for a man!'

She tore them all up and plumped for a dignified silence.

Bella was very understanding and very sad. Mog's mind was made up and when Mog's mind was made up, that was that. In the next few days her puppets were packed, her clothes, her paints and brushes, her needlework box, *David Copperfield*, her school books, the Christmas presents she had bought for home.

'I can always send a trunk on with your stuff,' said Bella.

'No thanks. It's all going when I go.'

With immense care she wrapped Edmund's cigars, Bella's crystallised fruits, Freda's gloves – she had gone home for the holidays – Mrs P's handkerchiefs and the bits and bobs for the children. She laid the gifts under the Christmas tree in the Great Hall.

Insistent that they wait until Edmund and the boy had gone off for their daily ride before making her departure, Mog went over to the stable to make absolutely certain that the coast was clear and nobody was there. She rushed out again hastily, and leapt into the loaded dog cart: 'Come on, Bella, let's go – quickly – I hate goodbyes.'

Thus, on that frosty Christmas Eve, Mog, Bella and Bess set off for the Halt where poor little Pete had deplored the lack of facilities so long ago. The Tillingham lions at the gate roared their angry farewell, St Mary the Virgin was sad – she hadn't had a soprano like that raising her rafters since the 1880s.

'I do hope we don't pass anybody en route.'

They didn't but, galloping along the ridge high above the lane was the baronet himself with his acolyte beside him. The dog cart was just pulling up at the station down below, piled high with luggage when he spotted it. He turned his stallion and started thundering down the hillside.

Bella was near to tears: 'I shall miss you, old girl. It's a slow train, you know – stopping at every piddling little place between here and Paddington.'

'That's OK – it'll give me more time to revert to being an East Ender.'

As she put her cases up on the luggage rack and leant out of the window to say her last goodbye, she caught sight of him, hopping along the platform as fast as he could manage. As the train drew out he tried to run: 'Come back. Come back. Don't leave me! Don't leave me!' Tears were pouring down his face. The engine let out a long whistle: 'I want my mummeeee.'

It heaved its mighty load up the slow incline, hissing and roaring its way out of the Vale of Tillingham, out of the Valley of the Shadow of Death, into the long, dark tunnel which led out of the enchanted forest, back home.

The train was crowded. Mog sat very still, clutching tightly the little parcel which Bella had thrust into her hand; she was afraid of tunnels – claustrophobia was endemic in the Smart family. They emerged into the daylight after what seemed an age and, with relief, she looked out at the countryside puffing by. 'Look at those cows, Miss – there's hundreds of them.' She recalled so clearly Pete's observation from her journey down to Somerset all that eternity ago. It all began to unfold, the fairy tale – the first sight of her dream Lord in the evening sunlight in the Great Hall, the wonderful Christmas of 1940, with the yule log, the dancing, larks with the children in the snowy woods, puppet shows in the village hall, thrilling the congregation at church when she sang on Sundays, the proposal in the rose arbour, playing the beautiful, adored mistress of all she surveyed, dispensing sweet condescension to the tenants, bringing light, joy, new paint and new curtains to the grand old stately home, becoming part of the pageant of English history – Lady Tillingham. Who was she kidding? Everything comes with a price. Take what you want said God. She thought of the Great Water Closet.

An East End girl with ideas above her station and fat legs, that's what she was, naïve and vain, taken for a ride by a bunch of toffs. How they must have gossiped in the drawing room at Tollington St Mary, beside the ha-ha at Nether Tillingham, in the solicitor's office in Midsummer Norton, how they must have despised common, silly little Rose Smart, prancing down the aisle, as cover for an effeminate who took his pleasures with a stable boy. Bella must have known.

They drew to a stop in no time at all, and who should get in to Mog's carriage but Pooty, briefcase and rolled umbrella at the ready.

'My dear Lady T – what a delight! May I join you?'

She nodded.

'Going up to town for Christmas?'

'Oh, yes.'

He settled down. 'Are you feeling OK? – you don't look too chipper, if I may say so. May I call you Mog?'

'Oh, yes.'

He looked at her intently. She was wearing a hat trimmed with black fur.

'Good lord alive – of course, of course – I've remembered who you remind me of – old Tilly's mater. You're the living, spitting image, her hair was black – coal black – that must have put me off the scent. But that hat you're wearing.'

'Edmund's mother? I've never seen a picture of her. No one ever mentioned the likeness before.'

'Well – they wouldn't, would they.'

'What d'you mean?'

'Well – perhaps I shouldn't say, if you don't know.'

'Pooty – come on – you can't leave it at that.'

'Well, swear you won't let on it was me who spilt the beans, old girl.'

'There is absolutely no chance of that. You might as well know – I'm leaving Edmund, for good – going home.'

'Well – she was er – a bit of a tart, it has to be said. Don't know where the Horror picked her up – she was on the stage, I think, sang and danced – that sort of thing. I say, are you really doing a bunk?'

'Yes, I am. I've gathered all that – he married beneath him, twice, they say.'

'It's not just that. I don't think she was quite the ticket.'

'Not quite the ticket?'

'Wonderful looking – like a film star – as a boy I used to drool. Gertrude she was called. They called her Gorgeous Gertie hereabouts. But poor old Tilly – he had a terrible time. He worshipped her, but she had taken against him from the day he was born. She was OK with Bella – but that poor lad, she beat the hell out of him, even when he was a tiny tot..'

'You mean she smacked him?'

'She laid into him with anything that was to hand – daily beatings for no reason at all. The Horror didn't like it, but did nothing, apparently, and nobody liked to intervene, although I have heard that the housekeeper they had in those days went to the rector about the bruising and the screams. She was sacked. And what d'you think that wonky leg's all about?'

'A riding accident, I was told.'

'It was one Easter holiday. Tilly was about eight, I should think. We'd been out on the ponies, Bella and Tilly and I, and she got it into her head that Tilly was not properly dressed. I shan't forget it in a hurry – she dragged him up the stairs by his scruff, set about him with a riding crop – we could hear the screams 'Mamma, no! Mamma no! I do love you – I do take notice of what you say ... I do ... I do.' Next thing she flung him headlong down the main staircase.'

'My God – what happened?'

'It was all hushed up, of course. I was sworn to silence. The worst of it was that the poor old devil went on adoring her – he'd do anything to try and please "Dearest Mamma", not that anything ever did. It was a great relief to those of us in the know when she abandoned ship.'

'She left?'

'Yes – bolted, taking the Tillingham diamonds with her. Tilly was about ten – he sobbed for weeks.'

'What about Bella?'

'She was always the tough one, very close to her Pa – anyway, Ghastly Gertie was nice enough to her daughter, quite the adoring mother.'

'Why was she like that? Aren't mothers usually more attached to their sons?'

'The Mater reckoned she didn't have all her chairs at home. Pa used to say that she'd probably been beaten herself, by her father, perhaps. He said she seemed to have a problem with the male of the species.'

'But she married Sir Horace.'

'For his title?'

'I suppose. So do you think Edmund married me because I look like his mother?'

'Well – wouldn't be the first man to have done that!'

'Yes, but in Edmund's case … I presume you, along with the rest of the county, are aware of his … his …'

'At Eton there was trouble, but that's not unusual, and one has heard rumours since, of course – that Canadian airman that got shot down, for instance.'

'Oh no –not him!' Mog was shaking now.

'Here – have a cigarette.'

'Am I to assume, Tilly, as you call him, took one look at me and said to himself "I'm going to marry that woman and keep my Mamma for ever, shut away, with no touching or anything unsavory like that, just the odd punch or slap, and no interference with my private life whatsoever."?'

'My good God – he didn't hit you?'

'Now and again if I got too close.'

'So you never …'

'No.'

'My dear girl, I am so sorry. You've had a beastly time. We all assumed that your beauty and charm would see him straight, if you see what I mean. Perhaps he did too.'

Their fellow passengers were all agog.

The paraffin sprinkled on the dry tinder had worked a treat, lit by the flame from the silver lighter, and, by the time Mog and Pooty alighted at Paddington the stable block at New Hall was burnt to the ground.

There was talk in the Tillingham Arms:

'Funny old business that fire up at the 'all – they're sayin' it were done a purpose.'

'And our lovely girl's taken 'erself off.'

'Gaahn off with that Canadian she was carryin' on with at the cricket dance I shouldn't wonder.'

'No – 'e were shot down.'

'Funny business that fire, though.' Meaningful looks were exchanged.

'Bobby from Magna came pokin' 'is nose in. I said nuffin' – fires 'appen, 'appen all the time, I says to 'e – where there's paraffin and straw together there be fire risk.'

'The Horror's missus took off too, o' course, back when Mr Edmund was a kiddie.'

'Weren't no fire then.'

'Only bonfires to celebrate!' Guffaws.

'She were a real good 'un, though, our little Lady T – not like Gorgeous Gertie – though she could 'ave passed for 'er – in looks I mean.'

'Mm. Reckon she's broke Mr Edmund's heart.

'Mr Edmund's got other fish to fry.' Wink, wink.

'Funny business – them getting' 'itched at all, if you ask me.'

'I've 'eard it was all to do with the old Horror's will,' he said, 'no marriage, no money,' he went on, 'Mr Edmund 'ad no choice.'

'Nah. That's a tale of the tub. Weren't no money to speak off. 'E just wanted to pull the wool over pryin' eyes.'

'Why didn't he wed someone of his own sort.'

'The county set knew all about his ways – none of them would touch him with a barge pole. That poor lass from Lunnun, she didn't know what was what – and 'e just thought 'e should make 'is self respectable when 'e was baronet an' all.'

'I reckon there were more to it than all thaat – 'e allays seemed so smitten. The way he gazed at 'er – like 'e was star struck.'

Chapter 32:

Christmas 1944 to January 1945

Fog swirled around the Christmas crush at Paddington. Pooty grappled with Mog's luggage:

'How are you going to get out to the suburbs with all this lot? Shall I try and get you a cab? – It may be a long, cold wait – they're not easy to come by these days.'

She was not listening. It was the sight of platform 1 that did it and the memory of dad's little choir singing their tribute to her:

'*Rose* of England breathing England's air
Flower of liberty beyond compare.'

They were all so proud of her. How could she tell them the sordid truth of it all? How could she just turn up after nearly five years of neglect, of swanning about playing Lady of the Manor, making feeble excuses not to see them, while they crouched in terror for their lives, managed on desperately meagre rations, longing for just a glimpse of the prodigal daughter.

'Oh, Pooty! Whatever shall I say to my family? They think I'm some sort of goddess – not a miserable, selfish dupe. And I've treated them so shamefully – mum was always sending met me biscuits and things and dad got me brushes and stuff for the decorating – and all I could do was put them off visiting me because I was …'

She sat down on one of her suit cases, put her head in her hands and sobbed as though her heart would break.

'Come on, old girl. They'll just be delighted to have you home, I'm sure. Look – why not hole up in my flat for a bit – get yourself sorted out – you're in no fit state to face the music at home. My housekeeper will keep an eye out for you – I'm motoring up to some of our folks in Norfolk tomorrow – the Mater's there already.'

Poor old Pooty. This was his chance. Mog was not paying any attention.

'And there's my sister with her perfect marriage and her perfect child – and I'm a failure – only going home because I need them – not because they need me, crying for myself and the shame of it – not for them.'

'I shouldn't worry about your sister,' offered Pooty. He wondered if he should let on about Ooly and Dougie, but decided this was not the time. 'Come on now, chin up – back to my place and when we've got you straight I'll come with you to your family if you like.'

'Oh, no – I wouldn't dream of putting you to the trouble.'

'Look – I don't give a hoot what your family background is. Your people are evidently kind, loving and generous. Tell you the truth – I'm more than curious to meet them.'

'Oh, Pooty. There I go again. All right – if you really don't mind – but they're ...'

'No buts.'

He called a porter and they made their way to the flat overlooking Regent's Park where the housekeeper took one look at the distraught Mog and switched the geezer on. She wallowed in a deep bath, scrubbing Lady Tillingham away.

When Pooty came back from Whitehall that evening she was sitting by a good fire, wearing her hat and coat, holding tight to her handbag. She looked pale and strained.

'Fancy going out for a spot of dinner? We could splash out and go somewhere special – if you like, or just somewhere quiet – I know a little place ...'

414

'It's very kind of you, Pooty, but I would like to go home now.'

'Okey doke. Home it is. We'll take the motor.'

'What about petrol?'

'I've got my sources.' He smiled.

'I don't want you to waste your precious petrol on me – we could go on the train.'

'Nonsense. Have a sherry to pep you up and then we'll be off. I can even take the masks off my headlights – from today restrictions are lifted. Whoopee!'

Pooty's Lagonda V12 (his pride and joy) nosed its way out of the park, shining its brilliant lights and illuminating a West End strange to Mog's eyes, picking out the dim shapes, the skeletons of churches, jagged, boarded up, eyeless buildings, landmarks, distorted and rendered surreal by the gaps and wreckage around them. Down Portland Place they went, and into Langham Place, the spire of All Souls was gone, only its stump remained, and next to it, was a wide empty space where the Queen's Hall and St Georges' Hall had been.

'Dad used to take us to concerts in Queen's Hall before the war and now it's gone. At least Boosey and Hawks is still there – we always used to get our sheet music from there.'

It was so quiet; there was no Christmas Eve bustle, no gathering of celebration in Piccadilly Circus, the restaurants in the Strand were half empty.

Mog gasped: 'Oh look at St Paul's! It's all alone. The buildings round it are all gone!'

The triumphant, blackened dome rose high above its flattened hinterland.

On they went, along what was left of Cheapside, past the remnants of Bow Church and towards the devastated East End. Mog gazed in horror at her home streets – dear old Bow Road – what wreckage, what desolation. They pressed on towards Chesnut Avenue and drew up outside number 29. Oh dear – so this was the much vaunted palace.

415

Dad opened the door.

'Mog! Mog! Well I'm blowed! Mates – come and look who's here! Welcome, Sir Edmund – you are most welcome to our humble abode. May I introduce my sister, Dorothy, my wife, my elder daughter Mrs John Bowyer, our granddaughter, Elizabeth.'

Dot, who was on the phone, hastily put the receiver down and did a curtsey. Ooly turned white.

'What about Uncle Ed?' said Todge.

'My brother-in-law, Edward Davids.'

'Dad, this isn't Edmund – it's Percy Poultney – we call him Pooty. 'He's very kindly escorted me here.'

'Baronet indisposed?' Asked dad.

'Oh my Gawd, Mog, why didn't you tell us you was comin' 'ome for Christmas.' Lil was in a flap. She hissed at Ooly, 'Go and get the lounge straightened up.'

'Cuppa tea your lordship?'

Ooly made herself scarce.

'Pooty isn't a lord, Mum – he's just Pooty.'

'Cuppa tea Mr Pooty? Mince pie?'

Dot wrote to Pan:

We do hope you had a good Christmas. We all missed you but dad thought it for the best that you stay away from here while all this is going on. There was no let up over the Christmas period – poor old Wanstead really got it in the neck. We seem to be getting the worst of it, I thought we came out here to get away from raids.

I'm sorry that your phone call on Christmas Eve was cut short – we had some surprise visitors – you'll never guess who! Mog turned up – quite out of the blue, with some chap called Pooty. Seems there's been some trouble down in Somerset and she's come home for good. I don't' know what it's all about – why she brought the Pooty person with her. It all seems rather fishy to me. She's got rather lah-di-dah and talks different. She didn't seem very impressed with the house – I suppose it's a bit of a come down after what she's got used to. Ooly was fed up –mum turned her out of her bedroom to put Mog in it.

Lil wrote the following week:

Well what a shock – my Mog come home. we had a lovely Christmas – all together. we missed you of course but it is lovely to have her back. Todge loves her – wont leave her be for a minit. she keeps going into her bedroom first thing – pulls out her curlers and gets her to sing songs to her. i think she is going to stay. she says she will help me in the garden when the bloody freeze stops. I don't know what happened with the lord but she's going for something called non-constipation, or so Ooly says.

Sid wrote:

We all trust you had an enjoyable festive season. We had a good sing song here – it's good to have Mog home again, but rather worrying. There's talk of some legal matters and she seems very down and is having pains from her operation, as she does when she's in a state.

It was a bleak New Year. Morale in the country at large was at its lowest ebb. Hardly any potatoes were to be had in the shops; there were no onions and no apples for sale.

The big new call-up, announced two days before Christmas, had brought the end of the official optimism that the war was entering its final weeks and the rockets were coming thick and fast. In Dagenham, East Ham, Barking Walthamstow, Romford, Leyton and Chigwell huge craters 25 yards across appeared. Fuel was in short supply; few buses were running, and down by Woodford Station women were queuing up with prams at the coal dump to try and get a sack or just a few lumps to keep their families warm; it was bitter cold.

Snow was falling, settling on the ground after a spell of hard frost, when, one January morning, Ooly met Dougie up at the George on the Green. They sat by the window.

'There certainly are some pr-pr-pretty decent houses round here.' said Dougie. 'Still standing! What d'you think of that one – it appears to be on the market. It's got a good size garden – and that looks like a swing over there – and a see-saw – Todge would love that. Let's go and knock on the door – see if we can have a look round. If you'd like to? There's even a school, right next door.'

'It's very grand. I love the mellow brick and just look at those pillars either side of the front door and those huge holly bushes all smothered in berries – I've always wanted a holly bush. There's so many windows – how many bedrooms d'you think there are?'

'Enough to accommodate all the m-m-mini-Mitchells that we can muster. The reception rooms must be big enough to entertain all of Todge's class mates for her fifth birthday and all the farthest reaches of the Smart clan, whenever they want to come. Come on – drink up and we'll go and see if we can have a dekko. I'm sure your people would love to have you living so near. If you like the house why don't we bring them to see it? It really is t-t-time I m-m-met them all.'

Ooly shivered as they crunched across the frozen grass and up the gravel drive. 'It's too soon – what with Mog's bombshell and everything. Let them get used to that before I drop mine.

When Pooty turned up I nearly died. I didn't speak to him – I just hid upstairs until he'd gone – he didn't stay long, but I gather he's coming back for a visit. The cat will be out of the bag soon.'

'Good thing too, but I d-d-don't see why – Pooty's been perfectly discreet so far. And, in any case, I would have thought that with your titled sister's marriage going up in smoke, your divorce won't seem so terrible. Come on, my darling, it really is time we came clean and made some plans – the war will be over soon. Have you seen anything of *him* recently.'

'No – I've had letters as usual – Nell seems to think he's over in Antwerp.'

He rang the door bell.

'Why don't you t-t-tell your sister – about us, I mean. It might cheer her up if she realises she's not the only one in a bit of a tangle.

'I'm not giving her the satisfaction. For once my sainted sister has got herself into a serious mess. You know I've been turfed out of my bedroom! I am sorry for her, though; it must have been terribly humiliating.'

There was still no reply from Holly House and he rang the bell again, long and hard.

'What finally made Mog get out of it? – she put up with the charade for three or four years was it?'

'I don't really know. She had a bit of a fling with a Canadian fighter pilot who got shot down – perhaps it was to do with that. But that was over a year ago and I don't think it amounted to much.'

Still no answer from Holly House.

'Beats me that she didn't twig – about her husband, I mean.'

'Our Mog's not very worldly. And perhaps she thought it was worth putting up with for the glory of being Lady Tillingham. Who knows. Come on, Dougie, there's nobody in – let's go.'

'Poor Mog,' said Dougie, grimly. 'Getting herself mixed up with the d-d-dastardly g-g-gentry. Doesn't do does it?'

Before she could answer there was a flash high in the sky, and almost simultaneously a deafening explosion. Ooly shrieked and flung herself on the ground, pulling Dougie down with her.

'It's OK, darling. If we can hear it like that, it's nowhere near.'

She clung to him: 'Oh, God. Oh, God. Oh Dougie. Let's get all this business over before it's too late, before we're all blown to smithereens.'

'Done,' said Dougie.

When Ooly got back to Chestnut Avenue Mog and Todge were sitting at the kitchen table, glove puppets on their hands, chatting away in funny voices. Lil was draining some nicely boiled potatoes – her very own, dug from her garden. Unphased by any threats of annihilation, now Mog was back, she was happy – happily thankful for her logs, for the apples from her orchard and the parcels of onions sent from Blacksmith's Cottage, even though she had plenty from her own vegetable patch.

'Where 'ave you bin, Ool, all done up? Dinner will be on the table presently. Did you hear that rocket ? We saw the bugger – like a giant red hot poker with a trail of sparks – it's the first one I've seen – what a sight!'

'I went to look at the house.'

'What 'ouse.'

'My house, of course.'

'Is it OK?'

'It's absolutely fine – wonderful, in fact.'

Lil and Mog exchanged puzzled glances. Dot came in from the shops and caught the drift of the conversation.

'Been over to Buckhurst Hill, have you?' she asked, taking off her hat. 'I suppose you're looking forward to getting moved in there as soon as the war is over? Having your own bedroom will be nice.'

'Well there's no rush, is there?' added Lil, hastily, putting her arm round Todge. 'Can't see no finish to all this yet. And even when it's all over you'll 'ave to get your tenants aaht.'

'Have you thought about a school for Todge? – she'll be five in May,' asked Mog.

'Of course I have,' snapped Ooly. 'I'm going to make an appointment to see the headmistress of the Stag's Head school next week, as a matter of fact.'

'But, that's up on the Green, isn't it?' said Dot. 'Just near the George. Hardly convenient for Buckhurst Hill, I wouldn't have thought. What does Johnny think?'

'Johnny's in Antwerp – or somewhere. I am quite capable of making decisions about my daughter's education.'

'Oh, yes, of course, mate,' said her aunt. 'I was only wondering how you would get her there. It would mean an early start every morning.'

'Is it a private school?' asked Mog.

'I should 'ope so,' said Lil 'We can't 'ave our Todge goin' to one of them rough council schools! And it's nice and conveniment for here.'

'Pricey,' said Dot.

'We can manage perfectly well,' said Ooly.

'Praps dad or Aunty or Mog should go with you to see the teacher,' advised Lil.

'Oh, Mum – for heaven's sake!' And she flounced out.

Mog had a letter from Bella:

Dearest Moggins,

Just a line to let you know that I have got Edmund to agree to an annulment. Hailshot from Midsummer Norton will deal with the legal side – you've met him, of course. Best keep the whole thing hush-hush. He's in a pretty bad state, as a matter of fact – Edmund, I mean – what with your absconding and the fire we had in the stable block. Quack is dubious about his state of mind.

It's not the same without you here, old girl. I hope you're keeping your head above water. Pooty keeps me informed. He's a good old boy. One of these days I'll run up to town and say hello – if you could bear to set eyes on me!

To be honest, Mog wasn't really sure about an annulment; it was Pooty's idea. It would be obliterating completely her time as a Lady, as if it had never been. It wasn't as if she had any thoughts of marrying again. Surely she could just stay as Lady Tillingham, estranged? When

Hailshot sent papers to sign she felt deflated and hopeless – not at all like a balloon with its string cut, dancing off into the blue yonder. But the deed was done.

'Good old Tilly. He's not going to make a fuss about letting you go, I gather.'

Pooty was ensconced in the best armchair at number 29; he was now a regular visitor. Sid was not sure about him and Lil had plans that she didn't want disrupted; she dug out the copy of *Far away and long ago* given to Mog by Poor Old Tom when she had left for Somerset, and put it on her daughter's dressing table. Dot, the while, was charmed by Pooty's attentions. He would sit patiently with her skeins of wool held out in his arms while she wound them up into balls, and even offered to help with the washing-up. Ooly, once re-assured that absolutely no beans were going to be spilled, was rather pleased to have Dougie's chum around the place. He played snap with Todge, did conjuring tricks for her and talked politics to Ed. As to Mog ... well ... it was nice to be adored and, it has to be said, she welcomed some link with New Hall and her erstwhile elevated status. Adjusting to life down in the lower ranks after three and a half years of privilege was proving difficult; the little house was so cramped, so mucky, the noise of the trains rumbling along at the end of the garden kept her awake, shopkeepers in the Broadway showed so little respect.

'Mum, that fat man in the butcher's was so rude to me. You'd think I was asking for the moon instead of a few sausages and he virtually accused me of queue jumping! I can't understand it – shop assistants used to be so deferential.'

'I dare say they was reverential to the likes of you when you was daahn in the country.'

'No – I didn't mean that, Mum, you know I didn't. I meant before the war, people in shops were always so polite, so anxious to please.'

'That's the way it is now, duck, with all the shortages. Shopkeepers are lording it over us all – it's a tip-top time for them. Keep the blighters queuing, make them beg. Anyway – don't you go upsettin' any of them with your – yer know – fancy ways!'

'I wouldn't dream of it, Mum.' Mog was upset.

'I know you wouldn't, duck. Come on now – look on the bright side – it's good for dad. 'E's doin' a roaring trade in paraffin what wiv coal bein' so short and as for 'is mended up pots and pans – they sell a treat wiv no new metal goods to be 'ad. Not to mention yer Uncle Billy – old Flo's got a new fur coat out of all this!'

'Is that how he paid for the Paddington party?'

'Lor' love you – 'e never paid for that. Now keep this to yerself – it were Uncle Ed – got a win on the pools!'

'Oh dear – poor Uncle Ed – he's never had a bean in his life and he spent his little windfall on a party for his stupid stuck-up, show-off niece. Oh, Mum – I've been so awful. What ever can I do to make up to you all?'

'Don't be so daft. You just stay 'ere at 'ome and keep your old mum 'appy.'

Mog needed a project. She scraped the paint off the bath taps and polished them up so they shone like stars. Ooly fixed her up with some singing engagements and she got herself a part time teaching post at Chadwell Heath. As the frozen earth began to thaw she got to work on the garden.

She wrote to Pan:

Moggo calling.

It looks as if I'm home for good. I'll tell you all about it when I see you. Last Monday I went to a music lesson – on sufferance because dad made me, Matthews gave me about an hour's lesson; he said he thought the crack I'd got had come through wrong breathing and production of B, C and D. So I'm on exciting exercises for some weeks! He told me not to sing, but I was singing at Stoke Newington on Thursday and at Woodford today and one of the Skoriers' gang has asked Ooly and me to sing at the Old Girls in a few weeks – so I haven't very much chance to rest it.

Aunt Flo' came to see us today, all done up in her new fur coat. I suppose Uncle Billy sent her to poke her nose in and find out what's going on. Poor old Flap Jack – I fed her on a lump of shop cake and a solid rubber bit of tart I'd made; that'll teach her she's not to come here too often. She said I've got thin and quite changed. Don't know what she meant – whether she meant I'm getting old and plain or, as Ooly said, I was a bit maggoty with her! 'Spect she didn't like my cake.

My new school is OK, my register last week was full of noughts because of the rockets and I did knitting and puppets all the week.

'What ever is going on with Mog?' asked Gif. 'Do tell, Piggo.'

'I really couldn't say.'

'You must have some idea? What does she say in the letter?'

'Oh – you know Mog – she's just burbling on about this, that and the other.'

'She must have said something about the circs?'

'Just that she would tell me when she saw me.'

'Why don't you give her a ring?'

'You know very well I hate talking on the phone.'

'We can't be kept in the dark!'

'For goodness sake, woman – it's no business of yours. You're so damned nosey.'

'I'd like to know who this Pooty person is that your aunt referred to – where does he fit in, I'd like to know?'

'How d'you know what Aunty said in her letter? Have you been looking at my private correspondence again? How dare you! How dare you!'

Und so weiter.

Chestnut Avenue was, of course, all of a twitter. What ever was happening at number 29?

Mrs Plunket was agog: 'Lady Tillingham staying with you, is she? Do bring her in for tea.'

'Will she be staying long?' asked Mrs Spoon. 'That's her husband, the baronet who visits so much, is it?'

The news had filtered through to the Emporium; not that Sid had said anything, but Ooly had told Maureen – no details, of course; she couldn't resist telling her mum and Mrs O'Brien passed it on in the chippy, overheard by Dai Lewis.

'Your Rose back 'ome then, Sid?'

'Oh – yes, brother.'

''Ome for good is she?' asked Fanny Bastaple, all ears.

'Time will tell, time will tell.' He went out the back to find the milk saucepan he had been soldering for her.

The company turned excitedly to Dai. 'What's 'appened? What 'ave you 'eard?'

'Poor old Sid. 'E must be worried sick. Seems sommat went awry down the west country. It's all in the hands of lawyers, they say.'

'What's it all abaaht?'

'Well, as I understand it, there was some bedroom trouble, if you get my drift. And there was something about a fire. There was another fellow involved, 'es a toff – very high-up in some Ministry or other – or 'e might be a Canadian – got an odd name – it'll come to me in a tick.'

'Crikey – did she do the dirty on the baronet?'

'Doesn't do tanglin' with toffs, that's what I say.'

Sid came back and the company speedily reverted to the usual chat about the potato shortage – would Sam the Chippy survive? Yes – he's got a black market supply. The triumphs of the Red Army got a mention and the rockets featured – Bert Gum reckoned that London might have cracked if there had been Jerry rockets in 1940. Vi Kerridge spoke of the wonderful things that were going to happen after the war – new

425

homes, jobs for all, holidays with pay, pensions for everyone. 'I should coco,' added Doomandgloom. Fanny wondered if any of that would this have come about without the war? 'Should we be raisin' a cheer for good old Hitler!' she cackled.

As soon as they got outside, the subject of Rose Smart was immediately re-introduced.

By the time the gossip had flitted along the stalls to the far end of Roman Road, Sir Edward Littleton had raped Rose Smart repeatedly and set fire to the bedroom. She had been rescued by a high-up in the Canadian air force, a friend of Winnie's, called Fruity, who had carried her off and was intent on bearing her away into the sunset. Good as the flics!

Mrs Tittler, sour and aching, wrote to her son, Tom.

That Smart girl that so took your fancy has got herself into a right old mess. Just as well you never got yourself mixed up with the likes of her. Too much of a looker for her own good. Handsome is as handsome does. They're saying she's taken up with a GI now, would you believe!

Poor Old Tom.

Chapter 33:

February to early March 1945

By mid February the weather was mild and spring like; Todge was helping Lil and Mog to dig over the vegetable patch.

'You do like Pooty, don't you, Mum?' asked Mog.

'He seems a nice enough chap,' replied Lil. 'But I would have thought you'd 'ad enough of 'is class of person.'

'I like Pooty,' said Todge. 'I like Pooty a lot. He's more fun than Daddy Johnny.'

'Hush, Todge. You mustn't say that.'

'Why? Mum wouldn't mind. She doesn't think Daddy Johnny's much fun either.'

'Todge, do be quiet.'

'Mum won't hear. She's just gone out, gone to see Nanna Bow – again.'

This time she really had.

By the time she got to Bow the sky had darkened and it had started to rain.

On the way from the station she passed by St Alphege. She had passed the church many times since the Blitz, and, of course, Todge's christening had been in the little chapel in the adjoining vicarage but, this time, she felt unaccountably drawn in. There was a hole in the make-shift fence that had been put up around the ruins; she stepped through it. The roof was off; rain dripped from the gaunt skeleton beams, the remains of the gallery on the north wall. Bits of plaster and brick dropped from time to time, and falling planks sounded like doors banging in the wind. Six foot high sycamore saplings choked the pulpit – there must have been twenty of them, at least. Every nook and cranny of the site was infested with rampant rusty buddleia, bracken and moss. Birds were nesting in a tall, bushy pussy willow which stood just in front of the lectern – she could see sparrows and starlings, mice scuttled about – theses were the only denizens of this little world, so full of memories.

She remembered the ethereal beauty of the daffodils in the early light on Easter morning, the sunny glory of Whitsun services, when the church was dressed in geraniums, marguerites and hydrangeas. Then there was Harvest, the fulfilment of summer, with its rows of shiny apples, sheaves of golden corn (always got from someone's country cousins), bronze, white and yellow chrysanthemums, purple grapes and Michaelmas daisies. Most magic in her memory were the luxurious clusters of white lilac in the flickering candlelight of Christmas morning with her and Pan and Mog giving tongue:

"Yea Lord we greet thee born this happy morning."

And then there was her wedding. She remembered the morning, vividly – in Vicky Park – the scratchy feel of the parched grass on her bare legs, the patches of peerless blue sky glimpsed through the screen of bushes, distant cries from the lido, the soft buzz of far away traffic, the hum of drowsy bees on that most glorious warm morning at the beginning of September, just before war broke out. As to the later ceremony, it was a blur. The odd image was there: mum and Dot with brimming eyes, in the front pew, the rows of tiny pearl buttons on her ivory velvet sleeves, the glitter of dad's diamond tie pin.

The mosaic tiles in the chancel were intact – even the most hardy plants seem to have found them too inhospitable to provide a foothold. Here she had stood and pledged herself to Johnny. The wells that had held the choir stalls between the mosaic paths had become rectangular green patches, a tangle of angry weeds.

She leaned up against a bit of charred wall and closed her eyes. How she was dreading the furore to come –dad's shocked horror, mum's concern for Todge, Dot's sneering disapproval, Pan's explosion, Nell's distress, Johnny's angry despair. If only there was some way to ease the situation – Dear God, if only there was some way, any way, that would save her from having to make this agonising choice. A robin hopped down from the remains of the altar and stood looking at her, his head cocked.

Nell was, as ever, delighted to see her daughter-in-law. 'Well, how are things with you, chick? Let me take your coat and dry it off – you're soaked to the skin. Heard from Johnny?'

'Yes, the letters are coming regularly. He seems quite cheerful – glad to be in the fray, I'd say.'

'Sit you down and I'll put the kettle on. Now – little Elizabeth? I suppose she'll be starting her schooling soon.'

'She's going, I hope, to a school up on Woodford Green. It's a nice private school, quite small and not too expensive. Actually it's a boys' school that started taking a few girls since the war started.'

Nell looked dubious: 'Woodford Green? But you'll be setting up home in your own house as soon as the war is over, won't you? How far away is it? Not far, I suppose.'

'No, not far. Nell ... I ...'

'What is it, chick? You seem a bit down – is that a stye you're starting?'

'Oh, yes. I always get one when I'm due to perform. I'm singing to the Old Girls with Mog on Wednesday.'

'How is your sister getting on – settling down all right? It must be so difficult for her after what she's got used to. And the shame of it – divorce is *such* a shocking thing – she is getting divorced is she?'

'Well – er – I'm not sure.'

'She has left him for good, though, hasn't she?'

'Oh yes.'

'Is there anyone else part of it?'

'Well – there's this chap called Poultney who's in attendance a good deal.'

'I see,' said Nell, peering hard at Ooly over her specs. 'I wouldn't have had your sister down as the flighty type. Rather serious minded I always thought.'

'No – it's not like that, Nell. He's just a friend, at present anyway – someone who has been giving her a helping hand, a friend of her husband's.'

She felt disinclined to tell her mother-in-law the truth about Mog's hapless marriage but didn't want her thinking that adultery was endemic in the Smart family.

'Mm. And what about you, me duck. How is everything?'

'Nell, I … I … the school Todge is going to …'

'Yes?'

'Well, it's not really near the house in Buckhurst Hill, if you see what I mean. I haven't told Johnny about it yet. I should tell him first.'

'Oh dear, oh dear,' Nell wiped a tear away. 'I suppose you better had, but can't you at least wait until he's safe back home?'

The purchase of Holly House was activated with war-time speed and Dougie redoubled his efforts to try and get Ooly moving on the divorce front.

'Nell wants us to wait until Johnny comes home.'

'So you have, at least, t-t-told her?'

'Well – not in so many words – I kind of hinted at it, just made it clear that I wouldn't be moving into the house in Buckhurst Hill – but she knows all right. She cried.'

'My darling girl, there's absolutely no r-r-reason why you shouldn't continue your friendship with Nell – I know it means a lot to both of you. I can't see the H-h-hawk taking her place!'

'Oh yes – that's going to be on the cards! How can I possibly keep Nell as my confidante and friend when I'm ditching her son who is out there fighting for king and country, taking her grandchild away, breaking everyone's heart?'

'You would rather br-br-break mine?'

'No, no, no – but rather than endure this on-going torment, anything! I would rather have my leg cut off, be mangled in an air raid.'

'Ooly, that is a cruel and stupid thing to say.'

Dougie was angry; he had never spoken to her like that before. He'd probably never spoken to anyone like that before.

'If you'd seen what I see practically everyday of my working life … Sorry, darling. I know very well this is all my fault. If only I hadn't been so f-f-feeble back in the early days – you know I can never f-f-forgive myself for that. All I want to do is make it up to you, make you happy, protect you – and all I seem to manage is to inflict more suffering. Would it be easier if I just took myself off and left you to … to … to …'

'How are we going to furnish Holly House – you can't buy anything these days?'

'Oh – there's a stack of family stuff going begging. There's even a Bechstein in one of their places, I seem to remember.'

'Really?' Ooly gasped. 'Oh my goodness!'

'I thought I might br-br-broach the subject with the Aged Ps this weekend.'

'Aged Ps? That's *Great Expectations* isn't it? Dad used to read it out loud to us. I didn't know you were a Dickens man. You're not going to tell them about us – not yet?'

'I was going to, but if you'd rather I didn't, so be it.'

'What if they create a rumpus and go and see dad or something.'

'I c-c-can just say I've bought a house and need some furniture, then.'

'Shouldn't we wait until the war is over. It can't be long now, surely?'

The greatest offensive of the war was afoot – "Never before", gloried the press, "Has the Reich suffered such a scourging of her cities, troop concentrations and supply lines." Marshal Zuchov's armies were on their way to Berlin, Monty and the Americans launched an attack all along the Western front, and the great and glorious city of Dresden was reduced to a smoking ruin.

Lil wrote to Pan:

well i thank you for those nice onions – they came sataday morning just in time for dinner. i had one with some cheese – it was nice with a glass of beer. i was by myself – Mog and Ooly took Todge to Maureen's for the day. so i had a nice quiet day – i enjoyed it much. it does one good to rest from it all. i get very tired sometimes. i shall be sending you one of your books back. i will send you a cake in it at the end of the week. Ooly has got Todge down for a school up on the green. i suppose that means theyll be stayin ere for a bit longer at least. war news is good dont you think. weer givin it to them good and proper now. what abaat dresden? some of them are sayin as how we shuldnt have done it Jerry is nearly beaten so we shuld leave the poor sods of ordinary folk and theare bootiful city alone. remember the blitz – that's what i say remember them baydickker raids.

'What's the news from Chesnut Avenue?' asked Gif, trying to get a glance at the letter.

'Nose out,' shouted Pan. 'My private correspondence is no concern of yours. I've told you before.'

'Anything about the Mog business?'

'Absolutely nothing. Mum's just thanking me for the onions.'

'That's a long letter if she's only thanking you for the onions.'

'Pig, do mind your own business. She's just writing about the war situation – Dresden and everything.'

'I really do think that was the giddy limit,' said Gif. 'No need for

432

it at all – no strategic value – just vicious, avenging vandalism. Helga and I went there in the spring one year. I shall never forget it – great wide boulevards awash with pink and white blossom, magnificent bridges spanning the Elbe, palaces, opera house, green copper spires, extraordinarily exuberant baroque and rococo – the whole place. As good as Florence –better, I'd say. It was largely the creation of Elector Frederick Augustus I, you know, he's said to have had 267 illegitimate children.'

'How disgusting,' snorted Pan.

'It was the high point of the Grand Tour – quite an English colony there. They used to say Winnie's aunt lived there and that's why it was left unharmed, until now. Wonderful whipped cream floating on top of cups of hot chocolate, scrummy cakes smothered with icing. Mm. What does your ma say?'

'Nothing about bastards and cream cakes, I can assure you.' She re-sealed the envelope and tucked the letter away a drawer of her desk and turned the lock.

The headmistress of the Stag's Head agreed to take Todge immediately; they were short of pupils. Lil was delighted that her granddaughter was being sent to a school nearby and not taken off to the dreaded Buckhurst Hill. Sid, however, was worried:

'She's not five yet, mate, and if it's mainly a boys' school, won't it be a bit rough for her? She's not used to other kiddies at all, let alone boys.'

'Dad, she's got to make her own way in the world. It's no good mollycoddling her.'

The first day came. Todge was proudly attired in a purple blazer with white antlers emblazoned on the pocket, a grey skirt, grey cardigan and white blouse with a purple tie. She liked the tie best and the draw string shoe bag which held her special indoor shoes; she was eager to be off. Her stumpy little plaits were tied up with pale blue ribbons and they bobbed up and down as she marched bravely up Chesnut Avenue, holding rather more tightly than usual to her mother's hand. Ooly had agreed to let Mog accompany them, but drew the line at mum and Dot.

Ooly's and Mog's eyes looked unusually glittery as they said goodbye and watched Todge guided gently by Miss Rover into a seething morass of boyhood.

'See you this afternoon.'

Ooly was there at three o'clock sharp. Todge rushed out like a shot out of a gun.

'What did you do?'

'We all sat at little tables and made plasticine worms.'

'Is that all?'

'There was another new boy. He is called Simon and he got red in the face, and cried for his mummy. Miss Rover had to take him down the garden to see the bunny rabbit in a cage to cheer him up. Boys are soppy, aren't they, Mum?'

'Aren't there any girls in your class?'

'No. There's some bigger ones though. One called Parcellary Wind. Well Barbara in the top class calls her that – the teachers call her Marcelle Breeze. She's got a big black handbag with two yellow coloured pencils in it. She said I shouldn't have blue ribbons in my hair – its against the rules. They've got to be grey.'

'What a cheek! The pale blue looks nice with the grey of your uniform. Was the dinner all right?'

'Yes. It was all right.'

They set off in the direction of home.

'See that house there, Todge?'

'I'm not Todge now. I'm Lizbeth.'

'OK. See that house there, Elizabeth ? The one with the holly bushes.'

'Yes.'

'D'you like it?'

'It's all right. But it looks a bit like my school.'

'Look there's a swing and a see-saw and a lovely big garden.'

'Why isn't Nan meeting me? Has she got some grey ribbon?'

What Ooly didn't know – and would not know for many, many years to come, was that Todge had, several times during that endless day, retreated to the lavatory, the posh one, up the sweeping marble staircase, reserved for teachers and the few girls. Miss Rover had taken her up there for the first time, urging her to hold tight to the bannisters as she clambered up the shiny, slippery steps. She shut herself in safely for a big private cry. It was an abiding memory with her, the sight of the great ornate gilt door knob against the white painted door – she could just reach it. There she would sob out her misery and fear for months to come, about twice a day. Nobody had any idea.

As the daffodils were beginning to bud and the forsythia bush brought forth its golden glory next to the holly bushes, the Bechstein was delivered at Holly House, along with a Regency mahogany dining table of immense proportions and all manner of fine Mitchelleana. A decorator was engaged.

'Why don't we spend a day at Harrods and you can choose curtain material and bedding?'

'Oh – you do that Dougie – it's not my sort of thing – Johnny used to …' Ooly's voice tailed off.

'What about p-p-paint and wallpaper – I suppose that's not up your street either! Perhaps we should consult your father.'

'Don't be silly. It's just that … well it's all so sudden – getting the house and everything before anything is settled.'

'Well – at least go and have a look at the piano – here take the key. You haven't even had look at the interior of the house yet. Why not take Todge and show her round – you don't have to tell her what's going on.'

'Good day?' asked Ooly when she picked Todge up from school.

'I made a friend – he's called Dennis. His mum says I can go to his house for tea. He says he's got a gramophone with 'The Teddy Bear's Picnic' on it.'

'That's nice. We're going to have a look inside that house with the holly bushes – that'll be fun won't it?'

'Why? I want to go home to Nan now.'

'It belongs to a friend of mine and I said I'd measure up the windows for him.'

'Why? Dennis lives in a big house – he says it's as big as our school.'

'Would you like to live in a big house too, Todge – I mean Elizabeth?'

'I like my Nan's house.'

Ooly turned the key in the lock and the door swung open into a vast square entrance hall with a marble fireplace. There, among rolls of Persian rugs and packing cases it stood in all its rosewood glory – the Bechstein, a concert grand, waiting for Ooly.

She sat down and ran her fingers along the key board and tried to conjure up her new life – but all that came was the Hawk in brown and gold lace, hovering over her with beady, angry eyes.

Todge sat down on the floor, crossly: 'Don't play the piano now, Mum. I want to go home ... I ...'

'Let's go and see how many rooms you can count – come on.'

She seized Todge's hand and pulled her up, and through a pair of double doors into what seemed like a ball room, with French windows opening onto a terrace and a lawn which stretched away into the distance of the afternoon.

'D'you want to have a go on that swing?'

'All right.'

She allowed herself to be pushed – higher and higher it went. She squealed with delight.

'Come on, Mum – let's try the see-saw.'

Up and down, up and down:

'You're too heavy, Mum. This is no good – I'm going to 'splore the house.'

In she rushed, wheeling around making a loud whining noise:

' I'm a spitfire – this is what the boys do at school.'

She flew up the grand staircase.

'There's hundreds of rooms up here, Mum – and 'normous windows. And there's more stairs up to a higher part!'

'Just come down and look at the kitchen – the size of it!'

'What's that row of bells for?'

'You press a button or pull a cord in one of the other rooms and that makes one of the bells ring, calling a maid or some other servant to bring you tea or make the fire up.'

'Why don't the people get their own tea?'

'Rich people like to have servants to do things they don't like doing.'

'Why?'

'I suppose they think they have more important things to do.'

'I think they're lazy. Does your friend have servants?'

'No – no. The bells are left over from the old days.'

'What – before the war? What was "before the war"?'

Ooly laughed: 'D'you like it here, Todge?'

'Lizbeth. It's all right.'

'Would you like to live in a house like this one day?'

'Yeah! I would ring a bell and Nan would bring me a spoon of syrup. Can we go home now?'

Ooly had been avoiding any tête-à-tête with Pooty, but one evening found herself alone with him in the lounge. The old 'uns had gone to the flics and Mog was late home from school – some meeting or other.

'How's it going with everything, Ooly? I hope you don't mind my asking. I haven't seen Dougie for some time.'

'Oh – OK.'

'Any progress?' Pooty was hoping for progress; he thought it might help with his bid for Mog.

'Dougie's bought a house for us, near here.'

Pooty, a cautious man, was startled: 'Good grief – that's a bit premature isn't, with nothing properly settled? Has he said anything to Sir Henry and the Hawk? No one here knows anything, obviously. And what about your husband – is he still in the dark?'

'Yes.'

'And your mother-in-law? You're very fond of her aren't you?'

'Mm. You haven't said anything to Mog, have you, Pooty?'

'Good gracious, no – cross my heart and hope to die. And what about Todge?'

'I've taken her to the house, but I didn't tell her about it all. I pretended it belonged to a friend – just to see if she liked it.'

'And did she?'

'Not much.'

'He's furnished it and everything – beautiful things from his parents, curtains from Liberty's, a Bechstein.'

'I thought they didn't know?'

'I think he's just told them he's bought a house – nothing more. He's pressing me to meet his father.'

'Well that's absolutely splendid! Why don't you meet the old boy. Henry Mitchell's a pussy cat – the Hawk, of course, is a different matter. You'll get along with Dougie's pa like a house on fire.'

'I don't know. How are things with you and Mog, by the way?'

Pooty pulled a face and shrugged his shoulders. 'I suppose it will take her some time to get herself together after all she's been through. Mustn't rush her. At least the annulment seems to be going through smoothly. It might help her if she knew that you were in a similar sort of boat. Bit of sisterly empathy – you know.'

'We've never been that close and I'm not ready for disclosure,' said Ooly, huffily, thinking, for a little longer, at least, let the perfect Rose be the one who was blotting the family copybook, she whose price was above rubies.

'If you knew what a to-do there was seven years ago when the God Almighty Mitchells made such a fool of me and treated my family with utter contempt. And it's not as if Johnny's done anything wrong – it's quite different from Mog's situation, as I understand it, though she hasn't really said all that much.'

'She's had a pretty ghastly time, you know,' said Pooty gravely.

'I dare say it had its compensations.'

'If you mean living in the lap of luxury, you've got it all wrong. The Tilly set-up is grim – they haven't got a bean and the mansion is crumbling before their eyes.'

She thought of well appointed Holly House.

'In any case,' he went on, 'I can't imagine any material benefits would make up for a hollow sham of a marriage like hers.'

'I didn't have you down as a "love on a crust' man", said Ooly. 'Actually I was thinking more of the Lady of the Manor bit. Mog's always had notions. She just loved being Lady Tillingham. You can't imagine what a coup it was for her to land a lord, to be scooped up out of the gutter by your Tilly, whatever he was like, whipped off into dreamland, courtesy of Hitler.'

Pooty looked crushed; he simply refused to believe that the object of his adoration was just a social climber but, nevertheless, couldn't help wishing he had a title.

'Oh God, Pooty – I'm sorry – really I'm no better than she is,' Ooly went on: 'Calmly planning to trample on my family's feelings just to get …'

'Some happiness?' offered Pooty taking off his specs and polishing them slowly with a large handkerchief: 'I would have said, as an outside but close observer, that you and Dougie were in the grip of a grand passion. Dougie is besotted with you. You evidently care for him or you wouldn't still be around after all this time – seven, nearly eight years. What more could you ask for? The Mitchells are rolling in it, to boot. Once the dust has settled your parents will be so proud. You'll be the Lady of the family now.'

Poor old Pooty. He was a such good bloke. It was a pity mum had taken against him. Dad wasn't keen either.

Chapter 34:
March 1945

As March drew on things on the Western Front were approaching a climax. The pounding of Berlin from the air continued and the Allied armies now occupied the west bank of the Rhine from the North Sea to the Swiss border; any hour soon the all-out offensive will break, said the press, and Zhukov, with the armies of Russia, will move in from the Oder "the doom of Hitler and all his works is sealed".

For the Flower Garden it was the birthday season, a most important time for the Smart family who held the anniversaries in great regard. Presents were always carefully chosen with scant concern as to the cost – that was Dot's opinion anyway. Ooly's most treasured gift this year had to be kept private, of course, it was a gold locket embossed with an "M"; inside were two tiny photos, one of Dougie and one of Todge. Where on earth had he got the picture of Todge from? Johnny sent a card. Pooty brought Mog some lapis lazuli earrings and Poor Old Tom came up with an embarrassingly lavish bouquet of red roses.

Pan's birthday was the last of the three; there was a shower of parcels and letters from home.

Mum wrote:

i hope you have a happy & peaceful birthday with lots of presents. Well the Girls received their parcels quite safe – Mog was thrilled with her bag purse and her lovely flowers. She has bought Ooly a tackey case (attaché) and filled it with cottons, tape pins needles everything she wants for needlework box. Todge wants to schare them. she gets so excited about it all.

They will write you. her school is a good one I think but dad is worried about it being all boys. Ooly was pleased with her little cut glass pot and think it so pretty she think it is lovely. she is going to save her powers (powder) and cream until she goes home to put on her dressing tabble. did you read about the rocket at Holborn – you know Farrondon Market? It was a heavey one and lot of lives lost. it was Thursday morning one oclock last week. I don't think they have a very long run now. we have had a hole quiet night an day. dont you think the news are good? Wish they would bash them out of Holland. I hope you are having it quiet. give my love to Gif and yourself.. I cant think of any moore to say the girls will write to you. Goodnight. God bless and keep you safe. Love mum and Todge xx.

Dad wrote:

Just a few lines to wish you a happy birthday. The big woman is writing at the same time. We have been quite alright this week. I think things have been a little quieter. Little Todge has been out twice to dinner this week. They don't seem to be teaching her much at that school Ooly has got her into. The almond tree is in full blossom. The trees all round begin to look well. Your flowers were wonderful. I think this is all for tonight. Good night God Bless you, Dad.

Dot wrote:

Birthday blessings to you, my dear and may this year see all your cherished dreams come true. If the blouse is not to your liking, just send it back and I will change it.

Mog gave Ooly a workbox, of all things. I doubt if she will get much use out of it. We are seeing a deal of Mog's friend, Pooty, these days. He is a very nice gentleman. He was here for Mog's birthday and gave her some beautiful earrings – they must have cost the earth! I don't know what's happening with the legal matters – they're keeping it all very quiet. Dad insisted on having a bit of a "do" for Mog's birthday and invited the Spoons and Mrs Plunkett to join us. I don't think Mog was very pleased though she put a good face on it. Billy and Flo'were over and mum invited that Tom Tittler – do you remember him? Mum makes such a fuss of him – you would think he was a member of the family.

Ooly wrote:

What a lovely buffday present. I felt all glamorous when I opened my parcel – like a film star. Just the sort of present I like, what you wouldn't buy for yourself but love to be given. The daffs are sitting on the table in the window in my green glass bowl as fresh as when they arrived ...

I had a very nice birthday. Mum gave me a nightdress and money for shoes. Dot gave me a silver serviette ring – ever such a beauty – Mog gave me a case (attaché case) full of needlework niceties – she said she's sick of me borrowing her things! The old 'uns threw a birthday party for Mog – she was fed up. I think she was hoping to go off to some swish restaurant with her chum Pooty.

Mog wrote:

Mog calling with birthday wishes. I loved my exquisite little evening bag – I took it when my friend Pooty took me to a very nice place in town. He was going to take me on my birthday but mum made it quite clear she wanted me at home, so we had a bit of a party here with Billy and Flo'. Dad even invited some of the neighbours in. I think Ooly's nose was put a bit out of joint – prodigal daughter and all! Mum even made a cake and iced it with some concoction or other. You should have seen it – patisserie is hardly her forte!

Do you remember Poor Old Tom Tittler? He turned up too. He chopped the logs for us – poor old devil – I made him, and then was

443

smitten with remorse when he had to get back to his barracks and didn't
even have time for anything to eat.

Gif prepared a special lunch (it was a Saturday) and carefully wove
a crown of primroses for the birthday girl. She got tickets for the two
of them to go to the theatre in the evening. Dom Sci. brought round a
magnificent confection and an extravagant bouquet of spring flowers
was delivered – from Jocasta. Offerings from various Pan worshippers
arrived at intervals during the morning and Teddy B sent a slim volume
which arrived by the second post.

'Haven't I got anything from you, Pig?'

'Wait and see.'

'What is it, Piggo. Do tell.'

'Wait and see.'

'You know I'm no good at waiting. Give me a clue, at least.'

'No.'

'Oh – go on.'

Just after lunch, a special offally dish, invented by Gif, followed
by some tinned pineapple kept for the occasion, a van appeared in the
drive. While Pan watched in stupefied delight as a large greenhouse
was put together in the garden; while the gleaming structure was being
assembled, another vehicle appeared at Blacksmith's Cottage. It was
Jocasta's Morris.

'What's she doing here?' grumbled Gif.

'She's taking me off for a surprise treat somewhere. Didn't I mention
it? Back tomorrow night. Oh – thanks for the greenhouse.'

At Pan and Jocasta's departure poor Gif wiped her eyes, and with a
mighty arm flung a stone at the greenhouse (a small one) and went to
her desk and got two letters out.

She re-read the first, with some pride:

Air Ministry, 6 November 1940.

Madam,

I am commanded by the Air Council to inform you that their attention has been drawn to your meritorious conduct when you went to the assistance of the pilot of a Royal Air Force aircraft which had crashed and caught fire near Harlow on Sept 15 last.

The Air Council wish me to express to you their high appreciation of your services and to thank you for your help.

I am, Madam, your obedient servant,

AS

Permanent Under Secretary of State.

She had been very hurt by Pan's dismissive response to its arrival and decided not to show her the letter which had followed it up, only recently:

Dear Miss Drayman,

At last we have been able to track you down. Our son's survival is thanks to your heroic efforts four years ago and although we can never, in any way, recompense you for what you did, we would be honoured if you would be prepared to meet us so that we can express our heartfelt gratitude in person. We have no wish to intrude upon your privacy, but would be inestimably grateful if you would consider meeting with us, at your convenience, perhaps at an hotel in your area? My wife and I await your response eagerly.

Your most humble and obedient servant,

Biggar.

Without saying anything to Pan she had telephoned Lord Biggar and an arrangement was made for them to meet for lunch at the Crown in Highbridge on Sunday (tomorrow). She supposed it was convenient that Pan was out of the way.

The prospect of the encounter filled her with unease; she had done what she had done, the like of which hundreds of ordinary people had been called upon to do during the course of this terrible war. It was satisfying to have her action recognized by the authorities, of course, but the personal gratitude of the family … it seemed wrong that she should be singled out.

In the event, it turned out to be a very jolly lunch with some absolutely top hole treacle pud and some scrumptious petits fours to finish off. A huge sum of money was tentatively offered and hastily declined. Lord B was desperate to reward the heroine and, having established that she was a teacher (and a brigadier general's granddaughter) even suggested that she might accept the headship of the that most celebrated of all girls' schools, Doevale – he was the chairman of the governors and they were, as it happens, looking for a new head at present. Gif explained that for a single woman teacher the friendships formed through school were in lieu of family and not to be lightly dismissed even when serious advancement beckoned. She really couldn't consider moving away from Suffolk, but was immensely grateful for the thought. Lady B was understanding – 'But surely there is something we could do to recompense you?'

There was. She thought of it on the way home. Jocasta was delighted and amazed when she heard from Lord Biggar and accepted the offer with alacrity.

On Saturday the 24th of March the press reported that General Patton with the American Third Army had crossed the Rhine, the traditional border of Germany that no foreign army had crossed in 140 years. Thereby was Monty's thunder stolen. On Sunday it was announced that Monty was over with the 21st Army Group; "Over – and on" was the headline in the *Sunday Pictorial*. In the greatest airborne operation of all time 40,000 British glider troops and US paratroopers had been dropped on the east bank of the Rhine to secure a bridgehead. "Once the river line is pierced and the crust of German resistance is broken," announced Winnie, "decisive victory in Europe will be near." The powers were converging on Berlin – the German army was crumbling. The "great and final assault" was imminent.

Meanwhile at home an Easter rush for holidays was in full swing; hotels and boarding houses in Bournemouth, Margate and Southend were all booked up, chock-a-block, even though the food offices warned there wouldn't be enough to go round and advised holiday makers to bring their own. It was exceptionally mild and, for the most part, sunny. Mrs Gum was doing a brisk trade in Cornish daffs and violets, not to mention flowers for the rash of weddings which erupted in anticipation of the coming peace. Among Sid's customers in the Emporium joy was not unconfined, however.

'It's all right for them as 'ave got the cash – rushin' off to Saaf End,' grumbled Will Kerridge.

'Some 'oliday when you've got to take yer own grub; yer own grub wiv yer!' added Doomandgloom.

'Yeah,' said Fanny Bastaple. 'I thought we was s'posed to be winnin' this flippin' war! No more meat from the Yanks, they're sayin'.'

A world-wide meat shortage threatened – the worst yet – rations would be cut.

'Them GIs get five times as much meat as our lads – did yer know?' said Will. 'No wonder they're nickin' our victory, getting their selves over the Rhine before Monty's lads.'

'Wot I say is feeding the starving Europeans is all very well,' went on Fanny, 'but what abaaht my old man? 'es no good wiv aaht is chops.'

'Cheer up, mates,' said Sid. 'Winnie and Monty have brought us through. Good old Winnie – he was over there, you know, when we crossed the Rhine. He even walked about on enemy soil, bold as brass. Soon enough we'll all be back to normal – no more rations, no more raids, the boys back home safe.'

'I've heard they're planning a wonderful celebration in Bethnal

Green,' said Ethel Jiggins, back from her sister in Grimsby. 'The council are really going to push the boat out. There's to be a grand victory dance on the Green, with concert parties, bands, processions, fireworks.'

'I'd 'ave thought we'd 'ad enough of bloody fireworks, bloody fireworks,' said Doomandgloom. 'Our chaps might be on their way to Berlin, but the rockets are still comin', still comin'.'

'Not thick and fast like they were, though, brother,' said Sid. 'Papers say the only way to stop them, is to smash the launching sites in Holland destroying the lives of thousands of our Dutch allies and ...'

Will interrupted: 'We don't want no streets full of iced buns and buntin', stuff their struttin' flag waving. The workin' man 'as won this ruddy war, and wot we want is safeguards against slavery and some steady, constant work, a roof over our 'eads and sommat 'arf decent to eat. All them bloody Tories can talk abaaht is liftin' controls; wiv aat controls the price of 'ousin', food and clothing will shoot up. Givin' us back our freedom! I should coco.'

'Yeah,' chimed in Dai Lewis. 'Like they did after the last show – I recall my old Da sayin' as 'ow they let South Wales become nothin' more than a dead land.'

Ethel Jiggins wasn't quite sure what controls were all about, but couldn't help thinking that it would be good to sink her teeth into an iced bun and have a bit of a dance.

Sid pinned up on the door a newspaper cutting about Winnie's trip to Germany.

At Chesnut Avenue the coming victory, the longed-for peace was looked to with mixed feelings. For Lil it would mean the loss of Todge, for Ooly the final curtain. As the Allies crossed the Rhine; Ooly approached her Rubicon. On 27th March, the day that the papers said that all the German defences beyond Monty's great bridgehead were collapsing, Ooly went to meet Sir Henry Mitchell. It was a Tuesday. She and Dougie and his father were to assemble at Holly House.

Everything would be fine. She was not to worry.

She was sick with nerves. Garment after garment was tried on and discarded. Should she go for glamour or tweedy respectability? The latter sat ill with Ooly – it became frumpy and ordinary. On the other hand the last impression she wanted to give was that of a flighty piece, East End trash done up regardless. But then Sir Henry was a man, after all. Eventually she started her momentous walk up Snakes Lane to the Green in a jersey dress to show off her figure, a sensible three quarter length tweed jacket and black suede sling backs to lighten the mood. The ensemble was finished with a small, black felt with an upturned brim and diamante earrings. Half way up Snakes Lane she removed the earrings and wiped off most of her lipstick.

She was, of course, terribly early and sat tinkling uneasily at the piano as the time crawled on.

From time to time she reapplied her lipstick and wiped it off again.

Sir Henry was an unknown quantity – he had not been at the fateful party at Barrington Gardens, of course. All the talk had been about the Hawk. The only photo she had seen was that one of him at the Mosley wedding and she had no recollection of what he looked like.

On the dot of noon the door bell rang.

'Oh God.'

'Mrs Bowyer, I presume? Lily, if I may?' Sir Henry was markedly unlike his son, a little rotund man, with a high colour and a tiny, sharp nose; he was sporting a rather unlikely red woollen waistcoat. It crossed her mind that he looked like the robin which hopped off the step as she opened the door.

'Oh yes, of course. Please come in. I can't offer you anything, I'm afraid. There's nothing in the house – and no water or gas yet.'

'Douglas not here ?'

'No. I don't suppose he'll be long.'

'Well, my dear' (he looked her up and down appreciatively), we could take a snifter while we wait.'

Out came a silver hip flask. 'Brandy, dear girl? I think we probably need some.'

They perched on packing cases and discussed the war and the weather, the weather and the war. Still no sign of Dougie.

'I expect he's got held up at the hospital.'

More swigs were taken from the flask.

'Damned uncomfortable these packing cases! What d'you say we try and unearth a settee or something – there's several here somewhere.'

'I think there's a chaise longue underneath a pile of stuff in the kitchen.' said Ooly. 'I'll try and get it out.'

'No, no, my dear, you sit tight and I'll have a go.'

Off he hopped and returned dragging the chaise.

'Sir Henry, do let me help you with it!'

'Certainly not – and no "Sir Henry" if you don't mind – if you're going to be my daughter-in-law I want you to call me Hal. Got it? Hal.'

'Well, in that case, you've got to call me Ooly.'

'Ully – that's an odd one!'

'No – Ooly.'

'Fair do's – Ooly it is.'

They sat down together on the green chenille and laughed and had some more brandy.

'Well – if Douglas is too busy saving lives to bother with us we'd better get on with it on our own. D'you care for him?'

'Yes, of course I do.'

'Husband?'

'Married him after Dougie took off – rebound I s'pose.'

'D'you care for *him*?'

'Yes and no.'

'More explanation needed.'

'He's a good bloke – handsome – well educated – no violence or drunkenness or cruelty or anything like that. He's in the RAF –

450

balloons.'

'Provides for you?'

'Oh, yes. It's just that he's so grumpy and sour.'

'So you propose to throw over your perfectly adequate spouse for my son, with no more complaint against him than that he is surly?' He twinkled. 'Doesn't light your fire, I imagine.'

Ooly blushed: 'I suppose that shouldn't matter.'

'Doesn't – until somebody comes along that does. Then the trouble starts. Mind you – I'm not saying that ignition is unconnected with behaviour. And, of course, Douglas did get in first, it has to be said. You two have been knocking around for nearly ten years, on and off, I gather. If it hadn't have been for my Hilda and her nonsense you'd have been safely tucked up together long before the war. Well ...' He leant back with a satisfied sigh, 'That seems to be that. Er – practicing Jews – your family?

'No. Not Jews at all. My father's a Methodist and all the rest of us go to church.'

'Not that I give a hoot, but its my Hilda – strange and difficult woman. Truth to tell we're terrified of her, Douglas and yours truly. But then she lit my fire – once upon a time. Children?'

'I have a daughter – she'll be five in May. She's at school just over there – my mother's picking her up today.'

'Good. Daughters are good – wish I had one myself. Close to her pa is she?'

'Well – what with war and everything, she doesn't really know him.'

'Good – I mean good under the circs. Will you have more?'

'I hope so.'

'Could do with some new life when this ruddy show is finally over. House suit? Seems to fit the bill. If you want anything changed, it shall be done. Women can be most particular about their billets – I know that.'

'Yes, it's fine, but I'm very worried about getting a divorce – my

451

family will be so upset – we were all so humiliated by that business in '37 when your wife tried to buy me off and treated dad and Aunty like so much East End rubbish. And now I am supposed to tell them that I'm proposing to ditch my good, solid Johnny and link myself to a tribe of toffs who took me for a gold digger. And then there's my mother-in-law – she's been such a wonderful friend to me. It will break her heart, I know it will.'

Oh dear. She hadn't meant to say all that – the kindly old gent had loosened her tongue, with his sympathy and his brandy.

Sir Henry put his head in his hands.

'What can I say? Winnie's daughter is divorcing that Vic Oliver fellah – it's all over the press – divorce is nothing like the scandalous rarity its used to be. And look at your sister. Douglas tells me she's disentangling herself from those weird Tillinghams. Damn good thing too – with their tumble down mansion and their odd ways. As to all that rumpus in '37 – it's all very well my blaming Hilda – and that Brackenthorpe piece, of course – she was pushing from behind – had her sights set on Douglas since they were knee high to a grass hopper – but, when all's said and done, I shouldn't have gone along with it. But that's the way it's always been with us, I'm afraid – Hilda says "jump" and poor, weak old Hal jumps. No backbone

'So what if Hilda says "jump" now?'

'I think we can dismiss any possibility of that. She dotes on the boy and even she realised she'd blundered. What a state he was in! Didn't speak to anyone for months. He wouldn't look at any other woman – she dredged up a whole string of 'em – not a flicker. I'm very sorry for what's happened – very sorry indeed. You're a brave lass, giving the boy another chance. If there's anything I can do to help things along with your people – er – should I have chat with your pa – man to man? I've got a decent little row of shops in Kensington – if he was interested …'

'Sir Henry – Hal – if you imagine you can bribe my father you'd better think again. I am not to be purchased like a prize cow. I thought we had made that quite clear …'

'No, no, no – please accept my apologies, dear girl. I merely thought such an offer would be an earnest of my good will. Forget it, please forget it. I have to say I'm looking forward to having such a talented and beautiful addition to the family. Now – let me, at least buy you a spot of lunch and show you off to the locals.'

'Shouldn't we wait for Dougie?'

'D'you know, I have my suspicions that he's not coming – I shouldn't wonder if he never meant to – thought it best to leave us to our own devices.' He smiled and tucked her arm in his as they set off for the George.

They parted company in high spirits and it was with a lightness of step that Ooly set off back to Chestnut Avenue. As soon as she got home she would write to Johnny. When dad got in she would break the news to them all, once Todge was in bed.

'You've been a long time,' said Dot. 'Over at the house again?' There was a phone call for you – some doctor.'

Ooly smiled to herself. She wouldn't ring Dougie back until the letter was posted tomorrow morning and she had told the family. Then she could assure him that she had, at last, done the deed and they were on their way to heaven.

By the time dad and Ed came in Ooly had screwed up several drafts of her letter. She would try again later after she had confronted the family. Dad and Uncle Ed were rather later than usual; when Ooly came downstairs, her speech prepared, they were all sitting round the kitchen table and her father was holding forth:

'Shocking thing in Whitechapel this morning. Annie, that girl who used to work for Vicar came into the shop in a terrible taking. A V2 hit a block of flats near the hospital –Hughes Mansion – you probably know it. It was named after Thomas Hughes, author of

Tom Brown's School Days – Mary Hughes, his daughter, was a social worker in those parts, saint of a woman, ran a hostel for the homeless there known as the Dewdrop Inn. Wonderful soul – died in '41. They say for 30 years she had had no new clothes, no holiday and no proper bed. Hundreds were killed – mainly Jewish families, they were, though not all. Poor Annie looked after a couple of doctors who lived there, cousins, she said, related to Mosley, by all accounts. One of them copped it – killed instantaneously they think – the other, mercifully, was on duty at the hospital.'

The phone rang again. Ooly flew into the hall and picked up the receiver. It was Archie's voice on the line.'

After the War.

'It was the best of times, it was the worst of times'.

So it was all over.

On the night of 1 May Big Ben was illuminated at 10.15; this was the first time since 31 August 1939. In Trafalgar Square the *Daily Express* staged an exhibition of photographs of the camps at Buchenwald and Belsen; it was called 'Seeing is Believing'. Pooty went to have a look; he and a thousand Londoners passed slowly by in horrified silence. Old Sarah Posnanzki remembered the little boy crucified by Stepney Church. It all might have happened here.

On 2 May hoardings proclaimed 'Hitler Dead

Lil wrote to Pan:

'Isnt it wonderful. The war I meen. We have taken our Schelter down the room looks nice. Ooly Todge and myself done it up on Friday. Dad and Ed took the schelter on Thursday afternoon. I wonder when we shall get the good news will you have time to go whoopee. It is lovely to go to bed at night & think you can rest safe know listning for bangs Todge said to granddad you are taking the schelter down because the war is over know moore bombs coming over she is a knowing kid.'

On 8 May Germany collapsed; there were queues at telephone boxes – everyone wanted to share the news. The Spoons rushed in to 29 Chetnut Avenue and even Mrs Plunkett (with whom relations been frosty since the cow incident) came in to talk about it.

Church bells rang and people danced all night on the bomb sites. 'Saturnalia came to floodlit London and the West End was a mad house' wrote the *Daily Mail*.They burned Hitler in effigy on Hampstead Heath; soldiers swung from lampposts in Piccadilly Circus. It was as bright as the Blitz with bonfires, fireworks and search lights criss crossing the sky in V signs. Even Mrs Doomandgloom Davies emerged from the funeral parlour -it was the first time she had been seen in Roman Road since 1939.

August brought the surrender of Japan, but at what cost! Doomandgloom reckonned the calamitous horrors at Hiroshima and Nagasaki was the shape of things to come. How long would it be before the great powers, armed with such weapons, would destroy the world?

It took a long time to end-months for the chaps to come home. When Johnny came marching home again Ooly was on holiday at Bognor with Pan and the rest of the family. Rationing was to go on for years. Food shortages were worse than ever, meat almost unobtainable. That Christmas turkeys were at a premium and Billy slept in his shop at Bethnal Green with a shotgun.

London was drained and exhausted, grey and dismal, hungry and threadbare. Shanty towns of prefabs appeared on every square inch of space, divorce was rife -couples had grown apart. Children resented the return of fathers they didn't know. There was no end for years to 'make do and mend' and the black market boomed. The East End had suffered most; it was left empty, torn and bleeding, a derelict place

The shattered plate glass of the windows were never replaced in the Emporium. It looked as if it was boarded up and only the customers from pre-war days, who knew it was there, came in these days. Sales had fallen off: Hitler's 'slum clearance' had done away with the bugs, many of the regulars had left the area and there was competition from new cut-price enterprises.

Sid often quoted Captain Cuttle, the Limehouse Rigger in Dombey and Son:

'..new invention, new invention - alteration, alteration ... the world has gone past me. I don't blame it; but I no longer understand it. Tradesmen are not the same as they used to be, apprentices are not the same, business is not the same, business commodities are not the same...'

As the grey years of austerity roll on and the new terror of total annihilation in nuclear war replaces the old fear of the Jack Boot, Johnny is often busy in the garden at Buckhurst Hill. These are probably his happiest times, lifting the heavy clay and doing his best to create a flower garden-it is not easy work. Afterwards, in the evening, he will sit in a steaming bath and have a dream or two –a car, a spaniel, a detached house, a greenhouse, a pony for the girls, love. Perhaps he will go down to the *British Queen* later on and 'have one', just one. He can hear Ooly rippling out her longing on the ebonised chapel grand Mr and Mrs S. gave them as a wedding present. Pity she doesn't do something with her music or join the *Roebuck Players*-they're meant to be rather good. It might buck her up.

Twilight is the worst time for Ooly. Oh - just to walk along a summer Suffolk lane and hear his far away, loving voice, calling her home! But Ooly never cries. At least she's got Todge; she's quite grown up these days, though Nell reckons she sprang fully mature from the womb. She loves listening to her mother's stories about the heady days of her youth when she was Queen of Bow. There's Todge's little sister now too, but her eyes don't tip down at the corners as Todge's do, so it's not quite the same.

The Smarts still assemble for musical evenings, especially when Pan is home on a visit. Mog's two little Tittlers are put to bed in their freshly painted bedrooms (pale turquoise) in the nice new semi, and she and Poor Old Tom set off for Chestnut Avenue; it isn't far. The childrens' godfather, Uncle Pooty, usually baby-sits –he's only a stone's throw away up at Holly House, on the Green. They sing the

Kerry Dance, well Sid, Mog and Pan do –Ooly can't join in with that, she gets all choked up:

> Loving voices of old companions
> Stealing out of the past once more
> And the sound of the dear old music
> Soft and sweet as in days of yore.

Even more difficult to bear is Dad's rendering of 'Oft in the stilly Night':

> 'Oft in the stilly night
> Ere slumbers chain has bound me,
> Fond memry brings the light
> Of other days around me:
> The smiles, the tears of boyhoods years,
> The words of love then spoken;
> The eyes that shone,
> Now dimmd and gone,
> The cheerful hearts now broken!
> Thus in the stilly night
> Ere slumbers chain has bound me,
> Sad memry brings the light
> Of other days around me.'

2017.

Number 29 Selman Street, still stands today, restored and tarted up taken over by some of the new Bow gentry. There is a tub of pansies at the front, a Chelsea Box of lilies at the back and the most glorious display of roses over the door, every June. Who won the battle of Selman Street? Suffice it to say that pansies bloom all year. Marigolds absolutely refuse to thrive.

They say it's haunted. Tristram, who owns it now, swears he is woken at night by the strains of the Alleluia Chorus and his wife says she hears some old Victorian parlour songs, but maybe it's in her head. Mary Portas, the media's Queen of Shops, tries to bring Roman Road market to life again, with artisanal bakers and cheese boutiques. The grandson of Angelo the 'Italiano'sells ice-cream. Up and down the street he goes, wheeling his grand father's little cart, with its two sunken tubs with handled lids. When they are lifted, there, glowing in the sunshine is the most golden ice-cream in the one, and in the other the glistening white lemon ice. You would have to be very old indeed to know that it doesn't taste like it once did. Never will there be such a summertime treat as that.

Should you ever find yourself in Tillingam in Somerset-you might-New Hall is now open to the public-do visit the *Tillingham Arms* and take a look at the sign board. It's rathered weathered, not having been re-painted since 1945 when the then baronet had it done. The landlord will tell you it depicts a Lady Tillingham who was around during the war. Most people think it is Greta Garbo.

Blacksmith's Cottage has been bought up by someone who could afford to refurbish and extend it beyond recognition. They still talk of Miss Smart in the village, and Miss Drayman. and the vicar, Billington-Smythe, who came to live in the adjoining cottage. According to the post mistress, who is a bit of a gossip, they were a rather un-holy threesome, with an intercom connecting the two households, which shared meals and goodness knows what else There was even a rumour, or so she says, that Miss Smart was once investigated by the police-years ago-just after the war. It was something to do with the vicar's wife being smashed to death by a poker –but nothing came of it. She has only been gone a few years - last seen by her gardener, riding up and down on her stair lift with a bottle of Johnny Walker belting out *Onward Christian Soldiers* at the top of her still magnificent voice.